# About Katie

I live in the beautiful Cotswold countryside with my family, and I'm a country girl at heart.

I first started writing when my mother gave me a writing kit for Christmas, and once I started I just couldn't stop. *Living Dangerously* was my first novel and since then, I haven't looked back.

Ideas for books are everywhere, and I'm constantly inspired by the people and places around me. From watching TV (yes, it is research) to overhearing conversations, I love how my writing gives me the chance to taste other people's lives and try all the jobs I've never had.

Each of my books explores a different profession or background and my research has helped me bring these to life. I've been a porter in an auction house, tried my hand at pottery, refurbished furniture, delved behind the scenes of a dating website, and I've even been on a Ray Mears survival course.

I love being a writer; to me there isn't a more satisfying and pleasing thing to do. I particularly enjoy writing love stories. I believe falling in love is the best thing in the v                            perience it, ar

*Also by Katie Fforde*

# The
# Christmas
# Stocking
### and other
### stories

arrow books

1 3 5 7 9 10 8 6 4 2

Arrow Books
20 Vauxhall Bridge Road
London SW1V 2SA

Arrow Books is part of the Penguin Random House group of companies
whose addresses can be found at global.penguinrandomhouse.com.

Penguin
Random House
UK

First published in Great Britain by Century in 2017
First published in paperback by Arrow Books in 2018

www.penguin.co.uk

A CIP catalogue record for this book is available from the British Library.

ISBN 9781784757274

Typeset in 11.58/15.7 pt Palatino LT Std by Jouve (UK), Milton Keynes
Printed and bound in Great Britain by Clays Ltd, Elcograf S.p.A.

Dear Reader,

Who would have thought there were so many different ways of experiencing Christmas? Although of course there are as many Christmases as there are people, I'm only used to having the one. I had great fun writing these stories; in fact I think I slightly prefer my Christmas to be in story form. I have a bit more control over events that way!

So here is a book of Christmas short stories for you. I did one a couple of years ago – *A Christmas Feast* – and that was such a great experience I decided to do another. Last time, all except one of the stories had been featured in magazines over the years. That little volume used up all my existing supply, however, so this time only two of the stories – 'Candlelight at Christmas' and 'A Christmas in Disguise' – have appeared before and that was in digital form only. All the others are brand new!

One of them was inspired by my grand-dogs, so called because although they belong to my daughter, I helped hand rear them when their mother died tragically a year ago. They are a joy to us all, even though they covered my house in mud regularly until finally we fenced off the pond. They also love to embarrass me in front of my daughter and her husband, by clambering on my furniture and generally doing things that they know they aren't allowed to do at home! Which proves I'm not a fit grand-dog mother at all!

I do hope you enjoy these stories, and that they may offer you a little light relief when real-life Christmas is getting a bit frantic!

With love and Happy Christmas
Katie xxx

*To Annie and Wilson,*
*my much loved grand-dogs.*

# Contents

# The
# Christmas
# Stocking

It was Saturday morning, the day before Christmas Eve, and the mild, damp Christmas weather had suddenly bucked its ideas up and turned cold. Romy was suddenly freezing.

She'd been selling Christmas decorations in an old station building at a bustling Cotswold Christmas market and she'd done well in the first two hours. But now, in spite of wearing masses of layers under her leather jacket (including her not-very-cool thermal vest), two pairs of socks under long-haired sheepskin boots, a pair of stripy leg warmers over her jeans (a later addition, courtesy of one of the other stalls), and a furry trapper hat, the cold was beginning to penetrate.

She looked longingly at the refreshments stall that was doing great business. She'd been up at the crack of dawn and she'd only managed to grab a banana and muesli bar on her way out. Also, her boiler had just broken down so the shower had been tepid and the flat freezing. A cup of something hot, and maybe a bacon butty, would give her stamina for the day ahead. But if she ran over to buy a cup of tea she might miss valuable sales from the group of people, mostly men, who'd just entered the building.

Although it was only about twelve o'clock they'd obviously just come from the pub. They probably thought they were getting their Christmas shopping done early, with Christmas Eve still to go, perhaps safe in the knowledge that they only had one present to buy. Adoring wives and girlfriends no doubt would be buying presents for mothers, sisters, 'Auntie Flo's and anyone else necessary.

She noticed a man come in behind the group and at first she couldn't tell if he was with them, or on his own. He was wearing motorbike leathers and had a sort of swagger about him. He had slightly long, dark blond hair and walked with determination. As he didn't appear to be drunk and wasn't wearing a crumpled suit, she decided he was on his own.

Romy reckoned he was here to buy a present for his girlfriend or his wife, and so she gave herself a minute to stop finding him rather attractive and think about her own boyfriend. Gus was waiting for her in France, with his parents, getting ready for a big family Christmas. She looked around her stall, wondering, for the seven-thousandth time, if his family would appreciate her presents, samples of which she was now selling. There was a difference between 'home-made' and 'handmade' and she was going for the 'handmade, personalised look'.

She'd met Gus's expat parents, who lived in France but didn't seem to speak a lot of French or have many French friends. His two sisters she had checked out thoroughly on Facebook. They were nice-looking, sensibly dressed and looked like advertisements for Boden with their shiny blond children, whose white teeth were evidence of regular trips to the dentist and limited access to fizzy drinks.

For the elder sister's three children, Romy had done a set of frosted-glass jam jars with silhouettes of Mummy and Daddy, all three children, and the dog (a Labrador). She had been aiming for a generic child but actually she felt she had achieved a likeness. It wasn't an ideal present to be carrying on a budget airline – she hadn't wanted to spend extra money on hold luggage – but she thought they were nice. For the younger sister's two little boys she had painted plain white lantern fairy lights with figures from Minecraft. Finally both women, and their mother, were getting silk scarves, hand-painted by Romy. Perfect for carry-on luggage. She would buy presents for the husbands at the duty-free shop. Alcohol was always acceptable.

As she ran through the checklist in her head whilst surveying her stall, Romy felt a swell of pride at her handiwork. She'd been working so hard this season, doing all the local markets and Christmas fairs, selling her Christmas decorations. It wasn't a major earner but, apart from the rent for the stall, it was almost all profit. And it topped up what she earned from her part-time job while she was doing a master's. She was proud of the decorations and only hoped Gus's parents would appreciate them when they opened their presents.

Thinking about them as a family she reflected that while they were all kind enough, they were very hearty and, going by the parents, had loud voices. She didn't really object to the volume, it was the backslapping and teasing that was only just the right side of cruel that bothered her. And they all thought that anything not entirely practical, like art, was a complete waste of time. To make matters worse Romy knew she had only been invited to France because Gus had told his family her own parents were going to New Zealand for Christmas. Really she would have preferred to spend Christmas with friends, but she would have felt ungrateful turning down the invitation.

Gus was lovely, of course, and Romy had been mad about him when they'd first got together. But a year in she sometimes wondered if she'd only been attracted to him because he was so different from her previous boyfriend. He'd once admitted to her that his friends were all a bit shocked that he'd chosen such an arty, indie type while at the same time envying him for having such a gorgeous girlfriend. When they first met he had asked her rather anxiously if she had any tattoos. She hadn't, but his question made her think of getting one, a bat perhaps, on her wrist. This trip to France would be a bit of test – if their relationship survived they were probably meant to be together. She wished she didn't feel so ambivalent about it all: the Christmas *and* the relationship.

'Here,' said a voice. 'I thought you could use this. You look cold.'

It was the man in leathers, handing her a mug of spicy hot chocolate.

She took it with a grateful smile. 'Thank you so much,' she said. 'I certainly could use it. I hardly had time for a cup of instant coffee this morning and my boiler has broken.' She took a heart-warming sip. 'Please, take a look round the stall and have something free. For your girlfriend, maybe?'

She hated herself for what must look like a blatant bit of digging but it was too late.

'I have actually got her present,' said the man. Judging by his expression, he seemed fairly confident that his girlfriend would like it. Romy knew it was silly to be disappointed – it wasn't as if she was free herself – but somehow she was.

'Well, that's good! Most men don't even start thinking about it until Christmas Eve so you're well ahead.'

'I do need some Christmas decorations though; my house is a bit of a shell at the moment. My girlfriend's been having an early Christmas with her family in Connecticut. I want the place to look amazing when she comes back. Make her really fall in love with it.'

'Well,' said Romy, having now sipped enough hot chocolate to warm her up. 'Christmas decs are what I specialise in. All made by me. And there are these, in case you missed them.' She gestured to a jar on the floor that contained white-painted branches. On the branches were decorations made to look like hot-air balloons. Every one had a single battery light so from a distance the branches looked as if they were dotted with stars. Close up you could see the individually painted egg-like shapes.

He inclined his head. He had a slightly unkempt look that seemed genuine and not deliberate. If it *was* deliberate, it was extremely effective. 'I have to say, I was drawn to them when I first came in.'

'But you stopped at the coffee stall first?'

'I saw you stamping up and down and flapping your arms. I guessed you were cold.' He was very twinkly, and impossible not to respond to.

Romy laughed. 'Was I that obvious? I am sorry.

I think this stall is in a bit of a draught or something. Everyone else seems fine.' In spite of his 'bad-boy' good looks, he had a very kind smile. She experienced a pang of jealousy for the girl who had parents in Connecticut. 'So!' she said briskly. 'What would you like?'

'I think I'd like all of them,' he said after some thought.

'I can – happily – give you one, but not all of them.'

'And I – happily – will pay for all of them. I'll have my one free one too, of course. And everything else you have left. I want to make a big impression.'

He grinned. Romy coughed and looked down at her decorations. He was far too attractive for her own good, she decided, but as a customer he was pretty much perfect.

'Well, the hot-air balloons are five pounds each,' she said. This had put people off, although the work and effort that had gone into them had been enormous. 'The bats are four pounds fifty and the jam jars with the tea lights – although they are extremely pretty – are only a pound.'

'In which case, I won't have a free balloon. A hot chocolate isn't worth a fiver.'

'Have one of these then,' suggested Romy. She held out a model bat made out of wire and black tights. She'd made several but they hadn't sold well. Bats were rather niche, she discovered.

'Oh, a bat!' he said, sounding excited. 'I like bats!'

'You do? Then have a couple of them. No one else seems to like them. I suppose they're more Hallow-een than Christmas. I think they're rather sweet.'

'I like them because they got me my house and music studio cheap.'

'Clever bats! How did they learn that trick? It's one I'd like to learn myself.'

He laughed. 'Sadly they didn't do it by being clever, only by nesting in the roof of the buildings, and as they're protected they can't be removed. And not everyone likes bats.'

'So what sort of a house is it? If bats want to live there? It's not an old church or anything, is it?' She had a vision of bats streaming from a narrow arched window at dusk, with Dracula following – from a larger window, obviously.

'It's an old mill but it was empty for years and years and the woods have grown up around it. It's going to be amazing when it's finished.'

'Sounds wonderful! I've always wanted to live in the woods, to wake up with the sound of the birds singing, to see the dappled sunlight filtering through the branches.' She stopped. 'Not in winter, maybe!' She laughed and pulled off her hat. 'It comes of having been nicknamed Goldilocks,' she said as her blonde curls revealed themselves.

'All is now clear!' he said, joining in her laughter. 'You were destined to live in the woods!'

'I have thought of dyeing my hair black so I could pretend to be a bat. Then finding myself a home in the woods might be easier.'

'Don't do that!' He sounded horrified.

'No, it's all right. A friend did it once and it took ages and hundreds of pounds for her to realise that, actually, blondes do have more fun. But now, your decorations? How many did you say you wanted?'

'I want them all.'

'Really? There are ten balloons, which is fifty quid straight off. I'd give you a discount of course.'

'No need for that. Just add up how much it all costs.'

Romy did the calculation. 'Let's call it eighty quid.'

He had done the sum a bit quicker than she had. 'I make it ninety-five.'

'No, with the discount for quantity, it's eighty quid.'

'Ninety!'

She shook her head. 'Eighty is my final offer.'

'Ninety! I want the branches as well.'

'The branches are free. You could find your own branches – especially if you live in a wood!'

'I suppose, but then I'd have to find white paint and a brush. I'd rather have yours.'

'Go on then.' This man had bought her entire stock, which meant she could knock off early and pack. Her flight was horrendously early in the morning and she had to catch a coach to the airport even earlier.

He frowned. 'I've just thought. I came on my bike. How would I get the branches home?'

'Well, how are you going to get the hot-air balloons and all the other decorations home?'

'In my top box but I couldn't manage the branches.'

'Then man up and make new ones! You wouldn't have to paint them white. Stick them in a bucket or something, like I've used. Fill it with sand, or earth or stones, and add the hot air balloons. That's your Christmas tree done. Just add presents and chocolate.'

He didn't respond but spent several seconds looking at her speculatively. 'Actually, I wonder if I could ask you a huge favour?'

'Ask away. I can say no.' But realised she probably wouldn't.

'I need to get some groceries – more than I can fit in the top box really. I was going to try and get the shopping delivered or hope I found a friend to get it back for me.' He paused. 'But would you take the groceries and the decorations?'

Romy didn't think for long. Apart from anything else – and there were a lot of things – he had bought her entire stock. Delivering it wasn't too much of an ask.

'OK, I'll do it. In exchange for a tour of your house.'

He gave a shout of laughter. 'Done! But don't expect anything too much. It's a work in progress. And now, let me pay you . . . ?'

'Romy,' she supplied.

'Felix. It's been great doing business with you,' he said, passing over some cash.

She accepted the notes he put into her hand and slipped them into her bag. Now she would have some spending money in France. 'You go and do your shopping.'

As Romy followed Felix in her car she felt skittish and excited. Because of Felix, she'd have extra time to pack for her trip to France tomorrow. She needed extra time. None of her clothes seemed suitable and her presents were bulky. And as Gus's parents had been kind enough to invite her for Christmas, she didn't want to shock them by wearing clothes they thought too outlandish. Her natural style was a bit Goth-like. It was going to be hard for her to fit in with the turned-up collars, Liberty prints and cashmere cardigans.

But she knew, as she followed the motorbike along the lanes, that she was using her excitement at packing as an excuse to cover her faint guilt at visiting a man to see his house, even in daylight. If he'd been an unattractive toad it would have been different; she wouldn't have felt guilty at all. But he was very attractive indeed. And not remotely a toad.

The bike turned off the Cotswold lane and she followed it along a tree-lined path. The trees grew thicker and became actual woods. The sky had darkened a bit as well and she knew she didn't have long before the daylight would be gone. She parked where he indicated, in a large lay-by.

'Oh wow! Real woods!' she said when she had got out. 'It's beautiful!' It was also quite a lot colder amongst the trees, and much crisper. In the town it had been chilly but damp.

'It is quite isolated but I like it.'

There was emphasis on the 'I'. Romy felt he should have said, 'We like it.' His words indicated his New England girlfriend felt a bit differently. But Romy was probably imagining things.

'Come on in and I'll give you the tour.'

'Let's get your stuff unpacked first.'

When she'd seen the decorations safely into the house, she took one of the food bags into the kitchen end of the big, open-plan room. There weren't any proper units, just a stainless-steel sink and a big cooker flanked by a couple of old cupboards, but she loved the way it was separate but also part of the room. It had so much potential it was hard not to squeak enthusiastically. The bag clinked revealingly as she set it down on a makeshift worktop.

'You don't seem to have bought a lot of food,

considering it's Christmas and people usually buy three times as much as they're likely to eat,' she said and then wondered if she'd sounded nosy and rude.

He didn't seem to object. 'Well, I was going to friends for Christmas and Boxing Day. I reckon it's best to buy everything when it's half price after Christmas.'

'Cheapskate! You're happy to bum meals off your friends so you can buy everything cheaper afterwards!' She was only pretending to be shocked. Really she thought it was a good idea.

'Hey! I was going to take both lots brandy, port, some of that vile cream liqueur that my girlfriend likes and some very nice red wine.'

Romy put down the box that contained food. She liked Bailey's herself and wondered if Gus would have bought her some. She suspected his parents would have referred to it as a 'stickie' and disapproved.

'OK,' she said, 'let's get your Christmas tree set up.'

They assembled Romy's painted branches in the corner by the huge glass wall that looked out on to the woods. It took a little while to add all the decorations as he'd bought quite a few but the effect was wonderful.

'This is lovely!' Romy said when they'd lit all the little battery tea lights. 'Handier if they were connected and you could just put them on with a switch but I designed them as individual decorations. I didn't expect them to be sold as a job lot.'

'So what is it you do, exactly? When you're not flogging tea lights?'

She laughed. He was teasing her and she liked that. 'I'm doing a master's in Art in the Environment. I've deviated slightly. I set out doing something sensible but got waylaid.' She laughed again. 'My boyfriend thinks I'm mad to have given up on something that would have given me a qualification – to teach maybe – but when I realised I could do an MA in a subject I loved, I had to give it a go.' It was why she was always looking for ways to make a bit of extra money.

'I think that sounds very cool,' said Felix, looking at her intently.

Embarrassed, she said, 'It does mean I'm always broke, of course. But I don't really mind.'

He seemed to pull himself together. 'Now let me show you my house before the light goes.'

The house was enormous and luxurious – or it would be when it was finished. The kitchen was positioned so it got all the views. Skylights above it meant it also captured every scrap of natural light. The sitting room had a huge wood burner, several tatty old sofas and not much other furniture if you overlooked the piles and piles of vinyl records. The walls were stone and desperately needed some large artworks (Romy's opinion, and she kept it to herself).

Upstairs there were three bedrooms with gorgeous bathrooms attached, with baths looking out into the trees: wet rooms with plenty of room for two; and a master bedroom so beautiful it made Romy catch her breath with admiration and envy.

'It's amazing,' she said. 'Absolutely amazing.'

'It will be,' said Felix. 'Sadly only the downstairs shower is plumbed in, the sitting room is still a bit of a mess and the kitchen hasn't even been started.' He sounded as if he were quoting someone. 'Oh, and the bedroom smells of bats.'

'Does it? I didn't notice. Mind you, I don't know what bats smell of. And a gorgeous scented candle would fix that, wouldn't it?'

He shrugged.

'Seriously, something from Jo Malone could make the bedroom smell heavenly. Your girlfriend will love it then.'

He didn't answer for a moment and then said, 'I hope so. Do you want to see the studio?'

Now she felt bad for suggesting the candle. It was none of her business. She was glad that he had changed the subject. 'Oh, yes please.'

'Though it's for musicians, not artists,' he added.

'I'm not fussy.'

Crossing the cobbled yard from the house Romy became aware it had got a lot colder, even since they'd been in the house. She slipped a little on a stone and she hoped it was water, not ice. She determined not to linger too long in the studio. She should get home and pack. The days were short and she didn't want to be driving through the dark woods in the dusk. And for some reason being at Felix's house in the evening rather than just after lunch would seem even more wrong than it felt already. And it felt wrong, she knew, because she fancied him.

The studio was far more complete than the house. It had beautiful wood floors, strange square boxes attached to the walls which she assumed were for soundproofing, a huge curved desk with hundreds of switches on it and a grand piano. There were some photographs of bands on the wall, one of which Romy recognised. Romy couldn't even guess how much it would have cost but it didn't look cheap.

She felt a flash of sympathy for his girlfriend. His priorities were for the studio, but if that was how he made his money it was fair enough.

'I expect you're thinking that I spent too much on the studio and not enough on the house,' said Felix, a touch defensively. 'But it is how I earn my living: producing music.'

'That's just what I was thinking,' said Romy. 'After all, you've got to earn money, you can't just spend it all on a fancy house.'

He grinned suddenly, his teeth flashing. 'Although part of the reason a lot of the house is unfinished is because a mate was doing the plumbing and he went and had a baby and he ran out of spare time.'

'Unusual,' said Romy solemnly.

'I meant – you knew I meant – that his wife had a baby. But you are right. I should stop being a cheapskate and pay someone to do it.'

'I absolved you of being a cheapskate when you told me how much alcohol you were giving to your friends.'

'That's all right then.'

'Look—'

They both spoke at once, but Felix motioned for Romy to continue.

'I really should be heading off,' she said regretfully.

Felix said, 'Why don't I make you some tea or something? And a sandwich?' She wasn't sure, but Romy had a feeling he didn't want their time together to end either. And she was hungry. It had been a horrendously early start and her banana and muesli bar felt like a long time ago.

'I've got bacon,' he added temptingly.

Romy succumbed. 'That would be great. Then I really must go.'

At Felix's suggestion, Romy lit the wood burner while Felix made bacon butties. He had proper rolls and toasted them lightly before adding the bacon. He also had a full range of sauces and while Romy liked hers plain, it was nice to be offered things. She also accepted a mug of tea.

They ate and drank their tea in front of the fire and the conversation flowed easily. They had so much in common: a love of the outdoors, bats, music, the same sense of humour and outlook on life in general. Romy felt so at ease; she could hardly believe they'd only met a few hours before.

'So, tell me why you've got a picture of Flying Angels on your wall in the studio?' she asked.

'The Angels? Old friends. They come here to rehearse sometimes and do a little mixing. Do you know them?'

'Well, they are quite local. I heard them in a pub.' She'd taken Gus along and although he pretended to like them she hadn't been convinced.

'That's cool! They've got a gig coming up. We should go and see it together.'

'Actually, we shouldn't,' she said, putting her mug on the floor by the fireplace and getting to her feet. 'And I should go home now.'

She didn't trust herself – and possibly not him either – to keep things friendly. She needed to get herself out of there before something happened that they would both regret.

'Are you sure? Are you sure you have to go?' He got up too and seemed distressed at the thought of her leaving.

'I am. I've got a ridiculously early flight in the

morning. And the coach before that. But it has been –
lovely. I love your house in the woods and I really
didn't think the bedroom smelt of bat poo.' She had
added this to lighten the tone but it seemed a bit
too intimate now.

He walked her to the door and on up the hill to
where her car was parked. He still didn't seem to want
her to go. And she walked as quickly as she could to
make sure she did leave and didn't give up on Gus,
her flight to France and everything sensible in her life.

'Well, goodbye,' she said, doing up her hat.

'Goodbye,' he said. He looked as if he might kiss
her cheek but she stepped back so he couldn't.

She got in the car and pulled out of the lay-by.

She found tears pricking her eyes as she drove slowly
away. That was possibly why she didn't see the bend
coming, just as she hit a patch of black ice, and when
the road curved her car went straight, over the slight
camber and into a tree. Because she was going so slowly
she wasn't hurt, but watching the front of her car crum-
ple, as if in slow motion, was acutely painful.

Her car was above the ground on the driver's
side, but she could still get out and lower herself
down. Then she clambered up the bank and back
on to the track.

Felix was there, panting. 'I was watching from

the upstairs window, I saw what was happening. Are you OK?' He took her into his arms without waiting for her to reply.

It was lovely but it didn't help. She felt more like crying than ever. 'I'm fine,' she said huskily.

Then her phone pinged; she could hear it in her car. 'I'll get it,' said Felix and ran off.

She was calm by the time he got back. Her father had bought her membership of a rescue service. They would pull her out and the car was probably drivable. It would be fine.

'Here's your bag,' said Felix. 'I didn't want to go in your bag and get your phone.'

There were two text messages. The first was from the airline to say her flight had been cancelled due to ice on the runways. The second one was from Gus, who'd obviously also found out about the cancellation.

'So soz about your flight! Nightmare! You'll have to try and rebook and come over the day after Boxing Day. But we're all leaving the day after that so maybe it's too far to come just for a day? You'll find some local friends to have Crimbo with? Catch up afterwards, OK? And very merry Christmas to you, lovely girl.'

'What is it?' Felix asked. 'What's the matter?'

'My flight is cancelled due to black ice. And Gus, who obviously has the app on his phone and so knew that, suggests I have Christmas with local friends.' She paused. 'I probably can't even drive to any of them now. I wonder if I could get a taxi?' If she could, it would cost a fortune.

'Spending it with local friends is a brilliant idea!' said Felix. 'Spend it with me! We're friends, I hope, and you couldn't get more local.'

While she couldn't help smiling, Romy said, 'I can't. And you're supposed to be going to friends yourself.'

'I could cancel them – they only asked me because they thought I was going to be on my own. Why not spend Christmas with me? Your flight is cancelled. What else are you going to do? Your car's not drivable and a taxi would cost an arm and a leg.'

'But you have a girlfriend. I should at least try to get home.' She remembered then about the broken boiler, no heat, no hot water and no landlord to fix it. (He'd gone away for Christmas.)

'Yes, but she's not due here until just before New Year and nothing bad will happen. You have my absolute word on that – scout's honour. We'll have Christmas together as friends.'

Suppressing a giggle at the idea of this music-producing biker boy being a boy scout, she looked for another reason to leave. 'But what about my car? I can't just leave it nose to nose with a tree.'

He smiled. 'I don't have a sticker on my motorbike but my other car is a Land Rover – you need one living here. When the black ice has gone, I'll pull you out, no problem.'

'It's Christmas Eve tomorrow. Maybe, if the weather improves, I could go home then.'

'Didn't you say your boiler was broken? You want to go back to a cold house?'

'The boiler heats the hot water, too,' she admitted.

'Then stay! I promise nothing will happen that would worry either of our partners. I really respect your feelings about this and they're my feelings too. Cheating is wrong.'

She felt a smile of happiness spread over her face. She had no alternative. She pushed aside the guilt and allowed the bubble of happiness to rise. She didn't have to spend Christmas with her boyfriend's hearty family but instead with a lovely man who was fun and interested in the same things as she was. She couldn't believe her luck, really.

'I do have to say,' she said as they walked, arm in arm (in case she was wobbly after her prang), 'I was rather dreading staying with Gus's family. They're terribly kind and all but I don't think I'd have fitted in. They're very into quizzes.'

'I like a quiz myself,' said Felix. 'Aren't you keen?'

'No! I like them too. But I'm hopeless at things I feel I should know about. I'm great at art and artists, indie bands, stuff like that. But mountain ranges? No!'

'But if there was one in the paper, you'd give it a go?'

'Only if competition rules don't apply.'

'You mean you google the answers?' He seemed a bit shocked.

'No – at least, not until the end when you're really desperate. I meant no one saying, "Didn't they teach you geography at that arty school of yours?"'

'They didn't say that!' Felix was appalled.

'To be fair, they didn't. But I was worried that it was the sort of thing they would have said.'

He pulled her closer towards him in a little hug. 'Idiot. It won't be like that if it's just us. Oh . . .' He paused, allowing Romy a couple of seconds to enjoy the 'just us' part of his sentence.

'What?'

'I called you an idiot. Not very friendly.'

'But you said it in a friendly way. It's fine.'

She felt a little pang of loss as they got to the house and he let her go.

'There's just one thing,' he said as they went in. 'I have an album to finish working on tomorrow. I really can't take the day off. Will you be OK looking after yourself?'

'I'll be fine,' she said. Then she had an idea. 'I know!' she said enthusiastically. 'Why don't you give me a job to do on the house? I'm good at those practical things – far better than I am at quizzes.'

'You don't have to – you could just veg out in front of the telly.'

'No! I'd rather do something. No point in making Christmas decs now, and my plumbing skills are non-existent, but if you've got something that's maybe a bit delicate for your average builder? I could perhaps do that?'

'Actually,' he said slowly, as if pennies were dropping in his mind, 'I have some lovely Art Nouveau tiles that were taken out of a bomb-damaged house in London. They've got cement on the back and they're all fairly damaged but I think they'd look lovely in the master bathroom. I know it's all very modern and high end at the moment but a little touch of Arts and Crafts would just make it a bit different.'

'I'd love to do that! Working with reclaimed things is what I like doing best. And if I'm doing a job I won't feel so – guilty.'

'I'll never give you any cause to feel guilty – or me to feel guilty. I promise.'

'But I'll feel better if I'm contributing in some way. My being here will be justified.'

'I think we should open one of the bottles,' said Felix. 'To celebrate. Then we should eat something.'

'I know what I want!' said Romy. 'The sickly cream liqueur that your girlfriend likes and you obviously hate.'

'No argument from me. We won't be fighting over that one. With or without ice?'

'Too cold for ice. On its own, please.'

'I'll have a whisky mac. It's my designated Christmas drink.'

They brought their drinks to the fireside, taking a sofa each. Romy had removed her boots at the door and was happy to be able to snuggle up.

'I'll get you another pair of socks, in case you're cold,' said Felix, and leapt up from his own sofa.

Romy loved the way he moved quickly, gracefully. Gus was a bit ponderous for someone of his age, she reflected.

Felix came back not just with socks, but with a lovely mohair blanket. 'I bought this locally,' he said. 'It felt wrong to leave it in the shop. It was so beautiful. Sadly,' he added, 'apparently it's not the right colour.' He paused. 'Wrong green.'

'As an artist, I think it's a perfect green. I never get why people seem to want everything to be the same colour. Brides who insist that their bridesmaids have their shoes dyed to the exact shade of turquoise when they could just wear bright pink shoes. It would look better.'

Felix looked at her, surprised. 'So you don't think everything needs to match?'

'Definitely not,' she said, 'but I do have to tell you that, according to the pictures on Facebook, Gus's parents are quite into matching.' She flushed guiltily, feeling suddenly disloyal to people who had, after all, been kind enough to invite her for Christmas. 'I ought to check my Facebook. See how they're getting on over there in *la belle France*.' She paused. 'Can I use your computer?'

When he didn't immediately reply she wondered if she'd asked the wrong thing. Some people didn't like other people using their equipment. But she hadn't got the impression he was like that.

'You can use my computer, sure, but unless you're going to write a novel or play Solitaire it won't be a lot of use to you.'

'Sorry?'

'No internet. I can get Wi-Fi on my phone if I go right to the top of the hill, climb a tree and the wind is in the right direction but not down here.'

Romy laughed. 'Really? I love that!'

'It's funny, but hellishly inconvenient. I usually just go to the pub and get it. I am sorting it,' he went on, still awkward, 'but it involves cabling. Is that a problem?'

She thought about it. Normally being without access to social media would have been shocking, but just now it seemed perfectly OK.

'Not really.'

'You can text all right, so we're not completely cut off from the world. But obviously, online shopping is out of the question. Hence my trip to town earlier.'

'You mean I won't be able to shop the sales on Christmas morning?'

He'd got her measure now and was laughing. 'No, you won't. You'll just have to open your stocking like every other civilised person.'

'Except I haven't got a stocking. Father Christmas thinks I'm in France.'

'You may have to have it late this year.'

She nodded. 'What about you?'

He frowned. 'Me too. I sent a stocking over to Connecticut in my girlfriend's luggage – last year we both spent a lot of time doing them.'

'Maybe she'll bring it back with her, when she's home.'

He frowned again. 'Actually, I think she is home.'

After a few moments she said, 'You mean, back with her parents?'

He shook his head. 'Not her parents so much, as Connecticut – America.'

'I think I'd find it hard to emigrate,' said Romy. 'I mean, Gus's parents can afford a mansion in France and it looks amazing. But I'd feel cut off from family and friends. My own culture.'

'Lauren seemed keen to be British when she first came over. Her family is very grand – definitely went over on the *Mayflower*, or one of those other early ships, so I think she felt she was coming back to the Old Country. But more recently – well, I'm not so sure.'

'Shall we find something nice to watch on telly?' she said after a little while. All this talk of Gus and Lauren was a necessary but unwelcome reminder that she and Felix had other halves to consider.

'Or a film!' His enthusiasm returned. 'I have a zillion DVDs.'

'Oh, no Netflix?'

He shook his head. 'No internet. Come and look through the selection and then we need to think about food. It's Christmas. It's the law.'

'I've got some lovely Cheddar in my car,' said Romy. 'It was going to be a present for Gus's parents. They miss Cheddar, apparently, in France.'

'I've got some basics, potatoes, some tins of things.'

'We'll be fine!' Romy had been a student for a few years now. She was confident that she could make something tasty out of random ingredients, even if Felix couldn't. 'Let's have a look at these DVDs then.'

He did have a vast collection, kept in shoeboxes. There were some lovely old films she'd either never seen or hadn't seen for ages, and box sets of TV series she'd never caught up with.

'I think it's got to be *Miracle on 34th Street*,' said Felix. 'It's Christmas. Then we'll make dinner.'

When he'd set it all up he plonked himself on the sofa next to her. 'I'm not snuggling up or anything, but if I sit over there I'll get a terrible crick in the neck.'

Romy wished he could snuggle up. She couldn't imagine anything nicer.

'Do you know, I'd never seen that before?' said Romy when the film had ended. 'It's lovely!' She tried to wipe her eyes without him seeing, and was caught out.

'It's OK. You're supposed to cry.'

'And I did! Now I'm hungry!'

'Let's make something to eat.'

Gus wasn't a great one for sharing a kitchen. He did like to cook, with a lot of knife sharpening and banging, and throwing used pans into the sink, but he didn't want Romy there while he did it. Felix, however, was much more relaxed in the kitchen. He was happy for Romy to chop and peel, or, when it came to the curry sauce, stir and taste and fiddle with the seasoning. (Gus despised tasting food while you cooked it. His theory was that if you knew what you were doing, you knew how the food tasted.)

Felix was even very forgiving when Romy added far too much chilli paste, insisting, between gulps of water, that he liked a bit of heat – especially at Christmas.

'What would you like to drink with that?' he asked Romy, when she'd found some yoghurt in the back of the fridge and had managed to cool it down a bit.

'Have you got any lager?'

He nodded. 'Over in the studio. I'll go and get it. It'll be nice and cold.'

While he was getting it, Romy took her plate with her to the sofa. It was so cosy there. Could she have done this with Gus? she wondered. And she decided no. Curry on your lap in front of the TV would never be allowed at Christmas, and if they had it at any other time, Gus would be watching sport. Romy didn't mind this so much, but she hated it when Gus kept getting up and punching the air, shouting 'yes!' or 'come on!' He would bounce back down on to the sofa, jolting her out of her little doze.

Felix sat down next to her and handed her a beer. 'So, what do you fancy now? Ever seen *Northern Exposure*? It's the best! I had to get this from Germany to get the original soundtrack.'

'Music is important, isn't it?' Romy took another mouthful of curry and then a sip of beer to cool her mouth.

'Very. Not everyone gets that.'

She didn't ask if Lauren got that. She'd be hoping for the answer to be 'no'. That would have been wrong for so many reasons.

Romy yawned widely. 'Oh, sorry!' She glanced up at the big clock that hung on one of the walls. It was only ten o'clock. She felt guilty. It was rude to yawn.

'Early start? Because of the market?'

'It was pretty early. And I was up late last night making things.'

'It was definitely worth it,' he said, indicating the branches with their little balloon lights. 'But I think you need to sleep now. The thing is I'll need to change the sheets on my bed—'

'I'd much prefer to sleep on the sofa,' she said quickly. 'I'll be very happy here. The sofa is comfy and the fire is cosy. I've always wanted to have a fire in my bedroom, so to speak, and now I've got one!'

Everything she said was true but really she didn't want him to go to a lot of trouble so she could sleep in his bed. She felt it would inevitably involve thoughts she didn't want expressed. If she didn't go near his bedroom she'd be less likely to imagine what it would be like if he didn't have a girlfriend and she didn't have Gus.

He frowned and considered. 'Oh, OK. It would be easier because I'm not sure if I've actually got any clean bedding to go on the bed. I'll put it in the machine and then back on when it's washed for when Lauren comes home.'

'She'll appreciate that.' Romy certainly would. It wasn't the kind of gesture that would occur to Gus.

'In the meantime, I'll find a sleeping bag and some blankets.'

It took a little time to do everything needed to get Romy ready for bed. She didn't have a tooth-brush and although Lauren had left hers, she'd rather her teeth all fell out than borrow it. She did borrow a smear of moisturiser though. Then she wished she hadn't. It smelt wrong. Lovely, but wrong.

The most intimate moment was when they were putting out the balloon lights, which took ages. When the last one had been switched off they were suddenly in darkness, very close.

Romy longed to move forward an inch. She knew he would put his arms round her and kiss her. She desperately wanted him to. But she knew if he did it would shatter the innocence of their time together. As it was, nothing had happened that they couldn't talk about to their partners. They'd watched telly, cooked, watched more telly and had a few drinks. All fine.

She sensed he felt the same because he didn't move for a few seconds while they stood in the darkness. She couldn't move first because she was in the corner, with her back to the big wall-sized window.

He cleared his throat. 'Sometimes, when all the lights are out, I see deer coming out of the woods.'

'I'd love to see that!' she said quickly.

'Maybe – if the roads are still icy and you have to stay – we could put food out for them? I don't like to do it all the time in case they get dependent. But they do like it.'

'What do they eat?'

He made a face. 'Deer food. I buy it.'

'Oh, can we do it? I'd so like to see them.'

'It is magical.'

It was no longer so dark. Ambient light now glowed from outside as the moon escaped from behind a cloud for a moment.

'I'll just go and put a light on,' said Felix. 'Then we can go to bed.'

Romy was aware how safe she felt. She didn't really know why, but she felt absolutely confident that Felix wouldn't do anything she didn't want.

Although she was blissfully comfortable on the sofa, her head on a pile of pillows, one of which had a silk pillowcase, her feet towards the fire that provided warmth and a comforting glow, it took Romy a little while to drop off, in spite of being very tired. For though she was aware of being very happy, she was also aware that this happiness was just for now, and for tomorrow night, if she didn't make herself try and get home. Just for the moment she lay there, appreciating her lovely day, the fire, and – she realised with something of a shock – being away from Gus. He was a lovely guy, she knew. But he wasn't the one for her.

Romy got up early on Christmas Eve so she could be showered and dressed before he appeared. She'd rinsed out her knickers the night before and put them on the wood burner to dry. She was pleased and a bit surprised to find them dry and she was feeling quite respectable when he appeared shortly afterwards.

'You're looking very bright and bushy-tailed. I hope that doesn't mean you didn't sleep and so had to get up at dawn?'

'I wouldn't be looking bright and bushy-tailed if I had. I'm up early because it's a work day and I want to do some.' She paused, aware she probably sounded a bit barking. 'So I don't feel guilty about being here.'

He nodded. 'No need to feel guilty as we have discussed, but I'm pleased you're keen.'

'I'd love a place of my own to work on. You just need to show me what to do.'

'Breakfast first, please!'

'Oh, OK. Slacker.'

She loved her day. There was a barn next to Felix's studio and this was where she worked. He lent her protective gloves, some headphones so she could hear music and there was a pile of lovely William De Morgan tiles to sort out.

He'd said he really only needed six but she had

knocked off the old cement and glued six by lunch-time, so she made it her mission to do them all.

Felix didn't look to see what she had achieved until he had declared his own work finished.

'Oh wow! You've done a brilliant job! You've cleaned all the tiles and glued the broken bits. You're amazing! Lauren would never have— Sorry, I shouldn't mention her.' He didn't say anything for a couple of moments. 'She wouldn't have done that.'

'It's my thing, that's all,' said Romy, trying to conceal how pleased she was with his reaction.

'Come into the house. I'm not going to let you lift another finger tonight!' He paused. 'I don't know if you noticed, working so hard, but the track is still covered with black ice. There'll be no point in trying to leave tomorrow.'

'I'll have to stay here then.' In her head she counted the days: tonight, and tomorrow, Christmas Day. Unless the freezing weather continued, after that this happy idyll would end. She smiled at him, hoping he didn't see the edge of sadness that she felt.

He was as good as his word. She showered and put on a pair of his joggers with a T-shirt and then his dressing gown. He seated her on the sofa in front of the wood burner with a very large glass of Bailey's.

Later he replaced this with a glass of wine and a bowl of coq au vin and mashed potato.

'The stew was in the freezer,' he said. 'Lauren isn't fond of "messed around with" food. She's a grilled fish and salad girl.'

'And I bet she looks amazing because of it,' said Romy.

'Yes, yes she does.'

In spite of herself, Romy yawned widely. 'Golly, you must be fed up with the sight of my fillings.'

He raised an eyebrow. 'Have you got any?'

'A couple.'

'I wasn't looking. Now, can I interest you in the Work, Rest and Play pudding? You've worked, I hope you'll rest and tomorrow we'll play.'

'What is it?'

'Melted Mars Bars with brandy and ice cream.'

Romy smiled. 'O.M.G.'

'I like it too. Lauren says—'

'Lauren is beautiful because she doesn't eat refined sugar and fat,' said Romy quickly.

'So why are you— Sorry,' he said, and went to fetch the puddings.

Romy was aware of the smell of toast and the sound of a crackling fire. For a few seconds she let herself enjoy both things and work out why she was experiencing them. When she remembered, she had to stop a smile spreading over her features.

'Hey! Happy Christmas! Sorry to wake you but I was excited.'

She smiled sleepily at Felix who was holding a pile of toast right by her nose and had obviously just made up the wood burner.

'Why?' Her voice was croaky and she was glad he wasn't going to kiss her because her breath probably smelt. She'd done the best with her teeth the previous two nights, with a towel, some toothpaste and one of those bottle brush things you put between your teeth.

'Because it's Christmas! I always used to get into my parents' bed on Christmas morning!' His expression changed. 'Oh God, sorry. That came out wrong.'

'It's OK,' said Romy. 'I understand completely. It's Christmas morning. I should get up.' Suddenly she became aware that she'd discarded his borrowed nightclothes when she got too hot during the night and was only wearing a strappy top and her knickers.

'No! Wait there! I've got you a stocking.'

'Really? But you didn't know I was going to be here!' While Felix was out of the way she grabbed the T-shirt he had lent her from the floor next to her and put it on. She felt better now she was more covered up although her muscles were a bit stiff from the work she'd done the day before.

He came back, looking pleased with himself, and

handed her a mug of tea. 'The fact I didn't know you'd be here is what made doing the stocking such fun. I'll go and get it,' he went on. 'It's only little things.'

She took a bite of buttered toast then a glance at the clock, which told her it was nearly nine. 'Have you been up for hours?' she said as he returned, holding a sock, the kind you'd wear with walking boots. It was full of knobbly things.

'Yes! I told you I was excited. Here!'

She took another bite of toast and gulp of tea and then took the stocking. She could see he couldn't wait for her to finish either before she opened it.

The first thing she took out was a CD.

'It's one of my band's. I hope you like it.'

'I'm sure I will!' She was delighted to have this. It would be something to treasure forever.

'Do finish your toast,' he said.

'I will, if you don't mind. I'm always starving first thing.'

'Oh me too! Lauren doesn't really get breakfast. She just has a slice of lemon in hot water.'

'Which explains her wonderful figure and amazing skin,' said Romy, helping herself to another slice of toast.

'Yes! You're right again. How did you know?'

Romy shrugged, still chewing.

Then she went back to her stocking. She didn't want to rush it.

The next thing to come out was a tin of sticking plasters.

'You have to remember, this is all completely unprepared,' said Felix, possibly slightly embarrassed. 'And you may have developed blisters yesterday, chipping away at the cement. It was quite a hard job.'

'I love plasters,' said Romy. 'But I never have one when I need one. Although I am a bit stiff today I haven't got blisters, but these'll come in really useful when I *have* got them.' She meant every word and hoped she didn't come across as gushing. She put her hand back in the sock and pulled out a lemon.

'Lemons always come in handy,' said Felix.

'They do!' agreed Romy, thinking: Especially if you eat them for breakfast. Out loud she said, 'We can make punch later. If you've got plenty of them.'

'Always,' he said.

The next item – which was nearly the last, Romy realised rather sadly; she'd been enjoying her stocking so much – was a bar of dark chocolate.

'Left over from a recipe, I'm afraid. It's probably too dark to just eat.' Felix was apologetic again.

'We can make brownies, or something nice with it, if it is too strong. Very good dipped in hot milk, I find.'

'We may not have spare milk for drinking just as is.'

'Brownies then.'

'Do you bake?' He seemed surprised and possibly pleased.

'A bit.' She considered for a few moments. 'If we want more breakfast later, I could make pancakes.'

His eyes widened in delight. 'We have real maple syrup! Amazing!'

Romy smiled and put her hand into the sock and pulled out an onion. 'Just what I always wanted!'

'I knew that!' said Felix.

The final present was wrapped up. As it was small and Felix had used wide parcel tape to secure the paper, it took a bit of time before she released it. It was a little pin with a stud at the back in the shape of a bat. 'I love it!' she said. 'I absolutely love it!' She looked at it again and then said, 'How did you know? I mean – I love bats,' she added quietly.

'I know you do,' he said, also quiet. 'I bought it a while ago because it was raising money for bats and I kept it—' He stopped. 'Just in case—'

'In case of what?' She knew she shouldn't push him but she couldn't stop herself.

He shrugged. 'In case Lauren ever got into bats, I suppose. Or cheap jewellery.'

Romy laughed; she knew she was supposed to. 'I should get up. But thank you so much for my stocking. It's one of the nicest ones I've ever had!'

'Surely not! It was only a few things I got together at the last minute.'

'It was spontaneous. I love that.' Gus, she realised now, wasn't great at the spontaneous gestures. Then she chided herself for having ungenerous thoughts.

'If you want a shower, I'll get you a better towel. I was a bit embarrassed with the one you used yesterday,' said Felix, suddenly in host mode.

He left to find a towel but also, she realised, to give her a bit of privacy.

They met at the door of the shower room. She was clutching her clothes to her and he was holding a towel and some bath products.

'Here,' he said, handing her the towel. 'I've found some of Lauren's shower gel. I'm afraid mine's only supermarket stuff.'

'Supermarket stuff is fine,' she said, managing to take the bottle in spite of her armful of clothes and towel. She'd managed with a bar of very old soap the day before.

'Really? I'm sure Lauren wouldn't mind you using hers.'

'Honestly.' Romy had used Lauren's face cream and it had felt uncomfortable all night, not smelling familiar. Besides, she'd wronged this woman in her imagination quite enough: stealing her expensive beauty products would compound the wrongness.

'Right!' Felix said. 'I think we should go and see what the weather is like, gather a few bits of wood for the fire and then have pancakes?'

'Yes, and then I must do some texting to tell

people I'm OK and explain that I haven't got the internet.'

'I've done my texting already. I think my friends were glad I wasn't coming. They were short of chairs.' He fixed her bat pin to her coat carefully. She could feel his breath against her face and the warmth of his hands where he brushed against her neck. She could also smell him. He smelt a bit better than she did. He'd obviously added a splash of cologne to the supermarket shower gel.

'Thank you so much! I really love it. Now, come on,' she said, the moment the pin was in place. 'Let's go out!'

Really she would have much rather they had stayed where they were, close to each other, breathing the same oxygen, but she knew they mustn't. She wanted him and she was fairly sure he wanted her, but they couldn't act on their feelings. And yet she knew this would always be a special, secret Christmas she would hold in her heart forever.

Although the road was still very icy, in the woods, where the frost had fallen on beech leaves, the going was crisp.

'If you're up for it, we can walk right up to the boundary?'

'So you've got lots of land?'

'Yes, but it's very steep. Only good to grow trees, really; we have mostly beech. They're lovely trees but shallow rooted. With the gales we've had recently, there are likely to be some down.' He shrugged nonchalantly. 'I don't mind. It saves me having to thin the trees and beech is great firewood.'

'Let's get gathering then!'

After a while, Felix said, 'Hmm, you know, actually it's quite far to the boundary. Shall we have pancakes and maple syrup first, and then make the trek?'

They went back to the house with some smaller branches, which they dumped outside, and then went into the living room, which was warm and very welcoming. As Felix went to replenish the fire, Romy plonked herself down on the sofa, accepting the time had come to get in touch with people. First she sent a text to her parents, and then a more carefully worded one to Gus. 'Hi honey, hope Christmas going well. Fine here except there's no internet! You have to climb a tree or something so I won't be doing that. Have a lovely time! Romy. Xxx'.

She didn't put lots of 'love you's because Gus didn't like too much of that sort of thing and at the moment it wouldn't feel right. The kisses would do.

Texting done, she looked around the kitchen-cum-living room. Romy had lit the lights in her balloon decorations before they left and they looked lovely.

'This is so Christmassy!' she said. 'Lauren is going to love it when she gets here!' She felt the need to mention her name, to remind them both that she existed.

'I hope so. It certainly looks festive. A bit like a

magazine.' He glanced at Romy. 'And I mean that in the very best way.'

'Good! Now show me the frying pan!'

They were full and thoroughly sticky when Felix said, 'Shall we have a drink? It is Christmas!'

'Actually,' said Romy. 'Don't let me stop you, but honestly? Unless we're going to spend the rest of the day watching TV I'd rather make the hike to the top of the hill? We were on a mission.' The moment she'd spoken, she worried that she'd sounded puritanical and boring.

'I never say no when people are prepared to go wooding, and after the amount of pancakes I just ate, I definitely need exercise.' He gave her a quick sideways hug and then let go of her again equally quickly. 'You're a great cook, you know that?'

'I'm OK at what I can do,' she said, trying to hide her pleasure. 'Now, let's go for that really big tree at the top of the hill.'

She was panting and very warm as they approached the boundary fence, high up by the road.

'This is why it's so quiet in my house,' Felix said. 'It's because we're below the road.'

'I thought it must be miles away from anywhere last night. It was so silent.'

'Come on. Last little bit to climb.'

When they got to the top there were three fallen trees. Huge giants lying prone, with vast flat roots like plates attached to the bottom of them.

'Unfortunately they look far too big for us to get down to the house, unless we go back and get the chainsaw? Well, thank goodness none of them fell on the road! I'm not sure but I think I'd have had to pay to clear them, if they had. And supposing they'd fallen on a car! It doesn't bear thinking of.'

'Well, it hasn't happened, thank goodness,' said Romy, understanding how he felt. 'Hey – I hope none of them were the one you climbed to get the internet!' she went on.

'No! I'm not a monkey. I couldn't climb one of those.'

'So which is the tree you climb, then?'

'I'll show you.'

There was a small tree that had obviously been pollarded at one time. It was quite easy to climb but then, scarily, Felix wriggled his way along a branch so he was above a steep gully. 'Look! No hands!' he said, waving.

'Agh! Don't! Hold on! You're making my stomach feel peculiar.'

'It's perfectly safe, I promise you.'

Just then, his mobile started to ring and he reached

into his pocket to get it. 'Hello?' he said, and then dropped the phone.

'Oh no!' said Romy.

'Find it! Quick! Before it gets lost in the leaves.'

She bounded into the gulley and scrabbled about, eventually finding the handset. 'Got it!' she called. 'Now come down!'

He lost his balance and fell off the branch.

'Noo!' wailed Romy. 'Are you OK?'

'What the hell is going on?' demanded the person on the phone. It was Lauren.

Realising that she couldn't pretend she wasn't there, Romy began to bluff. 'Hello?' she said into the phone. 'I'm just a passer-by. The man has fallen out of a tree and dropped his phone.' At least that was all true.

'Don't be ridiculous!' said Lauren. Her tone made Romy think of Katharine Hepburn – a woman who took no nonsense. 'Felix lives in the middle of a forest! There are no passers-by.'

'Um, in England we often go for walks at Christmas.' This was true too, but it sounded pathetic.

'No one knows that place is there! Let me speak to Felix.'

Felix, who seemed completely unhurt, was laughing hysterically. He seemed to think it hilarious that his girlfriend had called from America and was now talking to Romy, who shouldn't even be there. He was shaking his head and waving his hands, indicating he couldn't speak to Lauren in his hysterical state.

'He has just fallen out of a tree. He can't come to the phone right now.'

'For God's sake!' snapped Lauren. 'You mean he thinks this is funny! Well, give him a message for me. Tell him his Christmas stocking is in the airing cupboard, under the pile of laundry waiting to be ironed. I knew he wouldn't find it there!'

'I'll tell him,' said Romy meekly.

'You know? I did feel a bit bad about this whole thing. But not now!' She disconnected.

Felix came up to her. 'Are you OK? You look a bit shocked.'

'You're the one who should be shocked – you fell out of a tree.'

'But I didn't get an earful from Lauren. I expect she thought I was being childish?'

'She did, and she didn't believe me when I said I was a passer-by.'

Felix bit his lip.

'And she said that your Christmas stocking is in the airing cupboard, under the linen that's waiting to be ironed. She said you'd never find it there.'

'I did find it, actually,' he said. 'But I didn't look at it. It wasn't Christmas then.' He bit his lip again but this time he seemed chastened.

'Shall we take what wood we can and then you can find your stocking and open it?' suggested Romy.

'Good idea,' Felix said, visibly pulling himself together. 'Come on. Let's each get a big old log, and then I'll race you back.'

'That's not fair! I don't know my way!'

'Eat my dust!' he called, setting off with almost an entire tree.

Romy was more circumspect and took a smaller branch. She soon caught him up.

They laughed as they jogged through the trees, sometimes stopping to gather more wood, and sometimes falling over in the fallen leaves.

But although she was cheerful on the outside, inside, the day had been a little spoilt for Romy. Lauren's call had burst their bubble. She should be here, not Romy.

They dumped the wood where the sawhorse and the axe were. 'Come on then,' said Felix. 'Let's get my stocking!'

'Don't you want to open it in private?' said Romy, who had followed him in but was taking the time to get her dirty boots off.

'Nah, it might be a bit sad on my own.'

He waited until she was ready and then headed up the stairs.

'OK,' he said, stopping outside a cupboard that was unpainted and obviously new. 'Let's get it.'

His top half disappeared into the cupboard and he came out holding a bright red stocking made of felt, which was embroidered and covered with jewels and sequins. It was obviously quite heavy, too. It looked terribly expensive. She imagined it being full of carefully chosen presents. She wondered if he'd get as much pleasure from his elaborate stocking as she'd had from her makeshift one. Handmade always won in her book. She felt a wave of guilt for being the one to open it with him.

They went back downstairs and Felix made up the wood burner while Romy made tea for them both. 'Do you want anything to eat?' she called from the kitchen area.

'No! I want you to come and help me with my stocking.'

She had wanted to put it off for some reason, but came and sat down. Felix took out a bottle-shaped present, and set it aside for now. 'I think I can guess what this is. Let's see what else is here?'

He tipped out the contents on to the sofa. There were half a dozen little packages wrapped in gold tissue paper. He picked up the first one and unwrapped it. It was a little antique brooch.

'Jewellery for a man? Unusual,' said Romy, sensing something was wrong.

Felix didn't answer. He opened another package and revealed a friendship bracelet, the sort of thing you might buy at a festival. 'We went to Glastonbury this year,' was all he said.

One by one the parcels were opened and each one had a piece of jewellery in it.

'OK,' he said. 'That's all the jewellery I ever gave her. Let's have a look at the bottle.'

He pulled the paper off the bottle. It was Jack Daniel's and it had 'Felix' written in a Sharpie pen across it. There was a note attached by a rubber band. He opened it, read it quickly, and handed it to her. 'You read it.'

'Really?'

He nodded.

*Dear Felix,*

*I think we both know we've reached the end of the road. I don't want to live in your house in the woods. I need open spaces and sea and Connecticut gives me that.*

*I hope this doesn't seem harsh or cowardly, but I couldn't risk being talked around. I hope you'll see I've done the right thing. The bottle of Jack is to help you with that.*

*Goodbye. It was fun for a while.*

Lauren's handwriting was beautiful and her signature looked as though she'd practised it. Romy stared at the note as the silence stretched.

'Well, that's me dumped,' Felix said eventually.

Romy didn't know how to respond. She couldn't tell from Felix's expression whether he'd like to call Lauren every name under the sun, or beg her to change her mind and come back to him. It didn't seem like the latter to her, but she couldn't be sure.

She looked at him, trying to work out how upset he was. He looked back, his expression thoughtful, tender. Then he gave a quick, bright smile. 'Come on. Let's get some more wood in before the light goes completely.'

Felix obviously enjoyed the distraction of dragging huge logs through the woods, and Romy did too. She was at a slight loss to work out if his high spirits were put on for her benefit or if he was really pretty relaxed about being dumped in a truly heartless way.

How would she feel if Gus broke up with her? she asked herself. She realised she'd feel relieved. She knew she was going to have to have the 'it's not you, it's me' conversation when they next met. She just hoped he wouldn't be hurt.

'Right!' said Felix, slightly out of breath. 'It's nearly dark and I'm bushed. How about we put some food out for the deer, then go back in and open the Jack Daniel's?'

'Sounds like a plan. What can we have to eat? I'm starving!' She laughed. 'Not something I've ever said on Christmas Day before.'

He pulled her to his side in a quick hug. 'It's been a funny one,' he said. 'But I've loved it.'

She didn't mention the Christmas stocking. Was he happy in spite of it? Or because of it? 'I have too! The best Christmas ever. Well, since I've been grown up, anyway.'

'Me too! And don't worry, I won't let you starve, either. We've got plenty of food. I've got a wild boar salami I was giving my friends for a present. We'll start on that.'

Romy hadn't set her heart on seeing any deer. Her delight was in standing in the dark, the room lit only by her little battery lights, sipping sweet American whiskey, side by side with Felix.

He put his arm round her and hugged her to him, whether for comfort or just because, she couldn't tell. She wasn't going to question it.

And then the deer appeared. They saw them first when the light caught their eyes. And then they came closer, half a dozen of them, snuffling the earth and finding the food.

Romy and Felix didn't speak. They just stood there in the dark, in silence, watching the deer.

Romy added it to her mental store of delightful memories of this Christmas. Apart from the loveliness of being with Felix (and it was very difficult to set this aside!) it was so unusual. There were no presents, hardly, if you overlooked the lovely stocking she'd been given, and the toxic one that Felix had received. The food wasn't Christmas food but, although she liked turkey and roast potatoes, she had really enjoyed making meals with Felix.

And there'd been a lot of exercise. She'd loved dragging wood down to Felix's wood store where later he would turn it into logs.

She knew real life would be back – probably tomorrow – but she would always treasure this stolen, special Christmas Day.

Romy was awoken the following morning by the ping telling her she had a text message. Maybe Gus had finally got around to replying to her Christmas message. She found her phone.

No, not Gus. It was the budget airline. The country was no longer stalled by black ice, and if she wanted to rebook her flight, she could go to France the following day. She didn't want to and was pleased that she could get her flight money back. She wasn't going to fly to France just to finish with Gus. He could wait a few days!

She got out of her heap of covers on the sofa, dressing as she went, with a glance out of the big window that would have told her it was warmer if easyJet hadn't already done so. Then she went into the kitchen end and put the kettle on.

Felix, his hair sticking up at the back, joined her there shortly afterwards, smelling of toothpaste.

'Morning!' she said. 'The black ice has gone.'

'Morning.' He kissed her cheek carelessly, as if it were part of his routine. 'How do you know?'

'My flight has been reinstated. I got a text.'

'So are you going to go to France? We've eaten all your present cheese!' He didn't sound devastated but maybe he was hiding his feelings.

'It's hardly worth going to France now, but I should go home.'

He nodded. 'I'll get the Landy out and sort your car. It should still be drivable, but if it's not, I'll take you where you need to be and arrange to get your car back to your house.'

'That would be great. I mean, great if you could get my car back on the road. But there's no need for doing all that other stuff. I can do that.'

'I'd like to do it. It would be a sort of thank you for all the work you did on the tiles and being so . . .' He fell silent. He examined her as if she were a strange creature he was trying to identify. 'So lovely,' he finished eventually. 'I've just loved spending Christmas with you.'

Tears caught at her throat. 'And I've loved spending it with you. I adored seeing the deer.'

'I've loved every minute of it,' he said. 'Are you sure you have to go?'

She nodded. 'I've got to face real life now.'

'Me too.' He made a face. 'It sucks, doesn't it?'

She laughed in agreement but she wasn't sure what he meant. Was it real life he didn't like? Or the fact that they had to separate?

Her car took a bit of rescuing, but his Land Rover was up to the job and towed it out from where it was resting, its nose against a tree.

At last it was facing the right way, on the track, and it had all Romy's bits and pieces in it.

She got in and opened her window so she could say goodbye. Felix leant in.

'Hey – I've got a good idea! Let's go to the pub? It's on your way. It's still Christmas, after all, and you could use their Wi-Fi.'

'OK!' said Romy, her spirits lifting ridiculously at the thought of one last drink with Felix, albeit a non-alcoholic one.

He got to the pub before she did and was waiting by his vehicle showing her a space where she could park. The car park was quite crowded.

So was the pub, but full of Christmas cheer and bonhomie.

Felix was obviously known there. 'Hey – happy Christmas, mate!' the barman called. 'Your usual? Oh! What's the young lady having?'

'Ginger beer, please,' said Romy, admiring the way the barman had stopped himself commenting on it being her at Felix's side, and not Lauren.

'Same as himself!' said the barman. 'When he hasn't got a chauffeur, that is.' He winked. Then he slapped a couple of packets of crisps on the bar. 'Those are on the house. Christmas present.'

Romy couldn't help laughing as she followed Felix to a bench in the corner that was unoccupied. 'Do you think all his Christmas presents are packets of crisps?' she asked.

Felix shook his head. 'No, only people he likes get crisps. Everyone else gets pork scratchings.'

'It's weird we both like ginger beer,' said Romy, after they'd toasted each other.

'There are lots and lots of things we both like,' said Felix. 'Bats, for example. We can see them in the summer.'

Romy cleared her throat. Him using the word 'we' and 'summer' in the same breath was lovely.

'So, if it's really "back to reality" time we better get our phones out. Get that social media fix I've not been missing,' said Felix briskly. 'The Wi-Fi is strong here.'

Romy would have been happy to ignore the out-side world for a bit longer but as the Wi-Fi had been her excuse for coming to the pub and not just going straight home, which included having no heat or hot water, she produced her phone.

'I wonder how Christmas has gone in France,' said Felix. 'See if there are any pictures?'

There were loads. Gus's younger sister seemed obsessed with recording every moment of the Christmas holidays. Maybe she didn't feel she'd properly experienced anything unless she'd put it all on Facebook.

'So, which one is Gus?' asked Felix, poring over the pictures.

'That one,' said Romy, pointing him out with a finger.

They scrolled through the pictures for what seemed like a while. It was hard not to notice that in them was a woman Romy didn't recognise. It wasn't one of his sisters; it was someone else. And in every picture she was next to Gus.

'Do you know who she is?' said Felix.

Romy shook her head. She was feeling odd. It was quite obvious that this woman really liked Gus. She couldn't tell how Gus was feeling because he was always facing the camera, taking part in the explosion of photos proving what a wonderful time he and his family were having at Christmas.

'Want me to do a bit of internet digging?' asked Felix. 'Find out who she is?' There was an eagerness in his offer that made Romy smile.

'You can do that?'

'Probably. If she's not that up on internet security.'

She passed the phone over to him. She could see he was dying to investigate.

While Felix's fingers danced over her phone, Romy examined her feelings. How would she feel if it was proved that Gus had met someone else in France and had obviously enjoyed her company? The trouble was, she couldn't feel anything. If she really tried to feel something, she realised it was a sort of bland happiness for Gus.

'OK,' said Felix. 'She's called Samantha, and she gets on really, really well with Gus's family. Ah. Her most recent Facebook post – do you want to know what it says?'

'Of course! Why wouldn't I?'

'Because it's a bit – well . . .'

'Just show me.' She took her phone. ' "That moment when you're spending Christmas with friends and discover that your friend's brother is really cute." ' And there was an emoji of a happy, blushing face. Underneath the status was a picture of Gus beaming at the camera while Samantha planted a delicate kiss on his cheek, his hand on her knee.

Neither of them spoke for a few seconds. Then Felix said, 'Back to mine then?'

'Back to yours.'

'Great! There's a bottle of Jack Daniel's with my name on it!'

Then he turned her chin towards him and kissed her, properly, right there in the pub.

She didn't care how many people were watching them; she was lost in his kiss and the promise of what was to come.

'Get your coat, you've pulled,' she said, laughing, when he finally let her go and she'd got her breath back.

'Who'd have thought a Christmas stocking could make me so happy?' he said as they went to the car park.

'Have to say, it's made me very happy too!' said Romy.

# A
# Dream
# Christmas

Ginny had a headache and the taxi, ordered for them by the best man, smelt strongly of Lynx and pine-flavoured car deodorant. The smell made her feel sick, although that could have been from a mixture of too much Prosecco – which she never wanted to drink again – and general exhaustion. Across the car, Ben also looked worn out and nauseated. Considering it was supposed to be the happiest day of their lives *and* Christmas Eve, it was pretty bloody awful.

The day was over and, although she knew she probably shouldn't be, Ginny was glad; the whole thing had been more stressful then she'd ever imagined, but without the benefit of the wedding she'd dreamt of at the end of it – just the wedding everyone else had wanted. Still, she thought, not long now and they'd be at their honeymoon destination: the little luxury haven in the New Forest, deep in the woods, that she'd booked last spring when she thought getting married on Christmas Eve was a really good idea.

At least there was a silver lining to their unconventional timing: they were now on their honeymoon, and therefore didn't have to spend their first Christmas with either of their families, neither of which they got on with. The more she thought about it, the more relieved Ginny was that she didn't have to speak to her mother for over a week, and Ben's mother ever again, if she could possibly wangle that.

Both mothers had completely hijacked the wedding, guilt-tripping them into having people and things they really didn't want – or rather that Ginny didn't want. Ben had been mysteriously absent for all of the wedding preparations, leaving Ginny to try and fight alone for the wedding they wanted, and ultimately to lose the battle.

Ben hadn't even given Ginny a proper explanation for his absence, only vague excuses of being 'snowed under' at work, or being 'offshore' earning extra holiday time for their honeymoon. He was home for one weekend when he went on his stag do, which meant they hardly even saw each other, let alone had meaningful conversation. After months of the same, Ginny had drawn her own conclusions: Ben didn't like confrontation, and was happy to abandon her to it.

'*Oh, darling!*' *he said.* '*We have the rest of our lives together. Let's just let our mothers have what they want. I really don't want to fight with them just now!*'

'*Does that mean I have to fight with them?*'

'*No, just give in gracefully. Does it really matter, anyway?*'

With an attitude like that, Ginny really hadn't had a hope.

In a funny way the wedding would have been easier if Ginny's father hadn't been so generous. But while he was lavish beyond sense in some areas – he hired the most expensive videographer he could find – in other ways he was curiously mean. The wedding favours had been donated by a business acquaintance for whom it was a bit of useful publicity. This meant each guest received a miniature packet of cheese and biscuits to take home. Had there been some alcohol – a small bottle of port or something – Ginny would have been happier. But no, her father had discovered that if alcohol were included in the gift, the hotel would charge corkage. She could only be relieved that her father wasn't chummy with someone who produced ball bearings or there would have been a selection box of them on the tables.

Whenever she protested about any of the wedding plans, she was accused of being a bridezilla; in fact, this accusation was flung at her if she even expressed an opinion. 'What do you mean you don't want mustard on your sandwich? That's ridiculous! Everyone likes mustard with ham!' Ginny couldn't even say that she thought hiring white doves was a ridiculous extravagance. And her saying she didn't really like birds being too near her was dismissed as diva-ish nonsense. 'They'll be so pretty!' her mother had said. 'If you will get married in the middle of winter, you'll need something to make the photos look half decent!'

And so her wedding had turned into a giant showing-off fest by her parents for their family, friends and business acquaintances. If Ginny's parents had a hundred guests each, Ben's parents had to as well. Ginny hadn't had the strength to object; she'd been allowed a couple of her closest friends but no one else who wasn't in some way 'useful'. If she had, she'd have had another earful of 'ungrateful' and 'don't you know how much this wedding is costing?'

She dreaded to think how much the whole thing *was* costing and in some ways she felt she'd rather not know. However, she was fairly certain that if her mother hadn't been so set on having the wedding she'd never had, her father would have made a contribution to a deposit on a house, which would have been so much better than a massively expensive 'do'.

Currently they lived in Ben's flat. It was small, had no garden and, crucially, was within 'popping in' distance of his mother. And because she'd always 'popped in' when Ben was single, his mother didn't see any reason to stop when he had a girlfriend. Ginny didn't think their being married would stop her either. She felt spied on and criticised and was desperate to move. The cost of the wedding probably made this prospect even more distant.

All Ginny had wanted was a small wedding in their local church, followed by a reception at their local pub. This did really great food and could also put people up for reasonable prices. But no, Ginny's mother had not been satisfied by this idea.

She'd tried to talk to her dad about her feelings, but he'd brushed away her objections. He'd been brainwashed by her mother into believing a humongous wedding was every girl's dream, and anything Ginny said to the contrary was just her being silly. He took her protests that the wedding was getting out of control to mean she was secretly thrilled at the extravagance, but didn't want to show it. If Ben had been around more he might have been able to make her father see sense, but he was never there! Now the wedding was over she'd have to confront Ben about his recent behaviour, but not tonight. She didn't have the strength.

Not only had Ben ducked out of all the arguments and arrangements but he had chosen his best friend as best man. Any normal best friend would have been fine, but Eddie wasn't normal – unless you considered being a caricature of a best man was acceptable behaviour in real life. The jokes that were so off colour they created a whole new palette, the practical jokes that were about as funny as amateur night at the local pub, and the inappropriate asides that made everyone uncomfortable. Thank goodness her mother didn't know what MILF stood for.

'I suppose we won't have to invite Ed and my mother to the same social events, will we?' she said.

'What's that?' said Ben. 'What are you talking about?'

'I was just saying, it won't matter that Ed offended all of my family and most of yours. We won't want to bring them together socially ever again.'

'Ed is a good bloke,' said Ben, on the defensive. 'He'd do anything for you.'

'Except make a speech that is suitable for a wedding, rather than one that belonged at a stag do.' But she said it very quietly. She didn't want to fight about it. It was over, after all.

Ginny caught a hairpin that had slid out of her bridal up-do and down her neck and suppressed her desire to say 'Are we nearly there yet?' She closed her eyes. As she relaxed in the back of the taxi, slowly winding its way deeper into the heart of the New Forest, Ginny tried to pep herself up. After all, she'd just married Ben, the supposed love of her life even if he wasn't her favourite person at the moment; her parents had thrown them a fairy-tale wedding, even if it wasn't the small church wedding she'd wanted; and whilst she felt hurt and let down by all of them, she resolved to try to forgive and forget. She only hoped it would be possible.

❄

She awoke to Ben saying, 'Are you sure this is it?'

'The satnav says it is, mate,' said the driver. 'Withycombe Lodge.'

'It's in the middle of a wood!' said Ben.

Ginny cleared her throat. 'It's on the edge of an estate – a country estate –' she added just in case Ben thought it was the other kind. 'It was the house-keeper's cottage.'

She forbore to point out that when he had been consulted on their honeymoon destination, he'd just said, 'You do it! It's more your thing than mine.' She went on, 'And look, your car's here!' Thank goodness the best man hadn't messed up that bit. 'Let's go inside!'

She felt revived by her doze and got out of the car, eager to see the cottage that had been her 'happy place' over the past weeks, when the wedding seemed like the most expensive nightmare ever. She hoped it would be a sanctuary for her and Ben, where they could spend the first few days of mar-ried life getting to know one another again.

Ben dealt with the taxi while she found the keys that had been left, endearingly, she thought, under a plant pot. They were charmingly old-fashioned keys, no fancy seven-lever locking systems for this little establishment.

On the website the cottage had looked rural but very high-spec, with a Jacuzzi bath, every sort of in-house entertainment you could dream of, and a kitchen filled with glamorous, gleaming, intelligent appliances which could take the top off your boiled egg for you, if you knew how to programme them properly. There was even a hot tub somewhere in the woods.

Ben had gone straight to his car and so she let herself into the cottage, briefly wondering if Ben should have carried her over the threshold. But as in her eyes Ben had done nothing right for months, she wasn't surprised and only mildly disappointed. She also appreciated having a few minutes on her own.

It was the wrong cottage; she knew that the moment she was through the front door. The address was right but the interior most definitely wasn't. This wasn't high-end luxury, this was – she looked around – well, old. Not old in an outdated way, but old like cottages she had once seen in a living-history museum. It was out of a different century.

Firstly, it was cold, but she noticed it was very clean. There was a beeswax, lavender smell and she realised it must be polish.

She went from the little hall, complete with old-fashioned hallstand including a mirror with age spots, into the sitting room. This was simply, even sparsely furnished. There was an inglenook fireplace with space for a kettle to one side of it, and what would have been a bread oven. There was a settle, pulled in close to the fire, and two wooden chairs. There was a small bookcase, which seemed of a later period than the rest of the room. On the deep window-sill was an oil lamp which, when she checked, proved to be still run by oil – it hadn't been converted to electricity. The mantelpiece, too high to reach almost, had two candlesticks and a pair of Staffordshire dogs. There was a dresser with blue and white china plates on it. A couple of faded watercolours on the wall depicted scenes of farming life, haystacks, heavy horses, yokels wearing smocks. She realised it was probably the original room in the house; the little kitchen, which also led off the hall, would be a later addition.

The room had a lot of charm, she had to admit, but it was definitely not what she'd booked. And – she was quite sure about this – she was not going to admit this to Ben. She was too exhausted, and he didn't deserve an honest confession of the mistake she'd made when he'd contributed so little. No, she would tough it out and pretend it was what she'd intended for them all along.

She went upstairs to see if the bedroom was the cloud of Hungarian goose-down duvets and pillows, thousand-thread-count sheets and memory-foam mattresses she'd been promised. It wasn't.

There was a beautiful brass bed but it was covered in a patchwork quilt, made with tiny hexagons, not the bigger ones she was used to. Under it were sheets – linen sheets – and blankets. And a paisley eiderdown. Not a hint of what she'd been longing for these past difficult weeks.

The bathroom next door didn't have a walk-in shower big enough for two; it had a very antiquated lavatory with an overhead cistern and a wooden seat, a washstand with a matching jug and basin and a towel rail. There was also a large brass jug that could have done with some flowers in it. On the towel rail was an arrangement of linen face towels and a couple of very small ordinary towels. She knew by now there would be no fluffy bathrobes hanging on the back of the door but she looked anyway.

She went back into the bedroom thanking her lucky stars they didn't have to walk down a path to an outside privy, even if the bath was probably hanging somewhere and had to be filled with hot water from the brass jug. With her luck recently, an outside lavatory could have been considered 'charmingly rustic' and cost extra.

As she walked down the wooden stairs (no carpet, not even a runner), she realised she might have to admit to Ben there'd been a mix-up and sort it as soon as she could. Was it possible to live in a house like this without at least a decent sleeping bag to offset the discomfort? But there was no way she could face having a row with the house owner, or the agent, or whoever, now. And tomorrow was Christmas Day and then it was Boxing Day so the sorting out might not happen for three days at least. So she wouldn't say a thing to Ben until matters could be put right.

But the fire was going in the sitting room, and the brass candlesticks on the mantelpiece and the oil lamp were lit. Also, there was a vase of holly, bright with berries, she hadn't noticed before. It all looked very pretty, she decided, in an antique sort of way.

Ben must have done that, she realised, and reluctantly gave him a good mark. But lighting fires was macho and manly – and easy. Far harder to stand by her side and tackle her determined mother and her ridiculous wedding requirements. But the live flames and the crackling sound cheered her. She went out to help with the bags. He'd obviously done the fire and gone back out for them.

She was about to congratulate him on lighting the fire when he forestalled her.

'Idiotic Eddie! He forgot to put the box of food in the car.' He looked rueful. 'Sorry, darling. We'll have to find a pub, or maybe there's a takeaway we could ring. There's bound to be menus in a holiday cottage.'

Hadn't he noticed it wasn't the usual sort of holiday cottage when he went into the sitting room?

Obviously not. He apparently had zero observational skills.

'I'm sure we'll manage something.' Ginny had squashed some of the leftover goody bags into her case. The odd wedding favours might turn out to be very useful. If they had biscuits and cheese, they wouldn't starve.

'This is a bit different!' said Ben, dumping two cases in the hall. 'I rather like it! Sort of olde worlde. But not tacky.'

She didn't comment. 'I'll take my case up,' she said. 'I need to find a cardigan.'

Rather to her surprise, the bed was turned down, both sides, and very neatly. It was odd, but she'd remembered it being all tucked in. How strange. She must have spent so much time dreaming about this bedroom, when the wedding preparations were getting on top of her, that she'd forgotten what it really looked like.

Feeling better now she was wearing her favourite cashmere cardigan, she went downstairs to find Ben in the kitchen. She hadn't been in here before but it was perfectly in keeping with the rest of the olde-worlde feel. There was a range, which seemed to be lit, a butler's sink, and an enamel table as a work surface. There was a simple wooden table with two kitchen chairs drawn up to it. Another dresser stored more plates and some old stoneware jars, possibly containing basic ingredients like flour and sugar.

Then she suddenly wondered – didn't sugar come in cone form in the olden days? She chided herself for being ridiculous. However 'period' the house may have been it was still the twenty-first century.

'Hey!' said Ben. 'I've found a casserole! Piping hot and smells delicious. Baked potatoes to go with it.'

'Oh! That's a bit of a surprise!' said Ginny.

'Really? I expect it's one of those places where they deliver food without you noticing they've been; you know, the invisible butler or something. Specially for honeymooners.'

'I don't remember that being mentioned,' said Ginny, feeling anything but honeymoonish, 'or I wouldn't have bothered with that box of groceries that got left behind.'

'Bloody Eddie!' said Ben. 'He was a rubbish choice of best man, I do admit. But never mind, this is far nicer than having to cook for ourselves.'

Ginny didn't mention the special smoked salmon, the potted shrimps, the pâté with truffles in it. Just the thought of it made her mouth water. And they were having stew. Although it was better than just having wedding-favour cheese to eat. She wondered why her brain had been so wiped that she'd forgotten this detail about food being provided. She was tired, but this wasn't like her.

'And look!' he said. 'A bottle of wine!' He picked up the bottle. 'It has a handwritten label. Elderberry! Good God! I wonder if it's drinkable.'

Ginny didn't say anything; she just opened a cup-board and found some lovely glasses, obviously antiques. Everything was so odd, so not what she was expecting. She came to the conclusion that her nightmare of a wedding had addled her brain. 'Let's try it.'

Ben filled the glasses, which were sherry-sized, and they clinked. 'Well, here's to the rest of our lives!'

'The only way is up!' said Ginny ruefully. Things could hardly get worse, after all.

'Actually, it's quite nice!' said Ben. 'Full-bodied, probably quite strong but—'

'Delicious!' The warmth of it, fruity, a little sweet but not overpoweringly so, was extremely comfort-ing. 'It's like cough medicine without the nasty taste.'

Ben nodded. 'I always thought home-made wine was fairly vile, but obviously not always. Hey,' he went on, 'I think we should eat next door, in front of the fire. These old plates on the dresser are quite deep, aren't they? Perfect for a stew.'

'Good idea,' said Ginny, opening a drawer on the hunt for knives and forks. Just then a whiff of some-thing cooking caught her nostrils. 'Hang on, I think there's something in the oven.'

Taking an old-fashioned pot holder from a hook, she opened the door of the range. 'Yes! It's a pie! It smells wonderful!'

She took it out. 'Some sort of fruit, I think. Perfect

for a pudding. It just needs custard,' she added, looking at Ben.

'I'll manage without custard,' he said. 'Let's go through and eat this.'

They ate the stew with the baked potatoes and a slab of country butter put on the table by the 'secret butler'. Ginny might not have known he was coming, but he was jolly good at his job.

'I think this is venison,' said Ben. 'It's really tasty. Well done finding this place, Gin. It's brilliant.'

Ginny wasn't as confident although she had really enjoyed the stew. 'I'll go and get the pudding,' she said.

'While you do that, I'll put some more wood on the fire,' said Ben.

Ginny picked up their empty plates. She had eaten rather a lot and she wasn't sure if she could manage pudding as well. She went through into the kitchen.

On the table, by the cooling fruit pie, was a little jug covered with a beaded cloth. Ginny investigated. It was cream, thick and yellow.

'The secret-butler thing is *really* efficient,' she muttered as she found bowls and spoons and served the pie. 'It's just really odd I don't remember anything about it.' She added cream and carried their pudding back to the sitting room.

'Hey, darling!' said Ben excitedly. 'It's snowing!'

'Is it! How wonderful!' said Ginny. 'I didn't think it was that cold or even that snow was forecast.'

'Well, it's doing it. Maybe it's magic snow, just for us.'

'To go with the magic cream that just turned up in the kitchen.' She laughed, but not sincerely.

'Well! I do have to say again, darling, you've done brilliantly booking this place.'

'Booking here wasn't difficult. It was the wedding that was so hard.'

Ben looked away, possibly not wanting to talk about the wedding. 'This wasn't at all what I was expecting.'

'Nor me,' murmured Ginny. He probably wasn't expecting the wedding he'd ended up with, either.

'But it's great! Really different.'

'Yes,' she said, hoping the antique bed with its charming coverlet was comfortable. 'I'm not quite sure about the bathroom. It hasn't got a bath in it. Or a shower.'

'We'll manage. There's probably one somewhere. We can explore tomorrow.' He looked at her speculatively. 'Is it time for bed?'

Ginny was very tired. They hadn't made love for ages and she still felt too resentful about the wedding to want to change that. 'Absolutely, but I warn you, I'm not up for anything except sleeping.'

He didn't argue. 'It was a shattering day, wasn't it? I hadn't expected the wedding to be so – over the top.'

If Ginny had had a fraction more energy she might

have started to explain why the wedding was so over the top and how he could have helped prevent it. Instead she said, 'Me neither! Now let's put the candles and the lamp out and make sure the fire is safe.'

When the room was in complete darkness they gazed out of the window at the falling snow.

'It's coming down really thick now,' said Ginny.

'Imagine if we're snowed in,' said Ben.

If Ginny had been in a state of marital bliss, the thought of being snowed in with Ben would have been heavenly for so many reasons. Now, she wasn't sure she even wanted to be married to him, let alone snowed in with him. 'It is proper, Narnia snow,' she said, hoping he wouldn't hear that actually, she felt like crying.

'Come on, let's get to bed,' he said, putting his arm round her. 'We can play in the snow in the morning.'

Ginny hadn't noticed the little fireplace in the bedroom the previous times she'd been in it but now there was a fire burning brightly there.

'How charming!' she said. 'We can go to sleep by firelight.'

'The secret butler really has excelled himself,' said Ben. 'Though I don't suppose he'll manage to be secret tomorrow, with all this snow. He – or she – will leave tracks and he'll have to reveal himself.'

As she washed before bed (somehow there was hot water in the jug, all ready to pour into the basin, and a bar of perfumed soap next to the bowl) Ginny admitted to herself she hadn't forgotten about the secret butler; there'd been no mention of it on the website or in subsequent communication. She was tired, not stupid.

As soon as she'd finished, she went back into the bedroom. Laid out on the bed was an old-fashioned, Victorian-style nightie, with a high neck and long sleeves. When Ben was in the bathroom she found herself happy to put it on. She was sitting up in bed wearing it when Ben came back.

'Actually, that nightie is really pretty,' said Ben, 'but I do think the secret butler has a sense of humour! Does he know it's our honeymoon? That's not exactly sexy, is it?'

'It's warm! Now hurry up. I really want to go to sleep.'

Although she closed her eyes and listened to the occasional crackle of the dying fire, she didn't immediately sleep. There *was* no secret butler, and she didn't like the only other explanation that had occurred to her.

*She followed the footprints in the snow, winding through the trees, their boughs heavy. Each time she felt about to catch a glimpse of her guide, the figure would be lost*

behind another corner. But she kept going, spurred on by a sense that this journey was important; that this person wanted to show her something.

Eventually the trees thinned and she could see a church ahead, and a woman standing holding the door ajar. Immediately she knew this was the woman she'd followed. Dressed in a long, plain black dress – cinched at the waist and high at the neck – this was a woman she felt she'd seen before a thousand times, in school lessons, exhibitions, television shows. But it wasn't just the recognisable Victorian dress that made her familiar; it was the atmosphere around her, an air of benevolence and understanding.

'Happy Christmas, darling!' Ben's kiss woke her with a start. He smelt of toothpaste. 'I've made tea. It was ready on a tray; all I had to do was add water to the pot. It was even warmed!'

Ginny sat up slowly, rubbing her eyes of sleep and her vivid dream, pushing the memory to the back of her mind. She took the dainty teacup and saucer he was handing her. The tea was delicious, quite unlike the ordinary teabags she used every day. 'Breakfast?'

'Porridge,' Ben went on. 'I found it in a pot with the lid on. I don't usually like it but there was a bowl of brown sugar and the cream was there again. I'm prepared to give it a go.' He paused. 'There's a loaf of bread for toast, although I expect I'd have to do it in front of the fire. There's a toasting fork, so if you want it, just say the word.'

Ben was obviously trying very hard. 'How quaint,' she said.

'Do you want it in bed? I could easily bring it up.'

She thought about it. 'Is it cold in the kitchen?'

'No. The range is going full blast.'

'I'll get up then.'

'I'll start making toast. I fancy trying out the toasting fork.'

'After breakfast I want to go in the snow. Is it still there?'

He nodded. 'Masses of it! It's really amazing. I'll go to the car later and get our wellies. They are in there, aren't they?'

'Should be. But make sure Eddie hasn't put spiders or frogs in them. His idea of a joke.'

'I'll check. See you in a minute.'

Going to the window in her long nightie and looking out at the snowy landscape – more snow than she ever remembered seeing in England – made Ginny feel as if she were in a children's story. She loved it, letting her imagination drift just as the snow had done.

She stayed staring until she got cold and then she gathered up her clothes, helping herself to a couple of extra layers from the case, and then took them all back into bed and put them on there. She remembered her mother telling her that's what she and her brother had had to do when they were little. That was back in the days when Ginny was still a child, years before her mother turned into the mother of the bride from hell.

Ben called up the stairs. 'Hurry! I'm starving and I don't want to start without you!'

She came down to join him. He looked particularly fresh-faced and healthy, she thought.

'I've been to the car and got our wellies. I couldn't resist going out in it.'

'Don't blame you. I so love snow!'

He came round the table and kissed her cheek. 'I'm really glad it snowed then. Because the Christmas presents aren't in the car.'

'It's OK. I don't really mind.' They'd agreed on only giving each other small things. They were saving hard for their deposit.

'Right, let's eat!'

He put a plate of porridge in front of her and moved a bowl of brown sugar and the jug of cream so she could reach them.

'The other thing', he said, clearly puzzled, 'is that there are absolutely no tracks from our secret butler.'

Ginny wasn't really surprised. 'Oh! How odd! I wonder how all these things are happening then. The fires being lit, food being left.'

They regarded each other for long seconds. 'Well, what do you think?' Ben asked eventually.

Ginny didn't feel ready to share her thoughts with him. They were too – ridiculous.

It had been fun making toast with the toasting fork. It had a special flavour that was so much better than toaster toast. The butter was delicious too. Ben, who had investigated the jars on the dresser, found marmalade in one of them, thick cut and obviously home-made. And the porridge with cream was extremely filling but so delicious it was hard not to eat too much of it.

Ginny felt so full she could hardly move but she couldn't resist the snow either. So, wearing all their clothes, plus some hats and scarves that were on the hallstand, they set forth. Ginny knew they were meant to wear the hats and scarves because she was quite sure they hadn't been there the previous evening.

It was easy to see where Ben had floundered through the fresh snow to the car, and it was perfectly clear that no one else had been near the house. Ginny was reminded of her dream – wandering through woods in the snow, following footprints – and felt a chill go down her spine that had nothing to do with the freezing air. But Ben didn't seem to want to speculate on what was going on in the house. Ginny thought he had probably come to the same conclusions that she had, and didn't want to talk about it either. After all, nothing at all bad had happened – yet.

'This is paradise!' said Ginny. 'Really deep, proper snow, on Christmas Day, in England! It's unheard of!'

'I tried to look on my phone to see if the whole country is snowed in,' said Ben, 'but needless to say there's no coverage here.'

'I think I saw about there being no coverage on the website,' said Ginny. 'I thought we would enjoy being out of contact for a while.'

'Well, that part went right then,' said Ben. 'With our honeymoon accommodation.'

'Oh, shush! We've got snow, haven't we? And what could be better than that?'

'Having a Ski-Doo or a team of huskies?'

Ginny threw a snowball at him. Within seconds he'd got her right back and for a few frantic minutes they bombarded each other until, exhausted, they flopped on their backs into a patch of untrammelled snow and made snow angels.

'I'm loving this!' said Ginny. 'Being a bride was horribly grown up. This is being childlike in the best sense.'

'I agree,' said Ben. 'Even though there seems to be a little tiny gap between my jacket and my jeans. The snow is seeping in.'

Ginny stood up and held her hand out to him;

she helped him get upright. 'Come on, let's explore the woods. You never know, we may find a lamp-post and a family of beavers, all the lovely Narnia stuff.'

'More likely to find polar bears,' said Ben. 'Though I could certainly do with a fur coat.'

'You'll warm up when we get going.'

Ben kissed her cold cheek, took her hand, and they set off.

It was quite tiring, walking through deep snow, but it was a bit shallower when they got further into the woods. Ginny hung back a bit and let Ben lead the way. As they walked she considered telling him about the hot tub that was supposed to be quite near the house. But she knew they wouldn't find it. There was no such thing as a hot tub in this strange, snowy world.

'Hey! A building,' said Ben.

As she came up behind him into the clearing, Ginny was hit by a wave of déjà vu. 'It's a church!' she said; *the* church, she thought. 'Let's go and see if it's open. I love old churches.'

Although she spoke cheerfully, inside she suffered a wave of unease, quickly eclipsed by a pang of regret for the quiet church wedding she'd wanted. Basically it had been cheaper to do the whole thing at the hotel, but Ginny knew that it hadn't been the expense; it was because they didn't really understand her faith, or her wanting to bring God into a marriage ceremony. It was the biggest, most important of the fights for which she'd longed to have Ben beside her.

This was a little gem of a church. Ginny wasn't an expert but it looked early. It was grey stone and not very decorated except by ivy. Large yew trees stood in the churchyard, heavy with snow.

'I wonder if it was built here in the woods, or have the woods grown up around it?' said Ben quietly.

'Shall we see if it's open?' asked Ginny, half expecting to see the woman from her dream and now keen to go inside. She set off down the path where the snow was less thick for some reason.

Ginny stopped at the door. 'I can hear music!' she whispered. 'There must be a service going on.'

She looked around at the snow, clear of footprints, and didn't meet Ben's gaze. She knew he was wondering how on earth there could be a church service, with people in it, unless they'd all been delivered by Father Christmas's sleigh.

'Is it locked?' asked Ben.

Ginny tried the handle. 'No,' she said, 'we'll tiptoe in and sit at the back.' She opened the door.

The church was empty, and the music stopped the moment they entered. But it was lit. There were branches and sconces of candles everywhere, sending shadows up to the beamed roof, and while it wasn't a bright light, it was warm and somehow welcoming.

'There must be a service soon,' said Ben, still keeping his voice low. 'We're just early. It would take ages to light all these candles.'

'That's right,' said Ginny, not believing a word of it.

Together they walked up the central aisle to the altar. It wasn't very far.

They were at the chancel steps, admiring the beauty of the candlelit church, when Ben put his hand on her arm. 'Darling, I've been wanting to tell you something . . .'

Ginny was alarmed. 'What?'

He smiled gently. 'Nothing horrible. Only – well – how much I love you really. I know I haven't said that for a long time although I never stopped feeling it.'

'You've been away so much—'

'And I need to explain that, too.' He paused. He looked a bit guilty. 'I've been doing two jobs.'

'What?' Just for a minute, Ginny was furious. There she was having to handle a wedding on her own when he was – well, what was he doing? 'You'll have to explain.'

'It is quite complicated but I was given a contract, a one-off, which was really well paid. But because it was a one-off, I didn't want to give up my day job, so to speak, so I did both. And the contract was in Europe, which was why I was never here.'

'But, darling, you knew we were getting married—'

'The money! I'm not overly obsessed with it, you know that, but the money was so good . . .' He paused. 'I've got enough for a deposit on a house!'

'Oh, Ben!' She went into his arms and hugged him. 'Really? We can have a house?'

He held her very tightly. 'We can. Our own house. We don't have to live in my flat any more, which I know you hate—'

'Only because it hasn't any garden,' said Ginny, although this wasn't the only reason she didn't like it.

'Now we can have a proper little house. It'll be all we ever wanted.'

'Oh, Ben!' she repeated. 'I was thinking all sorts of horrid things about you! About how you were ducking out of the wedding preparations because it was so ghastly, when all the time you were working so hard for a deposit! But why didn't you tell me?'

'I wanted it to be a surprise, a wedding present of sorts. I love you so much, and I wanted our married life to start off on the best foot possible. But I've not been here for you the way I should have been. I just hope you can forgive me now you know it was for a good reason.'

'I love you so much, Ben. And I will forever, I know for a fact.'

'And me you! There'll never be anyone else for me now I've got you.'

They hugged for some time, then Ginny said, 'It's almost as if we've renewed our vows.'

'Only this time it's just for us, in this beautiful church.'

Maybe not just us, thought Ginny, but didn't say. She didn't think they were quite alone. But too many words might change the atmosphere.

Ben took her hand. 'We'd better go,' he said. 'There might be a churchful of people arriving soon.'

She squeezed his fingers. She knew there wasn't. She felt as though this church and this special moment had been prepared just for them.

The music started again just as they reached the door and they stopped to listen. It was an old carol, one of Ginny's favourites.

'It's "Tomorrow Shall Be My Dancing Day",' she whispered, scared that it would stop before it had finished.

As the last notes trailed away and there was only the organ's last chord to listen to, Ben opened the door. 'Let's go.'

While they were both hungry and wanted to see what, if anything, they would find for their lunch, they didn't rush. The country churchyard was so pretty, filled with snow, and now sunlight was coming through the clouds, causing the headstones to cast blue shadows.

'Look,' said Ben. 'This one hasn't got snow on it.'

'It must be in a specially warm place,' said Ginny, knowing her explanation sounded silly.

'Hey!' she said, having read the headstone. 'It mentions Withycombe! Where we're staying!'

' "Here lies Hannah Stanwick," ' read Ben, ' "faithful servant to her Lord in Heaven and to her worldly masters, Sir Terence and Lady Withycombe. 'Lord, now lettest thou thy servant depart in peace.' " '

'Look at her dates!' said Ginny. 'Eighteen fifteen to nineteen hundred. She was a good age, especially for those days.'

'Eighty-five,' said Ben.

They stood there for several minutes, looking at the gravestone in silence.

'Let's get back,' said Ginny.

They walked back through the snowy woods in silence, holding hands. Ginny felt uplifted and closer to Ben than she had done for months and months. A glance at him told her he seemed to feel much the same.

In the cottage, the kitchen range was blazing. There was a pan of hot soup on the stove. There was a new loaf of bread, butter and a plate of ham and pickles.

'I'm starving!' said Ben.

'Me too!' said Ginny. 'And weirdly tired. I suppose a wedding takes it out of you.' She didn't repeat what he already knew, that her wedding had been especially tiring.

'Do you think maybe it would be wise to have a little lie-down before we eat, revitalise ourselves?' Ben asked with a twinkle in his eye.

Ginny returned his knowing smile. 'I think forty winks would be an excellent idea.'

Later, after lunch, full of soup and ham sandwiches, they went back into the sitting room. The fire was blazing and there was a small table drawn up in front of it. On it were some old-fashioned games, a wooden jigsaw puzzle and a pile of books.

'The secret butler obviously expects us to curl up in front of the fire, play games and read,' said Ben. 'Which is not a bad idea.'

They made themselves comfortable, piling up the cushions (there seemed to be more cushions now than previously) and covering themselves with a couple of thick woollen rugs.

Ginny thought that the olden days were very good at some things, but they hadn't quite got draught-proofing worked out yet.

They hugely enjoyed themselves, first playing snakes and ladders and after that they did the jigsaw. As Ginny inserted the final piece – wife's prerogative – Ben picked up one of the books. 'Would you like me to read to you? You can shut your eyes if you're sleepy.'

'What's the book?'

'*A Christmas Carol*,' he said, 'perfect for the time of year and—' He didn't finish his sentence but began reading.

Ginny loved the sound of Ben's voice but she would have preferred something that didn't involve anything otherworldly. Yet she closed her eyes and let her mind drift. Would they ever have sat in front of the fire and read in their normal lives? No, she concluded. They might watch a box set, or a film, which was also nice, but being read aloud to was very special. This little hideaway might not have been Ginny's luxurious cottage, but it had done them a world of good. She let herself drift off, thinking exercise, food and blessed isolation had really worked their magic.

Ginny woke up on the sofa several hours later with a cricked neck and a cold draught nipping at her feet. The fire had gone out, as had the oil lamp, and the cottage was dark and cold. Ben was sprawled across the floor, *A Christmas Carol* on his chest rising and falling with the rhythm of his breathing.

Gingerly, not wanting to tread on any part of Ben in the gloom, Ginny made her way over to the window and the last of the wintery, afternoon light. She gasped so loudly that she heard Ben stir behind her. The snow had all gone, as if it had never been there.

'What is it?' Ben asked sleepily.

'The snow's gone.'

'How weird. And what's happened to the fire, and the lamp? God, it's chilly. Shall I see about some tea to warm us up?'

Ginny nodded, still unnerved by the sudden change in the landscape. Ben got to his feet, fumbling for the torch on his phone, and made his way out to the kitchen. Ginny had to stop herself crying out that she'd come with him; she suddenly didn't want to be left alone. But she was being silly – snow could melt, fires could die, and lamps extinguish all by themselves in the few hours they'd been snoozing.

Ben came back into the living room almost immediately. 'The range isn't lit and there's no hot water.'

Ginny's eyes widened in mock horror, trying to pull herself together. 'You mean, we have to make our own fires? That's awful!'

Ben grinned feebly. 'I'm happy to do it, love, but it may take a while.'

They looked at each other across the room, and an understanding passed between them.

'Gin? Would you mind if we left quite soon? It's not just that the secret butler has let us down . . .'

'No, that's fine.' She breathed a sigh of relief. 'I want to leave too.'

'We'll get supper somewhere,' said Ben. 'I'll go up and pack the bags.'

'I'll just clear up here and the kitchen. Meet you downstairs in five.'

Ginny lit the oil lamp and headed to the kitchen as Ben hurtled up the stairs guided by his phone. Something had changed and she no longer felt comfortable in the cottage. She couldn't wash the plates quick enough and was grateful that the secret butler (or whatever euphemism Ben wanted to use) had done the pots and pans. She dried the plates and replaced them on the dresser. Then she turned round to check everything was in order. That was when she saw it.

On the table was an old book, open. Ginny placed the oil lamp on the table and inspected the page.

In beautiful handwriting were the words 'I am now confident that the newly-weds will be very happy in their marriage.'

Ben came in, dropping the bags at the door, and looked over her shoulder.

'The ink's wet,' he said. 'Let's go!'

'Just hang on. I have to find out a bit more.' She

blew on the ink until it was dry and then she inspected the book.

Going by the name on the first page, it belonged to Hannah Stanway, housekeeper to Withycombe Manor. It was full of recipes and notes. The last entry before that day's was written in 1900, the year of Hannah's death.

'We saw her grave,' said Ginny. The implication hung in the air.

'I don't believe in ghosts,' said Ben.

'Nor do I. We need to leave!'

Ben reversed the car. 'Where to?' he said.

'Let's get back to the main road and think about it then,' said Ginny.

By the time they were out of the woods they'd started to laugh, the sort of laughter created by the release of tension. They'd escaped. But what they'd escaped from they didn't know.

'So, left or right?' asked Ben.

'Right,' said Ginny. 'We've got all evening to find somewhere to stay.' She was determined to find somewhere, even though she knew on Christmas Day it would be difficult. She really didn't want to have to go back to the flat. His mother would be over like a shot, wanting to know why they'd come home early. Ginny would have to say something went wrong with the booking and then have to listen to hours of comment on how she could have done things better.

'Well, that's weird!' said Ben. 'There's a sign to Withycombe! Isn't that where we just were?'

'I thought so. But we've driven miles, haven't we?' asked Ginny.

'We've been on the road for quarter of an hour.'

'Let's switch on the satnav; it may come up with a town we could go to . . .

'It's determined we're going to Withycombe,' Ginny went on. 'Look – there's a sign! Withycombe Cottages and Manor House. I'm sure that's what I booked!'

'Then let's go! They may still have our cottage available,' said Ben.

'We – er – I may not have booked it. There may have been a mistake.' Neither of them was ready to talk about where they'd spent last night, and what had happened there.

'Let's go anyway. Hang the expense. If they've got a room, we'll have it!' He paused. 'I really don't want to go back to the flat and have my mother interrogating us about our honeymoon.'

Ginny giggled. Hearing Ben talk about his mother like that made her feel better.

Soon after the turn was marked and they followed a drive down for a quarter of a mile or so until they came to a large, imposing manor house.

Ginny would have turned round and gone back by this time but Ben was on a mission. They got out of the car and he took her hand. He strode into the big house as if he had every right to, Ginny trotting slightly behind.

'Good afternoon!' said Ben firmly. 'We're looking for accommodation—'

Before he could finish his explanation and apologise for it being short notice and all the other things Ginny was certain he had in mind to say, the woman at the desk, whose badge said 'Sharon', looked up firmly. 'Name?'

'Andrews,' said Ben.

Ginny opened her mouth to speak but shut it again. Sharon was looking down a list. 'Ah yes,' she said. 'Honeymooners.' She smiled. 'You're in one of the cottages. Come with me.'

When she had summoned a minion to take over her duties Sharon collected a large metal key. 'Someone will bring your bags if you leave your car keys. Come with me, I'll show you where you're staying.'

They were escorted across the floodlit drive and a stretch of lawn to a path flanked with lampposts which led into some woods. It was surprisingly similar to the path to the cottage they had just fled from and yet, for some reason, Ginny was confident it was different.

Superficially the little house was much the same,

but this version had been updated. There was fresh paint in tasteful, muted colours. Two little bay trees stood on either side of the porch (which the previous house hadn't had) and although the key was still large and iron, Ginny doubted it was ever kept under a plant pot.

'I'll show you round. We're very proud of this little place; it's our most recently renovated cottage.'

This was the place Ginny had booked. She recognised it from the website. There was the tasteful sitting room, with a wood-burning stove. Comfortable tweed-covered sofas draped with cashmere throws, white painted bookcases, and an entertainment centre that could show anything from early black-and-white movies to the latest new releases.

'The kitchen is through here,' said Sharon. 'Oh, and your box of food has been delivered and the cold stuff put in the fridge.'

It seemed a lifetime since Ginny had packed that box – a lifetime she could hardly remember just now.

The kitchen was at least twice the size of the previous one and as high-tech as the first one had been simple. There were granite worktops, an island, a fridge the size of a family car and every gadget imaginable. Only a trained chef would get the best out of it, Ginny decided.

'Of course, you don't need to cook at all if you

don't want to,' said Sharon. 'You can either come over and eat in the dining room, or have meals delivered here.' She laughed. 'Don't worry, we're always very discreet. Now, I expect you can find the bedroom and bathroom on your own.' She paused. 'Any questions?'

'Yes,' said Ben. 'While we were on our way we came across another old house in the woods, very like this . . .'

'Oh? The old housekeeper's cottage? That's one we have yet to do up. The original owners had cottages for all their principal servants to live in all their lives, until they died. This is why we have five that we let and will soon have a sixth.'

'So do you know anything about the house-keeper?' asked Ginny. In some ways she didn't want to know but if she didn't ask she knew she'd be annoyed with herself.

'Her old journal is up at the house. You could read it if you come up for dinner,' said Sharon. 'We're doing a *Downton* night this evening. Every-thing is as it would have been at the turn of the last century. Some people dress up and really go to town, but you don't have to. But it is fun.'

'We'll see how we feel after a quick freshen up,' said Ben.

'Quite right. No pressure – just call on the house phone when you decide. Now, will you be all right lighting the wood burner? Or shall I send someone?'

'We'll light it ourselves,' said Ginny quickly. 'My husband's good at fires.'

Ginny and Ben exchanged a warm glance. It was the first time she had properly referred to him as her husband.

'Well, if there isn't anything else you need, I'll be on my way. Oh, and we're having champagne and Buck's Fizz at breakfast tomorrow if we don't see you for dinner. As it's Christmas Day.'

'Christmas Day tomorrow?' said Ben.

Sharon laughed. 'Yes, tomorrow. You've been so busy with the wedding you must be exhausted. I bet you could sleep for a whole day, but trust me, tomorrow is Christmas Day!'

When they were alone, Ginny and Ben looked at each other.

'We're probably really over-tired,' said Ginny. 'Me doing the wedding thing and you having two jobs. We've just had the same dream or something weird.'

Ben nodded but looked about as convinced as Ginny felt. 'That'll be it. It was a good dream though. I liked the bit in the church.' He put his hand on hers.

Ginny's fingers closed over his. 'That meant more than those stupid, soppy vows we made in the hotel, in front of all those people.'

'We didn't need to make our feelings sound good. We just spoke from the heart.'

'That's how I felt – feel.' She cleared the sudden tears from her throat. 'Shall we think about food? I'm starving.'

'Good plan. Shall we get dressed and go up to the hotel for dinner?'

'I'd like that.' Although she was so happy with Ben their recent experiences made her curious and also want a bit of company.

'I'll give them a call.'

The path to the house was well lit, making the walk through the woods exciting rather than spooky, but Ginny still held on to Ben's arm.

Under her coat, Ginny was wearing the clothes she had packed carefully for just this occasion. It was the dress she had bought in the sale the previous year, with her honeymoon in mind. It was cocktail length in dark green velvet, with long sleeves and a deep V-neck. She wore a string of pearls that Ben had bought her for her birthday just after they'd met and little pearl studs. She felt elegant and understated and Ben's eyes had glowed in appreciation when he saw her; he'd murmured a compliment into her ear.

He was smartly dressed too and she felt very

proud of him as they walked into the hotel together. Once beyond the efficient reception area, which they had already seen, the hotel was a period masterpiece. Everyone had gone to a huge effort to recreate Christmas in a grand country house. This was *Downton* with all the bells and whistles.

There was an enormous Christmas tree, decorated with old-fashioned glass baubles, miniature brass trumpets, wooden Father Christmases, fat little parcels, little plaster cherubs and crystal icicles. Swathes of tinsel added more glitter and the final touch was fairy lights that looked like real candles.

There were boughs of holly and ivy and other greenery draped with scarlet ribbons and golden bows on every mantelpiece and over every picture.

The female staff wore long black dresses covered with starched lace-trimmed pinafores and matching lace caps. The men wore tight black trousers and striped waistcoats, and highly polished shoes.

Some of the guests had gone to a lot of trouble to dress in period costume and had obviously hired outfits specially. But many were just wearing smart but modern clothes, something Ginny was glad about. She could do without too much authenticity.

After drinking glasses of hot punch they were summoned into dinner. The large, elaborately dressed table, with more glasses per place setting than Ginny had ever seen before, did seem very authentic with a grand centrepiece and beautiful crackers at every place.

It was fun, all eating together, and although no one really knew each other, soon conversation was flowing, aided by the wine, which didn't dry up either.

To Ginny's huge relief, there was no suggestion of the women leaving the gentlemen to their port. In fact, when they were all completely stuffed and had played a Victorian game involving burning fruits and nuts, it was suggested that people disperse to have port. Carol singers were due to arrive and most people drifted off to listen to them. Ginny and Ben went to find the library.

As expected, it was full of books and had a good fire, but it was also empty except for them.

'Right,' said Ben, 'let's find this housekeeper's book. I want to find out about her.'

'But didn't we agree? We just had the same dream?'

'I know,' said Ben. 'But I still want to find out more about her if I can.'

The book was easy to find: it was in a pile on a table, put there for guests to read. Ben picked it up.

'Come on. Let's investigate.'

Once they were established on a sofa near the roaring fire, glasses of port and a plate of home-made fudge and chocolate to hand, Ginny, who had been a bit reluctant, was more enthusiastic about reading the book.

'It says here,' she said, picking up a laminated card tucked into the book, 'that Hannah Stanway worked for the family for sixty years.' She read aloud, ' "She was a favourite of the family and much treasured. It was to her that they all took their troubles and she was always ready with wise words and comfort. After she finally retired, when she was seventy-five, she was still visited and consulted by the family until her death in 1900." '

Ben picked up the book. It was exactly the same as the book they had found on the kitchen table except that it was much older and faded. The writing inside wasn't always legible.

'That gives us a clue where to start looking,' said Ben. 'She wrote us a note in this book and I want to find it.'

Ben worked back in the journal from 1901 and it wasn't long before he found the entry they had read only that morning. Knowing it was written on Christmas Eve made it easy.

'Here it is,' said Ben. 'It's the note she left for us only the ink is really faded and there are a couple of splodges on it. And look, there are references to snow in the previous entry.'

Ginny didn't let herself process fully what Ben

was saying. She preferred to think the last twenty-four hours had been a hallucination, a joint dream they'd shared in a post-wedding daze. Even if that was unlikely, the other explanation was even more ridiculous.

'OK,' said Ginny, 'what I think happened is that somehow we had the same weird dream that was set in the past. But it didn't really happen.'

She was very definite about it and Ben, having looked at her steadily for a couple of seconds, nodded. He didn't believe her theory any more than she did.

'Agreed. Now, shall we go back to our cottage? We have a honeymoon to start!'

They drifted back, hand in hand, and Ginny was in heaven. They'd reached as satisfying and logical a conclusion as they could. She and Ben were together; they'd have their first Christmas tomorrow, far away from family, curled up in their snug, comfortable holiday cottage, with every modern convenience.

It was only much later, when she opened her overnight bag, the one she had used at the old cottage, that she found the nightdress. She knew perfectly well that she'd last seen it laid tenderly over the towel rack in the bathroom in the old house, on top of the linen face towels. She'd put it there herself.

She dismissed the frisson of disquiet that ran

down her spine. After all, the housekeeper and everything she had created had brought her and Ben together. Ghost or dream, it didn't matter. She and Ben would live happily ever after.

# Candlelight
## at
# Christmas

'They're your *parents*, Rupe! It's Christmas! I couldn't say no.'

'But you hate my parents,' Rupert pointed out.

Fenella sighed at her husband's horrified expression and leant on the big old kitchen table, currently pulled out near the big old Aga.

The kitchen was the centre of the Gainsboroughs' lives in winter at Somerby. It was Fenella's favourite room in their rambling old house. Huge and shabby but with a newly installed wood burner and a sofa and chairs it was always cosy. The stove was an early

Christmas present to the house because finally Somerby was earning its keep – only just – by being a wedding venue, film set and sometime cookery school.

Fenella pursed her lips. 'That's putting it a little strongly. But I'll admit they are challenging, and I was really looking forward to not having them this year, but . . .' She shrugged. 'But the friends they were going to have norovirus. And it's no joke when you're elderly.'

'It's no joke even when you're not elderly,' said Rupert, but laughing anyway. 'Did you warn them we had a houseful?'

'Yes I did, but with a house this size, you can never say you haven't got room. What I didn't tell them is that Sarah rang just before your mother. She says the twins are teething and are being really hard work. She and Hugo wanted to know if we still wanted them all to come for Christmas.'

'And you said, "Yes of course," I hope?'

Fenella nodded. 'Of course!' She bit her lip. 'I'm sure Christmas will still be lovely it's just . . . I was so looking forward to a cosy time; just us, our girls, Sarah and Hugo and their babies, and Gideon and Zoe who always love helping with the cooking. All of us old friends slobbing out in the upstairs sitting room, drinking and throwing clementine peel and nutshells into the fire.'

'Well, Zoe's pregnant, so she's not drinking.'

'You know what I mean,' she said glumly.

He nodded. 'And I know just how much you were looking forward to it, darling. I was, too. I was going to beat Hugo at poker or die in the attempt.'

'You can still do that, surely?'

Rupert shook his head. 'Nope. My parents will try and make me play bridge instead; that's all they want to do these days. Well, I won't. I've forgotten how anyway.'

'I'm not sure how your mother and father will cope with the babies,' worried Fenella. 'I'll keep Sarah, Hugo and the twins in the bridal suite and hope your parents are not too disturbed. There's plenty of room for the family to spread out and make a noise if necessary. That room does have lovely facilities though I say it myself.'

Rupert nodded. 'If there's one upside to two crying babies it's that maybe my parents'll stop nagging us about trying for a "son and heir". And blaming you for us not having one already.'

Fenella didn't comment and just said, 'That reminds me, where are the girls?'

'They're sorting out the cupboard in the larder. Glory's so excited about her godmother Zoe coming for Christmas.'

Fenella smiled. Her eldest daughter, Glory, was five and very good at guiding her younger sister, Simmy – short for Cymbeline – around. More like bossing at times. There was a special cupboard that contained only plastic things. Taking everything out and putting it back in again was one of their favourite games.

'Then if they are happy, I'll go and sort out the Pink Room for your parents. It's full of clutter at the moment.'

'Are you sure? You're looking a bit tired, honey,' said Rupert.

'It's the day before Christmas Eve. Of course I'm tired!' she snapped. 'And on top of everything else I had to check Gerald's house was fit for visitors this morning.' She frowned. 'I know in theory looking after the holiday rentals for him while he's away isn't much trouble, but somehow it is. Although the cottage was perfectly clean I had to put flowers and a bottle of wine in it, and arrange a hamper. He's a mean old thing not arranging for something a bit more at Christmas, the price he charges.'

Rupert looked knowing. 'And you're a bit grumpy. You'd usually enjoy doing those things. Is it PMT? Should I dig out the emergency chocolate?' he asked.

Fenella hadn't meant to tell Rupert what she was about to say but she decided she had to, really. 'Actually, Rupe, it's been PMT for a while.' She bit her lip, hoping she didn't have to spell it out.

'You're pregnant?'

Fenella nodded and watched her husband struggle for the right facial expression. He was very happy with his two girls and Fenella didn't think she really wanted another baby and yet, somehow, another one might be on its way. 'It's very early days,' she said.

'Have you taken a test, Fen?'

'No! We've both been so busy there hasn't been time to get to a chemist. Let's not think about it just now. My period may simply be late because I'm stressed. Now I must go and get tidying. Oh – could you give the girls something to eat? There are some spuds in the oven. You could give them baked beans and cheese with them. They love that.'

As Fenella left the kitchen she couldn't help feeling guilty for not being totally honest with Rupert. She had actually managed to buy a pregnancy test; she just hadn't had a chance, or the courage, to take it yet. And now with all this extra prep to do she wasn't sure she'd have the time.

Fenella went upstairs to the airing cupboard and gathered armfuls of bedlinen and towels. Then she faced the dumping ground that was known as the Pink Room. Luckily the mess was fairly superficial and she just hauled everything off the bed and stuffed it in a cupboard. Her mother-in-law would moan if she didn't have enough hanging space but if the chest of drawers was relatively clear and there was enough space for a few things in the wardrobe that would have to do.

Her phone vibrated in her back pocket. It was Zoe. Fenella sank down on the bed, her heart in her mouth in case Zoe was ringing to cancel. 'Oh, Zoe!' she said quickly, before Zoe had time to speak. 'How lovely to hear you! Last-minute change of plan – my in-laws are coming for Christmas too. You remember them – Lord and Lady Gainsborough? You met them when I was having Glory and you were at Somerby for the cookery competition?' Fenella tried to sound as if somehow this wasn't quite the disaster she felt it to be.

'I do remember meeting them, and I definitely remember the cookery competition,' said Zoe dryly, apparently not fooled by Fenella's feigned enthusiasm. 'Hardly likely to forget it in the circumstances. As that's where Gideon and I met I'd say the competition was directly responsible for my current condition.'

Fenella laughed. The cookery competition at Somerby had been enormous fun and extremely stressful. Zoe, one of the most promising contestants, and Gideon, the scariest judge, had met each other during it. Zoe had lost the competition but kept Gideon. 'So how are you? I do hope you're not ringing up to cancel. I'm totally relying on you and Gideon to keep me sane.'

'And cook?' laughed Zoe.

'That too, but not if you don't want to.' Zoe was the most wonderful cook, and Fenella was definitely banking on her help.

'I'm fine to cook and I'm not cancelling but I have got a bit of a big favour to ask.'

Now that she knew the friends she'd been so looking forward to seeing were coming, Fenella relaxed. 'Anything!' she said expansively. 'I'm sure it's fine.'

'It's Gideon's fault. There's a young Frenchman working with him in the food wholesaler's at the moment and he can't get home for Christmas. He's only twenty-one and it seemed mean to leave him on his own so Gideon suggested he could come to you, with us. It seems an awful cheek? Gideon said he thought there'd be plenty of room.'

An extra Frenchman seemed like nothing to Fenella compared to her in-laws. 'Of course he can come! No bother! Gideon's right, there's always room in this house. And if not, there's the cowshed. Gathering up waifs and strays is what Christmas is all about.' She sighed. 'If it wasn't, I probably wouldn't be lumbered with the two most difficult guests in the world.'

Zoe laughed. 'Oh, poor you! But I don't think you could describe this man as a waif and stray. I haven't met him but Gideon says he's quite aristocratic and lives in a château. His father is a famous wine producer.'

Fenella stopped feeling quite so relaxed about the Frenchman. 'Oh God, now I'm worried.'

'No need to be. You live in what would be a château if it was in France.'

'But it's only partly done up! A snooty Frenchman will despise our shabbiness.'

'I don't think he's snooty or Gideon wouldn't have wished him on you.'

They chatted on for a few minutes about what Gideon and Zoe were bringing with them as contributions and then said goodbye.

Then, looking about her, Fenella realised that not only did she still have to make up the bed, but the lighting in the Pink Room was a bit dim. Rupert's parents liked 100-watt bulbs in every socket. They had stockpiled high-energy light bulbs and had no truck with the other kind. Fenella would have to find extra lamps to make the room seem adequately lit for them and was slightly tempted to bring out the photographic spotlights she had somewhere. That would teach them!

She also had to think now where Zoe's Frenchman was going to sleep. Fenella suddenly felt a bit tearful and realised she probably was pregnant. She wouldn't usually be fazed by a little thing like finding places to put people.

❄

Rupert was looking pleased with himself when she got back down to the kitchen. The girls were eating baked potatoes and beans but, as they often did, this couldn't have been the reason for his smugness.

'I've saved the situation!' he declared with a triumphant gesture.

'Really?' She smiled encouragingly. Apart from persuading his parents to go to a nice hotel for Christmas she wasn't sure there was any way of saving it.

'I've got us a nanny to help with all the children.'

Fenella sat down and looked at the bottle of wine that was on the table, wondering if she wanted a glass or not. 'How did you manage that?'

By the time Rupert had finished explaining, her doubts were increased. The nanny Rupert was talking about was Meggie, the daughter of friends of theirs. Meggie was charming, young and pretty but very shy. 'But why is Meggie willing to spend Christmas with us?' continued Fenella.

'It's her dad's turn to have her for Christmas this year and Meggie hates going apparently,' Rupert explained. 'And as I'll be paying her handsomely, her father, who's very mean about paying for anything for her, couldn't object!' he finished triumphantly.

'I like Meggie,' said five-year-old Glory, putting a baked bean in her mouth with finger and thumb.

'So do I,' said Simmy, who habitually copied her older sister.

'That's all right then. I'm sure Meggie will be wonderful,' said Fenella, but really she felt that Rupert had just given her another person to look after at Christmas. However, as he'd obviously gone to a lot of trouble to try and help her, Fenella couldn't possibly say so. 'When's she coming?'

'She'll be here just after lunch tomorrow. In time to give us plenty of help.'

'You know Fenella and Rupert,' Meggie's mother, Amanda, was saying to her on the drive to Somerby. 'They're lovely! And Rupert's paying mega-bucks.'

Meggie smiled at her mother's outdated slang. 'Which I'm sure is why Dad agreed to it. But you are right, Christmas at Somerby will be so much better than Christmas at Dad's, with Ignatia.'

'The Iguana,' said her mother with a smile. That was what they'd called Ignatia when her husband had first left her for the younger woman.

'The stick insect more like, who clearly thinks I'm fat,' said Meggie.

'Darling, she's just jealous of your curves. Yours are real and hers are silicone!' said her mother,

shooting Meggie an anxious glance. 'You're a beautiful, lovely young woman with great skin—'

'I know I'm not *fat*! But the Iguana says – hints
heavily anyway – that if I were thinner I'd have
a boyfriend. She will say, because she said it the
last time I was there, that a girl in her first year
at university who hasn't got a boyfriend has
something wrong with her.' She paused, reliving
the humiliating conversation. 'Which is her way of
saying I'm overweight and lack social skills.'

'You're shy—'

Meggie sighed. 'But I'm good with children which is
why Ignatia tolerates me at all. I'm useful with her
little ones. It's fine. I can spend this Christmas being
a nanny instead of being at Dad's.'

'Oh, darling, you are happy about this job, aren't
you? It's just when I rang Rupert about firewood
and he mentioned about his parents coming and
their friends' babies teething he seemed so utterly
delighted when I suggested—'

Meggie patted her mother's knee reassuringly.
'It's OK, Mum, really. And you squared it with Dad
so I don't have to.'

'It seems awful that you'll have more fun being
a nanny than visiting your dad, doesn't it?'

'Obviously I'd rather be with you and Jim,' said
Meggie. 'But at least this way Dad can't get at me
for not working in the holidays.' She sighed. 'I think

he's forgotten where we live and as I don't drive it's not easy!'

'I know, darling. And I love having you at home, and you're so sweet with Petal . . .'

'Of course. She's my baby half-sister and I love her!'

Her mother shot Meggie a smile before checking the signpost and turning left. 'He said you can put the money towards driving lessons.'

'Kind of him to tell me how to spend it,' said Meggie. 'I'd planned to do that anyway.'

'He is mean,' her mother acknowledged, 'and a bit controlling. Always has been. Worse now.'

They lapsed into silence for a moment. Amanda broke it saying, 'Anyway, he said as long as you're there for New Year's Eve—'

'So I can babysit?'

'No, they're having a party—'

'So I can be a waitress then,' said Meggie. She preferred the babysitting option. She loved her half-brother and -sister and they loved her. Children didn't make judgements about people in the way that adults did. At her father's parties her step-mother spent a lot of time telling people Meggie was *not* her daughter, implying she'd have had to be about ten when she gave birth to her. Another, heavier silence fell in the car.

'I think it's this lane,' said Meggie. 'Just drop me

here or you may have to reverse out if there are a lot of cars there already.'

Meggie walked up the long sweeping drive, looking at the enormous old house that the Gainsboroughs were gradually restoring. It stood on a hill overlooking the surrounding countryside, wintery now but still beautiful. Apparently the house had been built in the Queen Anne period but had been added to over the centuries. The additions made it less elegant but somehow friendly – and of course bigger.

When she arrived she was startled to see the entire Gainsborough family on the doorstep to greet her. She was a little out of breath after the long walk up the drive.

'Sorry for the welcoming committee,' said Fenella, kissing her cheek. 'We spotted you from an upstairs window and the girls rushed down.'

'And I was coming up from the kitchen as they reached the front door,' said Rupert, taking her case. 'Thank you so much for coming. I can't tell you how grateful we are.'

'It feels like such a long time since we last saw you, Meggie,' added Fenella. 'You're in your first year at university now, aren't you? Goodness me, I wish I'd looked as lovely as you do halfway through my first year. Too many parties, not enough sleep! But you look absolutely radiant.'

'Oh, well, I'm not much of one for parties,' Meggie said. She smiled, but was unable to stop feeling nervous. The last time she had visited Somerby, some years ago, there had been lots of dogs, but there were none now. It felt wrong, somehow. 'Where are the dogs?'

Fenella looked a little forlorn. 'Our old Bessie died a couple of months ago. We're dog-free now.' She smiled briefly and then said, 'Come on, girls. Shall we show Meggie her room?'

'I'll show her!' said Glory, taking charge, heading inside and setting off up the stairs, Simmy close behind her. Rupert followed both girls with Meggie's case.

'When you're settled in we'll have a cup of tea,' said Fenella as she and Meggie went up the stairs a bit more sedately.

'Only if you're having one,' said Meggie, very aware that she was being paid and mustn't just be an extra guest. 'There's no point in my being here if you have to look after me.'

Fenella paused, laughing. 'I'm delighted you're here and I always want tea. Although as it's Christmas, we could have something stronger if we fancied. It's after lunch after all!'

'Definitely,' they heard Rupert say, 'it's almost obligatory.'

As Meggie and Fenella reached the landing, Glory took hold of Meggie's hand and led her to a small room squashed between two larger ones.

'I'll leave you girls to it,' said Rupert. 'I have to light a fire in the dining room. If I don't get the chimney warmed up the room will double as an ice house when we want to use it tomorrow.' He ran downstairs, his long legs making short work of it.

'I'm sorry it's so tiny,' said Fenella apologetically in the doorway of the room. 'It was originally a powder room, or an extra bedroom really, belonging to the suite where the girls are. Their suite has a beautiful bathroom with a slightly sunken double bath, perfect for bathing children. Once the wedding season starts they'll have to move out of it, but now, it's handy.'

Meggie looked about her. The room was small, but it was cosy and looked comfortable.

'The infamous bathroom is just here,' said Fenella, opening a door on the landing. 'The girls use it as a sort of heated swimming pool,' she explained, 'although it's not that big.'

'I want a bath now,' said Simmy.

Meggie tried to remember why she was called Simmy but failed. 'It's quite early for a bath, isn't it?' she said, bending down to the little girl. Meggie often wished she felt as confident talking to adults as she did children.

Fenella took her youngest daughter by the hand. 'Meggie must have a cup of tea and maybe some Christmas biscuits before she does anything else. The twins will be here soon.' Fenella looked at Meggie. 'They're about six months, and apparently they're teething. Just the thing to make my parents-in-law's Christmas perfect! Luckily they're sleeping quite far away.'

Fenella looked tired, thought Meggie. 'Let me know if you want me to make up beds or anything,' she said. 'I can stuff turkeys, too. I like to be useful.'

Fenella went ashen. 'The turkey! I've forgotten to pick it up! I wonder if Rupert can go?'

Meggie could see Fenella teetering between wanting to be a good and welcoming hostess and needing to collect the turkey. 'I expect the girls could take me down to the kitchen,' she said. 'And I could make my own tea. Then you could fetch the turkey?'

'Would you manage?' said Fenella, looking relieved.

'Of course. Glory and Simmy will show me where everything is if Rupert's not there,' said Meggie. 'Really.'

'That's so kind of you. I know he's got to extend the dining-room table, which means finding bits. We never use the dining room if it's just us and most of the people we have over are happy in the kitchen so getting the room fit for purpose takes a bit of doing.'

At that moment, Rupert reappeared at the end of the landing, carrying two bedside lamps. 'These are for my parents' room. You know how they like everything to be well lit and I remembered we were short of lamps in the Pink Room,' he said.

'Oh, you're brilliant, Rupe! I was going to do something about that but totally forgot! What time are you picking your parents up?' asked Fenella, looking at her watch. 'I've got to get the turkey.'

'I told them I couldn't pick them up.' He sounded pleased with himself. 'I've arranged a taxi.'

'Rupert! And they were OK with that?'

'Of course not. But it'll bring them from their door, so they have to put up with it. They know it's all very last minute.'

'So what time will they be here?'

'About six o'clock.'

Fenella's eyes widened. 'That late?'

'I told them it was because the taxis were busy but I wanted to give you maximum time to get ready. Which you'll need if you have to go out now.'

'I'll help,' said Meggie. 'Just ask me. I'm good at present-wrapping too.'

'Doesn't Father Christmas wrap his own presents?' asked Glory.

'No,' said Fenella, 'only the ones he puts in your

stocking. We have to wrap the others. And as I can never make myself do it as I buy them, I would be very grateful for some help, Meggie!'

It was dark and Meggie and the girls were in the bathroom. Glory and Simmy were splashing merrily in the huge bath and Meggie was reviewing the afternoon. She'd wrapped presents for Fenella, made another batch of biscuits with the girls and gone round the garden and done posies for the guest bedrooms using rose hips, rosemary and ivy, with wisps of old man's beard. She was enjoying herself. She felt useful and appreciated. And it was a welcome change not having her diet-obsessed stepmother hovering around making her feel inadequate.

The Gainsboroughs' Christmas promised to be heavenly too. The plan was that when the girls had stayed in the bath as long as they could before they became wrinkled they were going downstairs in their nighties to look at the tree. Fenella had explained that, in theory, they wouldn't have seen it lit up before. Of course they had, but this time, because it was Christmas Eve, it would be special. This long bath was to encourage them to sleep this evening.

Meggie was reading 'The Night Before Christmas'

to the children while they splashed when she heard noises, voices and greetings floating up from downstairs. They would be the other guests, she realised. She'd had time to feel comfortable with Fenella and Rupert but the thought of meeting their smart friends was daunting. Fenella had filled Meggie in earlier: Hugo was a photographer, his wife Sarah a wedding planner, and Gideon and Zoe a food writer and chef respectively. They were obviously old and close friends. Meggie would just shrink into the background and stay with the children as much as possible. It was what she did when she stayed with her father, or at least tried to.

Then there was more commotion, this time accompanied by the sound of crying babies. These must be Sarah and Hugo's twins that Fenella had told her about, part of the reason Meggie was there. The sound of crying got louder and she realised the twins were on their way upstairs.

'Hi!' said a posh male voice. Meggie turned to see a tall, blond man standing in the bathroom door, babe in arms. 'So sorry to intrude but Fen said we should come straight up. I'm Hugo, by the way, this little monster's dad. Sarah's got the other one.'

'Uncle Hugo!' said Glory.

Meggie had got up and automatically put her hands out to take the crying baby the man was holding.

He pulled away, laughing. 'I wouldn't take him if I were you. We have a nappy situation.'

Meggie laughed softly and went on holding out her hands. 'I'm an expert on nappies,' she said. Her father declared changing nappies was not part of his job description so Meggie had changed many a dirty nappy when she'd been staying and Ignatia was out.

'Oh well,' said Hugo. 'If you don't mind. This one is Ted, short for Edward. Fen suggested we put them both in the bath – which I now see is the size of a swimming pool – with these girls.' He looked at it.

'Ergh!' said Glory. 'Not if they're pooey.'

'They won't be "pooey" when I've finished with them,' said Meggie, who had laid Ted down on the bathmat and was taking off his clothes.

'I see you're an expert,' said the man.

A woman, elegant but a bit tired-looking, carrying another screaming baby, came into the bathroom. 'I've got the nappy bag.' She paused, seeing Meggie stripping off her son. 'Are you all right with poo?' she asked Meggie. 'I'm Sarah, and this one is Imogen. We call her Immi.'

'I'm Meggie and I'm fine with poo,' said Meggie, thinking that as a way of introducing herself it summed her up quite well.

Now Ted was free of his nappy and most of his clothes, the crying stopped. Meggie took Immi and laid her down next to her brother.

'You have got a way with them,' said Sarah.

'I'll go and get their bath seats.' She smiled at the little girls already in the bath. 'Don't worry, they'll be all cleaned up beautifully before they join you.' She put her hand in the water. 'Perfect temperature.'

A little later Meggie was on her own with the four children. The girls were delighted with their new companions. Simmy – short for Cymbeline, Meggie had remembered – was particularly fascinated by her new, real-life bath toys who kicked and gurgled in their seats in a very satisfactory way.

Rupert appeared in the doorway, assessed the situation, and then said to no one in particular, 'I'm going to organise drinks.' He ducked out of the room.

'Thanks!' called Sarah from her bedroom, where she was unpacking.

Meggie had found bath towels, thinking it was time the bigger girls got out of the bath. Once they were dry and dressed she could consult about the babies.

She had just done up the girls' adorable matching rose-patterned nighties when there was a cough in the doorway. The best-looking man Meggie thought she'd ever seen was standing there with a bottle of champagne in one hand and three flutes threaded between the fingers of the other.

'My goodness!' said Fenella to Zoe when she'd seen the Frenchman disappear up the stairs with the champagne. They headed into the warmth of the kitchen and Fenella added conspiratorially, 'Where did you find him? And will Meggie be able to cope?'

'Sarah said Meggie was brilliant with the babies,' said Hugo, father of the babies concerned, following Fenella and Zoe into the room.

Fenella made a face at Zoe, who was laughing. 'Not quite what we meant, Hugo darling.' They both sat down at the kitchen table.

Zoe's husband, Gideon, came into the kitchen with a huge pile of boxes that were obviously full of food. 'He's the son of a major wine producer and he's working with us for a bit to broaden his experience and perfect his English.'

'He likes babies,' said Zoe, unconsciously putting a hand on her own pregnant stomach. 'Apparently he misses his little nieces and nephews.'

'Oh!' Fenella felt suddenly sentimental. 'What a shame he couldn't get home for Christmas, then.'

'It's all right,' said Gideon, removing a huge dish full of something golden from a box. 'He's not that keen on his brothers and sisters.'

'Speaking of little people, I have to say I'm looking forward to seeing Glory and Simmy. They
must have grown so much since the last time,' said
Zoe.

'They have! And can I just say, I really appreciate
the fact that you give Simmy just as nice presents
as you do Glory, Zoe. When I was little my sister
used to be given amazing dresses from Harrods by
her godmother and of course I just had to watch
her getting them. I cried once and felt terribly embarrassed when her godmother, possibly prompted by
my mother, bought one for me, too.' Fenella cleared
her throat and told herself sharply to get her hor-
mones under control.

'Oh goodness, don't be silly, I love those two
equally. So why may Meggie not be able to cope with
Étienne?' asked Zoe, possibly sensing that Fenella
was feeling emotional and keen to get on to something more neutral. 'He's very nice.'

'Meggie's very shy,' explained Fenella. 'Her stepmother does all she can to demoralise her. Her
mother rang me while I was picking up the turkey
and told me all about it.' She frowned. 'Quite
frankly I think this stepmother sounds like something out of *Snow White*. You haven't seen her yet,
Zoe, but Meggie is absolutely lovely to look at. She's
petite but with an amazing curvy figure and so
pretty, and she has the most wonderful nature – no
wonder the children love her. Meggie may be here

135

as a nanny but at least we'll be nice to her this Christmas.'

'I have got her quite a nice present,' said Zoe. 'Lovely tights. I bought them for me but forgot I was pregnant and they wouldn't really fit.'

'I've got a cashmere sweater I bought in the Brora sale,' said Fenella. 'I'm giving her that. Not sure it's my colour and I think it would look lovely on Meggie. It's a sort of dark rose.'

'I'm afraid all my other presents are food this year,' said Zoe. 'Scottish tablet for most people. I know I won't be able to cook with boiling sugar for ages when this one comes.'

'I love tablet!' said Rupert enthusiastically as he came into the kitchen.

'I can't believe it!' said Sarah, who was just behind him. 'I've left the twins with those lovely young people and your two girls.'

'Which means us lot can have a quick grown-up drink!' said Rupert, producing more champagne and glasses like a magician.

'Before his parents arrive,' said Fenella, suddenly feeling a bit depressed at the idea.

'I seem to remember having quite a lot of fun with your parents, Rupes,' said Gideon, leaning against the Aga. 'Even if they didn't know we were. When we were looking after them while you were in hospital having Glory. Do you remember, darling?'

'I remember nearly poisoning them with very old

stew and that's about it,' said Zoe cheekily. 'Were they ill, do you remember?'

'Nope,' said Fenella, 'not that I'd have noticed, with Glory just having come into the world and that cookery competition taking up all my time.'

'And mine,' said Zoe, glancing at Gideon, who came to her side and pulled her against him.

Fenella, who had decided against having more than a sip or two of champagne, sighed. 'I was so looking forward to us all being together again for Christmas.'

'It'll still be fun,' said Sarah. 'We'll dilute the in-laws.'

'I know,' said Fenella, striving to be upbeat when she was feeling anything but. 'At least we had the carol service last Sunday, and not this afternoon. It's one of my favourite parts of Christmas. It's so lovely, with all the carols being sung by candlelight.'

'The twins would have screamed through it,' said Hugo, nodding. 'Just as well you've had it. None of us would have heard a note.'

'So maybe, with Lord and Lady Gainsborough coming, it's jolly good you've got it over with. I mean, that you've had it,' Zoe corrected herself. 'And you must admit, your in-laws have a certain comic value,' she added.

'Yes!' Sarah agreed. 'They were hilarious at Glory's christening.'

'It's different for you. They're not your in-laws.' Fenella would not be comforted.

'We'll protect you from them,' said Zoe. 'They think I'm your maid or your nanny or something anyway. It'll be fine!'

Gideon laughed. 'If you wore a maid's outfit, they'd suspect Rupert of getting you pregnant and insist that he turns you out of the house on Christmas Eve.'

'And on that note – happy Christmas,' toasted Hugo.

Fenella began to see the funny side, grateful that her friends had a strong sense of the ridiculous.

Rupert took a tray out of the Aga. 'Here, have some of these. Zoe brought them. Cheese straws, my favourite.'

Fenella got up. 'I'd better take some upstairs to Meggie and your Frenchman.'

'Do sit down for a few seconds, darling. You're looking tired,' said Rupert. 'I'll go.'

'Why don't I do it?' said Sarah. 'I need to go back up anyway and reclaim my children.' Before Fenella or Rupert could object she'd grabbed a plate of cheese straws and swept out of the kitchen.

Meggie had been unable to speak when first joined in the bathroom by a gorgeous man and a bottle of champagne.

''Ello,' he had said in an extremely sexy accent. 'I'm Étienne, but in England they call me Steve.'

'Oh? French for Steven, I see,' said Meggie, thinking she'd be sticking to Étienne.

Étienne, having put down the glasses, eased the cork out of the champagne and poured. 'What is your name?' he asked as he handed her a glass.

'I'm Meggie. I'm a sort of nanny.'

'Nanny? Like a female goat?'

She laughed. He was teasing her but so charmingly she didn't mind. And as she was already fairly pink from being in the bathroom for so long he probably wouldn't notice her blush. 'Probably, yes.'

Sarah came in holding a glass and a plate of cheese straws. 'Champagne in the bath! How decadent! Although I doubt Rupert and Fen had this lot in mind when they designed this amazing bathroom. Happy Christmas!'

They all clinked glasses. 'Now,' went on Sarah, 'I'd better take these two out—'

'Why?' asked Étienne. 'They are happy?'

'They are very happy,' Sarah agreed. 'But I expect you two want to go downstairs and join the party.' She put down a bag full of baby clothes and other paraphernalia.

'We want to stay here,' said Glory and her sister nodded.

'I'm quite happy here,' agreed Meggie. 'And the babies seem fine with me – with us.'

'I too am very happy,' said Étienne. 'I miss my sister's children.'

'Oh,' said Sarah, sympathetic, 'it must be awful not being able to be with your family at Christmas.'

He shrugged. '*C'est la vie.*'

'Why don't you both go down and have a quiet drink with the others?' suggested Meggie. 'I expect the babies will need you quite soon but you could have a few moments off.' Meggie knew very well how much mothers longed for snatched moments of baby-free time. Her stepmother never stopped talking about it and her mother looked grateful whenever Meggie held out her arms for her half-sister.

'Good,' said Étienne. 'You go, we will "babysit".' Somehow this very mundane word was rendered sexy by his accent. 'You don't have to stay with me,' said Meggie. 'I'll be fine.'

'And I will be fine with you, and the rest of this quite good champagne.'

Meggie wasn't quite sure why Étienne was happy to stay with her. He certainly didn't suffer from shyness and lack of confidence about joining the others.

'Can we come with you, Aunt Sarah?' said Glory.

'Of course! If I take Glory and Simmy with me, I won't feel so guilty about leaving you with my two.' Sarah picked up her glass. 'Are you really sure?

Shout the moment it gets difficult! Come on, girls, let's have a look at the tree. Father Christmas might have left something under it.'

'Silly Aunt Sarah! Father Christmas only does the stockings, not the other presents.'

'Sorry,' said Sarah. 'Forgot.'

'You really didn't have to stay with me,' said Meggie to Étienne when Sarah had gone. 'You could have a drink. Meet Fenella and Rupert.'

'I have met Fenella and Rupert and, charming as they are, I prefer to drink champagne in this very pleasant bathroom with a pretty girl and these babies as my companions.'

Meggie took a while to think up something to say in reply. 'You must like children.'

'I do.'

'So you must be sad you're not with them at Christmas.'

He shrugged. 'I will see them for Twelfth Night.'

He smiled (devastatingly, thought Meggie). 'Actually, everyone is sad for me because I couldn't go home for Christmas but I didn't want to go home for Christmas.'

'Why not?'

'It is a little embarrassing. There is a football match I want to watch the day after.'

'Oh.'

'But you are also not home for Christmas? If you are here? These people are not your family?'

Meggie nodded. 'They're not. My parents are divorced. This year I was to go and spend Christmas with my father and stepmother but then my mother heard that Rupert had a lot of people so she offered my services as a nanny.'

Étienne frowned, his arms crossed. 'And you are happy about this?'

Meggie nodded again. 'Actually, yes. I hate spending Christmas with my father. My stepmother . . .' She paused. Was it OK to slag off your stepmother to random Frenchmen? She decided it was. Her stepmother wouldn't have hesitated to slag her off. 'We don't get on. She's very critical. And I'd spend most of the time looking after their children anyway, although I do like them.'

'And what does she find to criticise? A lovely girl who looks after her children is a good thing, no?'

'She's happy about me looking after the children but she doesn't think I'm lovely. I'm not skinny enough for her.' If she hadn't had a glass of champagne she probably wouldn't have said that. Even she knew enough to know you shouldn't draw attention to your flaws.

'Really? Stand up!'

She was perched on the edge of the bath. He took her hand and helped her to her feet and inspected her. 'No, you are not skinny. You are perfectly lovely. This is why your stepmother hates you.'

Meggie was taken aback, and was about to protest but Étienne refilled her glass so she didn't. 'I am being paid to be Rupert and Fenella's nanny. My father likes me to earn money. He's rather lost interest in keeping me since he's got a new family. He thinks I should be more financially independent.'

'So they won't miss you not being with them?'

'Not really. As long as I'm there for New Year's Eve. They're having a big party and they want me to help and then babysit.'

'Do you want to spend New Year's Eve with your father? Don't you want to go out with your friends?'

'My friends don't live in London where my father lives. It's fine, really.'

'Something about you is a little unhappy. Tell me.'

She managed a smile. 'It's not unhappy, it's ironic. One of the other things my stepmother complains about is that I haven't got a boyfriend, but if I did have one, I wouldn't be willing to skivvy for her.'

'This is a new word! Skivvy?'

'It means do housework, like Cinderella. She was a skivvy before she met her Fairy Godmother.'

'Ah! I know this story. *Cendrillon*. But your stepchildren? They are not ugly?'

Meggie laughed. 'They're my half-brother and -sister, and no, they're sweet. They'll probably have food issues when they're bigger but they're fine now.'

'We will not concern ourselves with them any more.' He tipped the last of the champagne into his glass.

Meggie was surprised how quickly they'd got through the bottle and worried that she might be drunk in charge of children. 'I think we'd better get the babies out.'

Sarah had obviously had the same thought because she reappeared in the bathroom brandishing some more canapés. 'Here – have these to go with the cheese straws. Or do you two want to go downstairs and have a drink? The girls are looking at the Christmas tree and being so sweet. Hugo will be up in a minute to help me feed these two.'

Meggie glanced at Étienne. 'You go down. I'll help Sarah feed the babies.' She'd seen bottles in the baby bag.

His gaze lingered on her for a few seconds and then he shrugged. 'OK. I'll see you soon, Meggie.'

Meggie loved sitting on the sofa in the bridal suite with Sarah. They each had a baby and the dim lighting and the gentle sound of sucking were wonderfully soothing. She would have kept silent to help the babies drift off to sleep, but Sarah was more cavalier.

'Étienne is rather gorgeous, don't you think? Gideon was saying downstairs that all the girls in the office are a bit in love with him but that he's very aloof in that Gallic way.'

'He was very friendly to me,' said Meggie, 'and lovely with the children. Not aloof at all.'

'Fenella is delighted to have you to help with the little ones but having Étienne so good with them as well is a real bonus. Rupert's parents are a nightmare, and they'll be arriving any minute.'

Meggie wasn't sure Sarah should be gossiping with the nanny but wasn't going to stop her. 'In what way?'

'They come from another era – pre-war probably, when everyone had servants and didn't feel obliged to be polite to them. It's a miracle that Rupert is so lovely. His parents are so haughty! And they can't forgive Fenella for not having had a son.'

'But isn't it the man who determines—'

'Yes! But try telling them that! Or rather don't.' Sarah glanced across at Meggie. 'You seem to be a natural at this baby-feeding lark.'

Meggie laughed softly. 'I've had practice. I'm thinking about being a nanny. I love children.'

Sarah shook her head. 'You could earn lots of money but most of the time you'd be with children, other nannies and other women's husbands.' She paused. 'Although if you *do* decide to be a nanny, please let me know. I'm always on the lookout for good childcare, along with half London.'

'You're a wedding planner, aren't you?' Meggie

would normally have been too shy to start a conversation with someone like Sarah, but the intimacy of the occasion made it seem allowable.

'Yes I am, although I do lots of other event planning as well. I quite often need casual staff if you want to leave me your details.'

'I don't think I'd be any good at events. I'm too shy. Those sort of people are all glamorous and outgoing.'

Sarah laughed, causing her baby to open its eyes briefly. 'You're not exactly unglamorous, if I may say so, and sometimes a lovely sincere smile is more effective than all the eyes and teeth some events people go in for. And I bet you're reliable – turn up if you say you're going to.'

'Of course!'

'Then please let me have your details and I'll give you mine. I gather you're at uni? If ever you want work during the hols I'm bound to have something.'

'That would be very kind, although I don't live in London. I really only go there to spend time with my dad.'

'Well, the offer is there, and not all the work is London-based. If I had something more local to here I could let you know. Oh! I think I hear people coming!'

Although the babies were both sound asleep and could have been put in their travelling cots, by tacit agreement Sarah and Meggie didn't go down to meet

the new arrivals. They sat quite still as they overheard complaints about the journey and the coldness
of the house, and shortly the stump stump stump
of footsteps as Fenella's in-laws came up the stairs.

'I've put you in the Pink Room,' said Fenella. 'The
bathroom is through here. It has a walk-in shower.'

'How else are you expected to get into a shower?'
said an arrogant, impatient male voice. 'Crawl? Of
course it's a bloody walk-in shower!'

Meggie and Sarah exchanged glances and tried
not to giggle.

Fenella heaved a sigh of relief and caught Rupert's
eye. He was sitting at the other end of the kitchen
table. They exchanged little smiles. They'd got
everyone seated except the babies, who were asleep,
and the little girls, who were playing with a pre-
Christmas present provided by Zoe. Zoe and
Gideon's fish pie was in front of Rupert next to a
pile of roasting-hot plates that would be impossible
to pass but would satisfy his parents. Getting everyone sitting down, more or less in the places assigned
to them by Sarah's placement, had taken forever.
But soon, Fenella realised with relief, she could leave
the table to put the girls to bed. She knew she'd
probably fall asleep with them, reading a Christmas
story. She couldn't go to bed properly for ages – there

were stockings to organise – but a nap would be wonderful.

'OK,' said Rupert, plunging his serving spoon into the golden pastry that topped the pie. 'I hope everyone's hungry!'

'Shall I pour the wine?' asked Étienne.

'Thank you,' said Rupert. Fenella, up her end of the table, hoped the young Frenchman, whose family were great wine producers, approved of the vintage.

'I hope this fish pie hasn't got prawns in it,' said Lady Gainsborough. 'I'm allergic to prawns.'

Fenella's gaze shot in query to Zoe.

'No prawns,' Zoe confirmed.

'It's just it makes me terribly ill if I have prawns,' Lady Gainsborough went on, in case anyone was in doubt about what 'allergic' meant.

It was going to be a long meal, thought Fenella, plotting her escape.

It took Meggie a few moments to work out where she was. Then she remembered. It was Christmas morning and she was at Somerby. Then she became aware of a weight at the foot of her bed. A stocking! She was delighted. Her mother always did her one but her father and the Iguana thought she was too old for them. Feeling very happy, Meggie pulled the fat, stripy sock towards her and unpacked it. Fenella must have done it for her when she was feeling very tired and Meggie was touched. There was a chocolate orange in the toe (something her own mother always included – it took up a good amount of space), a miniature of Bailey's Irish Cream (a very nice touch), a packet of Father Christmas tissues, a pair of socks and a trio of toiletries.

She ate a slice of her chocolate orange (chocolate for breakfast was a family tradition in her mother's house) and let her mind drift to Étienne. He was devastatingly attractive, but in spite of this, and being French, he was extremely kind. He made her feel attractive. And he was lovely with the little ones. She gave a wistful sigh and decided he was just part of what was turning out to be a very special Christmas.

She pulled on her clothes and went downstairs to the kitchen. Rupert hadn't let her stay downstairs and help him clear up after dinner and Meggie thought that there might well be detritus from the fish pie she could deal with. Fenella and Rupert were going to a lot of trouble to make sure she had a lovely time; she was determined to do everything she could to make it all go a bit more easily.

She enjoyed having the big old kitchen to herself, though it seemed a bit empty with Bessie now gone.

She would have liked to put on some Christmas music but there was a quite complicated sound system and she didn't want to waste time working it out. Meggie wanted the kitchen to be gleaming before Fenella appeared. She switched on the chilli fairy lights that decorated the row of kitchen equipment above the Aga and set to.

She was giving the table a final wipe when Étienne appeared. 'Good morning! Happy Christmas!' he said.

In his tight navy blue jumper over well-fitting jeans and shiny leather shoes he managed to look incredibly smart and relaxed at the same time. He came over to her and kissed her cheek. He had obviously just shaved and smelt of something delightfully citrusy and sharp.

Offering a brief prayer of thanks that she'd brushed her teeth already, instead of waiting until after breakfast as she usually did, Meggie smiled shyly. 'Happy Christmas. Shall I make you some coffee?' There was a coffee machine in the corner and Meggie felt fairly confident of being able to make it work. Her father had one somewhat similar.

'I will make coffee,' he announced and moved towards the machine. 'Did you have a Christmas stocking?'

'Yes, I did! I wasn't expecting one but it was a lovely surprise. Did you have one?'

'Yes, but I think Father Christmas must think I am very dirty and also an alcoholic. There was a lot of shower gel and soap but also a small bottle of brandy.' He said all this completely seriously but Meggie knew he was joking.

'I had those things as well but also chocolate,' replied Meggie, realising suddenly that the toiletries were probably from a supply used to stock Somerby's guest rooms when they were rented.

'I also had chocolate.'

Rather to her relief (Meggie wondered what she could think of to say next) Rupert arrived. He looked bleary-eyed and his hair was ruffled; he was wearing very brightly striped pyjamas under his dressing gown.

'Morning! Happy Christmas,' he said with a sleepy smile. 'The girls came in to open their stockings at four o'clock this morning. Thank goodness they eventually went back to sleep. Fenella too. All my girls out sparko. Tea?'

Meggie had already slid the kettle on to the hot plate of the Aga and Rupert went to it. 'I'm going to take my parents tea in bed,' he said, 'then we can have Buck's Fizz.' He poured boiling water into a small teapot he'd taken from a hook. 'I wonder if I can persuade my parents to have breakfast in bed too? Then we can all be as raucous as we like.'

Rupert was just assembling a tray when Hugo appeared. He was dressed but also looked tired. He was carrying Ted, helpfully dressed in blue stripes.

'Morning, all,' he said. 'Good God, those PJs, Rupes! Bit bright, aren't they?'

'The girls choose me a pair of Christmas pyjamas every year from a rather smart catalogue,' Rupert explained. 'One day they'll be dark navy with a subtle bird's-eye spot but, currently, it's bright stripes.'

'Shall I take him?' said Meggie, going to Hugo, feeling the need to be useful and always liking to have a baby or small child to hide behind. 'Does he need a bottle?'

'Actually I was wondering if there was a banana or something I could mash up for him. I must get the high chairs in from the car.'

'No need,' said Meggie. 'I'll mash the banana and then feed him on my lap. What about Immi? She must be hungry too.'

'You are a star!' said Hugo. 'I'll go and get her. It would be lovely to give Sarah a bit of a lie-in. She feeds the babies herself in the night and although they went for nearly four hours at first, they've been snacking ever since.'

'Here.' Étienne, who had been sipping a tiny cup of coffee which probably contained more caffeine than an entire jar of instant, took Meggie's burden. 'You get Immi. I will hold this one while Meggie mashes.'

Hugo headed off to fetch his daughter. Seeing this desperately handsome young man holding a baby gave Meggie such a pang of lust she was glad she could turn away from the room and hide her blushes. She had to remind herself that she was only nineteen, far too young to even think about having babies, and that Étienne was so out of her league it was ridiculous.

She was still a bit breathless when he came towards her with an apron he had found hanging over the bar in front of the Aga. 'Here, put this over yourself. Babies are messy.'

'Right,' said Rupert, carrying a tray with tea and bread and butter on it. 'I'll see if I can persuade the aged parents to stay in bed long enough for us to have a jolly breakfast. Oh, hi, Zoe! Competing with me on the bright nightwear front, I see.'

Zoe came into the kitchen as Rupert left, smiling benignly. She was wearing red flannel pyjamas with dressing gown and slippers to match. Zoe still managed to look cute, Meggie thought, and with her baby bump she could be mistaken for Father Christmas.

'Happy Christmas, you two,' said Zoe to Meggie and Étienne.

'Happy Christmas,' they replied.

A few minutes later Hugo and Rupert were back in the kitchen, Hugo with Immi and Rupert rubbing his hands in satisfaction. 'Mission accomplished – the parents are staying in bed. I think we're OK if we have breakfast now. We can take Sarah and Fen some up too if they don't want to come down.'

'Sarah will want to come down,' said Hugo. 'I'll go in a minute and tell her breakfast will be ready soon.' Hugo handed Immi to Meggie with a grateful look and fell into a chair.

'Can't really see Fen and the girls wanting to miss it either,' said Rupert, 'but they were stirring when I went past so they'll be here soon. So! Who's for Buck's Fizz?'

'You know,' said Hugo, 'adding orange juice to perfectly good champagne is just making it sweet and we all know sugar is poison.'

Zoe shook her head at him. 'Hugo! Champagne is alcohol! Leaving the orange juice out of the Buck's Fizz doesn't make it healthy, you know!'

'You're just being priggish because you're not drinking,' he replied. 'I just prefer my champagne straight.'

'It's Christmas: you can have it just as you like,' said Rupert, taking the foil off a bottle.

'I seem to have arrived at exactly the right moment,' said Gideon. 'Bottles being opened and all that.' He kissed his wife and then Meggie on the cheek. 'So, what's for breakfast? Scrambled eggs and smoked salmon? Would you like me to make it, Rupes?'

'Yes, please,' Rupert said enthusiastically.

'I'm starving,' Zoe agreed.

'Me too,' agreed Étienne, tenderly scooping mashed banana off a tiny chin.

'Let's crack on!' exclaimed Gideon.

❄

Meggie was surprised to find herself so relaxed amid such cool people who knew each other so well. It was very unlike her. She'd given Immi to Sarah when Sarah'd arrived but didn't feel exposed.

When everyone was round the table eating breakfast – she had been thrilled to note that Étienne had made a big effort to sit next to her – Meggie asked, 'When do we open Christmas presents? I have a bit of wrapping to do.'

'Oh, that's because you spent so much time wrapping mine!' said Fenella, with her mouth full.

'There's a bit of controversy,' said Rupert. 'In my family we always had to wait until after tea.'

'And in mine we did them after breakfast,' said Fenella. 'And it's my house!'

It wasn't the first time they'd had this discussion, Meggie realised.

'Oh, OK,' said Rupert, 'we'll do some now but keep some back for later. Maybe the grown-ups' presents after tea?'

'So when do we have the turkey?' asked Gideon. 'And do you want me and Zoe to do it?'

'Yes please,' said Rupert and Fenella in unison.

'We're not territorial about it,' Fenella went on. 'We'll have enough to do. And we usually eat about three? We never seem able to get it together before then.'

'I can do the potatoes and sprouts,' said Meggie. 'If I'm not looking after babies.' Feeling slightly uncomfortable with everyone looking at her she felt obliged to explain. 'I do the potatoes and sprouts when I stay with my dad.'

'We'll all pitch in, otherwise you'd develop sprout-peeler's thumb or some such,' said Fenella firmly, 'although I suppose we'll let the grandparents off.' She paused. 'My mum and I always get just a bit drunk while we peel spuds and compete for speed. She likes a knife and I like a peeler.' She cleared her throat suddenly, obviously missing her mother.

Fenella was just drawing breath after breakfast, enjoying a few moments of solitude while people got their presents together and Rupert hustled the girls into their clothes, when she became aware of her parents-in-law, complaining loudly about the stairs, the slightly scuffed paintwork and anything else they passed on their way down to the kitchen.

Fenella nipped out and ran up the stairs to the ground floor and waylaid them in the hall. 'Good morning! Happy Christmas! I do hope you slept well. Let's go into the drawing room.' She'd learnt when Somerby first became a wedding venue not to ask people how they'd slept in case they told her.

'Where is everyone?' asked Lady Gainsborough frostily, and ignoring Fenella's 'Happy Christmas'.

'We're all just putting presents under the tree,' replied Fenella. 'The fire is going well in there.' God bless Gideon and Étienne, who'd got an inferno going, making other heating almost redundant.

Fenella herded them into the drawing room where, she was delighted and amazed to see, her children were dressed and playing prettily with a clockwork train set that had been a present from Zoe and Gideon. Meggie was on the floor with them, putting the trains back on the track as necessary. The babies, who had been quite vocal, were now sleeping happily in their enormous pushchairs that were up the quieter end of the room.

'Come and sit by the fire,' said Fenella. 'Children? Come and say happy Christmas to Grandmama and Grandpapa.' She smiled encouragingly, knowing her children would not want to do this.

Meggie, possibly reading the situation correctly, got up. 'Come on, girls! Let's go and say happy Christmas!'

Lord and Lady Gainsborough looked down at the

children. God, thought Fenella, they're like characters Roald Dahl would invent, looking at the children as if they were street urchins.

'Go on,' prompted Meggie in a whisper. 'Say happy Christmas!'

'Happy Christmas, Granny and Grandpa,' said Glory. Simmy gave a fair approximation of the same thing.

'Fenella!' said Lady Gainsborough. 'I thought we'd made it clear how we would like your children to address us! Grandmama and Grandpapa, as we addressed our grandparents!'

'They just got muddled for a minute,' said Fenella. 'No need to take offence.'

But her mother-in-law loved nothing better than to take offence, especially when none was intended.

'And who are you?' Lady Gainsborough asked Meggie.

Meggie, who seemed a bit taken aback, said, 'I'm Meggie, the "mother's help", just here for a couple of days while everyone's so busy. We met last night over supper?'

Lady Gainsborough just nodded approvingly and, dismissing her grandchildren with a flap of her veiny, ring-heavy hand, picked up the crossword, which had been left for her. Her husband grunted and did the same, picking up an ancient copy of *Punch*, which Fenella had found for him in a box somewhere.

Now that awkwardness was over, and the

children were back playing with Meggie and Étienne, Fenella breathed a sigh of relief. She took the
opportunity to go upstairs to her bathroom to brush
her teeth. She might be brave enough to take the
test that was hidden at the bottom of her handbag.
She'd been blaming not doing it on being so busy
with Christmas, but Fenella knew it was cowardice
really. She'd been feeling stressed, and the last thing
she wanted was for that stress to taint what would
be might be a very happy moment.

Half an hour later, Fenella went back into drawing
room feeling braced for the forthcoming day. She
had clean teeth, a little make-up on, and a new
jumper over her jeans. Everyone was sitting round
with drinks, chatting convivially, and she was
amused to see her starchy mother-in-law softening
in the warmth of the combined charm of Hugo,
Gideon and Étienne. Maybe it was because he was
French, but he managed to combine great respect
with a touch of flirtatiousness that Lady Gainsborough obviously adored. It was going to be all right,
she thought. Christmas was going to be perfect!

Then all the lights went out.

Fenella heard a four-letter word swiftly followed
by a lot of coughing from her husband. 'Must be a
fuse,' he said. 'I'll go and check.'

'I'll go with you,' said Gideon, 'just in case we need a plan B for cooking.

As quite a lot of the many sets of fairy lights that decorated the drawing room along with boughs of tasteful greenery were battery operated the table lamps weren't really necessary. But if the reason the lights had gone out was more than just a fuse, it could be a problem. The Aga had four ovens but they'd planned to use the electric cooker as well.

'How are everyone's glasses?' said Fenella, wishing she could fancy a drink herself.

'I'll do it,' said Hugo. 'You sit down for a bit.'

Fenella sat, but she was prepared to leap up at a moment's notice. The lights going out had not given her a good feeling. They'd recently had the house entirely rewired at vast expense. A power cut was more likely than a fuse. She pulled her phone out of her pocket. 'I'll just go on Twitter. That'll tell me what's going on.'

'Surely not on Christmas Day?' said Lady Gainsborough, sounding shocked.

'But yes,' said Étienne, 'my grandmother is also horrified by these things. However, phones are useful. I have photos of my family and our vineyard on it. Château de Saint-Vire – it is famous, *non*?'

Apparently it *was* famous. Even Lady Gainsborough, not as interested in wine as her husband, responded positively. 'Can I see the pictures?' said Lady Gainsborough.

'*Certainement.*'

Seeing Étienne at her mother-in-law's side, flicking through photos, Fenella hoped that ones of the château, which she and Rupert had seen, featured in the picture show. Lady Gainsborough would like that!

It didn't take Fenella long to realise it was a power cut, fairly localised, and as yet no one knew how long it would take to be fixed. It was Christmas Day and there was no bad weather predicted – there might not be many engineers on duty.

Rupert appeared shortly afterwards with the same information. They went into the passage so they could talk privately.

'What shall we do?' asked Fenella, thinking about parts of the house growing colder as auxiliary plug-in radiators grew chilly.

'Well, Gideon suggests we do the turkey on the barbeque but we should get going on that right away. Everything else will fit in the Aga, more or less, so we should be fine. Thank goodness we're not entirely dependent on electricity. And we've got a fair few camping lamps and things. I'll go and get them while there's still a bit of natural light.'

A thought shot through Fenella like a bolt. 'The cottage! Gerald's cottage! Those poor people! There are six of them and no way of cooking their Christmas dinner – or lunch, whatever they call it . . .'

Rupert's expression reflected her anxiety. 'And worse, that pathetic little wood burner doesn't push out any heat.'

'It's no good, Rupe. You know how I feel about waifs and strays. I wouldn't fancy cooking a Christmas meal in that cottage even if it did have electricity. We'll have to invite them here, for the meal at least,' said Fenella.

Rupert nodded. 'I know you wouldn't be happy if we just left them there. So, can you go and get them?'

Fenella was surprised. 'Can't you go? I'll have enough to organise here.'

'I'll have to find the barbeque for the lads—'

'No you won't! It's in the shed. Gideon and Hugo are more than capable. I've got the children—'

'The children have got Meggie.'

'I can't abandon Meggie! What about your parents?'

'They'll cope. Power cuts are nothing to them. I'll make sure they've got lanterns. The elderly are far more resilient about these things.'

'But why can't you go?'

Rupert looked very slightly guilty. 'I've got something I have to do.' He put his hands on her shoulders and kissed her. 'I'm really sorry, darling, but you've got to go to the cottage.'

Although she had been annoyed with Rupert for not going, Fenella found being out in the fresh air and away from the hurly-burly of Christmas Day very pleasant. She usually organised a walk but with so many people and babies in the house, this year she hadn't.

She could have walked down to the cottage, in fact, but decided to take the car in case the people needed anything carrying up to the house. If the cottage was completely freezing and uninhabitable she could just about put everyone up, using the recently converted stable. And as she remembered hearing herself say gathering up waifs and strays was what Christmas was all about, she had to be prepared to put her money where her mouth was, so to speak. At least the stable had a good wood burner.

The door was opened by a woman about her own age. She looked harassed and not pleased to have her door knocked on.

Fenella put on her best 'really, I'm here to help' smile. She used it a lot when there were events on at the house. 'Hi! Happy Christmas! I just came down to see if you had a power cut. I'm Fenella. We live at the big house? It was me who left the welcome pack, such as it was. We keep an eye on the cottage for Gerald, who owns it, while he's abroad.'

The woman nodded. 'Hi. Yes, we have. And everything in this wretched cottage is electric! I'm Sam, short for Samantha.'

'Well, why don't you come up and have Christmas lunch with us? We're having it at about three – just after the Queen's speech. But if you're freezing to death you could come immediately.'

'Come in,' said Sam. 'This is so kind of you. But maybe if you haven't got a power cut, ours is one that could be fixed.'

Fenella went into the cottage and saw a gloomy little family huddled round a wood burner that was more for decoration than for giving out heat. There was a worried-looking husband in a Christmas jumper, a couple of small boys playing on hand-held games machines, not bothered by the lack of electricity, and an elderly couple who looked miserable and bad-tempered at the same time.

'Hi, everyone!' said Fenella. 'Ghastly time for the power to go off. I'm just suggesting that you all come up to us? Our lights are off too, but we have a huge Aga, oil-fired central heating, and my macho male guests are planning to cook the turkey on the barbeque.' She paused. 'Apparently it works really well.'

The elderly woman, who was sitting so close to the stove she was almost touching it, said, 'We couldn't possibly impose on you and your family at Christmas.'

She sounded so like Lady Gainsborough that Fenella almost laughed. 'It wouldn't be an imposition at all,' she said firmly. 'We'd love to have you. And as we're quite a big party already, we might as well add you to the mix.' She realised too late that she should probably have expressed this a bit differently. She put her hand on Sam's arm. 'Shall we go into the kitchen? I can explain –'

'Oh yes, let's!' agreed Sam quickly. 'We could have a glass of sherry.'

The tiny kitchen could have doubled as a cold-room in a restaurant, Fenella thought as she went in. There was an open bottle and a half-full Paris goblet of sherry on the side.

'To be honest, going to you would be a lifesaver,' said Sam. 'Apart from the fact that we can't cook the bloody dinner, my parents-in-law feel the cold terribly and while they are really difficult, I don't want them getting hypothermia and dying just this minute.' Sam picked up the sherry bottle and waved it at Fenella in invitation. 'I've turned into a secret drinker. Henry, that's my husband, doesn't dare have a drop in case he has to take his parents to hospital or something.'

'Well, I've got my in-laws too, and they're also really difficult. Fortunately I also have good friends who are being amazing and there's loads of food and lots of room. It would be no trouble to have you, and you wouldn't have to be a secret drinker. My lot started at breakfast.'

'But not you?'

Fenella shook her head. 'Not at the moment. I have to keep my wits about me a bit. I'm afraid my children are too young to be of interest to yours and there are a pair of six-month-old twins, but we have lovely Meggie to help with them, and a gorgeous Frenchman who seems very into kids. He's also probably rather into Meggie; I haven't had time to work it out. He'd be cool with your two, I'm sure.'

'In which case, we'd love to come. It's so kind of you. I know Henry will be really grateful, and if his parents aren't, well, they never are!'

'Just the same as my in-laws. I do sympathise. But the house is big enough for people to get away from each other if they need to. We have a games room with a table-tennis table in the barn.' Fenella paused. 'You probably want to sort yourselves out a bit, but come up as soon as you're ready. You know where we are?'

Fenella set off for home, having been assured that the family would be able to find Somerby without difficulty, wondering how everything had been going on without her.

She went into the kitchen to find Zoe, Sarah and Hugo preparing vegetables by the light of a hurricane lamp, which wasn't giving out a lot of light. Meggie was on the sofa holding Immi and jiggling Ted, sitting in his chair, with her foot. But in spite of the dimness, it all seemed very merry. Her daughters must be with Rupert.

'Well, they're coming,' she announced. 'Poor things! Even with heating the cottage would be far too small for them really and Sam – she's the mother – has got her in-laws too, and they seem to have been carved from the same stone as mine are. Is Rupe up there with them?'

'Not sure where Rupe is,' said Zoe, digging the eye out of a potato with care. 'Why don't you sit down for a bit? Have a drink!'

'Well, if the in-laws are settled upstairs and have drinks handy, I'll get on with the snacks we're having to keep us going until the turkey.' She went over to a big fridge and opened the door. 'It's hard to know what to do about food when you're eating such a huge meal at three. But you need something between breakfast and turkey. Rupert's parents love sandwiches. I've bought fillings. Don't tell them! They'd be horrified. We're having smoked salmon and the blinis you made, Zoe.'

'Oh, do sit down, Fen!' said Zoe. 'I'll make the sandwiches. When are our new guests coming?'

'Not entirely sure,' said Fenella, finding herself surprisingly pleased to be made to sit. The lamplight was soothing. 'We'll hear them arrive, I expect. Although now we haven't got dogs going mad whenever anyone turns up, it's harder.'

About twenty minutes later, Hugo had left the party and gone out to see how the barbeque was getting on; Sarah had taken over holding a sleeping Immi; Meggie and Zoe had made a mountain of sandwiches; and Fenella, feeling unable to sit down for long, had dolloped sour cream on several dozen portions of smoked salmon and blinis. Now they were decorating the top with tiny black pearls of caviar. 'Right,' said Fenella, 'let's take these up.' She picked up a plate.

'I'll take them!' said Zoe and Meggie simultaneously.

'OK, you two, keep your hair on. I'll take the sangers and one of you can take the blinis. I think we'd better have them up there in the drawing room, don't you? I can't have Sam's in-laws in the kitchen when I hardly let my own in here.' She paused. 'At least it's too dark to see the mess.'

'Meggie and I will take the food,' said Zoe firmly.

'Well, you can't take it all,' said Fenella, frowning

slightly. 'And you're pregnant, Zoe. I don't want you tripping on the stairs in the dark. Besides, you should take things easy at this stage. Although I admit it's a bit late for me to be telling you that.'

'Really, stay here!' said Meggie, sounding a bit desperate. 'You might be needed. If the neighbours arrive.'

Fenella wondered if it was her, or if everyone else had gone slightly mad. 'We can hear the door perfectly well from the drawing room.' She picked up a plate. 'Come on.'

Lord and Lady Gainsborough were sitting by the fire, which was roaring away happily, reading by the light of a camping lantern. Otherwise the room was empty. Fenella thought how pretty it looked lit only by fairy lights, candles and the lamp.

'Oh, where's Rupert?' she asked. He was better at leaving his parents to get on with it than she was. He'd probably sloped off to wrap a present or something.

'We haven't seen him all day,' said his mother, sounding aggrieved.

'So, has he got the girls with him?' Fenella asked, suddenly worried.

'The girls are playing with the dolls' house,' said Meggie quickly, 'with Étienne. They're making decorations for it out of tinsel. Not sure how they're managing with just a big torch to see by, but they're happy.'

What a star, thought Fenella and decided that the minute she could see to go down there, she'd find a bottle of good brandy in the cellar to add to Étienne's present, which was currently a cashmere scarf she'd bought for Rupert and he'd never taken out of the cellophane. Étienne was worth his weight in rubies.

'Meggie,' Fenella said, 'would you be a dear and get the men in, if they can leave the barbeque for a second? They need sustenance and we need them to help with drinks.'

Meggie ran down the stairs and outside into the courtyard where Gideon and Hugo were standing by the barbeque wrapped in scarves and wearing woolly hats, with glasses in their hands, laughing.

'Break time,' she said. 'Fen needs you.'

'Oh, right,' Gideon said immediately. 'Let's go.'

Meggie took the time to find the downstairs cloakroom so she could tidy up a bit. Everyone seemed to be very casual about clothes for Christmas down here. At her father's, her stepmother always wore a new little-black-dress, littler and blacker than the previous year's model, and had to be in killer heels and full slap. She and her mother used to make bitchy remarks about the pictures the Iguana put up on Facebook, looking as if she'd never been near the kitchen. Which was pretty much true.

But here everyone seemed to be wearing jeans and jumpers, which were lovely but also very relaxed. But Meggie wanted to make sure she didn't look too sloppy. She had Étienne to impress. He, being French, looked incredibly stylish in his casual clothes. She had to try and keep up as best she could. Annoyingly, when she found the loo, she could hardly see a thing even though someone had thoughtfully put a few tea lights by the wash-basin. She could just make out her reflection: dark, slightly wavy hair, caught up in a scrunchy with escaping tendrils falling over her shoulders. The cosy red jumper she'd put on this morning looked OK, making the most of her curves. Or maybe she thought that just because she could hardly see!

But the more Meggie was around these lovely people, Étienne in particular, she realised that her lack of confidence was caused by her stepmother's constant criticisms. Those came from Ignatia's own insecurities, and shouldn't feed Meggie's. Encouraged, Meggie took one last look at her reflection, and then headed back to the drawing room and the rest of her Christmas Day.

Meggie rejoined the party in the drawing room in time to hear Fenella saying, 'So where is Rupert?'

Everyone else was there, Meggie realised, the little girls hanging on to Étienne's fingers and looking up at him adoringly.

'Well, I don't know, Fenella,' snapped Lady Gainsborough. 'He's your husband, but we haven't seen him since he brought us the lamp.'

'Helpful,' Meggie heard Fenella mutter under her breath. 'I am getting a little worried now though,' continued Fenella.

'No need,' said Hugo. 'I had a text from him just now.'

'You had a text!' said Fenella. 'Saying what? For God's sake!'

The little girls looked at their mother and Meggie realised they didn't often see her agitated. Meggie went over to them. 'Shall we find you something to eat? Do you like smoked salmon?'

'Just saying he'd popped out,' replied Hugo, sounding desperately guilty. He went over to the elderly Gainsboroughs with a bottle of champagne in his hand.

Lord Gainsborough waved it away. 'Whisky,' he said. 'Or, better still, whisky punch. Hasn't Rupert made any? It's one of the few things he's really good at.'

'Rupert seems to have gone missing,' said Fenella, obviously struggling to keep her feelings hidden.

Zoe went to her side. 'Really, it's all right, Fen. He's not missing. He's just out, like Hugo said. Let's get everyone fed and then maybe we can have presents.'

'We never have presents until after lunch,' said Lady Gainsborough, 'and by that I mean the turkey, not a sandwich.' But as she had at least four sandwiches on her plate she obviously liked them.

This remark seemed to galvanise Fenella. 'Right! Presents! Let's get them handed out and we can start opening. Glory, darling, you can read the labels? Can you put everyone's presents into piles.' She paused. 'Of course our guests might come in the middle of it – in fact they probably will – but we can't hang around any longer. Bloody Rupert,' she added, probably intending to say it a bit more quietly than she in fact did.

Meggie helped the girls and Étienne joined in. Remarkably quickly, Meggie thought, they had all the presents in piles. It turned out that the adults, apart from the in-laws and she and Étienne, had done a Secret Santa, which meant they only had one present each. Meggie was very touched and surprised to see that her own pile had five presents on it, considering no one had known she was coming until the day before Christmas Eve.

She had only given a present – a box of home-made biscuits – to Fenella and Rupert and a selection of colouring books, wigs and dresses to Glory and Simmy, thus ensuring both little girls could dress up as the sisters from *Frozen*. Meggie hoped her mother was right and that a home-made, edible present would be far more acceptable than something that would have to be found a home for.

Meggie could tell Fenella was on edge. She kept looking at her watch, obviously wondering where on earth Rupert was. Then, just as Fenella said, 'Right, eldest first. Grandpapa, open your first present!' the doorbell jangled.

'I'll go!' said Fenella, before anyone else could offer, and disappeared out of the room.

Meggie took an executive decision. The little girls, who, she felt, had shown the patience of saints, were getting restive. She whispered to them, 'Open your presents from me. It's those two. Do it quietly though so your grandmother doesn't get upset.'

Lady Gainsborough was already upset. Hugo had bravely explained who was about to arrive and she said in a loud voice, 'I really don't see why we have to have strangers in the house at Christmas! Although possibly that ship has sailed!' As she looked around the room it was clear they were all designated as strangers in her eyes.

How unfortunate, thought Meggie, that Lady Gainsborough's lordly statement was also heard by the family trooping into the room, obviously embarrassed by the situation.

Fenella did rapid introductions ending with 'Here, Mr and Mrs Williams, come and sit by the fire with my parents-in-law.'

Meggie braced herself to hear Lady Gainsborough say something sniffy, but instead she picked up the camping lantern and inspected the couple she was being presented with. 'I don't suppose you play bridge, do you? My family are about to open their presents and I can't imagine anything more tedious than having to exclaim rapturously over every pair of socks or tie that's opened.'

Meggie realised she was clutching Glory's hand a bit too tightly and released it.

'We do play bridge!' said the elder Mrs Williams. 'And are cursing the day our son married a woman who didn't. Do you have any cards?'

Fenella pounced. 'We have cards!'

Her mother-in-law shuddered. 'We don't mean the cards you play snap with! Fortunately, my husband and I always travel with our own in the hope we might be able to make up a four.'

'We have a card table!' said Fenella eagerly, snatching at this golden opportunity to keep all the elderly and difficult among them happy. 'I'd have asked Rupert to fetch it but—'

'Just tell me where it is,' said Hugo. 'I'll bring it in a tick.'

'And I will fetch your playing cards, Lord and Lady Gainsborough,' said Gideon, 'if you would like me to?'

Meggie focused on the children as everyone else sprang into action and, in minutes, the new family were settled with drinks, a card table and their own Christmas presents, brought by Sam, who seemed hugely relieved not to be solely responsible for everyone's happiness. Étienne was talking to the boys, who seemed to be around ten, about sport.

'I think I'm almost too frazzled to open presents,' said Fenella, collapsing in a chair with a sigh.

Just then the door opened. 'Well,' said Rupert, carrying a box, 'you'll have to open this one!'

He put the box on Fenella's lap and before she could do more than look at it, it opened of its own accord and out scrambled a black Labrador puppy. Fenella picked it up and held it to her. 'Oh, Rupert,' she said with tears in her eyes, 'you idiot! Wonderful – but an idiot!'

But she said it in a way that it made it clear it was the best present in the world and buried her nose in the squirming bundle. 'Don't puppies smell heavenly? What shall we call him, my darlings?'

'Something Christmassy,' cried Glory.

'Yes – definitely something Christmassy,' agreed Rupert.

'Rudolph,' said Simmy timidly.

'What a brilliant idea, my little Cymbeline,' cheered Rupert, lifting her into a giant bear hug. 'Only maybe we'll call her Rudie – seeing as she's a girl. Now where are my presents?'

A couple of hours later Meggie felt as though she was in a painting by one of the Dutch masters she was studying for her degree.

The huge table in the dining room had silver candelabra, each holding four candles, marching down it. In between were dishes of food: roast potatoes, roast vegetables, sprouts cooked with pancetta, sprouts cooked plain (Lady Gainsborough only liked them plain). There were plates piled with Yorkshire puddings mainly for the children, a random plate of fish fingers and another of baked beans, brought by the Williams family, in case their sons refused to eat turkey. There were mashed potatoes and mashed swede so Sarah could give the twins some solid food and there were silver dishes with nuts and raisins, crisps and cheese footballs (Lord Gainsborough's favourites). It all looked absolutely beautiful.

There were candles on every surface but this was the only room where Fenella hadn't run riot with the fairy lights. There was an antique mirror over the fireplace reflecting the flickering candles in front of it. The fire, which had smoked for quite a while, was roaring away.

Apart from the people, in a selection of jumpers, scarves and ponchos, making the scene contemporary it could have been a scene from a costume drama, only without the servants.

Up the children's end of the table, policed by Meggie and Étienne, there were a couple of large jam jars filled with battery-operated lights that acted as lanterns. There was enough light to see by but not enough to notice the random cutlery and china. Both little girls were now dressed as Disney princesses, including blonde wigs; the babies wore crowns from out of the crackers. They were in high chairs, one modern and one antique, and everyone was very, very relaxed. Rudie, the puppy, exhausted with being adored, was asleep on a velvet cushion in front of the fire.

'Well, my dear,' said Lord Gainsborough, addressing Fenella who was seated at the head of the table. 'I think we should propose a toast to you, for providing us with such a splendid Christmas.'

'Yes,' agreed his wife. 'I think this has been one of the best Christmases ever. And it's so lovely to have candlelight at Christmas!'

Fenella looked flabbergasted at this praise from such an unexpected quarter. Meggie knew by now that the Gainsboroughs were not ones for showing gratitude.

'Oh, thank you!' Fenella said, trying to hide her astonishment. 'I'm just glad it worked out so well.' She looked at the older Williamses, who also looked content.

'Splendid to be able to get a decent hand of bridge,' went on Lady Gainsborough. 'Such a stroke of luck. Nice to find fellow players but ones on the same level is more than one could have expected.'

'Well, come on then,' said Lord Gainsborough, who was in very good spirits owing to the quantity of them he had consumed, 'have a glass with me!'

'Oh, I won't, thank you,' said Fenella, 'I'm off it for the moment. Actually, I suppose there's no better time to announce this: I'm pregnant.'

The stunned silence was quickly followed by many voices congratulating her.

Fenella quickly sought to catch Rupert's eyes, realising it might have been an idea to speak to him first. But Rupert was looking back at her with such a beaming smile that she knew he was just as thrilled as she was. What a perfect Christmas present for them both.

'Good show, old girl!' said Lord Gainsborough. 'Maybe this time you'll be lucky and have a boy!'

To Meggie's huge relief Glory, who usually had the ears of a bat, didn't seem to have heard this objectionable comment. Instead she said from the other end of the table, 'Does that mean you're having a baby?'

'Yes, darling,' said her mother fondly. 'Is that OK with you?'

'Yes,' said Glory, 'because it means that next year we can have our own baby Jesus at the carol service and not have to use that horrid pink dolly with the broken arm.'

'Jolly well done, darling,' said Rupert, kissing his wife. 'You've saved the girls from the horrid pink dolly.'

'There's no effort I won't go to to make my family happy,' she said, having kissed him very thoroughly back.

Meggie stood in her father's house holding a tray of champagne glasses. It was New Year's Eve and she was wearing the cashmere jumper in a very flattering pink that Fenella had given her for Christmas. With it she had on a mini skirt with a wide, tight belt and Zoe's tights, which made her legs look amazing. She felt so much sexier and confident than she ever had before. Sadly at the moment it was being wasted on one of her father's friends.

'So what are you reading at university, Meggie?' he asked, inspecting her chest.

'History of Art with French,' she replied, trying to move away with her tray.

'Speak much French, do you?' the man went on.

'A bit.' She actually spoke it quite well but wasn't one to boast. 'I should really—'

Just as she was about to say 'circulate' the bell to the flat rang and her stepmother, head to toe in black fake leather, opened the door. It was Étienne.

'Good evening,' he said in his wonderful accent. 'I am Étienne de Saint-Vire. I am here for Meggie? You must be her mother.' He took Ignatia's hand and kissed it. 'It is cool that she invited me?'

'Yes, of course!' said Ignatia. 'But I'm not Meggie's mother!' She gave a little laugh. 'I'm hardly old enough!'

'Oh, excuse me!' said Étienne, all apology. 'Now I look I see you don't have her beautiful eyes.'

'No, but I do have—'

Meggie could see her stepmother stretching and purring in the presence of a supremely attractive young man. It made her cringe. She couldn't wait to tell her mother how creepy and embarrassing it was.

Étienne didn't wait to be hit on by the Iguana. 'I see Meggie over there. I will talk to her. *Enchanté, madame.*'

He was with her in a very few strides. ''Ello, Meggie.' He took the tray of glasses from her and set it down. Then he helped himself to two of them and handed one to her.

Meggie thought she would die of happiness, for many reasons. Firstly, he'd accepted her embarrassed-sounding email invitation; secondly, he was even more gorgeous than she'd remembered, which was quite difficult; and finally, he had obviously annoyed her stepmother, which was excellent.

'Hi,' she said, hoping her smile of sheer joy wasn't making her look desperately silly. 'You came.'

'Of course I came. I was delighted to have the opportunity to see you again so soon.'

The Iguana, obviously not happy about Meggie having all this divine young man's attention, swanned up. 'Meggie! You didn't tell us you had a boyfriend.'

'Meggie and I are not yet boyfriend and girlfriend,' said Étienne smoothly. 'Although I'm hoping that may change soon. *Madame*,' he addressed the Iguana, 'may I convey a message from my *grandmère*, asking permission for Meggie to stay with her, with us as a family, at our château, for Epiphany – Twelfth Night – what do you call it here?'

'Twelfth Night,' said Meggie.

'Oh,' said Ignatia shortly. 'You'd have to ask Meggie's actual mother for that. Although I suppose her father would do. Darling!' She summoned her husband to her side.

'Meggie?' said her father, surprised. 'Who's this?'

Étienne introduced himself. 'I am very much

hoping that it will be permitted for Meggie to join us at my grandmother's home for Twelfth Night?'

'It's a château,' said Ignatia.

Meggie's father seemed unfazed. 'It's Meggie's mother you should be asking. I suppose visiting a French château would be good for her French.'

Meggie herself wondered why Étienne felt obliged to ask permission from her parents and assumed it was a French thing.

Étienne turned to her. 'You speak French?'

Meggie shrugged. She didn't want to confess that her French was quite good – she would be too shy to try it out in front of him. 'A little.'

'She got an A star in her A level,' said her dad.

Meggie shrugged again, assuming confidently that this information would mean nothing to Étienne.

This was not the case. '*Ah bon!*' he said. 'This is very good news. My grandmother prefers to speak French.'

'Not unreasonable,' said Meggie. 'If she is French.'

Meggie's dad took Ignatia's arm to lead her away. 'Ask your mother, Meggie, but absolutely fine with me,' he said.

When they had gone Meggie cleared her throat. 'I'm going home tomorrow. If you don't have to go back to work, would you like to come with me?

Meet my mum and my stepdad? Then we can tell them about France.'

'Good idea,' said Étienne. 'I will ask Gideon if it is possible. The food-importing business is quiet just now. It should be fine. Now . . .'

He looked down into her eyes and Meggie's stomach did a back flip.

'Soon it will be midnight, *non*?'

'*Oui.*'

'And people kiss?'

'*Oui.*'

'We should practise.'

'OK.'

He put his arm round her and found a corner by a huge pot plant. 'This will do.' Then he lifted her chin, looked into her eyes, glanced down at her mouth and kissed her.

Meggie had been kissed before but never like this. Never with such a combination of passion and skill. Her eyes closed, her body felt as if it would hardly support her and she clung to him. She wanted it to go on forever.

While they were kissing, Meggie became aware of someone taking their photograph. Often the pictures the Iguana put up on Facebook were really annoying. She had absolutely no problem with this one.

Eventually they paused for breath. She swallowed and looked up at him. 'Is that a French kiss?'

He nodded. *'Certainement.'*

'If I'm going to visit you in France, maybe I should practise French kissing some more?'

He smiled. 'Very sensible.' And proceeded to help her do just that.

# Dogs
## Are for
# Christmas

It was very, very early on Christmas morning and pitch dark. Stella walked slowly up the hill to the common. She had forgotten just how steep the hills were in her father's bit of the Cotswolds. She was getting quite hot, with her hair tucked into a woolly hat and a couple of jumpers on under her jacket.

She carried her father's old Maglite to guide her. As she walked she imagined all those households where over-excited children were waking exhausted parents, wanting to open their presents, while the parents were desperate for another couple of hours' sleep. Considering it was only five a.m., there were quite a few houses with lights on, as well as the Christmas lights that flashed away all night, making the valley look like a slightly kitsch greetings card. It made Stella smile.

She was glad of the twinkly, cheery lights this morning, as her own mission was fairly gloomy. What she really needed, she felt, was a dog. A dog would make this trip normal and not a mad, sentimental whim. Also a dog would protect her from any possible muggers. Not that she was really frightened of being attacked, but she was a woman in her thirties and although fairly fit, if there was some opportunist – and optimistic – thief around she could be quite vulnerable.

Stella was heading for what was known locally as the Dog Walkers' Christmas Tree, which was more than just a jolly, outdoor Christmas tree. For many it was also a memorial to much-beloved pets who had died. It was a hawthorn – small for a tree, large for a Christmas tree – in the middle of the common, well away from any houses, and every year it was decorated by dog walkers. Stella never knew who put on the initial tinsel and plastic baubles but other dog walkers came up and added their own decorations and by Christmas Day it was a mass of mostly hand-crafted ornaments – to be collected afterwards. There was also a box for donations of dog food. This tree was both a sad and a happy place.

Stella had in the pocket of her father's old coat a little tin model dog that he'd made years ago. It was a fairly generic dog, her father had explained, but it represented all the dogs he'd had in his long life. Besides, his skills weren't up to anything much more specific.

Apart from the model dog, which was quite pitted and bent out of shape from years of being hung in howling gales, snow and rain, Stella had a box. In the box were the ashes of her father's last dog, Geoffrey, and (she would never, ever confess this to her sister, Annabel) some of her father's ashes too.

Stella knew he would have liked being mixed in with his companion Geoffrey, and would think it amusing to be scattered under the weathered old tree. But Annabel would be appalled at the idea, and would say that Stella was too sentimental and the whole thing was dreadfully whimsical. Because of Annabel's terribly sensible outlook, the rest of their father was in something like an urn and in the summer, on what would have been his ninetieth birthday, she and her sister were going to scatter the ashes together.

Stella knew putting some of him in with his dog was fanciful but she didn't care. To avoid upsetting anyone, and risk covering them with human and dog remains by mistake, she had set off for the Dog Walkers' Christmas Tree really early, certain there wouldn't be anyone else here at this time. Especially

on Christmas morning, which was so busy for so
many.

She had just successfully seen the ashes swept away
cleanly by the wind, and was thinking about her
much-beloved dad, when she was nearly knocked
over by a dog bounding up to her and planting its
paws on her chest. She staggered and braced herself,
just in time to avoid being knocked over by a second
dog.

A man came running up behind them, sweating
and overcome with embarrassment. He obviously
didn't know what to do first: shout at the dogs or
apologise to Stella. As the dogs were really just huge
puppies, and were now chasing each other round
and round the tree, the man cleared his throat and
addressed her.

'I am so desperately, desperately sorry,' he said,
pulling off his beanie hat and revealing a lot of
thick dark hair. 'Not only have my horrible dogs
nearly knocked you over, they have covered you in
mud.'

One of the dogs came bounding up to him and
his hand automatically went out to stroke the head
that pushed at him. Stella could tell that while he
was extremely embarrassed by them, he loved the
dogs very much.

British to the core and observing his feelings for the animals who were now clowning around, Stella nearly said that being bounced on was nothing, no trouble and probably her fault for standing with her head in the clouds. But as her father's fawn jacket was now covered in muddy paw prints, honesty forbade her.

'This is awful!' he went on. 'You must let me pay your dry-cleaning bill. You're covered! They're not even my dogs!'

The man, who was only a bit older than she was (though possibly nearer forty, Stella realised), couldn't stop apologising.

'They belong to my mother, really. She had them foisted on her when she was in no state . . .' He paused. 'I've just had to put her in a care home.'

Stella and her sister had managed to look after their father at home and had felt so lucky. She decided to keep the mood light-hearted. 'Well, it is probably hard for her to give them enough exercise from there.'

It took the man, who had stopped panting quite so hard, a nanosecond to realise she was making a joke. Processing that Stella probably wasn't going to sue him for damage to designer clothing, he relaxed a little. 'It is. Even if she put them on one of those really long leads.'

Stella laughed. 'Imagine them getting it tangled up in people's legs, felling them like ninepins.'

'I'd rather not, if you don't mind. It's bad enough what they did to you.'

'Don't worry about it,' she said. 'This coat will go in the machine. It's my dad's old walking jacket so it's seen plenty of mud in its time.'

'Well, if you're sure. I'm still mortified. I'm Fitz, by the way. My real name is Patrick Fitzherbert but everyone calls me Fitz.'

Now she knew he was Irish, she could hear the faintest of brogues in his voice. It was very attractive.

'Stella. Oh, and happy Christmas!'

'Happy Christmas to you.' He sighed.

'Christmas not going well for you?' said Stella.

He laughed. 'Not really. So far my dogs have nearly knocked you over and covered you in mud.'

'But they didn't knock me over and my coat is washable.'

Possibly hearing the word 'dogs' one of them came over and nuzzled Stella's leg. She stroked the head, happy to have it there.

'What sort are they?' she asked.

'Horrible,' said Fitz. 'They're horrible. A mixture: we have no idea what ingredients went into them.'

Stella studied them. 'There's a bit of Lab in there, I'd say.'

'And a bit of thief, a bit of high jumper and some marathon runner,' said Fitz. 'And a pinch of collie, which explains the white patches.'

'A handful?'

'A very big bit of handful,' he agreed. 'My poor mother! How she let herself agree to take them on God only knows. I suspect blackmail, otherwise there's no sense to it.'

'Is your mother – OK?'

'She's fine but frail physically, and her house is totally unsuitable for anyone elderly. I'm not sure *I* can manage to live in it without injuring myself. But did you mean, has she got her marbles? Technically yes, but obviously not really or she wouldn't have taken on the dogs. To be fair, she's always been a bit eccentric.'

'I like that. My mother is rather serious. She left my father, who was about thirty years older than she was, because he was too flippant and childlike. My sister takes after her.' A rush of guilt overcame her. 'That sounds horribly disloyal! I love my sister, I really do. She always looks out for me. But she doesn't think I can run my life without her advice.'

Fitz cocked his head. 'Is your dad . . . ?'

Stella nodded. 'No longer with us. But he was ancient and had a very good life.' She knew what his next question would be after the slip about her parents' age difference, but he wasn't rude enough to ask it. 'He had his children very late in life,' she explained. 'Mum was wife number three. Actually I came up here this morning to scatter Dad's dog's ashes. And a bit of Dad as well.'

'I'm sorry.'

'Not at all.

Tears suddenly gathered in her throat unexpectedly. She coughed. Her father had had the perfect end, dying at home, with Geoffrey on his bed. Geoffrey had died a few minutes later. They looked at the tree in silence. Stella was thinking of her father's parting with this world and the little dog decoration she still had in her pocket.

'It is a wonderful tree, isn't it?' he said, giving her a chance to get herself together. 'I came up this early in the hope there'd be no one about. I wanted these two tired out so I can concentrate on cooking.'

'And I came out early because I didn't want people seeing me scatter the ashes. Mission accomplished.'

'I'm not entirely sorry mine failed,' he said. 'Hey, let's sit down and admire the view, like old people? I know it's still fairly dark but the dogs are playing nicely at last and the walk from my house is pretty well perpendicular. I could do with sitting down for a bit.'

Feeling better instantly, she nodded in agreement. 'I can't quite say that but it's jolly steep from my house too. I come from London and it's a bit of a shock.' She sat next to him on the bench. 'The view is amazing though, even in this light.' The bench was facing the far Welsh hills outlined against the sky. A glimmer of moonlight that had just appeared showed where the River Severn snaked its way in front of them. 'It is worth the climb!'

'It is,' Fitz agreed.

One of the dogs was now lying across Stella's lap, while the other leant against her knee, so they were both warming her up. She liked the comforting weight of them although she was sure she should make them get down. She was teaching them bad habits.

'What are their names? I haven't heard you call them anything?'

Fitz laughed. 'Except "those bastard animals", you mean?'

'I haven't heard you call them that! So, have they got names? Proper ones?'

'I'm embarrassed to tell you. My mother is a little eccentric.'

'And?'

He looked sheepish. 'Tristan and Isolde. I call them Tris and Izzy. The one on your lap is Izzy, with the purple collar.'

'My, those are elaborate names – I wonder how they would have got on with dependable Geoffrey. I hope they wouldn't have looked down their wet noses at him,' she teased.

'They have their faults, but they're not snobbish.' He was fondling Tris's ears absent-mindedly. He paused for a couple of seconds. 'So you're not spending Christmas with your sister?'

'Not this year, no. I decided to come down to Dad's cottage, although it took some fighting for, I can tell you. She thinks I'll die of loneliness and no one should be without family on Christmas Day.'

'She has a point there, to be fair.'

'Yes I know, but it's only this Christmas! I really want to spend time in my dad's cottage – which is now actually *my* cottage – and see if I want to live in it permanently.'

'The place is yours completely? Annabel doesn't have a say in what happens to it?'

'Dad decided to leave his money to Annabel and the cottage to me. It came to roughly the same value in the end, and it might sound awful but we each got what we'd prefer.'

'So you mean to leave London? That would be a big decision.'

Stella had rehearsed this argument with her sister many times so knew her lines. 'Yes, but I'd be living rent-free and I could change my life, probably for the better. I could work part-time as a supply teacher and study something at the same time.'

'What would you study?'

'Not sure. But it could be anything! Imagine!' She found the prospect hugely exciting. Her teaching job in London had been brilliant, but exhausting and stressful. She wanted a change of lifestyle, and her father's death could give her the opportunity to make this happen.

'You're obviously someone who embraces change.'

'I think I am. Now,' she went on, feeling it was his turn to be questioned, 'are you spending Christmas with your mother?'

'I am. I'm cooking lunch and then I'll collect her and bring her home for the meal.'

'Will she mind going home and then having to leave again?' Stella could imagine this might be hard.

'I don't think so. I hope not. She's very pragmatic and, as I said, her cottage is very unsuitable for someone elderly – steep stairs and uneven floors. Besides, she has a great social life in the care home.'

'That's good then. So, are you living in your mother's house?'

He sighed. 'Currently. My girlfriend doesn't really like dogs. I'm going to have to rehome them soon, but it does break my heart.'

Stella had been stroking Izzy's head absent-mindedly, and was very glad she didn't have to make Fitz's decision. 'But if it was a good home? After all, you did put your mother in a care home.'

'She made that decision herself. Being human has its advantages. No, what's really worrying me is them being separated. Tris and Izzy are so close, and as far as we know they haven't had a great life, but they have always had each other. But who would want two of these beasts?' He sounded wistful.

'Would you keep them if your girlfriend did like dogs?' A small, ridiculous part of her was saddened by the mention of a girlfriend. She wasn't sure why.

'Oh yes. They're awful but I do love them.'

'Where are you based?'

'Bristol. I could commute easily enough from here into work but . . . I don't know. I'm going to try and work out what to do over Christmas, while I'm here. My girlfriend is coming up the day after Boxing Day. She may come round to the dogs, if they behave themselves. And I'll have to discuss it with my mother.'

'Well, if your girlfriend doesn't fall in love with them, I'm sure someone will want them. They're young; they will be trainable.'

'You're a woman of great faith, I can see that,' said Fitz.

Stella let the comfortable silence settle around them as she left Fitz to muse. Eventually she said, 'It's weird, isn't it? We're complete strangers and yet we're telling each other all about our lives in a way we never would if we, say, worked together.'

'It's like people you meet on trains.' He paused. 'While we're over-sharing, can I ask, have you got a boyfriend? Just so I can get the full picture.'

'If I stay in London I have a boyfriend, not if I move down here.' Stella thought about Piers, and their relationship that was hanging in the balance.

The last time they'd spoken they'd decided to take a break while Stella spent Christmas in the cottage working things out. Piers had lots of good points, but he didn't want to settle down yet. And while Stella wasn't sure where she wanted to settle, she knew that she was ready in principle.

'How could anyone not want to live here?' Fitz gestured to the view again, more of which had emerged as the light grew.

'How could anyone not like dogs?' said Stella.

'Touché. Well, seeing that you're such a fan of these two, would you consider coming and spending Christmas Day with us and my mother? She's a very sociable soul and it would make Christmas so much better if it wasn't just me—'

'Her beloved son?'

'—to talk to.'

'It's really kind of you—'

'Please don't say no! I know we've established we're complete strangers and we've shared all our secrets and so should never see each other again, but we could do that after Christmas? We should do slightly mad things on Christmas Day.'

'My sister considers sitting at home alone with a tin of Roses and a bottle of Prosecco quite mad enough.'

'That's not mad at all!' he went on. 'What's mad is taking pity on a poor Irishman who's cooking Christmas dinner for the first time ever!' He paused for dramatic effect. 'For his poor old mother who's in a care home!'

She couldn't help laughing. She was tempted. He'd made her laugh when she thought she'd only be crying.

'I'll make it worth your while,' he went on, obviously seeing her considering the idea.

'How?'

He thought for a moment and then shrugged. 'I'll work out something. I'm very resourceful.' He considered some more. 'Think how warm and fuzzy you'll feel if you sacrifice your solitary Christmas Day for a poor man and his widowed mother. Did I mention she was widowed?'

'I had sort of assumed . . .'

'So you'll come? I'm not a bad cook on the whole. And I'll do Yorkshire puddings? Come on now, you know you want to.'

'Yes, but—'

'The dogs would really like it if you came. You can tell how much they love you.'

She couldn't resist any longer, and she did love his dogs. 'OK! I'll come.'

After they had exchanged contact details and discussed what she should bring as a contribution (a conversation which was mainly 'nothing, you're doing me a favour' followed by 'I have to bring something! It's Christmas'), Stella suddenly remembered.

'Oh, before we go, there's something I must do.'

The little tin dog was a bit more out of shape than it had been but Stella bent it back again as best she could.

'Did your father make that?'

'He did. He was aiming for a generic dog, rather than a particular breed of dog. The fact that it's recognisably canine was good enough for him.'

Fitz laughed. 'I think I would have liked your father.'

'He would have liked you.' Piers, her current boyfriend, had met her father once and her father had done his best but they hadn't really hit it off.

'So are you going to tie it on then?' Fitz went on more gently.

'Yes.'

Tris and Izzy made it quite difficult, wanting to get their noses into what she was doing, but at last the decoration was securely attached.

'It looks grand there, doesn't it?' he said.

'It does. I should have brought some dog food really, for the animal sanctuary, but there's only dry food at home and I didn't have anything watertight to put it in. I'll buy something and bring it another time.'

'Don't worry about that. I've got some tins of food that came with the dogs. It gives them terrible diarrhoea.' He seemed quite pleased about this.

Stella made a face. 'That's a kind and generous gesture at Christmas.'

He shrugged. 'Well, it won't give all dogs diarrhoea! It's a premium brand.'

She tried not to smile. He shouldn't be encouraged in his flippancy, which reminded her a bit of his dogs. 'I'll be getting home now. I've got to bake something to bring with me or it wouldn't be a proper Christmas visit.'

But she started to smile as she walked home. Although the prospect of a Christmas Day on her own had been fine – pleasant, even – the thought of spending it with an attractive man, his jolly-sounding mother and his adorable, if very naughty, dogs was better than pleasant.

She'd made a batch of Welsh cakes (quick and sort of festive because they included dried fruit) and was about to have a shower when her sister rang. As she was feeling pleasantly Christmassy she answered enthusiastically.

'Hey, Annabel! How are you? Happy Christmas!'

'Stella? You're sounding over-excited. You haven't opened the Prosecco already? It's only eleven o'clock in the morning and when you're on your own . . .'

Stella's mood deflated almost instantly. Her sister obviously predicted a life of alcoholism and lonely spinsterhood for her. 'I know what time it is, and no, I haven't opened anything.'

'Sorry. It's just you sounded a bit – bubbly.'

'Natural bubbles only, I assure you,' said Stella, beginning to feel pleased with herself. 'I've been for a walk, made some Welsh cakes and, more importantly, got myself an invitation for Christmas lunch!' That'll show her sister that she was perfectly capable of starting a new life on her own.

'Aw! Nice!' Annabel was pleased, Stella could tell. 'Is it with Dad's old neighbours? They're a lovely couple!'

'No—'

'Or that nice family with children? Down the hill a bit?'

'Not them either, but it's lovely there are so many good people just near me, should I decide to live here.'

'So, who are you having Christmas with?'

'A really nice man I met on the common—'

All trace of Christmas spirit left her sister's voice as she rattled off questions. 'What? Are you mad? You're thinking about spending Christmas with a man you met on the common?'

'Yes,' Stella said slowly. 'The common is just the name for a bit of land. It doesn't mean the people on it are common, in Mummy's use of the word.'

Annabel took a couple of moments to take this in. 'Don't be silly, Stella! You know perfectly well what I mean. You can't go and have Christmas with a perfect stranger. It wouldn't be safe!'

'His mother is coming. She's in a care home. He's fetching her and cooking her Christmas dinner. She's a widow,' she added for effect, as Fitz had done.

'That's just some story he's told you! Don't do it. Have some sense for once in your life.'

'Listen, I'm taking the car. I won't drink. If it's dodgy, I'll just leave!'

'You won't mean to drink, but you will and then you'll have to stay . . .'

'I could walk home! In fact I might leave the car there—'

'Stella! You've got to promise me you won't go!'

'Annabel! Why are you being so unreasonable about this? You went ballistic when I said I was having Christmas on my own and now you're going ballistic because I'm not!'

'If you were having Christmas with someone sensible, instead of some random man you know nothing about, I'd be delighted!'

'I know lots about him. We bonded by the Dog Walkers' Christmas Tree.'

'What are you talking about?' There was noise in the background. 'God! Bloody Christmas! Apparently the turkey won't fit in the oven. Can't stay chatting. Just promise me you'll ring and cancel?' Then she disconnected.

While Stella certainly hadn't promised she'd cancel she did feel a bit thrown by the call. Was she mad to have Christmas with someone she'd met in – fair play to Annabel – a very random way? She felt a bit depressed by the thought, and wondered if her sister was right and she'd be better off staying at home and eating the Welsh cakes herself. She decided that Annabel was right, and picked up her phone to look for Fitz's details. Just as she found them her phone rang, vibrating in her hand. It made her jump and she dropped it. It was Fitz.

'Oh thank God you're there and haven't run off!' he said. 'I didn't know who else to call! There's been a disaster.'

All thoughts of cancelling went out of her head. He obviously needed help. 'What's happened?'

'Those bastard dogs! Scuse my language. They've trashed the place. I need a hand clearing up. I can't have my mother coming here and seeing it destroyed. It would break her heart.'

'So what happened?'

'Can you just come over? You'll see soon enough and I don't want to lose a second trying to clear it up. There isn't much time.'

He sounded really desperate and Stella packed up her Welsh cakes and the bottle of wine (she left the Prosecco: Fitz didn't seem a Prosecco sort of guy and she wasn't planning to drink) and then, as an afterthought, a pair of rubber gloves and some cleaning products. She had quite a lot because her father's house had taken a fair bit of sorting out after he died.

❄

'That was quick!' said Fitz the moment he opened the door.

'It's really near. Now show me what's happened!'

He showed her into a small but pretty sitting room that led off the little hallway. It took Stella a few seconds to work out what the problem was. Nothing was ripped to shreds (which she'd been dreading and expecting) but everything, from the sofa covers to the walls, to the rug to the cushions, was covered in mud.

'I went upstairs to a spare bedroom to stuff the turkey,' Fitz explained. 'It's only a little bird but the dogs are terrible for jumping up when I'm preparing food. So I shut them in the kitchen, then I heard a bit of noise and came down to this.'

'But how? This much mud? How did they do this? And where are they now?'

'On the way back from our walk they got into my neighbour's pond and it's full of mud. I thought I'd shut them into the kitchen until I could unlock the shed and put them in there but I didn't close the door properly, *et voilà.*' Fitz gestured despairingly with his hands. 'I've shut them in the shed now that the horse has bolted, so to speak. I've hosed them off and it's freezing out there but I have to get this cleared up before my mother sees it.'

As she looked, Stella took in the extent of the devastation. It seemed that having covered themselves in the contents of the neighbour's pond, the dogs had taken it upon themselves to spread the mud over every surface. It was like an art installation.

But her heart went out to the artists concerned. They were only young. 'You can't leave the dogs wet and cold in the shed. They'll freeze to death. You go and dry them while I think how we should tackle this.'

'I love that you said "we" just then. We hardly know each other but we're already a team.' There was a warmth in his brown eyes that made her heart do a little flip.

But she couldn't encourage it. He had a girlfriend and she sort of had a boyfriend herself. 'Off you go!'

While her father's house had needed cleaning – and it had been a labour of love – the dirt had only showed when you cleaned a bit and saw the contrast. This was all fresh mud and it looked terrible. She started on the two little sofas and an armchair. Tris and Izzy had obviously rolled around on all of them. She pulled off all the covers she could remove and bundled them up. There might or might not be a washing machine but there'd be a launderette at least. Then she went into the galley kitchen and found a bucket and a scrubbing brush. If she was going to really clean this place, she'd need hot water and lots of it.

Fitz came back into the house. 'Well, they're drier now. I'll put their beds in the shed for the time being. How are you getting on?'

'What time were you due to pick up your mother?'

'In about an hour. It takes half an hour to get there.'

'So we've got a hour and a half?'

He paused. 'Do you think we can do it?'

'Honestly? Not really. But I'll do my best. Unless . . .' Thinking about cleaning her father's house had given her an idea. 'Unless we go to my house instead? What would your mother think about that?'

He didn't rush into his conclusion. 'Well, they are her mad dogs; it was them that made the mess. And if she thought I'd met a nice girl on the common who'd invited us for Christmas, she'd be delighted.' He paused. 'We won't be able to stay for long though, because of the dogs. They're too young to be left for more than a couple of hours, at the most.'

She overlooked his reference to her being a 'nice girl', not because she didn't appreciate the compliment but because it implied his mother thought he was single. That wasn't a conversation for now.

'Oh no, you could bring the dogs. My father's house – my house – is very dog-friendly. We have a boot room full of rugs – we could put them in there until they dry off. And if you've stuffed the turkey already, it should be fine in my kitchen although it's not huge.'

'I haven't done the spuds yet. And I promised you Yorkshires.' Fitz wasn't yet convinced.

'You can do it all in my kitchen. I'm not at all territorial.'

He grinned suddenly and it dawned on Stella again how very attractive he was. 'Then we're on! I'll make a list of what we need to take.'

'Just one thing – and this may sound a bit weird and neurotic . . .'

'What?'

Now she was about to say it out loud it seemed even more weird and neurotic than it had in her head, but she took a deep breath. 'Will you tell your girlfriend about the change of plans and venue? It's just the sort of thing that if you told her about it later could be misconstrued. And then, although it is all perfectly innocent, you start to over-explain and it all gets silly.'

It took him a few seconds to make sense of this. 'Well, I suppose I sort of see what you mean. "Oh, by the way, I didn't spend Christmas in my mother's house, we went to a lovely woman I met out walking's house instead."'

She ignored this 'lovely' and nodded. 'After the event it would seem odd.'

'I'll ring her now.' He hesitated. 'Are you going to tell your boyfriend?'

Stella flapped a dismissive hand. 'Nah! We're on a break! He doesn't care anyway.'

Stella took the food in her car and Fitz brought the dogs in his. As he had a little dog wrangling to do she got to her house a bit before he did.

She realised she didn't have a lot of time to make the place look festive and was grateful for her habit of draping her homes with fairy lights even when it wasn't Christmas.

She rushed into the back garden and detached a length of ivy from the garden wall and tucked it behind everything on the mantelpiece. Then she lit the wood burner.

'Are you sure these hounds from hell can come in?' said Fitz when he arrived a little later, holding them on leads, looking like a charioteer behind a team of eager horses.

She nodded. 'I said the house is dog-friendly and I can't bear to think of them being alone. It is Christmas, after all.'

'I'll go and get their beds.'

Stella made a fuss of Tris and Izzy so they wouldn't notice that Fitz had left them. He was back very soon. 'Just take the beds through there.' She gestured the direction he should go in.

'That's just grand for the dogs if you can get them

to stay there,' he said a minute later. 'The trouble is, they prefer to be with humans.'

'It's probably full of doggy smells which should be comforting for them.'

Fitz looked down at her, half smiling, half frowning. 'My mother is going to love you!'

Although she'd invited him, Stella found his presence in her space rather unnerving. She needed to get him out of the house for a bit. 'And I'm sure I'll love her right back. Is it time you went to get her?'

'Yes. Can I leave the dogs with you, then?'

'Of course. Now off you go!'

Tristan and Isolde were not pleased to have been abandoned by Fitz. It was, Stella realised, possibly the second time they'd been abandoned by their owner in a very short time. They yelped and barked and tried to scratch their way through the front door.

Stella didn't have a lot of experience with dogs. Her father's dog had been trained by him and was always fairly well behaved. However, she was experienced with small children and decided she might as well treat Tris and Izzy the same.

'Now listen, you dogs, I know you're upset that Fitz has gone but he will be back and in the meantime we need to keep very calm. Follow me!'

She didn't know why but she wasn't going to question it: the dogs followed Stella into the boot room. It was dusty, full of boots, ancient fleeces and anoraks, dog leads, bowls and beds. Stella hadn't even begun to tackle it yet. And now it had their dog beds in it.

'And now, my darlings,' she went on – it wasn't quite professional to call schoolchildren 'my darlings' and Stella enjoyed not having to be professional – 'you're going to stay here while I get ready for Christmas.'

They weren't convinced. They whined and jumped up at the stable door as if about to climb over it. If they did manage to scale it, she was sunk.

'We're going to be very calm,' she said, very calmly, 'and I'm in charge so you don't need to worry. You can just lie in your beds.'

She pointed to their beds and eventually they got the message and lay in them. However, they didn't look as if they'd stay there without an incentive.

Stella found some dog biscuits (probably years past their sell-by date but who cared?) and they inhaled them in seconds. Then she spotted her father's old slippers on a shelf. She brought them down and gave one to each dog. 'Chew on these and don't get into mischief.'

She left the dogs happily occupied and could almost hear her father laughing from on high. She wouldn't tell her sister though; Annabel wouldn't think it funny at all.

As she went through to the kitchen the landline rang. 'It's Annabel, checking up on me,' said Stella out loud. And it was.

'Thank God! You're there! You haven't gone to that man for Christmas!' she said.

'It could be I just haven't left yet. It's only a quarter to twelve.' She needed to get the turkey in but she couldn't resist the temptation to tease her sister.

'Nope. You'd have gone by now. You can't bear being late.'

Stella sighed. 'Oh, OK, I'm not going to a strange man's house for Christmas. Satisfied?' She kept her tone casual, hoping that she sounded innocent. She was telling the truth, but it wasn't really the whole truth.

'But you won't be lonely?'

'No, I'll be fine,' said Stella, thinking it was typical of her sister to be so contrary. 'But I'd better go. I've got spuds to peel.'

'Really? You're doing Christmas dinner just for you?'

Again, Stella had done the wrong thing in her sister's eyes. If she'd said she was having Prosecco and a tin of Roses for dinner, as had been her declared plan, her sister would have said that was pathetic and she should have something proper. But now she'd talked about peeling potatoes she was going to too much trouble. There was no pleasing some people, particularly not if they were Stella's sister.

'Roast potatoes are my favourite part of Christmas dinner,' said Stella. 'I just thought I'd do a few.' Both statements were factually correct, but neither was absolutely true.

Fortunately Annabel's own Christmas duties saved Stella from more interrogation.

'I'm coming, darling,' Stella overheard Annabel coo. This told her that her sister's mother-in-law was within earshot. Normally Annabel was quite brisk with her children but she always wanted to be the perfect mother in front of her husband's (quite wealthy) family.

'I'd better let you go, Bells,' said Stella. 'Have a lovely day!' Annabel never liked having her name shortened but Stella thought it was good for her to have to put up with it sometimes.

By the time Stella heard voices at her door the turkey had been in the oven for nearly an hour, the potatoes were parboiled and she'd done the sprouts. She went to the front door to welcome her guests – the first she had had since the cottage had become hers. She suffered a flurry of nerves and hoped the house looked Christmassy and welcoming.

'Hello! I'm Stella. Do come in!' she said.

Fitz was escorting a tiny old lady dressed in a bright red skirt and coat, to which she'd added a large bunch of holly which at second glance proved to be fake.

'Mother of God! This is kind of you!' she said. 'Taking us in on Christmas Day, and all because of those naughty puppies of mine!'

'You had been going to take me in,' said Stella, standing aside so her guests could get through the door.

Fitz gave her a casual peck on the cheek as if she were an old friend. Considering they'd been survey-ing incredibly muddy sofas earlier in the day she supposed they were now friends. 'So what have you done with the brutes?' he asked.

'They're in the boot room,' said Stella. 'I'm unwill-ing to check on them as they're being so quiet but I know Mrs – um – your mother, Fitz, will want to see them.'

'Call me Mac, darling.'

'That's unusual!' said Stella. 'What's that short for?'

'Immaculata,' said Mac. 'A fine old Irish name. Now let's get a look at the dogs. But wait until I'm sitting down.'

'Let me get you settled,' said Stella, slightly con-cerned that their quietness might be sinister. Supposing the 'past their sell-by date' biscuits were poisonous and they'd died?

When Fitz's mother was settled in the armchair next to the wood burner, Stella went to fetch the dogs. She opened the door to the boot room. Tristan and Isolde looked up when they heard the door open and then, half-eaten slippers forgotten, looked intelligent.

Stella was not fooled. She knew this look just meant 'Is there any food involved?'

She put them on their leads. She was not going to have their erstwhile owner crushed to death on her watch.

'Darling child!' said Mac when Stella appeared in the sitting room behind animals that could have out-pulled Thomas the Tank Engine when he was trying really hard. 'They are allowed off the lead in the house.'

Since she lost her grip on them at that moment, Stella didn't have to reply as Mac disappeared under a flurry of paws and fur. She was just grateful Mac had been sitting down or she would definitely have been knocked over.

There was a lot of shouting and remonstrating until Fitz pulled them off, revealing his mother, who brushed herself down.

'Mother, dear,' said Fitz, 'those dogs—'

'I know! I know!' said his mother. 'They're too much for me.'

'Let's open a bottle,' said Stella, aware that Fitz's mother wouldn't want to talk about her precious dogs being rehomed on Christmas Day. 'It is Christmas, after all.'

'Good idea,' said Fitz. 'We brought plenty of them, Mother, so no worries there.'

'I drink very little myself these days,' Mac confided to Stella when Fitz was in the kitchen, having insisted that getting drinks was 'man's work'. 'But I do like to see people have a good time.' She paused. 'I was so delighted when Fitz told me all about you.'

'We only met this morning, so he doesn't know that much,' said Stella.

'You like dogs, which is a grand start.'

Stella felt a pang of sympathy for Fitz's girlfriend, who didn't. Fitz loved his mother and would want to please her but he shouldn't have to restrict himself to the animal-friendly when it came to choosing a potential life partner.

Fitz appeared with a tray of glasses and a couple of bottles in his pockets. One of the bottles contained sherry, which Fitz must have brought. On the tray was a tiny liqueur glass that Stella recognised from her father's cabinet.

'OK,' said Fitz. 'This is just the first pass at the drinks. I know my mother will have a glass of sherry—'

'I'm sure there's a better glass than that in the cabinet,' said Stella.

'That wee glass is the perfect size for me,' said Mac.

Fitz gave Stella a self-satisfied nod that made her smile. There was something irrepressible about him she couldn't help warming to. Rather like the dogs.

'And so to our lovely hostess?' Fitz said. 'I have wine in the kitchen and beer. Otherwise it's whatever you already have in the house.'

'I'll have a glass of sherry, please.' She'd always dismissed sherry as an old person's drink, but thought that actually she might quite like it.

When he handed her a wine glass full of it she really hoped she did like it. 'Fitz? Surely there's a middle way between the thimble you've given your mother and this?'

'I'm sure there is, but I'm a man of extremes.'

'Just sip it, dear,' said Mac. 'It'll be fine.'

Fitz produced the other bottle from his pocket. 'It's stout,' he declared. 'I can't be drunk in charge of a cooker that's not my own.'

He was obviously determined to cook Christmas dinner even if it was no longer to be served in his mother's house. 'Shall I come and show you where we're up to?' Stella suggested.

'Not at all. I'll find my way around and get on with the Yorkshire puddings. I brought your tin, Mother, so I'm confident.'

Stella looked at her guest and thought she was almost like a Christmas ornament, she was so small and perfect.

'You don't mind a man ferreting around in your kitchen?' asked Mac.

'Nope. It was my father's kitchen for years and years. It's only very recently become mine.'

'You miss him.' It was a statement, not a question.

'I do. Very much. But being in his house, with guests, helps a lot.'

The two women took sips of their drinks and looked at each other, not speaking and content to be silent.

Then Fitz came in. 'I am so sorry!' he said, possibly for the seventeenth time that day. 'I've just discovered these! Your father's slippers! They're destroyed.'

He was mortified and Mac put her hand on Stella's knee in a gesture of comfort.

Now it was Stella's turn to be mortified.

'Actually, that's fine. I gave them to the dogs earlier. To keep them quiet.'

Stella realised she was being regarded reproachfully by two pairs of eyes. 'I know! How are they supposed to know the difference between shoes they can chew and those they can't, if I give them slippers to chew?'

'But you thought, they're being rehomed so that's not my problem?' suggested Fitz. There was a protective edge to his tone that Stella hadn't heard before, and she suspected he was more dedicated to his pups than he was letting on.

'I did not!' She was indignant, partly because she was in the wrong. 'And I refuse to talk – or let anyone else talk – about rehoming on Christmas Day!'

Fitz shrugged. 'Fair enough.' He went back to the Christmas dinner.

With Fitz having taken over the kitchen, refusing to let Stella do any more cooking, it was up to her to entertain his mother.

'More sherry?' she said politely.

'Tell you what,' said Mac with a charming smile. 'Let's find something nice to watch on telly then we don't have to make polite conversation for however many hours it takes my son to get that turkey out of the oven and on to the plates?'

'Oh!' said Stella, surprised but relieved. She felt as though she'd been up for days and it was still only early afternoon. 'Let's see if we can find *Roman Holiday*. I've always loved Audrey Hepburn and one can get a bit fed up with Christmas films. They always have proper snow and I get jealous.'

'Perfect. I'll have a little nap while it's on. The marvellous thing about being old, dear, is that you lose your politeness filter. Instead of being tactful and careful not to offend people, you say exactly what you think.'

Stella couldn't help smiling. What Mac had just said was undoubtedly true, but Stella was certain Mac hadn't lost her filter at all: she was just using old age as an excuse to be as blunt as she liked.

As Stella allowed her eyes to close, cosy on the sofa with a dog on each side of her, she realised there was a disconnect. Fitz had implied the dogs had been wished on to his mother almost against her will, but surely this feisty woman wouldn't be bullied into anything? Something was up.

'OK! It's on the table, folks!' said Fitz some time later.

The poor man had done his best, Stella realised. Christmas dinner was a big ask, but while the meal he presented looked perfectly edible it didn't look festive or particularly appetising. The plates had slices of turkey on them and there was a bowl of roast potatoes and some sprouts, but there were none of the little extras: the pigs in blankets, roast parsnips, several sorts of stuffing or cranberry sauce.

Stella's sister Annabel (who did go over the top with these things) always had at least four different vegetables: carrots, celeriac with chestnuts and peas cooked with lettuce, as well as several vegetarian options for the main course. Stella usually felt slightly put off by so many dishes on the table all at the same time, but now she realised that without them, the occasion did seem a little flat.

'This looks lovely!' said Stella. 'Shall I find some napkins?'

She was not at all sure her father had napkins, paper or otherwise, but she might be in luck. As a single man, even one as old as he had been, women gave him presents. It was worth a hunt in a few kitchen drawers.

She came back with a roll of kitchen towel.

'Let's start,' said Mac. 'The turkey isn't going to taste any better for us having looked at it for a few minutes.'

'Hold on!' said Fitz. 'Just hang on a giddy minute!'

He left the room and came back with a baking tray full of a Yorkshire pudding looking like a small golden pillow, only with crispy bits at the edges.

'That looks amazing!' said Stella, hoping she didn't sound surprised.

'Oh, now we're talking,' said Mac. 'I was just missing the frilly bits, you know?'

'Actually I did buy all those extras we all love at Christmas, including gravy made by some famous chef and stuffing with truffles in it. And the dogs enjoyed it all very much. Including the "Bag for life – Christmas edition" they came in.'

'Oh no!' said Stella. 'I hope the plastic won't be bad for them!'

'And I hope', said Fitz, 'that it gave them a stomach ache to end all stomach aches.'

Mac began to laugh. 'Of course you were a fool to leave the bag where the dogs could get it, but now I know my Christmas dinner went to a good home I don't mind missing it.'

When Mac and Stella were on their second glass of wine (Fitz had moved on to water) Stella said, 'I have a mad idea.'

'Join the club,' said Mac. 'You fit right into this family.'

'I've got some bits and pieces. I bought a bumper pack of butcher's sausages from the farmers' market and put them in the freezer. And there are some posh sausage rolls – also from the market – and all sorts of vegetables. We could have another Christmas dinner tomorrow, with all the usual trimmings? We'd have to use today's turkey though.'

'Well, there's a lovely suggestion. Can I come?' said Mac. 'I do have a lot of fun in my care home but my partner in crime has gone to her family for Christmas and won't be back until the day after Boxing Day.'

'Of course! I meant both of you.' She turned to Fitz. 'Or are you going to your girlfriend's for Boxing Day?'

'Not at all,' he said. 'I'd be delighted to come back tomorrow, if you can stand another day of doggy hell.'

'I love dogs, and I think Iris and Izzy are just misunderstood,' Stella said. 'Now I'll go and get the puddings,' she added, thinking her unexpected Christmas was a lot nicer than her expected one.

'That was quite the loveliest Christmas meal I've had for a long time,' said Mac. 'Last year we had it with Fiona – that's Fitz's girlfriend – and it wasn't nearly such fun.'

'Mother!' said Fitz, more exasperated than offended.

'Everyone had gone to a lot of trouble,' his mother explained, 'and it was the perfect Christmas, it's just I've had more fun this year. But can you take me home now? I'm tired and I need my bed.'

But Fitz made his mother sit down by the fire, both the dogs' heads on her lap, while he helped Stella ferry the detritus into the kitchen.

'This has been so kind of you,' he said. 'My mother really has had a brilliant time. She speaks her mind so we'd know if she hadn't.'

'She explained to me about the filter, how when you get old you lose it and say exactly what you think.'

Fitz laughed loudly. 'I'm sure that's all true but I promise you, my mother never had a filter. She's always made her feelings clear about everything.'

'I rather thought that was the case. She's so bright I'm sure she's got every one of her marbles.'

'She has but they've always been in a very random order.' He sighed. 'I'd better get her back. Would it be all right if I left the dogs here until I can pick them up later?'

Just for a few seconds Stella let herself imagine what might happen. He would come back, it would be late, she'd offer him a drink – he could walk home from here and had only had a glass of stout to last him all day. They'd sit in front of the fire, the room lit only by fairy lights and flames. One thing would lead to another.

'Don't worry!' she said brightly. 'Why don't you leave the dogs here overnight? I'm sure they'll be fine. They can sleep in the boot room. The garden is dog proof for when they need to go out.'

He frowned down at her. 'Are you sure?' He seemed to think she was making a generous gesture when, in fact, she was just protecting herself, and him, from something bad happening.

'Absolutely! Now what time will you bring your mother? And it might be an idea to tell your girl-friend you're coming here again tomorrow? She's coming down the day after tomorrow, isn't she? Really, it's one of those situations—'

He put up a hand. 'I know. That if you don't say something right at the start, it all gets misconstrued.'

'So, would about twelve o'clock work for you both, do you think?'

'It would be perfect.'

He kissed her cheek. But it was only a peck on the cheek, she told herself. Nothing to get worried about.

※

When Stella had closed the door behind Fitz and his mother she had intended to finish the clearing up but instead she found herself in the sitting room on the old leather sofa in front of the fire. Both dogs had snuck up beside her, seemingly fine about being abandoned by their owners.

Stella had a lot to think about and today had somehow made the decision harder. She felt so torn.

In some ways it would have been easy for her to look back on the day and think how lovely it had been – because it had been. But was one lovely Christmas Day with strangers, who had rapidly come to feel like friends, really a sign that she could be happy in the country, in this house? Or was it just a weird blip and would the rest of her life here be lonely?

Fitz and her feelings for him definitely complicated matters. He was so much fun, witty, warm, kind to his mother (always a sign of a nice boy) and he loved animals. They seemed to have a connection. But he wasn't free and so was completely off limits.

But even if he had been free, and had reciprocated her feelings, it wouldn't be right to give up everything and move just because of that. After all, he might sell his mother's house, and not even be around at weekends. She'd be left alone, far from her support system.

No, she had to take him right out of the equation. She had to move down here because she wanted to, because it was the right thing to do.

Tristan's head moved so it took up even more of her lap. What was she going to do about these dogs?

Stella decided not to tell Mac and Fitz that the dogs had spent the night on her bed. It really wasn't important. She did, however, intend to boast about getting up early and letting them drag her up on to the common for a Boxing Day walk.

At first she'd been a bit worried about letting them off but she'd filled her father's old coat with dog treats, so they came back willingly every time she called. She had really enjoyed the experience.

She hadn't quite decided if she should report that the dogs had turned the television on for themselves by stepping on the remote, in order to get at a couple of Welsh cakes that had been left in the sitting room. Technically this was quite clever but morally it was frowned upon.

Once home, and in spite of her inability to shut the dogs in the boot room (even with the stable door open, they howled heartbreakingly), Stella managed to prepare a passable meal. It was putting it on the table that would be the real challenge, she realised, and decided to wait until people were there to guard it before she did so.

She was just putting the finishing touches to her make-up, glad to think that Fitz would see her looking a bit better than she had the previous day, when the bell went.

Fitz and Mac were a bit early, but that was a good thing. They could look after the dogs while she basted the roast potatoes and got the sausages in the oven. She'd finally coaxed Tristan and Isolde into the boot room (their prison, as they saw it), surrounded by biscuits and ancient dog chews, but now they were trying to make a break for it by jumping over the top of the stable door. The house was filled with their deep barks, which made them sound as if they were enormous.

She opened the door with a happy smile, only letting it falter for a nanosecond when she realised too late that it was a total stranger on the doorstep. She had a fair idea who this woman was. Stella did slightly wish she wasn't still wearing the casual black cords and deep pink sweater she'd walked the dogs in but it was too late to worry about that.

'Hello?' she said.

The woman was a little younger than she was, possibly about twenty-eight, Stella reckoned, and a bit thinner. Also, she looked properly groomed and elegant in a new-looking Barbour jacket, long boots and a handbag with a lot of gold bits on it. However, as glamorous as she was, she did not look comfortable. 'Er – hi – you don't know me but I'm Fiona, Fitz's girlfriend.'

'Oh! Come in! Fitz has talked a lot about you.' This wasn't true but it was only a white lie. 'Have you come to join us for our second go at Christmas lunch?'

'Is that all right?' Fiona seemed surprised.

'The more the merrier. It's all a bit makeshift, I'm afraid. Let me take your coat.'

The dogs were going mad but the one thing Fitz had impressed upon Stella about Fiona was that she wasn't keen on them. They would have to stay where they were. And at least they'd stopped barking, and were just flinging themselves against the door in excitement to greet the new arrival.

'Did you tell Fitz you were coming?'

There was a tiny, very revealing pause. It meant Fiona wasn't entirely sure how Fitz would react. 'No, I thought I'd make it a surprise.'

'Lovely! I'm sure he'll be thrilled. Now what can I get you to drink? I've got a bottle of Prosecco?' she went on.

'It's a bit early—'

'Just before twelve, not at all early considering it's Christmas.' There was no way Stella would get through this without alcohol, but she hadn't quite sunk to the level of tippling in the kitchen. Yet.

Having checked that nothing was burning, or likely to give anyone salmonella, she brought the Prosecco and a couple of glasses through to where Fiona was sitting huddled next to the wood burner.

'I haven't got champagne flutes, I'm afraid. This was my father's house and I'm just staying in it for Christmas. I think. Now, let me get a look at the fire. It's not really doing its thing, is it?'

Fortunately the stove was obedient and more flames flickered the moment she opened up the draught. If only the dogs were so biddable, she thought, straightening up.

Prosecco poured into Paris goblets (Fiona winced only slightly as Stella handed her one), the two women sat opposite each other while the dogs bounced against the door of the boot room. Stella took a sip of her drink and then realised that making conversation with a complete stranger (who did seem just a little anxious and possibly a bit hostile) while the dogs were so unsettled was impossible.

'Excuse me,' she said, 'I'll have to see if I can shut them up. Although,' she added hopefully, 'they would be calmer if they were with us?'

'I'm sorry, but I can't cope with dogs unless they're really well behaved. My father has shooting dogs and they hardly ever come into the house. Only for photos. But they never make a sound.'

Stella wondered what the hell she could do.

Yesterday having her father's slippers to chew on had calmed them down. She ran upstairs to see whether she could find any other old shoes of his.

She peered into the wardrobe to see what had escaped the charity-shop bag. (The slippers had been deemed too disreputable to put in.) Shoe-wise, there was only one pair of very good leather shoes, hardly worn. Now why had her sister not sent these off to Longfield Hospice? It was, she realised, because Annabelle planned to put them on eBay. They were very nice shoes, weighed a ton and had possibly cost hundreds of pounds.

Stella gulped, picked up the shoes and took them downstairs. She'd have to make some excuse to Annabel. Maybe she'd have forgotten about them, Stella hoped.

Stella rejoined Fiona by the fire.

'So what did you do to quieten the dogs?' Fiona asked. 'It seems to have worked.'

'I just gave them something to occupy them. I wonder where on earth Fitz and his mother are? They're late!'

'They're always late if his mother is involved,' said Fiona. 'I think it's something to do with me.'

'So as she doesn't know you're here, that can't be

true. More Prosecco?' Stella didn't wait for her to answer, she just filled up her glass.

She'd gone back into the kitchen ostensibly to check on the dinner but really to escape Fiona, with whom she seemed to have nothing in common, when she heard them arrive.

Fiona had answered the door.

Stella hovered, listening to the 'Surprise!' and 'Oh, hello, darling' which had more surprise than delight about them, as long as she could. Then she emerged.

'Isn't this lovely!' she said, her voice full of welcome and Christmas spirit. 'Fitz and Fiona can be together for Christmas after all!'

'Delightful,' said Fitz's mother. 'Now where are my dogs? You haven't shut them in the car, have you?' Mac's blue eyes pierced Stella's. 'They hate that.'

Just then, possibly hearing the voices of their loved ones, the dogs started to bark.

'I'll sort them out,' said Fitz.

'I'll go with you,' said Fiona.

'I'll get you a drink,' said Stella to Mac.

Stella chose to ignore the shouts of dismay that were coming from the boot room. It was Christmas, she was doing her best, and she had given the dogs the shoes – it wasn't as if they'd stolen them.

She and Mac were sitting on the sofa when Fitz

came in with one of the dogs on a lead. Fiona brought in the other.

Fiona was seething with indignation. 'You'll never guess what we found them doing.'

Stella didn't have to guess, she knew perfectly well. 'I gave the shoes to the dogs,' she said defiantly. 'I knew it would keep them quiet.'

Fiona turned on her. 'But have you any idea how much those shoes cost? What a waste.'

Stella took a breath but was saved from having to answer by the doorbell ringing.

'Who on earth can that be?' said Fitz, who didn't seem to be having a nice time.

'I'll open it and see,' said Stella, who'd have welcomed even a chugger collecting money for a phony charity just then. But as she got nearer to the front door she realised that on Boxing Day it probably wasn't someone who could be sent away with a couple of pounds.

It was her boyfriend from London.

'Piers!' she said. 'What on earth are you doing here?'

He smiled, his charming, slightly crooked smile that never failed to make her stomach flip. He'd grown a beard since she'd last seen him and seemed to be developing a bit of a hipster look with skinny jeans, a lumberjack shirt and braces. 'Annabel called me. She thought you needed rescuing. And by the sound of it, you do!'

But this time her stomach didn't flip. It could have been his new look, or because she was too annoyed with her sister and him. 'I don't need rescuing at all!' she said sharply. 'But I suppose you'd better come in.'

'Yah!' he said, his upper-class charm fading a bit in the face of her irritation. 'I've driven down from London just to see you, to be with you at Christmas.'

'We were on a break, Piers! And you showed no interest in spending Christmas with me when I sent you an email about my plans at the beginning of the month! In fact you said you'd rather stick pins in your eyes than spend Christmas in the country.'

He shrugged. 'Annabel said you needed me. Of course I came!'

'You'd better come in then. Put your coat on one of those hooks.' She flipped a hand. 'Now, come through.'

There seemed nothing to be done about it. She brought him into the sitting room where at least the dogs were now quiet. Izzy was sitting with her head on Mac's lap, and Tris had snuck up on the sofa behind Fitz. Fiona, sitting next to Fritz, was looking pained. Stella felt a flicker of sympathy for her. She didn't like dogs and one was sitting very near her.

'This is Piers, come to join us for the day,' Stella announced.

'And who is Piers?' asked Mac, very stately all of a sudden. 'Is he your man?'

'Yes,' said Fiona, suddenly looking a bit happier. 'Please introduce us properly.'

'OK, but I'll have to be quick, there's a meal to be served. Mrs Fitzgerald—'

'Fitzherbert,' corrected Fitz.

'Call me Mac,' said Mac, examining Piers intently.

'And this is Fiona, who's Fitz's' – she gestured with her hand – 'girlfriend. And this is Fitz, short for Fitzherbert, obviously. Now I must get back to the dinner.'

She allowed herself a small panic attack in the kitchen and soothed herself by tasting the gravy, which was spectacular. Strengthened, she added another plate to the pile she was warming by turns and wondered if she'd have enough chairs. She'd remembered there was one in the spare room when Fitz came in.

'Well! This wasn't what we expected, now was it!' he declared. 'Two unexpected guests!'

Because he was indignant, Stella felt more generous. 'No, but we've got loads of food and it's Christmas: we can't turn them away.'

'Indeed not. Now what can I do to help?'

His matter-of-fact presence was very soothing. 'If you could just go upstairs and get a chair out of the spare room. It's the one opposite the bathroom. And actually, maybe you'd better get the one out of the bathroom too. Not both at the same time, obviously.'

No sooner had Fitz gone than Piers appeared. 'So, Stellar Stella? What do I have to do to get a drink?'

She used to love this pet name for her but now it fell flat. 'Oh, sorry. I was preoccupied with chairs. Help yourself.' She gestured to the array of alcohol on the dresser. It was a combination of what Fitz had brought and what was left over from her father's time. 'I'm not sure what's there but there's wine on the table in the dining room, if you'd prefer that.'

'I could do with a Scotch,' said Piers. 'The traffic was surprisingly bad on the way down.'

'Have a look.' It had suddenly dawned on her that he was expecting to stay the night and planned to drink all day. Well, he could go in the spare room.

'Oh!' said Piers, sorting through bottles. 'There's the remains of a really good bottle of Madeira here. Shame there's only a drop left.'

'Mm,' said Stella, who'd put most of it in the gravy, which was why it was so sensational.

'So, how's it been down here on your own? Lonely, I bet,' said Piers.

Stella thought about it. 'A little lonely. At first.'

'And who are these mad people you've hooked up with?'

'I did introduce you. And they're not particularly mad.' They were fairly mad but Stella felt protective and defensive. Piers gave a short, derisive laugh.

Stella couldn't help noticing how helpful Fitz was in the process of making this second Christmas meal happen. Piers, on the other hand, who, Stella felt, might have shown some loyalty, spent his time chatting up Fiona. But as this made her laugh and generally cheer up, Stella decided he wasn't a complete waste of space.

But at last everything was on the table, everyone had turkey and all the peripheries and a great many thank yous and how marvellouses had been said.

Mac was particularly appreciative, saying how interesting it was to meet everyone, but something about her made Stella worried that she might pull her 'I'm old, I've lost my filter' card at any time. Judging by the looks her son was giving her, Fitz felt the same.

'So, Piers,' Mac said when everyone was chewing away at their turkey. 'What do you do with yourself in London?'

Piers liked talking about himself and did it well. He was expert in the art of the 'humble brag' and spent five minutes telling everyone about his job, his smart connections and, subtly, his income bracket.

Stella silently fumed away at him for gatecrashing her Christmas and being so boastful but Fiona seemed charmed. And Mac didn't object either, although she might at any moment.

'So, Stella,' Piers went on. 'Have you decided if

you should give up your job and come and live down here yet?'

Before she could answer, he went on, 'Stella is a really great primary-school teacher. She works in a tough area but at the last inspection her school was rated excellent.' He did seem genuinely proud of her.

'Well—' she began.

'So basically, she'd be barking to want to leave all that to live in an area which may be very pretty, but is pretty much nowhere.' He smiled at everyone to indicate he'd finished talking, oblivious to the fact he'd offended three inhabitants of 'nowhere' in one sentence.

'You know?' said Fiona. 'You are so right? I love the countryside – long walks, cosy fires – but after a couple of days I need city life!'

Stella could see Piers and Fiona considered they'd had the conversation about Stella's career and future for her, and she didn't need to add anything to it. 'Did you get any bread sauce, Mac?'

'I did, thank you,' said Mac demurely, but with a dangerous twinkle.

'So what do you do, Fiona?' Stella said quickly.

'Advertising. It's just a fairly small agency in Bristol but we do great work and one day they might move to London.' Fiona smiled. 'And if they do, I'd deffo want to move with them.'

'If you do,' said Piers, producing a business card

from out of the air with the skill of a professional gambler, 'look me up. Or even if your firm doesn't move, you may want to.'

Fitz hadn't said a lot and Stella felt obliged to bring him into the conversation. Somehow they hadn't discussed their jobs the day before so it seemed a good topic. 'So, Fitz? How do you earn a crust?'

'Journalist by trade but I work for a magazine. I do a bit of freelance on the side,' he said.

'Fitz is amazing,' said Fiona, 'but he gets paid buttons. He's worth so much more!'

'Indeed he is,' said Mac, looking at Fiona.

'Who'd like second helpings of anything?' said Stella anxiously.

'I'd love some gravy,' said Fitz. 'It's absolutely epic!'

Fiona and Piers declared that they would do the clearing up. As Stella was on her knees with exhaustion from being a hostess, she decided to let them. She could sort it all out later. Mac was dozing by the fire, probably worn out by good behaviour.

Fitz had been banished from the kitchen too and said, 'I should take the dogs for a walk, or they'll get restive.'

'God! What I wouldn't give to go for a walk just now!' said Stella. 'A bit of fresh air—'

'And no conversation,' said Fitz. 'Let's do it!'

'I can't! I should stay and be the hostess.'

'Of course you can. Do you think I have to invite the others? I suppose I'd better ask. The way they feel about the countryside makes me think they'll say no.'

They didn't say no. Maybe it was because clearing up a big meal in a galley kitchen with very little space to put anything was extremely difficult, but they both said they'd love to walk off their lunch.

It took an age to get out of the house. Fiona didn't want to ruin her boots so Stella had to find something to lend her. Fortunately her walking boots fitted Fiona and Stella could wear her wellies. Fitz borrowed her father's boots. Piers was wearing boots already and Mac was staying behind to doze by the fire.

The dogs dragged Fitz and Fiona up the hill, Fiona mentioning several times how well trained her father's dogs were. 'He just wouldn't tolerate a badly behaved dog,' she said. 'Working dogs have to be obedient.'

'I think these are playing dogs,' said Fitz. 'We'll let them off the lead when we get well away from the road.'

'They'll be in the next county in seconds flat,' said Fiona derisively.

Stella wanted to defend Tris and Izzy; then she wondered why. They weren't her dogs, after all.

The four of them stood by the Dog Walkers'

Christmas Tree and Stella explained it to Fiona and Piers. She didn't point out the battered little dog that had been her contribution but they were both suitably charmed.

Izzy and Tris bounced around them, managing to get quite a lot of mud on Fiona's Barbour.

'It's fine!' Fiona snapped when Fitz apologised. 'It'll brush off, I'm sure.'

Stella felt for her. She was obviously really fed up about it but couldn't complain or she'd risk looking a bad sport. On the other hand, it was a country coat: it was designed to get mud on.

'You're being very good about it,' said Fitz, 'and I am really grateful. I do love these dogs.'

'So they live with you in Bristol?' asked Piers.

'No,' said Fiona. 'We can't have them in Bristol.'

'So—' Piers went on.

'They're going to have to be rehomed,' said Fiona. 'Fitz's mother obviously can't look after them.'

'Actually, if you don't mind,' said Stella, 'we made a pact not to talk about that over Christmas.'

'Fine!' said Fiona and brushed at her coat.

'Actually, I don't think I can ever talk about it,' said Fitz as Tris came up to him and pressed his head against his master.

'You'll have to think about it soon,' said Fiona, nearly sharp in her tone. 'Before you go back to work.'

'You can't have dogs in a city, it's not fair to them,' said Piers.

'The pact?' said Stella. After a moment, she added, 'Let's go back now. I'm desperate for a cup of tea.'

Stella was in the kitchen, in her socks, having put the kettle on, when there was a scream: a wail of agony that could have indicated someone had died it was so full of woe.

Her first thought was that Mac had suffered some sort of dramatic collapse and she rushed through, trying to remember her father's postcode for when they called an ambulance.

But Mac was sitting by the fire, looking in good health.

Fitz was holding the dogs by their collars and was on the way to the boot room with them.

In the middle of the sitting room, having hysterics, was Fiona.

'Those bloody dogs!' said Fiona through tears of rage. 'They've eaten my handbag and my boots!'

Stella was shocked. They'd only arrived back in the house about five minutes ago, hardly time to have eaten a biscuit let alone illicit leather goods. At least she'd put the kettle on; maybe Fiona needed something for the shock.

'Piérs?' Stella said. 'Could you make tea? We could all do with a cup.'

Almost making Stella fall in love with him all

over again, Piers went to the kitchen straight away. Almost.

Fitz had restrained the culprits and returned to the room. 'Oh come on!' he said, trying to be placatory. 'It's only a little nibble!'

Fiona held up her beautiful handbag and Stella could see the tooth marks. It may have been a nibble but the bag was still ruined.

'Oh my God, I'm so sorry!' said Stella.

'And my boot!' Fiona held it up.

This had also been chewed – a large hole just above the heel.

'This is awful,' said Stella, for want of something better.

'It's more than awful!' shouted Fiona, turning her wrath on Stella. 'It's a disaster!'

Stella thought. 'I'm sure there's house insurance. That would—'

'It's not your fault, Stella,' said Fitz. 'I'll handle this.'

'Yes!' Fiona was less distraught now but more angry. 'You will handle it! And you'll find a home for those dogs! Or have them put down!'

'Darling, you're hysterical,' said Fitz.

This was true but astoundingly tactless. Stella was extremely relieved when Piers came in with a tray of tea. He took the first mug to Mac, who seemed faintly amused.

'I may be hysterical, but I'm right!' said Fiona.

'Either you have those hell hounds put to sleep or sent to a home for delinquent animals or we're through. You have to choose!'

'No!' said Stella, almost as loudly as Fiona. 'You don't have to choose! You can't let the dogs come between you.'

'They are already between us! They have destroyed my bag and my boots! I'm never going to forgive them, never!'

'I'm going to have the dogs!' said Stella, aware that she was shouting. 'I mean' – she lowered her voice – 'I will keep them here, look after them, train them.' She heard her voice crack and took the mug of tea that Piers offered her.

'You have to think very carefully before making a decision like that,' he said, looking a bit shocked. He gave Fitz his tea and then perched on the sofa with his own mug. 'You can't make it on impulse.'

Having had a few sips of tea Stella felt calmer. She looked at Piers. 'I'm not making it on impulse, I've been thinking about moving down here for a little while. And I'd like to have the dogs, if Mac and Fitz are happy about it.'

'You'd give them a lovely home, to be sure,' said Mac. 'I'm just sorry that Fitz had to choose and made the wrong choice.'

'He didn't have to choose,' said Stella, 'because I'm having them!'

'I can't believe you want them,' said Fiona, 'even

if it was your fault they ate my things, giving them those good-quality shoes to chew.'

'Don't take it out on Stella,' said Fitz. 'She's got us out of a very difficult position.'

'But how will you manage?' said Piers. 'You can't just give up a well-paid job and a good life in London.'

'I can. Without my massive rent to pay, I can just do supply teaching,' said Stella, feeling completely calm and happy about her decision.

'How will you work, if you've got dogs?' asked Fiona.

'Part-time will be fine. I'll sort something out for days that I'm not in the house. I want time to study anyway. Living here, without having to pay rent, I can do that.'

Fiona was relaxing now. She no longer had to hope her boyfriend would choose her over the dogs. 'Well, you'd be getting us out of a hole if you would take them.'

At that moment, Fitz caught Stella's eye. She couldn't interpret his expression. It was so complex. Gratitude, sadness, speculation were all there. 'Are you absolutely sure about this?'

'Never been surer in my life,' she said.

'Actually?' said Fiona to Fitz. 'Can we go? I don't think I can stay in the same house as those dogs a minute longer.'

'I have to take my mother back first,' said Fitz.

'I could go to your mother's house and wait for you there,' suggested Fiona.

'No,' said Stella, who could remember just how muddy it had been the last time she had seen it. She doubted if Fitz had had a chance to do much about it in the meantime. 'It's a bit doggy,' she added.

Fiona shuddered.

'I've an idea,' said Mac. 'Why doesn't Stella take me to the care home? We can have a bit of a chat.'

'So we can go?' said Fiona to Fitz.

He shook his head. 'We can't leave the dogs on their own.'

'Tell you what,' said Piers, 'why don't Fiona and I find a nice pub? Then Fitz can stay here with the dogs while Stella takes Mac back?'

'Sounds like a plan!' said Stella. Once again she acknowledged that while she didn't want to be with him any more, Piers did have his good points.

'So, Mac,' said Stella when they were in the car, 'tell me. Why did you get Tristan and Isolde? I'm not buying the whole "poor old woman, didn't know what she was doing when she took them on" thing.'

Mac laughed. 'Well, you've caught me there, although I did fall in love with them and I'm so grateful that you've agreed to take them.'

'But why *did* you take them?' Stella persisted, aware that Mac would avoid answering her if she wanted.

'To be honest, I'm not sure Fiona is the right girl for my boy.'

'And?'

'I thought the dogs would break them up. He's always loved dogs and those two had a very bad start in life. They deserve a bit of fun, a proper home. I thought if Fitz fell in love with them, he'd fall out of love with her.'

'That was very wrong,' said Stella. She wouldn't usually have said this to a much-older woman who was nothing to do with her really.

'It was, but I do want to see him settled before I die.'

'You're not going to die anytime soon,' said Stella.

'I know. There's still time for the right girl to come along.' She winked.

Stella kept her eyes on the road and didn't comment.

One year later, on Christmas Day in the morning, Stella walked up to the common. It was just getting light. In her pocket she had a battered tin model of a dog and at her heels she had a pair of perfectly trained dogs. A lot had happened in the year since the first time she came up here.

She had studied and trained and become a dog behaviourist. She had turned her father's cottage into her home and she loved it. She managed well on a few days' supply teaching, and a friend she'd met through her behaviourist training looked after Tris and Izzy while she was out all day. Even Annabel had come to accept she had made the right decision. There was very little wrong with her life, she was aware, and she was grateful.

She let the dogs off the lead when they reached the common and carried on walking up the hill.

Suddenly they started barking. As she'd more or less trained them not to bark she was surprised and a little concerned. Maybe there was something wrong?

'God! I've been here for hours waiting for you!' said Fitz, just making himself heard over the joyful shouts of the dogs.

She began to smile. She would have been lying to herself if a part of her hadn't hoped she'd meet Fitz again but she hadn't let herself think it might happen.

'Why are you so late?' said Fitz, coming up to her, rubbing his hands together against the cold.

'No need to come early like last time,' she said. 'I had no ashes to scatter and the dogs are very good now – well, usually.'

'I've been waiting, hoping to see you. I drove up first thing.'

Stella was trying very hard to stay controlled. 'Why?'

'You know why! I want to – I'd love to – take you out sometime? What a ridiculous situation.'

Inside, Stella was bursting with happiness but she was determined to keep it under control for as long as she could. 'How's your mother?'

'You know perfectly well how she is. You see her far more often than I do.'

This was true. She saw Mac every week and they were very firm friends by now.

'I've been finished with Fiona for a couple of months now,' said Fitz. 'But I expect you knew that too.'

She had known.

'I wanted to leave a decent interval before I started courting again,' he said.

Now she started to laugh, unable to restrain herself any longer. 'How are you going to go about that then?'

'Like this.'

He took her into his arms while the dogs jumped around them. They hugged for a long time, like lovers who had been parted. And then they kissed until the dogs sat down, bored.

'That'll do,' said Stella. 'And happy Christmas.'

# A
# Christmas
## in
# Disguise

*To the lovely A. J. Pearce who told me about the*
*organisation described in the book.*

Cooking Christmas dinner for a group of strangers was an odd way to be spending the morning, but at least it was warm.

Jo looked around the huge, glittery kitchen (sparkly marble, high-gloss cupboards, lots of glass) and smiled. It was so different from her mother's house and on a completely different planet from where she sometimes spent Christmas Day. The difference made her giggle. 'If my friends could see me now!' she hummed.

Because, for the past two years, Jo had spent either Christmas Day or Boxing Day helping out at the animal charity where she was a volunteer. The charity cared for brood bitches and puppies rescued from puppy farms, and one of the things the volunteers did was take over the charity at Christmas so that the paid employees could have some precious time off. She had learnt to manipulate a hose and a shovel with flair and, when she wasn't cleaning out kennels, she sat quietly with frightened dogs, reading her book, just being there, so the animals could get used to human company.

This Christmas would be very different indeed.

Andi had invited Jo out for a drink, to make her request – plea, rather.

'I wouldn't usually ask you this, but what are you doing for Christmas?' said Andi, pouring wine into Jo's glass with a generous hand.

'I agree that isn't what you'd usually ask me, so why do you want to know?'

'I want to know if you're doing something amazing, in which case we'll finish the wine and then I'll go back and write my resignation letter.'

'Oh my God! Why?' Andi had an amazing job as cook to an A-lister, who, while she could be tricky – very tricky sometimes – paid well and wasn't around a lot. It was a dream job.

'Because I really want to be at home for Christmas and she really wants me to cook for her and her friends.' Andi sighed, looking worried and suddenly a bit close to tears.

'Oh, love,' said Jo. 'Tell me.'

'My sister's just had a baby, as you know, and all my family are going to be down in Cornwall with her, and I really want to be there too!'

'And Caroline won't give you the time off? You explained?'

Andi nodded. 'She said, "Andi ..."' – she could do a pretty good imitation of her boss's crisp tones – '"I ask very little of you. You get very well paid and I'm rarely here. When I do want you, I expect you to be here, doing your job." So that was me told.' She paused. 'Although Caroline has had quite a lot of dinner parties recently, which makes it feel even more unfair.'

Jo sighed in sympathy. 'I see.'

'So, what are you doing?' Andi went on. 'If it's skiing with a wonderful new boyfriend, tell me now and I'll write my letter and brush up my CV. I won't get a reference, so I'd better make it good.'

As she was a trained chef herself (although not currently working as one), Jo knew what her friend was going to ask. She put Andi out of her misery. 'Actually, I'd quite like something to do. Unlike you, I don't really want to spend Christmas with my family.'

'Why not?' Andi obviously found this hard to understand.

'Because – my mother would say – I lack family feeling, and I'd rather look after smelly old dogs than spend time with them.'

Andi bit back a giggle. 'That's a bit harsh.'

'And while we don't get on brilliantly – unlike you – that isn't always true, but it is true this year.'

'Why? Has there been a row?'

'Yes, but only after I said I wouldn't spend Christmas with them.'

'But why did you do that?'

'Because they're all going to New Zealand for Christmas, to spend time with my aunt. And while my mother's family feeling is obviously massive, it doesn't run to helping me out with the fare – not even a contribution – so I said I couldn't afford it and now they all hate me.'

Andi giggled and added more wine to the glasses. 'So you'll stand in for me then? Yippee! And when your charity next needs catering done for an event, or cakes for a raffle, or anything that involves food, you can ask me.'

'I'm more than happy to cook, but is Caroline OK with this?'

Andi bit her lip and shook her head. 'Jo, Caroline doesn't know and she mustn't find out.'

Jo froze. 'What?'

'You did hear right. She mustn't find out. Not only must you do the cooking, but you also have to pretend you're me.'

'Andi, I'd do anything for you, you know I would, but I really don't think I can do this.'

'Please, Jo! If you don't, I'll lose my job for sure,

and it's really well paid. I wouldn't mind so much, but I'm finally managing to pay Mum back the money she lent me ages ago. Really, I wouldn't ask you if I wasn't desperate.'

Jo gulped, a light sweat breaking out over her forehead as she realised what Andi was asking. 'But, Andi, we don't look anything like each other. The moment she sets eyes on me—'

Andi took a breath. 'It's OK. I've thought about this a lot, as you can imagine. For a start, you'll be wearing your chef's gear, including a cap. Secondly, she doesn't want all that much served. She'll get one of the men to carve, so all you have to do is rush in with dishes, with your head turned away.'

'Rush in with a turkey weighing about five stone on a platter – that'll be easy. Not.'

'No,' Andi protested. 'A three-bird roast—'

'That doesn't really make it any easier.'

'Listen, she never seems to look at people she doesn't think are important. I'm sure it'll be fine.'

Jo gave up trying to make her friend see sense. 'Well, it's your job on the line and not mine. I'll give it my best shot.'

Andi hugged Jo so hard it hurt.

Cooking for Caroline wouldn't have been a problem on its own, but not letting her know it wasn't her usual cook at the wheel, so to speak, was going to be harder. But, as Caroline insisted on Andi wearing chef's whites and a cap, Andi had continued to assure Jo that the chances of Caroline noticing were minimal.

'It is a shame you've just had your hair cut,' said Andi. 'Although it does really suit you. Caroline is used to my frizzy mass billowing out from under my hat.'

'Well, maybe she'll think you've had *your* hair cut,' said Jo. 'In fact you'd better cut it or, when you come back, she's going to wonder.'

'I'm sure she won't notice. Honestly, when she's with her fancy friends she'd notice me more if I was a speck of dirt on the heel of her shoe! And she'll be with her fancy friends.' Andi indicated they'd be very fancy indeed, and Jo began to hope for major A-listers: maybe the Beckhams; or possibly minor royals not invited to Sandringham.

'So, who's coming?'

'I don't actually know, but it'll be people you can brag about cooking for – promise! And, of course, I'll give you my wages. At the very least.' Andi paused. 'It's up to you if you want to give the money to your charity. I know what you're like.'

Jo laughed. 'Well, I may not give it all to them. There are plenty of things I need, too.'

'Good for you; you will have really earned it.'

When she'd arrived at Caroline's on Christmas Day and taken in how much was involved, Jo had begun to think that Andi was right. This was a bit more than just an enlarged Sunday lunch.

Having put the oven on, so that she could get the promised three-bird roast in as soon as possible, Jo went out to the garage, where the spare fridges and freezers were. She was a bit surprised to discover there was a need for them, given the size of the one in the kitchen, but Andi had said that was where the langoustines were, and Jo wanted to get as much prep as possible done before Caroline was likely to emerge. Andi had assured her this wouldn't be until two minutes before the guests were due to arrive, as Caroline's make-up – which she referred to as '*maquillage*' and was applied with a brush with only about two hairs in it – took so long. It was effective, though. Caroline was a gossip-mag regular (never knowingly under-papped) and this made her a very tricksy employer. According to Andi, she was all charm and expensive gifts one minute and ice-cold tyrant the next. It was the 'ice-cold tyrant' bit that Jo was dreading. She really didn't want to lose Andi her job.

She had three polystyrene boxes and two bags of *moules* under her chin and was just swinging her hip in the direction of the door, in order to shut it, when she became aware of a car that hadn't been there before, and a man getting out of it.

She raised the boxes in front of her face – it would be just too unfair if her cover was blown by nine o'clock in the morning. The mussels slipped a bit.

'Can I give you a hand with those?' said the man.

Just for a second, Jo considered trying to stay hidden behind the boxes but decided that was silly. 'I'm OK, thanks,' she said.

'No, you're not; those mussels will be on the floor in a minute.' He took hold of them.

'Thank you very much,' said Jo. 'Er – if you don't mind my asking, who are you?' He was helpful and quite nice-looking and she hoped Andi had forgotten to tell her there were waiting staff to assist her. It would make her life so much easier.

'I'm one of Miss Calander's guests,' he said. 'Who are you?'

This was a bit heart-sinking. Why was he here so early? No one was due to turn up until after midday. 'Oh, I'm the cook.' She smiled brightly.

'No, you're not,' he said. 'I know Andi.'

Jo's optimism vanished. 'Oh, well, she's not here. And, if you wouldn't mind, I'd better get this lot into the kitchen. So if you could put the mussels back on the boxes?'

He took no notice. 'I'll take them.'

She followed him across the yard and through the back door. 'Look,' she said, 'I know it sounds crazy, but would you mind not telling Miss Calander that I'm not Andi? I mean, that Andi's not here?'

He put the bags of mussels on the island – big enough to rival actual islands, Jo was convinced – and walked across to the coffee machine. Watching him switch it on, find capsules and cups, she realised he was very familiar with the kitchen. He was probably one of Caroline's toy boys – she had a reputation as a cougar; although, to be fair, she had a reputation as a woman who attracted older men, too.

'You mean, Andi's gone home for Christmas without permission?'

Jo nodded. She could have said that Andi had been called home for a family emergency, but it didn't seem worth the trouble.

'Let me guess: Andi asked permission and Caroline went ballistic?'

'Yup. Andi had thought Caroline was spending Christmas on someone's yacht, but no.' Jo decided it was better to shut up now. This man was one of Caroline's guests and it wasn't a good idea to slag off his hostess, however much the hostess deserved it.

'I can imagine the conversation. "I pay you to do sweet FA most of the time, so when I want you here for Christmas, I expect you to be here. So bloody inconsiderate!"'

Jo suppressed a giggle. 'That was pretty much how it went, though I only got the expurgated version.' Then she realised this man could lose Andi her job and it stopped being funny.

'And you stepped in?'

She nodded. He didn't look disapproving; in fact he looked quite nice, if you liked very well-groomed men. Jo's job as a receptionist for a guest house that catered to walkers and backpackers, and her hobby – passion really – as a volunteer in an animal shelter, meant men in suits didn't really feature in her life.

'How do you like your coffee?' he asked.

It was a nice suit, she realised, in a very pale grey, and he was wearing a pale pink tie. 'Oh, I'll have a latte, please. But I should be making it for you – you're the guest; not that I've had time to work out how to use the machine yet. And why aren't you wearing a Christmas jumper?'

He laughed. 'I'm hoping someone will give me one later. But, as I've invaded your space, the least I can do is make coffee. I'm Matthew Farley, by the way.'

'Jo White.'

He handed her a tall mug full of foamy milk, just how she liked it.

'So, are your family all wondering why you're cooking for a superstar when you should be at home with them at Christmas?'

'Well, my mother did tell me off for having no family feeling, and asked if I didn't want everyone to be together at this special time, yes.' She paused.

'Go on.'

'But as her "family feeling" didn't include helping me out – or even *offering* to help out – with the fare to visit my aunt, I decided it was fine to help Andi out instead. My aunt, where they are all having Christmas, lives in New Zealand,' she added.

'And you're not going to your boyfriend's family instead?'

She shook her head. 'I'm single.'

'So how do you and Andi know each other?'

'Catering college.' She frowned. 'Do you think we'll get away with it? We don't look all that much like each other, but when I put my chef's cap on, maybe Miss Calander won't notice? I'm not doing much serving, apparently.'

He sipped his coffee, looking at her. 'She may well not notice, but you do have very short hair and, unless I've got her muddled up, I thought Caroline's cook had billowing curls.'

'I know,' Jo said. 'I only had mine cut on a whim, and if I'd known . . . but of course I couldn't have known!'

'And Caroline won't be thinking about the staff.'

'So what will she be thinking about?'

He shrugged. 'Well, there's the man she wants to put up money for her new business – she'll be wanting to make sure he's well and truly wooed. And she'll be looking at me and thinking that I'll finally succumb to her invitation to join her between her silk sheets.'

'Does she really have silk sheets? I'd worry that I'd slip out of them.'

He laughed. 'To be honest, I don't know. I only know that whatever kind of sheets she has, they'll be expensive; and I don't want to sample them unless they're on the spare bed.'

'So why are you here then? If she wants you, and you don't want her?'

'It's complicated, but basically she's my mother's best friend – although my mother is a bit older – and I thought I'd be safe.'

'Because? She knew you in nappies?' Jo had taken the top off the box of langoustines. They were huge: too big for canapés really, but as Christmas dinner was going to be served at three, the guests would need to mop up the alcohol with something.

'I was a teenager when my mother and Caroline met. No, it was because I was bringing my girlfriend with me.'

Jo looked at him with sympathy. 'And she couldn't get away at the last moment? Oh, shame!'

He didn't reply immediately. 'Actually, it's a bloody disaster.'

'Come on,' Jo said bracingly. 'There are lots of days at Christmas when you can see each other.' He looked more annoyed than upset, she felt, but she didn't know him; he might be really disappointed.

'Well, we won't be seeing each other on any of those days – we've split up.'

'Oh, I am sorry. Extra-sad for that to happen at Christmas.' She gave him a penetrating glance, before going back to pulling the heads off the giant prawns.

'I'm not sad at all, to be honest, but I did hope we could hold it together until today was over.'

'But you couldn't?'

'Obviously not. And it's left me in serious trouble with Caroline.'

'Really?' This sounded extremely unlikely. 'Why?'

'I thought I said. She – Caroline – told me that if I turned up on Christmas Day without this girlfriend she'd heard so much about, she wouldn't believe I'd ever had a girlfriend and . . . well, I won't go into details, but believe me, it'll all be extremely awkward and upsetting.'

'She'd cut you out of her will?'

He made a face and nodded. 'That would be the least of it!'

Jo smiled into the langoustines. 'Poor you. My heart bleeds.'

She heard him chuckle. 'It would if you knew quite how awkward it will be for me. Caroline won't like being turned down. It will be very hard for us to be friends afterwards. My mother won't speak to me, either, even if I could bring myself to explain why I'd so mortally offended someone I've known half my life.'

'Oh dear, I actually am sorry for you now.' She smiled, a little ruefully. 'I'm often at odds with my mother and it isn't fun.'

'So why do you and your mother fall out?'

'She's never approved of the choices I've made. She wanted me to go to university and get a "proper job", but I wanted to cook; and recently my jobs haven't been "proper". She also wanted me to join the family in NZ for Christmas, but I told you that.'

'My mother can be tricky, too. Although she's older than Caroline, they've always been close and she'd be devastated if there was a falling-out. Not entirely unconnected with the fact that Caroline is famous and gets all sorts of nice little gifts – tickets to West End shows, free meals in top restaurants and weekend trips to spas, et cetera – that she sometimes passes on to my mama.'

'Oh, well, let's hope they get over it and forgive us.' She looked at him. 'I should cook now. Andi's prepared a lot already, but there are some things I have to do.'

The three-bird roast, which she'd taken out of the fridge the moment she arrived so that it wouldn't be too chilly when she came to cook it, she had seasoned and added an extra layer of butter to. She reckoned it would take about four hours to cook, so she was planning to get it into the oven as soon as it came up to temperature. It could rest for as long as she needed it to, leaving her time – and oven space – for other things.

'I've had an idea.'

Matthew's voice broke into her calculations. He

was staring at her intently and she realised she found it very unnerving.

She decided to treat it lightly. She gestured to the oven. 'Ooh, we had one of those once, but the handle fell off,' she said, to stop him making her feel as if she was a laboratory experiment.

'Seriously! You could help me out. It could help you, too.'

She shot him a disbelieving glance. 'Really? Well, if you want a dinner party, picnic, banquet or anything along those lines, I'm your girl.'

'Actually I'm more interested in your gift for subterfuge.'

'Subterfuge?' Jo almost wasn't sure what he meant – it sounded nothing to do with her.

'Yes. Pretending to be someone else. Pretending you're Andi. If you can do that—'

She interrupted him. 'Hang on. We don't know I can do that yet.' The thought of it suddenly gave her a pang of anxiety. It wasn't just the thought of Andi losing her very good job, it was the embarrassment that being found out would create. 'Oh God! What have I let myself in for?'

'I think you'll be fine,' he said soothingly. 'You're more or less the same build as Andi and with your chef's cap on, to hide your hair, no one will notice. Or at least no one will notice unless they're looking, and Caroline won't look.'

'Thank you. That's what Andi and I thought.' She

sensed there was something else coming and waited, wondering if it was too soon to start making blinis. The batter was done already – she only had to cook them.

'So think how much easier it would be if no one knew what you looked like.'

She frowned. 'Well, no one does know what I look like.'

'More to the point, no one knows what my girl-friend looks like.'

Jo gave Matthew a smile that should have told him she had no idea what he was talking about, and would he please leave her alone to get on with her work. In fact she did have an inkling – and no intention of going along with his idea. But she didn't want to offend him. He was Caroline's guest, after all.

He either didn't read or chose to ignore the signal. 'You could pretend to be my girlfriend.'

She rolled her eyes. 'Really? Why would I want to do that?'

His attempt to look pathetic made her smile. 'To help me out? Stop my mother's celebrity cougar friend pouncing on me?'

'Look, I am sympathetic. I realise how awkward it must be for you, but you're asking the impossible.'

'No! Don't you see? This will make things easier for you. You could be a very helpful sort of girl-friend, who rushes out to help, which means that she – you – will be able to bring things in, take things out, without having to dress up as Andi.'

'No. I'd have to dress up as Seraphina, or whatever your girlfriend is called.'

'Lulu. She's called Lulu, but as Caroline won't remember that, you can call yourself anything you like.'

'There is no name I like! I'm not doing it. And if you don't go away and stop making ridiculous suggestions, I'll make you de-vein langoustines.'

'Perfectly happy to do that.'

To her surprise, he took off his suit jacket and found a tea towel that was hanging from the range cooker and tucked it round his waist. He helped himself to a knife from the knife-block and was soon slicing and de-veining at an impressive rate.

'You're good at that,' she said.

He nodded. 'Misspent youth in Oz.'

'Not that misspent. You've learnt a skill and you're still quite young, so lots of time to learn more.' She didn't look at him while she said this. She didn't want him to see that she was sending him up a little.

'Still quite young, but quite old enough to have a girlfriend.'

'Don't worry – you'll get one! You could go on Tinder, or a dating website. You'll have your pick.'

'Really?' He seemed amused at something; perhaps it was her confidence in his ability to get another girlfriend.

She nodded. 'You're posh and quite nice-looking.'

'But obviously not posh enough or nice-looking enough for you!'

She giggled. 'You're certainly posh enough.'

'So, too ugly?'

She met his gaze and saw that he was laughing, too. 'Not too ugly, no. But I'm busy. I can't be your girlfriend *and* cook Christmas dinner.'

'But don't you see? It would be easier. As my helpful girlfriend, you can appear as *you* far more often. Think about it?'

She gathered up the non-edible remains of the langoustines and did think about it. 'I sort of see what you mean,' she said. She remembered Andi saying she wouldn't need to serve that much; and having one of the guests onside would definitely make things easier. 'But why would your girlfriend turn up for Christmas in chef's whites?' She was teasing him, but she wasn't sure he realised.

'She wouldn't. She'd be wearing the hideously expensive cashmere cardigan with matching camisole that I gave her. And that I happen to have here, gift-wrapped at vast extra expense.'

She was coming round to his way of thinking, but she didn't want Matthew to know that just yet.

'You could keep the presents – all of them. There's even a nice little blue bag from Tiffany's.'

'You must think I'm very mercenary,' she said, wondering if she could sell the contents of the blue bag, and how much would it raise for the charity.

'Actually I don't think you're mercenary at all, otherwise you'd just say yes to the presents and put them on.'

She laughed. 'It won't work.'

'It will, if you give it a go. So, what can I offer you that would make it worthwhile?'

'I thought the expensive presents were supposed to be enough? If I'm not mercenary?'

'They're not enough. If you did this for me, I'd like you to have something you really want, and not just money.'

'I do want money! Well, my favourite charity always does.'

'Tell me about it.'

'Only if you help with the sprouts. Andi didn't get time to do them and there's a sackful.'

While they both peeled sprouts, Jo told Matthew about the charity: how it rescued bitches and puppies from puppy farms, and how sometimes the dogs were so unfamiliar with human company that they needed someone to just sit in the kennel with them, reading, so they could get used to being with a person.

'Hmm,' said Matthew. 'What you really need then is a big event – like a ball or a fun day or something – with a big celebrity to host it.'

'That sounds good. Can you arrange that then?' She was openly teasing him now.

He smiled. 'I could, if I had time, but I haven't. What I *can* do for you is supply a really good celebrity, though.'

'Really?' This was quite interesting. 'Who?'

'Euan Donavan,' he said calmly.

Jo wasn't much into celebrities. She hardly ever recognised anyone when they turned up on TV programmes, even when they were apparently universally famous. But she had heard of Euan Donavan – actor, film star and more recently singer-songwriter. Briefly she considered pretending not to be impressed, but gave it up. 'You could get him? How?'

'We were at school together and have been mates ever since.'

'Yes, but – surely you couldn't get him to commit to doing some charity event?'

'I could actually. And with someone like him, at the right event, you could raise a hundred grand.'

Jo went hot and cold and didn't know if she should take Matthew seriously or not. 'You must have some amazing dirt on him!' she said, sweeping sprout peelings into the compost bin.

'I couldn't possibly comment,' said Matthew. 'But, apart from that, I think he'd really relate to your charity. He is a big animal-lover.'

Jo nodded. 'That's probably why I've heard of him. I've never usually heard of anyone.' A thought struck her. 'You do look a bit familiar. You're not famous, are you? Not in *Made in Chelsea* or anything?'

He seemed to find this hilarious. 'No!'

'And you'd really do this for me? For my charity?'

'Yup. If you pretend to be my girlfriend.'

She studied him. He seemed to be completely genuine. His gaze was honest and straightforward and, if he did let her down, she'd still have the Christmas presents. She could sell or raffle them to raise money. There'd be something for the charity in it, even if not the main prize.

'There's one thing – well, a couple of things really. Suppose it all fails? That Caroline discovers I'm not Andi? And not your girlfriend?'

'If she discovers you're not Andi, I'll do my best to get Caroline not to sack her. But as for you not being my girlfriend – well, why can't you just be my girlfriend? I'm single; you're single. I'll take you out for dinner next week.'

Jo laughed; it was funny, and she was looking forward to telling Andi about it. 'Because I do not look like someone who'd be your girlfriend.'

'And what do you think she'd look like?'

'Well ... groomed, made-up, sophisticated and not wearing chef's whites – and clogs.' She laughed even more. It was so ridiculous.

They both looked down at what she was wearing on her feet: chef's clogs, brilliant for standing in all day, but not so good for masquerading as an It Girl.

'Ah,' said Matthew, 'bit of a problem. I did buy

275

my ex the cashmere and jewellery, but she would have worn her own shoes.'

Jo suddenly felt very depressed. 'Oh no! I wasn't really looking forward to doing it, but the thought of having Euan Donavan, and the money we could have raised—' She also felt that if she had masqueraded as Matthew's girlfriend and was discovered also to be pretending to be Andi, he could (and would) have convinced Caroline it wasn't a sacking offence, provided the food was good, and as ordered. It would have been nice to have that bit of job security for Andi.

He put his hand on her shoulder. 'Don't despair. I'll think of something.'

'Matthew, no one – let alone Caroline – is going to believe I'm your girlfriend, even if I did have the right shoes. I'm just not your type.'

'How do you know? I think you could be exactly my type. Nice-looking girl, great haircut, animal-lover, I assume a non-smoker – perfect!'

'Sweet of you to say that, but let's face it, no one will be convinced.'

'Of course they will. I'll sort the shoe thing.' He frowned for a second. 'I know, I'll tell Caroline that a heel came off one of your shoes, and can she lend you a pair. That should be OK.'

'Ooh. It rather depends on me and Caroline having the same-size feet. Give or take.'

'Your feet look quite small,' he said, 'as far as I

can tell in those clodhoppers, so it should be fine. And if Caroline has smaller feet – well, she'll have to lend you some slippers or something. Don't worry.'

But Jo was now convinced the plan would fail. She was disappointed. It wasn't just the money for the charity that she regretted, she realised, but the fact that pretending to be Matthew's girlfriend would have made it easier to pretend she was Caroline's cook, and now that seemed difficult. Being a girlfriend would also make it more fun.

'I'll leave it a bit longer, then I'll arrive officially,' said Matthew. 'Caroline's not expecting me until after eleven, but she won't mind or be surprised if I'm a bit earlier.'

Convinced that none of the subterfuge would come off, Jo referred to her list. She had to make choux buns filled with mushrooms, as a hot vegetarian canapé. She'd never made them before, but they'd probably be fine. She sighed, without realising she was doing it.

'Come on, Jo. We can do this! Shall I open a bottle of fizz? We could have a glass to stiffen our sinews.'

This made her laugh. 'Matthew, we don't live in the same world – really we don't. First of all, any cook who opened and drank the boss's champagne would be instantly dismissed ...'

'Not on Christmas Day, they wouldn't be.'

'. . . and secondly, champagne wouldn't stiffen my

sinews; it would turn them to rubber, which would not help me – or us – in any way.'

'It was only a suggestion. I would have told Caroline it was me who opened the bottle; she probably wouldn't mind – I'm sure there are dozens in the fridge.'

'There are, but I'm still not letting you open one now.' He looked a bit disappointed so she went on, 'Oh, I suppose you *could* open one, as long as you made sure Caroline knew it was nothing to do with me.'

'You could have a sip from my glass, and Caroline would never know you'd had some,' he suggested.

'No! It's already going to be hard enough, without me being tipsy. I have to serve canapés with my head turned away from my boss, so she won't see who I am. I have to get food to the table and serve it, ditto. Not at all easy.'

'No! My girlfriend – my very helpful girlfriend (not that she was in real life, actually, otherwise she wouldn't have dumped me at such an inconvenient moment) – will hand the canapés round. Then she'll "pop downstairs to see if the cook needs a hand" and will reappear, in your disguise, and be helpful.'

'Wouldn't that look weird? Why would she be helpful?'

'Because she's incredibly nice and wants to impress my celebrity friend, hoping for some unobtainable tickets to something.'

'Not that nice then – definitely on the make.' Jo frowned at her list, wondering what to prioritise.

'Maybe she's just doing it to be helpful. Some people are.' He nodded towards Jo. 'Like you, helping your friend Andi.'

'Oh, OK, she's kind! But I have to say that if this mythical girlfriend thinks Caroline would be impressed by her helping out the staff, she obviously hasn't read what the gossip mags say about Caroline.'

'Mythical, extremely kind and extremely naïve?'

Jo had to laugh. It was all so ridiculous. 'You forgot to add "dresses in strangely austere clothes that look uncannily like a chef's uniform".'

'Come on! Where's your imagination? You're wearing black trousers – anyone could wear them.'

'Humph. You were lucky. I usually wear very loud checked trousers, but Andi doesn't, so I wore black ones today, like she does.' She went across to the larder cupboard to find flour. 'I don't think Caroline likes loud checks.'

'Certainly doesn't.' Matthew Farley studied Jo while she measured out flour and then tipped it on to a piece of baking parchment. 'I've got jewellery and I've got clothes.'

Jo went to the fridge for butter.

'I'm going to get the presents,' said Matthew, 'and see how well we can dress you up.'

She shrugged and carried on with her measurements. She wasn't convinced.

She was beating the eggs into the flour and melted butter in a pan when he came back with a pile of boxes. 'Golly, you do give lavishly!' she said.

'I do. You really should think about becoming my girlfriend. You'd do well.'

Eyeing the boxes, she remembered that last year her then-boyfriend had given her 'on offer' body wash and hand cream and a bracelet that made her wrist itch. Posh boys obviously gave much better presents.

'Take them into the downstairs bathroom and put it all on. When we see what you look like, I'll telephone Caroline and ask her about the shoes.'

'OK,' said Jo, taking the boxes and feeling unexpectedly excited.

'Oh!' He put a detaining hand on her arm and extracted one of the boxes from the pile. 'I'll have that one back. You haven't been my girlfriend long enough to give you that yet.'

Jo laughed. 'Saucy underwear?'

'Come on, we've got a lot to do.'

The downstairs bathroom was attached to a sort of boot room, where Andi changed and kept her outdoor clothes. Jo was hoping – though not really believing it would happen – that Andi had left a bit of make-up in there. A stub of pencil, some mascara, maybe a lipstick. She found hand cream and lip balm, but that was it. She sighed. However she looked in the clothes and jewellery, no one would believe she was Matthew's girlfriend if she didn't have on a scrap of make-up, apart from well-moisturised lips.

Since he had confiscated one of the parcels, there were two boxes and a little blue bag. The boxes had been wrapped in-store by someone who took pride in their work. Had she been at home, Jo would have saved the pale pink tissue paper that cradled the contents of the first box: the cashmere.

It was a V-necked cardigan, fairly short, in a soft teal blue – almost the same colour as the little blue bag. She pulled off her chef's jacket and put it on. She loved the colour, and the cashmere felt wonderful against her skin. Excited, although she tried not to be, she opened the other box. It contained a silk camisole in the same blue. Hastily she took off the cardi and put on the cami, and then put the cardigan back on. It felt even nicer!

She turned to the little blue bag, the present from Tiffany's. Although Matthew had said she could keep the presents, she had no intention of doing so – certainly not the jewellery. In the bag there was a box, and in the box was a pair of diamond studs for her ears and a diamond pendant. Jo looked down at them, feeling slightly faint. If they were real diamonds, they represented an awful lot of money; and she didn't think Tiffany's – or Matthew, come to that – would deal in fake ones. She couldn't wear them. She wrapped up the box, concealed the other wrappings in Andi's cupboard and went back into the kitchen.

'What do you think?'

'You're not wearing the earrings or the pendant. Didn't they fit?' He feigned a look of horror.

'No. Yes! Of course they'd have fitted. But they're far too expensive. I couldn't wear them. It's against my principles.'

'Oh, don't be silly.' Somehow, the way he said it meant Jo didn't feel the urge to hit him. Matthew took the bag from her and rapidly extracted the goods. He put the pendant round her neck and turned her, so that he could do it up. 'Here, you have to put the earrings in. Do you need a mirror?'

'It's OK, this cupboard has a very high-gloss finish – I'll manage.'

'Wow!' he said when she'd fiddled them into place. 'You look stunning.'

Although extremely tempted to run back to the boot room, where there was a real mirror, she said, 'I'm not wearing make-up, and I'm not going to look the part without it.'

He stared down at her, frowning a little. 'You have a point. And I still have to get you shoes.' He glanced at his watch. 'I'll ring Caroline.'

'It seems ridiculous to ring her when you're in her house.'

'Not at all! I wouldn't dream of disturbing her when she's getting ready, even if I did want to—' He stopped, possibly to spare Jo's blushes, although she felt it was a bit late for that.

'Caroline. Good morning and happy Christmas,' he said into his phone, which he'd put on speaker mode.

'Darling,' said his hostess. 'Where are you? I can't even remember what time I invited you for, but I hope it isn't now, because I am not ready. I've had a hair disaster.'

He laughed indulgently. 'I know you'll look stunning, as usual; but talking of disasters, Jo's had one.'

Jo jumped. What had he done? Why was he mentioning her? She was supposed to be a secret!

'Jo?' asked Caroline.

'My girlfriend? The one I told you I was bringing?'

'Oh. I thought she was called Lulu, but you know me – hopeless with names.'

Thank God she was hopeless with names, thought Jo. Otherwise they were in trouble.

Matthew laughed softly. For someone who didn't want to sleep with his hostess, he was sounding very sexy. 'Lulu was *so* last season! Anyway, when we stopped for fuel, Jo went to the loo at the petrol station and broke the heel on her shoe.'

'Oh, nightmare!' Caroline obviously felt this was a genuine disaster.

'Yah, and worse – she was so fed up about it, she got distracted and only realised too late that she'd left her make-up bag in the loo, which I gather wasn't exactly nose-friendly—'

'What?' asked Caroline.

'It stank,' said Matthew. Jo was glad of the explanation, too.

'Oh God. Of course.'

'Anyway the poor girl is here—'

'Here? Already!'

'It's OK. Andi let us in, and I'm about to raid your fridge for a bottle of fizz – but Jo is so embarrassed about having no make-up and no shoes. Could I pop up and borrow a pair? And something – a bit of mascara? Just to make her feel a little better?' He lowered his voice, as if to protect his mythical girlfriend. 'You set a very high standard for glamour. Jo is nervous enough about meeting you. She's quite shy.'

Jo nodded. It might help; it might explain her being so helpful. It might also make it easier for her to run out of the room for no apparent reason. That would be handy.

'Sweet!' said Caroline, in a way that made Jo feel patronised even when she was a fictional character. 'Tell you what, darling,' Caroline went on. 'You pop up here and find some shoes, and I'll let Jo have my travel make-up kit.'

'Perfume?' Jo mouthed. Matthew nodded.

'I'll pop up,' he said to Caroline and disconnected.

While he was away, Jo looked at her watch and realised that unless she really got a move on, everything was going to be late. It was always the way, she realised as she flew around, putting the three-bird roast in the oven and adding cheese to her choux pastry: you think you've got lots of time and then something happens that means you're suddenly up against it. It made her feel she was in some ghastly cooking competition and was going to have people counting down the time and clapping as it came near to service.

However, with the oven on, she consulted her list and realised she didn't need to panic just yet.

It was a challenging menu, and Andi hadn't been able to prepare as much beforehand as she would have liked, being so taken up with Caroline's entertaining. What made it tougher was Caroline's understandable desire to offer less-fattening alternatives. Hence the langoustines and *moules* alongside individual cranberry-and-brie quiches (fortunately already made) and the blinis with caviar and sour cream. (Andi had told Jo that a low-fat yoghurt option had been considered and rejected.)

Then there was a game terrine with brioche and chutney, or smoked salmon. The three-bird roast was considered to be healthy enough for anyone. And then there was the pudding. Annoyingly, the details for this were missing, and Jo looked in vain for mention of it on another sheet, but no. All Andi had written was: 'you won't need to worry about the pudding', and then she had obviously been interrupted, because there was a dot on the page where she might have been about to start a new paragraph, but then nothing more.

Jo was just checking for the fourth time that the notes had come to an end when Matthew came back with a handful of shoes and a make-up bag. Seeing them, she said, 'Oh God, I don't think I can do this dressed up as someone else. This is not your normal Christmas dinner – it's very posh cooking. I'll have to concentrate!'

'Just get into the make-up and see if the shoes fit, and we'll make a plan.'

It was nice to feel she wasn't alone in this. 'OK.'

'So which ones do you fancy? Caroline found a bag of shoes that was due to go to the charity shop and I said you'd be fine with that.'

Jo grinned. 'I get most of my clothes from charity shops anyway,' she said, 'so perfectly fine.'

She chose a pair of tasselled loafers over the ballet flats, and ignored the heels. Caroline's feet were a bit bigger than hers, but that wouldn't matter because she wasn't pretending they were hers. 'These feel OK.'

'We'll tell Caroline you're frightened of heels since yours broke,' said Matthew, picking up the pairs with stilt heels that had probably cost three figures.

'I'd forgotten that was the excuse for my needing to borrow some,' said Jo. 'Now for the hard part: I don't wear a lot of make-up and I haven't time to experiment.'

'So don't. Just wear what you usually wear. You've got lovely skin – you don't need a lot.'

Jo's lovely skin evinced embarrassment at this compliment with a delicate flush, but she didn't comment and just took the bag.

She was back in the kitchen a couple of minutes later. 'OK?' she said. 'I just put on the usual, although Caroline has got wonderful make-up.'

He studied her. 'You look lovely.' Then he tucked her hair behind her ear. 'Simple but elegant. I have very good taste when it comes to women, it seems.'

She blushed again. 'So when do we have to appear upstairs?'

'Not for a while. I'll open a bottle of fizz.'

'Matthew! We're not really Caroline's guests, you know. At least I'm not. I'm going to put my clogs and jacket back on and get to work, as soon as ever I can after I've been presented as your girlfriend.'

He responded calmly to her mild panic. 'If I'm going to peel potatoes, I'll want something to keep me going. It's Christmas, after all.'

'You really don't have to peel—'

'The alternative is going upstairs to read *Hello!* magazine while Caroline gets ready. And I'd have to take you with me.'

She bit her lip. 'I never thought of that.'

'So what can I do?'

'Well, if you'd like to find all the right wines – there's a list – and open the reds, that would be great. Andi said they were in the cellar, but couldn't tell me where exactly.'

'That's OK, I know my way round Caroline's cellar. And after that I'll get on with the potatoes.'

Jo's fingers flew, peeling and shaping the veg into perfect little examples of their kind. She was doing a tray of roast vegetables as well as the potatoes, and it all took a lot of preparation. She did it on autopilot while she worried about the pudding.

Apart from that, Andi had given pretty detailed instructions about what was needed, what she had prepared and what had to be done at the last minute. And Jo didn't need to worry about the pudding just yet. Lunch was due to be served at three and it was only half past ten now. There were plenty of opportunities for other things to go wrong before they reached that stage. She assumed she'd find a Christmas pudding somewhere, which she could just put into the microwave and serve with whatever sauce seemed appropriate. If necessary, she'd offer brandy butter, rum sauce and plain cream. The fridge was groaning with ingredients.

Jo enjoyed cooking and, while her knife flew, she forgot there was a reason she was wearing cashmere under her chef's jacket and so was rather warm.

Matthew's phone ringing reminded her. 'Darling?' Caroline's voice was heard. 'I'm beautiful now. Come up and see me. I can't wait to meet your girlfriend.'

Jo's eyes flew to him. 'Oh God, I'm not sure—'

'Come on,' he said urgently. 'Remember your reward: the biggest fundraiser your charity will ever get! Now wipe your hands and get that jacket off.'

Together they left the kitchen and walked up the stairs to the first-floor drawing room, which had a view over the surrounding parkland to rival many other grand vistas.

Caroline stood in the curve of the bay window, looking sensational. She was wearing tight trousers in the softest caramel-coloured suede, which showed off her exquisite legs and which ended in shoes that, to Jo's inexperienced eye, seemed to be studded with diamonds. A blouse made of very heavy silk showcased her famously enhanced cleavage to excellent effect. She wore a huge square-cut emerald ring and several heavy gold bangles.

Although close up she was a little more lined than her photographs showed, she was still extremely beautiful.

Jo's tongue stuck to the roof of her mouth and she deeply regretted not having had any champagne.

'This is Jo,' said Matthew, leading her forward. 'Jo, this is my absolutely favourite "almost-relation", Caroline.'

Jo held out her hand, knowing it would feel like sandpaper in Caroline's. She spent so much time with her hands in water – very often cold water. But she needn't have worried. Caroline ignored the hand and instead took her by the shoulders and brushed her cheek against hers. Then she pulled back and studied her.

'Darling,' she said to Matthew, still holding on to Jo. 'She's adorable! Quite unlike your usual type, I'd have thought.'

Jo decided not to be insulted.

'If you mean she's a non-smoker who loves country walks and snuggling up in front of roaring fires, then she is a bit different.' He twinkled at Jo. 'But you'll admit she's extremely pretty.'

Jo blushed again, hoping her change of clothes and the jewellery would make this at least partly true. 'I wish you wouldn't talk about me as if I weren't here,' she said.

'Quite right.' Caroline took her arm and led her over to one of the many sofas. 'Let's go and get to know each other. Matthew, ring that bell. Get Andi to bring up some champagne.'

'I'll get it,' said Matthew. 'Andi's got enough on her plate.'

Jo suddenly felt like one of the charity dogs, rescued from years of continuous puppy-bearing, encountering a strange being – a human – for more or less the first time. She had no idea what Caroline might do and wished she could escape. She managed a smile.

'This is a really beautiful house,' she said. 'The views from here are stunning.'

'Yes. I bought it for the views, partly. But also it's handy for London, and a lot of my friends have places nearby – or nearby for Gloucestershire.' She laughed.

Jo felt she had to keep up the conversation. If she fell silent, Caroline might ask her a question she couldn't answer. Her mother's criticism that she spent so much time with dogs that she had almost forgotten how to communicate with humans seemed almost justified. Although she did work as a receptionist, she reminded herself. She had *some* people skills. 'Are you working on any exciting new projects at the moment, Caroline?' she asked. Why was Matthew taking so long? It was only one flight of stairs to the kitchen, after all.

Caroline smiled. 'I have plans.'

'Can you tell me what they are?' Jo was proud of

herself. She was doing social chit-chat as if it was second nature.

'No.'

'Oh.' Then she said, 'Sorry, I just have to go and look at the view again.' She got up and walked to the window. The view could keep things going for a while longer, she hoped. 'So, what are those hills in the distance?'

'I'm not sure. So, tell me, Jo—'

Jo was spared telling Caroline anything by the entrance of Matthew, who had filled a tray with champagne flutes. 'I'll just go and get some bottles,' he said.

'No, really, Matthew! Just ring for Andi – here, I'll do it.' Caroline walked across towards the fireplace, but before she could press the bell Jo intervened.

'Goodness me,' she said, 'I thought those logs were real!' She pointed at the fireplace. 'I have never seen such a realistic fake fire. If I hadn't noticed that none of the logs had moved, I would never have guessed.'

She didn't know if Caroline would be hugely insulted by this or not, but it was too bad.

Fortunately, Caroline wasn't insulted. 'It's good, isn't it? It's made by a firm that has a real log fire burning in its showroom and they get you to tell them – or even take a picture of – the moment you like best as the fire burns, and then they reproduce it.'

'It's a miracle,' said Jo. What she meant was that it was a miracle she'd managed to keep going with the small talk this long.

Then Matthew came in with the bottles. He had three of them. 'When are you expecting the rest of your guests, Caro? Will this be enough fizz?'

'I wasn't specific about time. And I should think that'll be enough. For us, anyway. Get a bottle open and we'll have a Christmas wish as we drink it.' Caroline glanced at Matthew meaningfully.

Jo knew what she'd be wishing for: she'd be wishing for the meal to go well and for her not to be discovered, either as Matthew's fake girlfriend or as the stand-in cook.

'So, here's to our Christmas wishes coming true,' said Caroline. 'Goodness me,' she said to Jo a few moments later, 'you drank that quickly. Matthew, fill her up.' She drained her own glass. 'Fill us both up. Although maybe I should ring for the canapés. We don't want to get legless before the other guests arrive.'

'Might be more sensible to wait until they're here, or we'll have eaten them all before they arrive,' said Matthew.

Caroline shrugged. 'Whatever you think, Matt. So, tell me, Jo, what do you do?'

Matthew said, 'Well—' but before he could go on, Caroline held up a hand.

'She can speak for herself, you know, Matthew.'

Jo felt reasonably calm about this, although she realised – and possibly Matthew realised too, which was why he'd tried to step in – that they should have spent some time thinking up a fictional CV for her. 'I work as a receptionist in a hotel,' she said, upgrading the small guest house where she also did cleaning and breakfasts, if the need arose.

'Oh! And is that satisfying for you?' Caroline seemed to suggest it couldn't possibly be satisfying.'

'I like it,' said Jo. 'It isn't terribly demanding, but it'll do for now.' And they were very understanding about her needing to work flexible hours, so that she could spend time with the charity.

'And do you live nearby?' Caroline went on.

'Caro, I told you,' broke in Matthew, 'her parents live near mine.'

'Did you, darling? Oh, shame! I need a personal assistant – I thought Jo might be perfect. Especially if she's a bit understretched where she is at the moment.'

Jo swallowed, glad that Matthew had interrupted. In fact she lived perfectly close enough to Caroline's mansion to work for her, but she knew enough from Andi that she wouldn't like it one bit, even if she wasn't sacked on the first day. Andi only coped because Caroline wasn't there all the time. She'd want her PA at her side, constantly, being run ragged.

'Oh, goodness,' said Jo, who had walked across to the window again. 'A Rolls-Royce is coming up the drive.'

Caroline laughed. 'That'll be Cindy and Max. They are a little bit "nouveau", but great fun. He's a Formula One driver,' she went on, for Jo's benefit. 'And she's a trophy wife from God-knows-where, but, as I said, fun.'

What on earth would she say about me, if she really knew me? Jo wondered. 'Poor but honest' was probably the best she could hope for.

'I'll go down and let them in,' said Matthew.

'No need. Andi will do it,' said Caroline with calm certainty.

Jo considered, knowing very well that Andi wouldn't. 'Actually,' she said, 'I need the bathroom. Maybe Matthew could show me where it is and let Max and Cindy in at the same time? Andi was pretty busy when we last saw her.'

Caroline shrugged. 'The guest bathroom is on this floor. If you go along—'

'I'll show her,' said Matthew. 'It'll be quicker.'

'Oh my God! This is a nightmare,' said Jo as she ran down the stairs as fast as her too-big loafers would let her.

'It's fine,' said Matthew calmly. 'You go and do

what you can in the kitchen. If you're a bit slow coming back up, I'll just say you didn't feel well.'

'I *don't* feel well!' said Jo and flew into the kitchen. 'I'll get the canapés on a tray and you can take them up. Come back and get a second tray, and then we don't have to worry about them any more.'

While she heard Matthew greeting Cindy and Max with enthusiasm, she whacked a tray of quiches into a low oven – thank God this kitchen seemed to have dozens – and put on the striped apron Andi had left behind the door. Putting her chef's jacket on would take too long. She'd keep that for when she needed to be on show.

The canapés were laid out on a large silver platter by the time Matthew had taken coats and sent Max and Cindy up the stairs. 'Come up as soon as you can,' he said to her as he took the tray.

While she didn't hang around, Jo didn't rush. It would be so annoying to make a mistake, when a few moments' thought could have prevented it. Having checked the quiches, she went back to the list. 'Quiches, take them out of the oven when Matthew comes back, fill up the tray with other stuff,' she said to herself, aware that the quiches were a bit pale, but deciding they would do. She worked as she thought, filling up another tray with blinis and prawns and adding a couple of small bowls of olives that she'd found in the fridge, to fill up the tray. She spotted a bag of Kettle Chips and opened them, putting them in some pretty bowls. The tray was short only of the quiches, as she waited for Matthew.

She turned her attention to the starter. 'OK, the terrine can come up to room temp; the brioche I'll warm nearer the time. Smoked salmon needs bread and butter and lemon wedges.'

She found talking to herself really helped, and she would consider whether or not it meant she had gone mad when she had more time. She glanced up at the clock. 'Twelve thirty – lunch is due at three, but I'll serve it when it's ready; put the veg in now. Find the meat thermometer—'

'I think you should come back up now.' Matthew stood before her some time later. 'People are threatening to come and check up on you. Everyone's here now and they want to drink toasts.'

'Damn! I was getting along nicely. But thank you for getting the door – it really saved me some time.'

'I was thinking: I don't reckon you need to appear in the dining room very much. I'll say Andi is stretched and I'll carry stuff in,' said Matthew.

'I agree; if I can mostly hand things to you, you can whisper to Caroline that things are going a bit pear-shaped, and she'll be so anxious for everything to turn out all right that she won't be so fussed about me not serving. Andi said I didn't have to serve all that much anyway, or we wouldn't have attempted this malarkey.'

'And I had a look in the dining room. The table's all set.'

'Thank goodness! For the first course, I'll just put everything on the table and then ring the bell for you all to come. The other courses will be trickier.'

'So are you OK to leave things now? I could tell a few more lies about you if I had to, although I'd rather not.'

'Well, everything is in the oven or waiting to go, except the pudding. I don't know where or what that is. I tried ringing Andi, but she's obviously in an area with no reception.' Jo went across to the wash handbasin and turned on the tap. 'What did you say was wrong with me?' She undid her apron and found the earrings, where she'd put them on the side.

'I looked embarrassed and whispered to Caroline about women's problems. They'll think it's a period.'

'Thanks a bunch.' She found a towel and dried her hands briskly. 'Couldn't you think of anything more embarrassing?'

'Well, I could have tried a stomach upset, but I thought that might reflect on the canapés. Now come on. Just let me check you. Lovely!' he said.

'Matthew,' she said quietly as they went upstairs.

'As I said, I can't get through to Andi and I need to know what the pudding is. If I know *what* it is, I've a better chance of working out *where* it is. Can you ask?'

'Don't worry, I'll find out,' he said.

When they entered the drawing room together everyone looked up, concerned.

'She's fine,' said Matthew, supporting Jo's arm. 'She just came over a bit faint.'

'You do look a bit flushed,' said Caroline. 'Come and sit down. Have a glass of fizz.'

'Actually, I'd rather have water,' Jo said. 'I've taken some tablets – I'd probably better not drink alcohol.' She felt a bit prissy saying this, but it would mean no one would press her to drink when she wanted to stay sober. She'd already had a glass of champagne.

Everyone else had had their glasses filled. 'I hope no one minded about not having presents,' said Caroline. 'There'll be a little thing for you all on the table, but that's pretty much it.'

Jo closed her eyes and swore to herself. Table presents. Where the hell would they be? She looked across at Matthew who, having finished pouring champagne, came and sat next to her.

'So, are there place names?' he said. 'I might go and put them round for Andi. She won't have time.'

'Yes, there are and they're in my desk drawer, with the presents and the list about where people are to sit. Pink for girls, blue for boys.' Caroline laughed. 'Bit of a cliché, but it seemed easier.'

'You should have let us bring you presents,' said a man called Justin, 'but you were so strict about it, none of us dared.'

'I'm not the easiest to buy for,' said Caroline. 'I prefer to buy my own presents.'

'I can think of something you might like,' said Justin suggestively.

Caroline glanced at Matthew and then said, 'I bet you can, but we'll leave that for later, hmm?'

Matthew got up and left the room.

Without Matthew there to do it for her, Jo felt she should try and find out about the pudding herself.

'So,' she said, 'what are we having to eat? I feel quite hungry now that I'm feeling better.'

'A lovely terrine, followed by a three-bird roast,' said Caroline. 'Ubiquitous, but delicious.'

Jo knew this much. 'And a traditional Christmas pudding to follow?'

'With custard?' said Justin. 'I love custard.'

Jo sighed inwardly. Did he mean proper custard or Bird's? Probably Bird's. It was a man-thing. But as long as Caroline had Bird's in the cupboard, she'd make it.

'The pudding is a surprise.' Caroline laughed. 'But a really good surprise! Possibly a bit explosive.'

Jo was annoyed that she knew no more than she

had before, but it ruled out a flaming pudding and holly, which was something.

'Are you being clever there, Caroline?' asked Justin, looking thoughtful.

'Maybe, just a bit.' She laughed coyly. 'I know you're a fan of crossword puzzles.' She made it seem like a secret and faintly wicked vice.

'I love surprises,' said Cindy, ignoring the crossword reference – it obviously wasn't a vice she indulged in. 'I really want a surprise party, but so far Max hasn't done one for me.'

'It's not going to be a surprise now, is it?' he said. 'If you've asked me to do it.'

Jo, not much caring what sort of parties people she didn't know had, was thinking. Had Caroline actually told her what the pudding was? The moment she could escape again, she'd have a look in the many freezers. She might find what she was looking for.

A discreet glance at her watch told her she should really get back into the kitchen. She needed to baste everything and poke the roast with the thermometer. She got up. 'Excuse me,' she whispered to Caroline, 'I need to find my handbag. I left it downstairs.'

Caroline raised an eyebrow, but although it was embarrassing to have her think she was having a period, it was as good an excuse as any for getting out of the room. As she left she heard one of the younger women say, 'So, tell me? Did he really appear on the main stage at Glastonbury?'

Who the hell were they referring to? she wondered. Maybe the Formula One guy was in a band or something. How odd!

After a cursory glance in the oven to check all was well, Jo went out to the big chest freezer. If she'd worked out Caroline's not-very-subtle crossword clue, she'd find it in the big freezer and not the upright in the kitchen. And yes! There it was, a Bombe Surprise. Good for Andi.

She took it out and studied it through its layers of wrapping. She decided it had a chocolate shell with something underneath. It could be ice cream or it could be mousse. She couldn't tell by looking, but mousse seemed the more sophisticated option. There was probably something gooey in the middle that would need to be at room temperature. She hoped she'd be able to work it out better later on.

She left it out, on top of the freezer. Later, she could check the defrosting process. Now she needed to spear the roast with the thermometer, to make sure it wasn't overcooking, and she hadn't got much time.

As she sprinted back to the house she reflected that it was just as well she'd really left her handbag downstairs. It was a very utilitarian backpack and not something Matthew's girlfriend would use to visit her boyfriend's mother's friend.

When Jo got back upstairs she was aware that she'd been away longer than she should have been. 'Sorry,' she said. 'Andi was having a bit of a nightmare in the kitchen. I gave her a hand.'

'You shouldn't have to do that,' said Caroline crossly. 'She's perfectly capable, and God knows I pay her enough!'

'I really like cooking,' said Jo truthfully. 'It's going to be a lovely meal.' Tell them that now and they'll be enjoying it even before they get to eat it.

It all went unexpectedly well. Caroline and the guests were no longer surprised at Jo being absent and she managed to get all the starters out, the candles lit, the fake fire lit and the dining room festive and cosy. Then she rushed upstairs.

'Andi says it's ready, if we'd like to go down.' She was a bit breathless.

'I know you like helping,' said Caroline. 'Matthew has explained that you're keen to learn cooking, but I think we should let Andi do the job on her own now.'

Jo nodded. She'd been told. She looked across at Matthew and caught the eye of Cindy, who seemed sympathetic.

'Andi has done brilliantly, though,' said Cindy. 'We usually hire a waiter when we've got this many for dinner.'

Caroline made a face. 'Have you any idea how expensive it is to employ staff on Christmas Day? Andi is my regular chef, so she is paid anyway.'

'But you'll have to give her a massive bonus, won't you?' said Justin. 'For working at Christmas?'

'I'm away a lot,' said Caroline. 'I won't be here for six weeks when I go to Necker for some winter sun. Andi won't have to do anything then. That makes up for working over Christmas, surely?'

Justin shook his head. 'Not really. You'll need to slip at least a monkey into her pay packet.'

Caroline looked horrified. 'A monkey? How much is that?'

'Five hundred,' said Matthew. 'I must say, Justin, that is a really generous suggestion.'

'That much?' Caroline couldn't believe her ears.

'That or a really expensive handbag,' said Cindy. 'I've discovered that if you're generous, your staff really stick by you. Our driver is getting a week in our London flat with his family – all expenses paid – for working today.' She suddenly looked embarrassed. 'It's what seemed right to me. They're taking the kids to *The Lion King*. We got them really good tickets. They've never been before.'

'I'm sure the extra cash would cover it,' said Matthew. He gave Caroline a smile. 'You wouldn't want to come across as a cheapskate or Andi might leave you, and she's such a great cook.'

Caroline became thoughtful and looked at her guests as if gauging the mood in the room. 'Oh, very well. I suppose I have spent more than that on a handbag before now.' She paused. 'But if I'm going to give her such a big bonus, I insist that she serves the pudding.'

Jo smiled. 'I might just help bring in the plates and things.'

Caroline raised her eyes to heaven.

Jo couldn't avoid absenting herself yet again, but this time she felt Cindy's sympathy follow her, which helped. She went to the garage for the pudding.

Back in the kitchen, she unpeeled the silicone mould carefully and regarded the Bombe Surprise. It looked like a huge Tunnock's teacake – 'None the worse for that,' she said out loud. Then she found a skewer and very carefully made a hole in the top of the pudding and inserted it. It went through nicely and came out again with some salted caramel on the end. 'Hmm, delicious,' she said. 'Well done, Andi.'

Then she wrapped a bit of kitchen foil round the stem of a sprig of holly and inserted it in the hole.

Suddenly the pudding looked festive and Christmassy. She was proud of it.

But the thought of bringing it in – actually pretending to be Andi in public, and most importantly in front of Caroline – was terrifying.

She knew Matthew would do all he could. He'd already moved up to sit by Caroline and, when Jo had last seen him, he was talking to Justin across the table, distracting Caroline, if not actually blocking the view.

She decided to bring the pudding in before the various forms of cream, the platter of fresh fruit and the cheese board. She checked that her chef's cap was pulled well down and picked up the plate.

Jo put the pudding on the table, her head turned carefully away from where Matthew had engaged Caroline and Justin in intense conversation. He had them both leaning into him, actually putting his arm on the table and curving his body around so that Jo was partly hidden. It was going to be OK, she thought.

Then one of the women's – Abbi was her name – voices rang out. 'That's funny – Andi has the same earrings as Jo!'

Before she could stop herself, Jo had glanced up at Abbi and found everyone looking at her.

'You're not Andi,' said Caroline, icily furious and getting to her feet. 'Where the hell is she?'

Jo cleared her throat. She'd been discovered, and

all because she'd forgotten to take off the earrings. And she'd done so well up till now!

'What the hell is going on?' demanded Caroline. 'Is Andi here? Get her up here immediately.'

'Steady on, old girl,' said Justin, patting Caroline's arm.

'She's not here,' said Jo croakily.

'So she ran off to spend Christmas with her family, did she? Well, she can say goodbye to her job.'

'Really, Caro, that is overreacting a bit,' said Justin. 'It's not as if she just didn't turn up. She did provide a replacement, who's given us some pretty fine nosh.'

Caroline glanced at him and then turned back to Jo. 'So, who are you?'

'Jo's a friend of Andi's,' said Matthew, obviously trying to save the situation.

'Let her speak!' said Caroline.

'Matthew is right,' said Jo, thinking to confess everything and then she could go home. Andi would have to take her chances at getting her job back. 'I am a friend of Andi's. She really wanted to go home for Christmas' – Jo managed not to say how vile Caroline had been about it all – 'and so she asked me if I'd step in and cook the Christmas dinner.'

'I don't understand,' said Max. 'Why didn't you and Andi just tell Caroline you were going to cook it, instead of her?'

Jo's mouth had gone completely dry. She longed

for a sip of water, but didn't dare pick up the nearest glass and steal one. 'Erm . . .'

Matthew weighed in again. 'Jo told me Andi was worried that it would give Caroline extra stress, if things weren't as usual in the kitchen at Christmas. Andi knows how much Caroline likes her cooking.'

Justin gave a shout of laughter. 'You mean you thought Caroline would go ballistic if Andi took time off when she'd been told she couldn't have it. I bet she threatened Andi with the sack, didn't she?'

Caroline shot Justin a glance, possibly trying to judge how he regarded this.

'No worries, darling,' Justin reassured her. 'I like a tough woman and, if I'm going to do business with someone, I like to know they're as cut-throat as I am. But it is Christmas, and we haven't been let down.'

Cindy looked at Jo with sympathy. She might be a racing driver's wife now, but she had probably had to deal with difficult employers in the past.

'Go on with your explanation,' demanded Caroline, glaring at Jo.

'There's nothing much else to say. I cooked the dinner instead of Andi, although she prepared a lot of it – this pudding, for example.'

Caroline made an irritated noise. 'I got that part. But you're Matthew's girlfriend! How can you be Andi's friend, too?'

'Isn't that just the most amazing coincidence?'

said Matthew to the table, as if was a wonderful thing. 'I asked Jo if she could spend Christmas with me, but she said no, she was doing a favour for a friend. When I came here and found her in the kitchen, I couldn't believe my eyes.'

'But why didn't you tell me?' went on Caroline, slightly less brittle now, but even more confused.

'Because—' Jo was about to confess that she wasn't really Matthew's girlfriend either, but he broke in.

'She felt you would feel awkward about effectively employing my girlfriend as your cook. And I agreed with her.' He gave Caroline a fond and slightly teasing smile. 'You would have done, wouldn't you?'

Caroline sighed. 'Possibly.'

'But the food has been superb, hasn't it?' said Abbi.

'Absolutely,' said Justin. 'You're a lucky man – er, Matt.' He winked at Matthew.

Matthew laughed. 'As I told you all, Jo and I haven't been going out long. I had no idea she could cook like this.'

Now Jo realised that Matthew had managed to keep up one of their pretences, she was happy for him. At least one of their subterfuges had worked. She was grateful too. He'd done so much to help her pretend to be Andi. She relaxed.

'Matt, darling,' said Caroline, holding his wrist

across the table, 'did you tell me: how did you and Jo meet?'

Jo tensed again, but left it to Matthew. He seemed to have taken to pretence like a duck to water.

'Oh, you know – what you'd expect.' Matthew laughed. 'It was at a charity do.'

Caroline joined in the amusement. 'You and your animal charities! I expect you to be opening a donkey sanctuary any minute.'

This was a bit of a shock for Jo. So he really was an animal-lover? Doing things for her charity wasn't only so that she'd cooperate with his mad scheme. It gave her a sudden warm feeling.

'Come on,' said Justin, taking control. 'Sit down, Jo, and have a drink. It doesn't really matter who's who. We've had a fantastic meal, cooked by you – come and join the party properly.'

'Yes, and take that ridiculous cap off,' said Caroline.

Jo obeyed her and sat in the chair that Geoff, Abbi's husband, found for her. She didn't know if Andi would keep her job, but there wasn't anything else she could do about it, and when they'd worked out the plan in the beginning they had both known that discovery was likely.

She accepted the large glass of wine that Geoff poured out for her. She had a teetotal friend whom she could ask to pick her up, if she had to. She raised the glass to take a sip when Caroline said,

'Actually, Jo, if you wouldn't mind serving the pudding first, before you get plastered?' There was enough chilliness in her tone to tell Jo that, if she was standing in for Caroline's cook, she'd better do it all.

She stood immediately and picked up the cake slice.

'Come on, Caro,' said Justin. 'That's a bit harsh.'

Caroline laughed, trying to pretend she'd been joking. 'Oh, you know, Jo's a professional – she'll know best how to serve it.'

'Just get it on the plates, girl,' said Justin. 'I can't wait to eat it.'

It took Jo a little time to relax into being a proper guest, although the wine did help. But the moment the first person got up to leave, she leapt to her feet.

'I'm going to revert to being Andi,' she announced, 'and clear up.'

'I'll help,' said Matthew instantly.

'So will I,' said Cindy.

'And me,' said Abbi.

With everyone, apart from Caroline and Justin, helping, it didn't take long for everything to be piled on to trays and carried to the kitchen. Cindy loaded the dishwasher as though she'd done it many times before; Abbi found the stripy apron and attacked the surfaces, while Jo and Matthew did everything else. Geoff and Max, having brought in the dirty dishes, went back to the dining room to carry on drinking port and nibbling at the cheese while they waited for their wives.

The kitchen wouldn't be exactly as it should be, Jo realised, but at least when Caroline came down in the morning (possibly to make Justin coffee to have in bed) she wouldn't feel obliged to have a screaming fit that no one could hear.

While they were all wiping and storing and stacking, Cindy said, 'Do you guys need a lift afterwards? We've got our driver, so we could drop you off somewhere.'

'Actually, I'd love a lift home,' said Jo. 'I'm shattered and am probably over the limit. I don't live far away – just about ten minutes from here. I could walk it, but I'd rather not.'

'Have your family been waiting for you to get back so they can open the presents?' said Cindy kindly. 'We did ours this morning.'

'My family are in New Zealand. We're going to have another Christmas when they get back, when we can all be together,' said Jo. This wasn't actually a plan, but it sounded a nice idea.

'So, what are you doing for Boxing Day? Putting your feet up in front of the telly, with a big box of chocolates? That sounds fab!' said Cindy. 'I sort of wish we didn't have to go my parents.'

'Actually, I'll be standing in for the regular helpers at the dogs' charity I support,' said Jo. 'So the staff can have the time off.'

'That sounds fun,' said Matthew. 'Can I come?'

Jo was a bit taken aback and didn't reply immediately.

'It would mean me staying over in this part of the world, so you might have to lend me the use of a sofa.'

She *really* hadn't expected this. He'd been incredibly helpful and kind and had even flirted with her a bit, but she didn't actually imagine Matthew would want to spend time with her. What she did know was that she definitely wanted to spend more time with him.

'Well,' said Jo carefully, 'it isn't huge, but the sofa is fairly comfy, and extra help tomorrow would be very welcome.' She smiled quickly at him. 'Then I can see if you can do more to help an animal charity than supply celebrities for events.' Even though the event in question would raise an enormous amount of money.

'Deal! Let's call it a day here, and get our lift.'

'OK, but we must go and say goodbye to Caroline,' said Jo. 'And I want to try and get her to promise that Andi will keep her job.'

'But she's gone upstairs and is probably making out with Justin on the sofa,' Matthew protested.

'Well, they can break off just for a moment, to say

goodbye.' She set off for the door and noticed Matthew wasn't following. She stopped.

'Really, there's no need to do that,' he said.

'Yes, there is. Andi's job is on the line.' Jo set off briskly, anxious to get this possibly difficult task out of the way.

Matthew joined her halfway up the stairs and they entered the room together.

Caroline and Justin were indeed on the sofa but not, currently, 'making out', much to Jo's relief.

'We've come to say goodbye,' said Matthew quickly. 'But we won't linger – we can see you and Justin want to be alone.' He took Jo's arm and made as if to hustle her out.

Jo stood her ground. 'Caroline, thank you for having me.' She decided that was appropriate – as Matthew's girlfriend, she had received hospitality. 'And thank you for lending me shoes and make-up.' She cleared her throat. There was no amused smile in Caroline's slanting eyes, and she'd been hoping for that. There had been a certain comedy in the situation, after all. 'And will you forgive Andi, and let her keep her job?' She nearly went on to say how much the job meant to Andi, but decided not to. Caroline was looking so frosty.

'I don't know,' said Caroline thoughtfully. 'I hate being deceived, you see. I find it rather difficult to forgive.'

'It was only fairly minor, surely,' protested Jo.

'Does it really matter who cooks your Christmas dinner?' She should have known by now that of course it mattered, but it was too late.

'You won't like it when you find out that *you've* been deceived, too.'

'Come on, Caro,' said Justin in a low voice. 'Keep it clean.'

'What do you mean?' asked Jo.

'Come on, love,' said Matthew, pulling harder on her arm. 'Time to leave these young things alone.'

Jo didn't move. 'Caroline?'

'That lovely young man you've snagged for yourself isn't quite the animal-loving innocent he pretends to be. Although, to be fair, he is an animal lover.' Caroline was smiling now, possibly at the prospect of Jo bursting into tears.

Justin broke in. 'Come on, woman – he swore us to secrecy!'

'Yes,' came voices from behind her. 'We all promised not to say anything.'

Now Jo did feel deceived. Everyone knew something about her supposed boyfriend except her.

'Maybe you'd better tell her, Matthew,' Caroline said. 'Unless you want me to?'

Jo turned to Matthew. He was looking down at her apologetically. Then he took her hands. 'You know I promised to get you Euan Donavan to do an event, so you could raise thousands for your charity?'

'Yes. Are you saying you can't get him, after all?'

There was a crack of laughter from one of the men, and the girls all giggled.

'No, I can,' said Matthew.

'Tell her!' said one of the men. 'Put the poor girl out of her misery.'

Matthew held her hands very tightly. 'I am Euan Donavan.'

It was just as well he was holding on to her. She might have fallen over otherwise. 'But how can you be? You don't look anything like him.' Then she thought about what Euan Donavan looked like. Grungy, beanie hat, meltingly gorgeous singing voice. She felt dizzy. It could be anyone under those clothes.

'Now you know how I feel,' said Caroline with silky triumph.

'I don't know how I feel,' Jo said truthfully. What she did know was that she didn't want to give Caroline the satisfaction of seeing her crumble. 'Except it's rather marvellous that my boyfriend has turned out to be famous.'

'So,' called someone, 'give him a kiss, to show there's no hard feelings.'

She caught Caroline giving her a quizzical look, as if Jo might now be daunted by his celebrity and not dare kiss him. But, of course, only Jo and Matthew knew it would be the first time they had kissed.

She reached up to him and pulled his head down to hers and kissed him firmly on the mouth. He

316

took up the challenge, wrapped his arms round her and took charge, kissing her thoroughly and intimately and – Jo realised – knee-weakeningly.

'I think that means you're forgiven, mate,' said Geoff.

Jo and Matthew exchanged looks. His expression was rueful, amused, apologetic. 'Am I?'

'Possibly – if you're still up for helping out with the animals tomorrow?' she asked. Or was that amazing kiss just part of his pretence?

He nodded. 'I'm absolutely up for it,' he said.

'Oh, for God's sake,' said Caroline, obviously put out that her big reveal had ended with a kiss, and not tears and foot-stamping. 'Both of you, get out of my sight! You're nauseatingly loved-up.'

'Andi's job?' asked Matthew. 'Secure?'

Caroline glanced at Justin and possibly read something in his stern expression. 'She can keep it. Oh, and Jo, you can keep the shoes. No one with any sense of style would wear them any more.'

'Come on, you guys,' said Cindy, 'let's find our limo and all get home. The driver needs to get back, even if we don't.'

After the car had left them at the door of the little terraced cottage that Jo rented, Matthew said, 'I know it's Christmas night, but if you don't want me to come in – let alone stay over – I can easily organise a lift.'

Jo had been worrying about bringing Matthew – Euan Donavan even – into her small and far-more-shabby-than-chic little home throughout the journey. Now she realised that if he'd taken one look at it and run, she'd have been devastated.

'I'd like you to come in. I'm not going to offer you half my double bed, obviously, but the sofa is quite comfy.'

'And we can snuggle up and watch a movie, before I sleep on it?'

'Sure. I've got some wine.' She put her key into the door. 'Come in. And you can tell me why you didn't want me to know you were famous.'

'It's to protect my family from all the nonsense, mostly,' he said, following her into the little hallway. 'And I didn't think you were the sort of girl who'd go for . . .' He hesitated, as if not knowing how to describe himself.

'Someone who performed on the main stage at Glastonbury?'

'You heard Abbi say that? I was so worried my cover was blown.'

'Join the club! You're not the only who had to spend Christmas in disguise.'

She switched on the fairy lights and the table lamps and went towards the fire. It was all laid; it just needed a match.

'Apart from deceiving you, which I hated,' he said, taking the matches from her and squatting down so that he could light the fire, 'I loved it all. It was so much fun, being with you.'

'I had fun, too.'

'So you'll consider being my girlfriend for real?'

She nodded. 'If you wield your broom and bucket well, and keep up that standard of kissing . . .'

He laughed and took her into his arms. 'That can only improve with practice – lots and lots of practice.'

Later, when she'd rather reluctantly left Matthew in front of the dying embers of the fire and gone up to her own bed, she got out her phone. Rather to her surprise, there was a text from Andi.

'Hope it all went OK and you don't want to kill me! I'll give you a really amazing Christmas present.'

Jo texted back. 'Don't worry, hon, you already did. He's about six two, dark blond hair and is currently drifting off to sleep on my sofa. Oh, BTW, his name is Euan Donavan.' Then she found an emoticon that meant 'very, very smug face'.

# The
# Christmas
# Fairy

Ella waited on the doorstep hoping someone would let her in soon. It was the day before Christmas Eve and trying to snow – not, unfortunately, in a way that would turn this little corner of Scotland into a winter wonderland, but in a way that just made it cold and miserable. She loved Scotland, and this part, Crinan, was her favourite, but she had to be honest. Although she'd added many layers over her top, including a parka with a furry hood, on her bottom half she was only wearing a tutu and stripy tights, and she was freezing.

Her grandmother, Ella knew, would say she

should have worn a thermal vest, to keep her kidneys warm. She thought about her grandmother now, preparing to spend Christmas with her parents, at home in Surrey. They would no doubt be talking about this mad business idea and sighing, half proud, half despairing. But they'd been doing that ever since Ella had decided she wanted to go to drama school, and even though she was now twenty-three they probably wouldn't stop.

Ella adjusted the tiara, which kept slipping down over her eyes, knocked out of place by the parka hood, and banged on the door again. The family weren't expecting her, but she knew it was the right address and she knew there were people inside, she could hear them. The Christmas spirit she had dug down deep to find was rapidly departing. She sighed. She had dragged two very large, very heavy suitcases behind her some little way from where she was staying, and she needed to get inside as soon as possible, before she froze to the spot.

At last the door was pulled open. A harassed-looking man glared down at her, and Ella's first thought was that he looked all wrong. When Jenny had enlisted her services she'd given Ella the lowdown on her three children and their uncle – Jenny's brother. She'd created an idea of what sort of man he'd be and he wasn't conforming.

He looked around thirty, not quite old enough to be an uncle, she felt, and he certainly wasn't jolly. For an uncle (in her book, always older with dubious breath and taste in tweed jackets) he was quite attractive. He was tall, dark and OK-looking, wearing a Christmas jumper she could easily have chosen herself. Pushing her tiara back yet again, she wondered if maybe she should have left it off until she was inside.

'Hello!' she said as brightly as any children's TV presenter. 'I'm Ella. I'm your Christmas Fairy!'

If anything, Brent Christy – and it must have been him – looked even more grumpy. It made her feel like an unwelcome trick-or-treater.

'Really?' he said, with the upward inflection that expressed complete incredulity. 'Is that even a thing? Well I'm sorry, I haven't got time for anything like that now. I've got a house full of kids, no central heating and no Wi-Fi, so if you don't mind—'

As he moved to shut the door again, Ella put her wellington-booted foot in the way so he couldn't. 'No! It's not like that. I'm not just a passing lunatic – your sister hired me. To help you!'

It was supposed to be a surprise, but a happy one. Jenny and her husband Graham had had to leave the country to go and look after his parents, who were elderly and lived in France. Graham's father had debilitating Parkinson's, and when his mother had had a nasty fall only five days before Christmas there'd been no one else around to help. It was a crisis situation, and it had chosen Christmas to occur.

The children had really not wanted to go with

their parents. Their grandparents' elegant apartment was too small for the whole family. Their mother had valiantly tried to find somewhere they could all stay but it was Christmas, everywhere was closed or full.

'It was then I had to ask Brent to step in,' Jenny had told Ella on the phone, obviously glad to get it all off her chest. 'And, bless him, he said he'd take the children up to Scotland, to where we were all supposed to be having Christmas. The kids are thrilled!'

But she had gone on to say that while she was touched and grateful she had felt it was a big ask for a younger brother and wanted him to have help. She had found Ella's website during a desperate Google search, trusting there would be someone out there who could assist. And she'd been right: the Christmas Fairy.

Annoyingly, instead of throwing himself on her neck in gratitude, Brent was just disbelieving and annoyed. 'Jenny did what?'

'Booked you your own Christmas Fairy!' Ella persisted. 'She found out about me and booked me to help you through the festive season. Please can I come in?' He didn't appear to even begin to appreciate his sister's generosity; Ella was getting very well paid for this gig.

He was resistant. 'It's really not a good time. We've had a very long journey, the kids are all starving and I can't find a corkscrew.'

Ella made a ta-da gesture to the suitcases. 'I can sort all that, if you only let me in.' Her smile barely disguised her gritted teeth.

He shrugged, as if to say that her presence could hardly make things worse, and let her drag the first of the suitcases into the house. After the initial shock, he finally seemed to remember some of his manners, and picked up the second bulging suitcase and brought it in behind Ella.

From the outside the house was similar to the others Ella had seen dotted around Crinan, but inside it was obviously a holiday let, which stopped it being cosy. Challenge number one, thought Ella, get some Christmas spirit in here!

A little girl of about seven appeared. This must be Mia, Ella realised. She'd been given a rundown on everyone so she could spread her fairy magic. Although she was tempted, Ella didn't think she should demonstrate her fairy magic by greeting her by name – that could be scary – so she just smiled. 'I've brought your supper! In my suitcase. How about that?'

'What is it?' The little girl gave her a stare that reminded Ella how unnerving small children could be. She wished she could say it was cupcakes for dinner.

'It's delicious!' She forced enthusiasm into her voice. 'It's boeuf bourguignon. It's got little tiny onions, squares of bacon, mushrooms, all sorts of delicious things. And on top—'

'I don't like stew,' said Mia.

Ella took a breath. 'But don't you like getting a big pile of mashed potato, turning it into a mountain range with your fork and making a lake for the gravy? Then arranging peas on top of the mountains to look like trees?' She paused to give time for Mia to picture the scene. 'Then, when you've done all that, you mash it all together with your fork and the potato tastes really yummy.'

She did realise that on the whole children weren't encouraged to play with their food, but she wasn't a parent-substitute. She was a fairy, and fairies were supposed to be subversive.

The tiniest hint of amusement lifted the corner of the un-jolly uncle's mouth. 'It sounds amazing,' he said. 'I'm Brent.'

'And I'm Ella.'

'Let me help you with your things.' He paused, his hand on the handle of the heaviest case. 'You weren't expecting to stay the night, were you? All the bedrooms are taken.'

'No, no,' said Ella hastily. 'I'm staying very nearby. Now, where's the kitchen?'

While she was unpacking the slow cooker containing the stew, which, thank goodness, hadn't leaked, an older girl appeared. She must have been Judith, sixteen and serious, who played the violin.

'Who's this, Brent?' the girl asked.

Ella put an ice-cream container full of very buttery

mashed potatoes on the counter. How would Brent describe her? He didn't have all that much to go on. She was looking very silly: stripy tights, sagging tutu, a lopsided tiara in her damp and tangled blonde hair. But she'd been given a job and she was going to do it.

'This is Ella,' said Brent, getting a tick from Ella for good manners. 'Your mother hired her. To help us.'

'I'm your Christmas Fairy,' said Ella, waving from the kitchen sink.

'A Christmas Fairy? What is Mum on? We're too old for fairies!' Judith was disgusted by the very thought.

Judith, Ella had been told by Jenny, had a very overdeveloped sense of responsibility and would turn into the 'third parent' given any opportunity. Her mother didn't think this was a good thing at Christmas: Judith should be allowed to be a child, or at least a teenager.

'She just thought it was all rather tricky for your uncle,' Ella explained. 'There's a lot of you, you're far away from home and staying in a strange house. That's a big deal at Christmas.' She let this summing up of their situation sink in. 'Now if you would all like to go away, I'll get supper on the table. You go into the other room – see if the fire needs another log . . .' She hesitated. 'Did you manage to get it going?' Ella had a bag full of firelighter's cheats she could produce if necessary.

'Yes,' said Brent. 'I'm not completely incompetent.'

'I didn't mean to imply anything,' said Ella, reminding herself that while he could probably be snappy with her, she couldn't retaliate. 'But you never know how well these holiday houses are set up for winter.' She was fairly confident, actually, given that they were in Scotland, where they knew about cold winters. 'I'll get your supper ready.'

Obediently, they went. Ella realised that Brent was rather young to be an uncle in charge of three children. (She knew there was a boy, who was fourteen, who was probably in his room, on his tablet, playing Minecraft. 'As long as it's only Minecraft,' his mother had said.)

Twenty minutes later she went into the sitting room. Brent, Judith and Mia had been joined by Bill, a good-looking boy with dark blond hair, carefully ruffled so he looked like a teen idol. They seemed awkward and unhappy, as if they didn't know what to do with themselves. Ella imagined the reality of the adventure – an unfamiliar Christmas without their parents – was beginning to hit home. But at least the wood burner was doing its job, and pushing out a fair amount of heat.

'Hi, guys!' said Ella, including Bill in her embracing smile. 'Supper's ready!'

Still despondent, they trooped back into the kitchen. There was a collective gasp, and then:

'Oh wow!' said Judith. 'You really are a fairy. It looks amazing!'

'It is kind of cool,' said Bill.

Mia, the youngest, was even more impressed. Ella watched her eyes shine as she took in the fairy lights decorating the walls, the candles on the table and the little figures apparently holding the dishes, the place mats like stars, and the cards with their names on in beautiful calligraphy.

Ella nodded in satisfaction. Desperate for money and something rewarding to do while she waited for her big break (any break, frankly) as an actor, she had conceived this idea of being a Christmas Fairy. The work was strictly seasonal of course, but she thought being a Valentine Cupid, or an Easter Bunny, could be a way to develop her business. Basically, she would be the person who would make any occasion magical. Brent's sister was her first client and she was determined to give complete satisfaction.

'It smells delicious!' said Brent. 'I didn't know fairies could cook.'

'It's the first thing they teach us at fairy school,' said Ella. 'Now I'll just pop off next door now.' She had the rest of the house to decorate.

'Won't you stay and have a glass of wine?' said Brent. He seemed disappointed to think she was about to leave them.

Ella shook her head. 'That's the second thing they teach us, don't drink on the job.'

She hoped they'd dawdle over their supper to

give her more time to work her magic; she had a lot to do in the sitting room. Her choice of pudding – sticky toffee pudding, one of the favourites listed by their mother – did the trick, and she was ready for them before they finished eating. She went back into the kitchen, pleased to hear happy chatter and laughter.

'When you've finished, there's a job that needs doing next door. I think you can see what it is. I'm going to clear up here.'

'No you're not,' said Brent firmly, not intimidated by her gentle-but-determined instructions. 'We'll all clear up. Come and show us what the job is.'

Ella could have argued, but preferred not to.

'A Christmas tree!' said Mia. 'With a zillion lights!'

'But no decorations,' said Ella. 'There's a box here. It's your job to decorate the tree.'

'And you've put lights up all round the walls and things too!' said Judith. 'In fact' – she took a few moments to take in the changes to the room – 'you've made it look amazing.'

Brent and Bill seemed outwardly less impressed but still happy.

'The lights will be handy if there's a power cut,' said Ella, knowing she shouldn't feel the need to justify herself but doing it anyway.

'Won't the fairy lights go out too?' asked Bill.

Ella shook her head. 'Most of them are battery operated.' She'd spent a small fortune on them but she'd known they were essential to create a magical Christmas.

'Is the power likely to go off?' asked Judith.

Ella gave a fairy-sized shrug. 'This is Scotland; anything can happen.' Having spent every holiday since she could remember in different areas of the country, she knew nothing was certain and she did like to manage expectations. 'Now, I should leave you to decorate the tree while I do the washing up.'

'No!' said Brent firmly. 'Fairies are an essential part of Christmas trees.'

Ella looked him firmly in the eye. 'I will help you decorate but I'm not climbing on top.'

He definitely twinkled. 'Glad to hear it!'

Ella relaxed her rules about not drinking on the job and accepted a glass of wine to sip while she helped with the tree decorating. Although they were reluctant   typical men   Brent and Bill soon got into placing the decorations. Ella had spent some hours on the internet sourcing them. Jenny, throwing money at this bad situation, had given her a big budget to buy anything she needed.

'I think that's the best tree we've ever had!' said Mia ecstatically.

'That's because it hasn't got all the home-made crap we've had for years,' said Judith. 'Cotton-wool-covered toilet rolls and goggle-eyed Santas made out of crêpe paper.'

Bill, equally impressed, nodded. 'And those really

heavy salt-dough stars covered with glitter that make the branches all bendy.'

Mia's face suddenly crumpled. 'I made that Santa, and I like our home Christmas tree better!' she wailed, her previous enthusiasm for the tree forgotten.

Ella had been warned this might happen. Mia was much younger than the others, Jenny had explained, and she was a bit clingy. 'Would you like a story?' she said, taking the little girl by the hand. 'It's a special story and it involves dressing up. Come with me. We'll go where we can be private.'

'Hey! I want to come!' said Brent.

Ella regarded him sternly. 'You have to dress up.'

'OK.'

'We'll come too,' said Judith. 'Come on, Bill.'

'Can I bring the wine?' asked Brent.

Ella didn't reply to this, she was intent on capturing Mia's interest so she would forget to be sad.

An hour later, everyone was weak with laughing and wearing a very strange selection of clothes. They had been donned to act out the various characters in a ridiculous tale, guaranteed to cheer up the most homesick child.

'That was brilliant!' said Brent, tipping the last of the wine into Ella's glass. He was wearing monster feet and a pirate hat, an eyepatch and a hook at the end of his arm. 'Who wrote it?'

Ella took off the fairy crown that was quarrelling with her fairy tiara and decided to go bareheaded from now on. 'I did.'

'Really?' If Brent had been surprised to see her when she first arrived on the doorstep it was nothing to his astonishment now. 'You wrote that?'

'I looked all over for something suitable but nothing seemed right. I had to have a part for everyone, you see.' She sounded apologetic.

'But you didn't know we were going to join in!' said Bill indignantly.

'No, you didn't!' his big sister agreed.

'I hoped you would. If you hadn't I'd have had to do all the parts myself, which would have been quite hard work. I did have a fall-back position.'

'It was probably quite hard work with us doing it,' said Judith.

'It was much more fun with you doing the parts,' said Ella.

Mia suddenly yawned enormously.

'I think you need to go to bed, Mia-woosy, it's almost nine o'clock,' said Judith. 'Would you like me to play you something on my violin?'

'Not really. You only play sad stuff,' said Mia.

'I don't! But a jig at this time of night would over-stimulate you,' said Judith, obviously feeling underappreciated.

Sensing a potential falling-out, Ella intervened. 'If you go quickly, I'll come and read you another story. A proper one this time, from a proper book. I have a few with me.'

'I'll read to her,' said Judith with a sigh. 'If she hates my playing so much. I quite often read to her and you must be tired, Ella. We'll ring Mummy and Dad when you're all tucked up, Mia.'

As Bill went upstairs with his sisters, possibly to listen to the story and join in the phone call to his parents, Brent and Ella were left alone. She felt suddenly awkward. She was here for the children, not for him unless he needed help with something specific.

'I should go. I think my fairy duties are over for the day. Lots more planned for tomorrow.' She got up and straightened her tutu.

'Please don't! Stay and keep me company for a bit,' said Brent. 'You've been so brilliant and I want to apologise for being churlish when you first arrived. I was a bit taken aback.'

She laughed and sank back down on to the sofa. 'I'm not surprised. Finding a fairy in a parka on your doorstep would be a shock for anyone.'

'I didn't know you could hire Christmas Fairies like you,' Brent went on.

'Well, I think I may be the only one. I thought up the idea a few months ago, when I just wasn't getting work as an actor. I felt I had to do something that was original and fun so I spent ages trying to find a service that people really wanted.' She picked up her glass, saw that it was empty and put it down again. 'I think maybe your sister will be the only person ever to hire me, but I'm very happy to have a client.'

'I'm sure that's not true – once word spreads that there's a fairy playwright available for hire you'll be run off your feet. Don't move! I'm going to get another bottle, unless you'd rather go on to whisky? Wine of the country?'

Ella shook her head, knowing she should go home but not wanting to leave the wood burner and, she admitted, the man currently in charge of keeping it going. 'Fairies never drink spirits. It's against the rules.'

'You seem to have broken a few rules already. Now stay there.'

While he was in the kitchen, Ella took a moment to check her appearance in the mirror over the fireplace. While not overly vain she was aware she'd been romping with children wearing a large selection of bizarre clothing, much of it animal-inspired, so she was bound to be a mess. Wishing she had the time and equipment to give her hair a wash and blow-dry, she did her best with her fingers before sitting down again. She'd been a mess for hours, she shouldn't really care.

'So,' said Brent when both their glasses were filled. 'How did you prepare for being a fairy?'

'Well, your sister was really helpful because she knew exactly what she wanted me to bring, and she knew what *you* might find difficult, especially staying up here.'

'Jenny did help bring me up, being quite a lot older than me,' Brent explained. 'But I think she forgets I'm now a thirty-three-year-old man – she thinks I still need my frozen pizza put in the oven for me.'

Ella laughed. 'No! She didn't think that, but she did think feeding hungry people after a very long drive wouldn't be easy.'

'So, she found you online, you said? And you happen to be based up here? What a coincidence.'

'No. But I know the area well and lots of local people. My family have had holidays up here – and in other parts of Scotland – for years. I put Crinan into my ad as one of the places I could be in.'

'That explains that then. And so what happened after Jenny got in touch?'

'She gave me details about all of you, what you liked, didn't like, and what was likely to cause problems. She told me Judith couldn't be parted from her violin, Bill mustn't be allowed too much screen time and that Mia might get homesick and miss her parents, so that's why I had the story all prepared.'

'I'm so impressed you wrote it yourself! With parts for everyone.'

Ella shrugged. 'Making stuff up is easy! It's real life that's tricky.'

'Actually, making up stuff is not that easy; not everyone can do it.' Brent frowned slightly. He looked as if he'd been about to say more but thought better of it.

'I did illustrations for it too, in case I couldn't get you all to dress up,' said Ella, partly to cover the awkward pause. 'But I'm glad you did. The interactive version of that story is so much better!'

'Can I see them? The illustrations?'

Ella shrugged again. 'If you really want to. But they're very basic.' She got up and found the pictures and brought them over.

'They're really good!' said Brent as he flicked through the pages.

'No they're not!' Ella looked at him as if he were mad. 'They're terribly naïve. I loved doing them though. Any excuse to buy new felt-tip pens.'

'Seriously, they're good! Better than a lot of the children's books I've seen. Didn't anyone ever suggest you should go to art school?'

'Not really. My heart was set on being an actor.' She brought her hand to her mouth suddenly. 'Whoops! Notice the past tense there? I still want to be an actor!'

'But not as much as you once did?'

Ella frowned. 'Really, you are asking a lot of questions.'

'I'm interested,' said Brent. 'I've never met a fairy before. I want to know how they tick.'

Ella looked at him, her head on one side. 'I'm not really a fairy, you know. I'm just pretending.'

'Never! You had me fooled! But seriously, I love these drawings and I love the story. I think you've got something, a real talent. Maybe that's the way to go rather than acting.'

'And I think you've had too much to drink and that it was time I was getting back.' She got up again, gathering up the folder with her drawings.

'I'll walk you home.' Brent got up too and Ella was suddenly aware of how tall he was.

'No! You're in charge of the children. It's really not far. I came on my own with those enormous suitcases.' She paused. 'Is it OK if I leave them in the utility room? But if they'll be in the way – or rather if you mind them being in the way – I'll take them back. They're not so heavy now.'

'Of course you can leave the cases and I will walk you back. Judith is sixteen, she can be in charge for a few minutes.'

'It's really not necessary!'

'I know. Just indulge me. I am "the client" after all.'

'Technically, you're not the client, your sister is, but I will let you walk me home. But first we must discuss tomorrow. When would you like me to come over? I can come any time but I do have to be here before bedtime because I have – elfly duties.'

He laughed. 'I think we'd like you to come in the morning.'

'For breakfast? Home-made crumpets are my signature dish – well, I can make them.'

'Wow. Aren't they quite hard to make?'

'Not at all – and even easier because I've pre-made the batter!'

'Come for breakfast. About eight thirty? Too early?'

'Not at all, as long as you don't need me to dress up as a fairy again.'

'I think your fairy credentials are well established, but having someone with local knowledge—'

'That's why I was hired.'

'Then come on. Let's get togged up in our arctic clothing and get you home.'

'So, how did yesterday go? I've been dying to find out!' asked Rebecca, the owner of the little house that was Ella's home for Christmas as well as the famous Crinan puffer. Ella had met Rebecca only once before, but had got in touch when her Christmas Fairy job became a reality. She'd been amazingly welcoming, insisting Ella stay with her over Christmas. She put down a jug of milk, along with a loaf of home-made bread, on the kitchen table in front of Ella. It was Christmas Eve morning.

'It was good, I think. The boeuf bourguignon was a hit, tree decorating went off with only a minimal hitch, and then the play swooped in to save the day.' Ella felt rather proud of herself, an unusual feeling, and she wondered if Brent might be right about writing, rather than acting, being for her? 'Thank you for all of this. I'm going over to make crumpets at eight thirty, but I'll need a gallon of tea and toast to sustain me before then.'

'All part of the service.' Rebecca had been brilliantly helpful when Ella was preparing for fairy duties. 'What are you going to do with them all today?'

'I've got loads of indoor stuff I can do with them if they want me to but it's a glorious winter day. I think we should go outside if they're up for that.'

'We've got some lovely beaches, although you would have to drive a little. Or walks over the moors?'

'I know about the beaches, but I'm not sure if they'd have the right shoes. If I was a proper fairy I'd magic some but, sadly, I'm only pretending.'

Rebecca stood up. 'Come with me! I am the real thing.'

Two minutes later Ella was looking at a row of wellington boots large enough for a small primary school. 'Wow! Where did you get all those?'

Rebecca laughed. 'Well, you know, it's like that

dog charity, we never throw away a healthy pair of wellies. And people donate them. Just like the dogs really.'

'But why on earth would you need so many pairs? I know you've got three children but—'

'For the puffer. When we visit some of the more remote islands, there isn't much for people to do once they've got there – and for puffer passengers it's often all about the travelling. So James takes them on hikes. That's why we need so many pairs of boots.'

'But lots of these are children's wellies—'

'I know, but once people know they've got a good home for their old pairs, they bring them all along.'

Ella laughed. 'If we need them, can I bring the family down to find a pair to fit them?'

'Absolutely! I've been dying to get a look at them all!'

Two hours later, Rebecca was granted her wish. They arrived sticky with golden syrup and slightly sick from eating too many crumpets.

'Oh, Brent is quite nice-looking,' she murmured to Ella as everyone tried on boots.

'It would be unethical for me to fancy him, though,' said Ella wistfully.

'Would it? Why?'

'Because I'm the Christmas Fairy! We don't fancy people!'

'To be honest, honey, there would be no point in fancying him if he was a fairy and not a person.'

Ella giggled. 'You know what I mean!'

'And I think you can fancy him if you want to, or if you do, if you know what I mean.'

Ella sighed. 'He's quite a bit older than me; we don't exactly run in the same circles. I probably won't ever see him again after Christmas, so no point.'

'You don't know that,' said Rebecca. But she gave Ella's arm a rub, indicating she understood and probably agreed.

Ella parked her car behind the big old Volvo that had brought the Phillips family from the south of England to Scotland. She retrieved her backpack, which had equipment for various beach games in it, including a microscope that she'd borrowed from her brother and a book about seaside life so there was no excuse for anyone to get bored, even if they didn't like playing rounders or beach quoits. She had more equipment in her car and many more ideas for activities.

The Phillips family exploded on to the beach, energised by the sight of clean sand and waves. Ella hurried and caught up with Brent. 'Good day for the beach, don't you think?'

'Definitely. Good to get them out of the house to have a run around,' Brent agreed.

'Good for me too,' said Ella. 'I mean, good for me in that I can tell Jenny that Bill didn't spend all the time playing Minecraft, or whatever.' She looked up at him questioningly. 'Hang on, I thought you said there was no Wi-Fi at the house? But he was definitely playing on his tablet when I arrived this morning.'

'You can play it offline,' said Brent. 'Now, I want to talk to you about something.'

'If it's plans for this afternoon I was going to see how everyone felt, but if they're up for it, I thought we could cook sausages over a fire. Here, on the beach. What do you think?'

'I think that's an excellent idea, but that wasn't what I was going—' He broke off. 'Oh look, another family. And they've got a puppy!'

Ella looked and saw a girl, who seemed to be a little older than Mia, running along with an Irish setter. Behind them, jumping and cavorting, was a puppy of indeterminate breed, and a couple who were presumably the girl's parents.

Mia instantly ran towards the puppy, which caused the other girl to approach them.

'I'm Kate. This is Rupert,' the girl was saying to Mia, indicating the Irish setter. 'We've had him since

345

before I was born so he's quite old now, and that's Hamish. He loves meeting people.'

'I'm Mia,' volunteered Mia shyly.

Judith and Bill knelt down at once so they could play with the pup, who made tiny whimpering noises as he jumped up to reach them. 'He's so sweet!' said Judith.

'Aye,' said the girl. 'But he does chew things.'

'You must be the family who are renting Arden House for Christmas,' said the woman. 'I hope you're having a nice time.'

'Great, thanks,' said Bill, who was also cuddling Hamish.

Ella noticed the girl look at him admiringly, and saw that Mia was looking at the girl, also admiringly. Ella decided to bite the bullet. 'Does anyone fancy a game of rounders or French cricket or anything?' she suggested.

The couple looked at each other, silently conferring. 'Well,' said the woman. 'You've time for a quick game, Kate. We'll take the dogs along to the end and back. If you'd like that.'

Kate made 'I don't mind' gestures that Ella interpreted as 'Yes please, but I just don't want to show too much enthusiasm'.

'So, rounders or French cricket?' said Ella, swinging down her backpack and rummaging about. 'Oh, here are some sausages. I thought they were in the car.'

'You have sausages in your backpack?' asked Kate. 'You're like my dad. He has things like that with him.'

The man shrugged. 'Never travel without a pound of bangers is my motto. Are you planning to cook them on the beach?'

'I think we are,' said Ella, 'if everyone's not too freezing cold. Would you like to join us? There's plenty.'

'What do you think, darling?' the man asked his wife. 'Fancy a hot sausage on a cold day?'

'I certainly do. But let's work up an appetite first.' She smiled. 'I'm Emily, by the way, and this is Alasdair. You know Kate, and the dogs.'

After an exchange of introductions and a quick run-down of the rules, there was a very hectic game of rounders that everyone joined in with except for Rupert, the senior dog, who observed it all from a safe distance.

Ella withdrew from the game early, and started to light a fire, using useful things from her backpack. (Rebecca had been very helpful, and generous with her firewood.) Emily joined her and found a good amount of dry driftwood. Soon the sausages threaded on sticks were sizzling away.

'You're very good at this!' Ella said to her, impressed.

'We like outdoor cooking and it's a good idea at Christmas, when there's always so much clearing up to do.' She paused. 'So, if you don't mind me asking, are you all related?'

Ella laughed. 'The children – young people – are Brent's nieces and nephew, but I'm the hired help.'

'Golly! You're good! Where does one hire someone like you? And what's your job title? Mother's help? Au pair? Surely you're not a nanny.'

'I think I'm all those things,' said Ella, 'but also party organiser. I'm the Christmas Fairy.'

Emily laughed. 'Is that a thing?'

'It is now. I invented it. I'm an out-of-work actor and wanted to find a way of earning something while I waited for an acting job. I've got a website.' She frowned. 'This is the moment when I pull a business card out of my back pocket, but I haven't got one. This is my first job.'

'So, how did you get it?' asked Emily, turning the sausages.

'Jenny – Mrs Phillips – was desperate and found me online. She and her husband had to go to France to look after his elderly parents. The children really didn't want to go as the grandparents live in quite a small flat. Brent offered to take on the kids and give them Christmas. Jenny thought it would be far too hard for him on his own and hired me.'

'And is it going well? If you don't mind me asking?'

'Brilliantly! I love them and I love being a fairy. It would be easier if I actually was a fairy, of course.'

She got up and brushed the sand off her knees. 'I'll just pop back to the car. I've got rolls for the sausages, and ketchup.'

❄

'I've never had a barbeque on Christmas Eve before,' declared Mia, wiping her mouth with the back of her hand.

'Nor have any of us, have we?' said Brent. 'I think it should be a new family tradition.'

'Eating on the beach is great,' said Bill. 'No vegetables.'

'You could have vegetables,' said Ella, wondering if she should have provided some and then deciding that no, fairies were for fun, not for broccoli.

'Except there aren't any beaches near us at home,' complained Mia. 'I like Christmas at home.'

Mia was shivering and her expression told Ella that a change of activity was required.

'Tell you what, let's take some seawater back to the house with us, and we'll examine it under the microscope,' Ella suggested. 'Brent will get the wood burner going and help you, and while all that's going on, I'll make special hot chocolate.'

'Why is it special?' asked Bill.

'Wait and see!' said Ella. 'And then maybe we can ring your parents, see what they're up to.'

'Probably something quite boring,' said Emily,

349

getting the message that Ella was trying to make the children's Christmas seem preferable. 'It would cheer them up to hear from you lot.'

'You can tell them about the barbeque on the beach,' suggested Kate. 'Are they near a beach?'

'Not very,' said Brent. 'But that all sounds like a plan. So, come on, guys. Seawater and hot chocolate!'

'Great combo, Uncle Brent,' said Judith witheringly.

'It's time we were off, too,' said Emily. 'Oh, and happy Christmas!'

'I do have to say, Judith,' said Ella, whisking hot chocolate in a pan, 'being the Christmas Fairy is a lot easier with you around. Not sure how I'd have managed without you.'

Ella glanced at the girl, who was leaning against the kitchen counter, staring into space. Ella could tell her heart, if not her mind, was somewhere else.

'Well, I'm glad it's worked out well for someone,' said Judith.

'Is it not working out for you? I thought we were having fun.' Ella managed not to sound resentful, although she'd tried so hard to keep everyone happy. This wasn't about her.

'It's not your fault, Ella. Even fairies can't sort out everything.' Judith sighed hard and then sniffed.

'Are you missing your parents? Worrying about your grandparents?'

'If it was that, I wouldn't feel so bad about not being happy!'

'So, what is it? Listening to people's problems is part of my remit.'

Judith couldn't answer immediately. Eventually she said, hesitantly, 'It's this party. I've never fitted in that well at school but I was invited to a party. There's a boy I really like and he'll be going. If I'm not there he'll get off with Sylvie, who's the girl everyone wants to be like . . .' Once she had started, Judith let it all out. 'By the time I go back to school they'll be a couple. No chance for me.'

Ella didn't rush to reply. She needed to think. 'I so remember that!'

'What, you? I can't imagine you were ever unpopular. You're so pretty and cool and everything!'

'Really, I'm glad you think that about me, but it's mostly pretend. I went to drama school. I learnt acting. And being cool is a lot about pretending that's what you are. People believe the act.'

'You haven't got spots.'

'Nor have you! At least, not more than a couple, and I had my share of zits in my time. Thank God for make-up, is what I say.'

Judith tried for a chuckle. 'I know I'm not the spottiest, or the fattest, but I am a bit fat and a bit spotty.'

'You've got a lovely figure! Trust me, men – boys – don't really care about girls not being a size zero. It's just not on their radar. What you need is a good old dose of confidence.'

'You've got a shot of that, have you? In your magic bag of fairy equipment?'

It was Ella's turn to sigh. 'Well, no. But it doesn't mean I can't arrange such a thing. It'll just take some thought, that's all.'

Although she kept up her air of the calm but constant provider of fun, her mind was churning away. She totally understood Judith and her disappointment. You get invited to the one party you want to go to and then you get dragged off to Scotland so you can't go.

And it wasn't just a case of her missing one party that was troubling her, Ella was sure. She did need her confidence boosted.

Having dispensed special hot chocolate – topped with whipped cream, marshmallows, chocolate sprinkles and the secret ingredient: popping candy – Ella left Brent in charge of the roulette wheel and gambling set she'd brought with her. The seawater seemed to have fallen by the wayside in favour of this more subversive but immediately popular entertainment. She needed to go back to Rebecca's, and Ella hoped Rebecca wasn't too busy to see her.

James, Rebecca's husband, showed her into the bedroom, without explanation. Ella went, worried she'd find Rebecca in bed. But no, she was sitting on the floor surrounded by wrapping paper and presents, a harassed expression on her face.

'Oh, hi!' said Rebecca, taking a dangerous-looking penknife out of the hands of her toddler, Nell. 'Did James headhunt you to help me? If ever I needed a Christmas Fairy it's now.'

Ella laughed and joined Rebecca on the floor. 'Well, no, I came because I need your help – advice really – but I'm more than happy to wrap.'

After Nell was handed over to James, instructions as to wrapping paper and items were delivered and another pair of scissors and roll of sticky tape were found. When they were ready Rebecca said, 'OK. What do you need?'

'It's Judith.' Ella went on to explain her party disappointment and her lack of confidence. 'I know you won't be able to do anything about it – if the Christmas Fairy can't help, I don't know what a mere mortal could do – but I thought talking it over might be useful.'

'Tell me a bit more about her,' said Rebecca, starting to stuff a stocking, having put an orange in the toe.

'She's quite reserved. I think she probably spends more time playing her violin than socialising, which is why it was so important for her to go to this party. She's very pretty – well, you've seen her—'

'She plays the violin?'

'Yup.'

'To what sort of standard? I mean, is she still just scraping away or can you recognise the tune?'

'Oh no! You can definitely recognise the tunes and I think her mother said she was Grade Eight or something.'

'You know what? I think the mere mortal can crack it this time!'

'What do you mean?' Although pleased for Judith, Ella would have liked to be the one to sort this out.

'My brother-in-law Alasdair – actually I think I heard from James that you met his family on the beach earlier?'

'Oh yes. They shared our barbeque.'

'Well, he's got a band.'

'I thought he was a doctor?'

'And he has a band! It just so happens they could use a fiddle player. It's for a gig tonight, and their usual guy has been – um, struck down, shall we say.'

'But how on earth—' Ella, although excited by the coincidence, didn't see how it could help Judith.

'I'm not sure,' said Rebecca, 'but leave it with me. I'll tell Alasdair, and, who knows, maybe they'll want her for the gig. But even if she only tried out with the band, before the gig, she'll have fun. They're a great group of lads, they'd make her feel special.'

'Especially if you told them they must?'

'That would help, yes,' Rebecca confirmed, 'and if they want some casual work on the puffer in the summer.'

Ella smiled. 'Well, it's a great plan!'

'You leave it with me and I'll be in touch. But if she's going to try out it'll have to be soon. It's an early gig, starts at seven o'clock, and it's four now.'

'Well, I won't say anything to Judith in case Alasdair says no way is he having some random teenager in his band.'

'I'll let you know as soon as possible,' said Rebecca. 'And thank you for helping me here. You're a demon wrapper, I'll say that for you.'

'I'm a fairy wrapper! They're the best kind! But please don't ask me to sing about it in rhyme.'

Ella left, Rebecca's laughter following her out of the room. She was smiling herself as she headed back to Arden House. She had a weakness for puns.

Ella hardly had time to wash the hot-chocolate saucepan she'd left soaking before there was a knock on the door. She went to open it. It was Alasdair, the man they'd met on the beach and – she now knew – Rebecca's brother-in-law. She looked up at him with a welcoming expression.

'Hello,' said Alasdair. 'I'm hoping you can help me.'

'I'm sure I will if I can. Why don't you come in?'

'I don't want to disturb you.'

Something about him made you instinctively trust him, Ella thought. It was probably something to do with him being a GP.

'Oh, it's all right. The family are playing roulette. Brent is a surprisingly good croupier. That's probably part of the job description for an uncle.'

Alasdair laughed. 'Then I'm afraid I'm not a good uncle. I have no gambling skills whatsoever.' He paused. 'I am in a band though.'

Ella sent him a conspiratorial smile. 'Which makes you perfect for my purposes.'

'Hello,' said Alasdair, walking into the casino-cum-living room. Everyone looked up. 'I'm hoping one of you can help me. I'm looking for a fiddle player.'

Judith gasped. 'What sort?'

'Well, it would help if you can read music, but I have a band and some of the things we play are traditional. Our violin player has a nasty case of D and V. Er – that means tummy bug.'

'Oh!' said Judith.

Ella studied her intently. Was she excited? Or terrified? Would she give this a go?

Alasdair went on. 'Ella happened to mention to Rebecca that you played, Judith.' He addressed her directly now. 'When she was helping Rebecca

356

with . . .' He hesitated, looked round and noticed Mia. ' . . . Christmas stuff.'

Ella was grateful he knew not to mention stockings. She'd asked Jenny if Mia still believed in Father Christmas and Jenny thought she did, but wasn't sure. The very worst crime in the Christmas Fairy rule book was breaking this trust.

'I play,' said Judith, half proud, half nonchalant.

'Would you be willing to help us out?' asked Alasdair.

'I won't be good enough,' said Judith.

'She's good enough!' said Bill and Mia together, openly proud of their older sister.

'I'm not!' said Judith, blushing.

'Why don't you go into the kitchen and play something for Alasdair?' suggested Ella. 'Then he can decide if you're good enough.' And if he makes the wrong decision, she thought, I'll arrange for his stocking to have nothing but coal in it.

Brent, Bill and Ella listened intently. They hadn't actually gone into the hall so they could overhear what was going on in the kitchen, but no one stirred.

First they heard a mournful 'Skye Boat Song' (her favourite, said Mia), and then a cheerier 'Marie's Wedding' when Marie did seem to be 'stepping gaily', and then something that made Ella want to cry although she didn't know if it really was sad or not.

' "The Parting Glass",' whispered Brent. 'I didn't know she could play all this!'

'Nor did I,' said Bill. 'And I live with her!'

Finally came an extremely fast and furious piece that no one knew the name of but was very impressive.

'Wow!' said Brent. 'She's brilliant!'

Judith and Alasdair joined them a little later. 'Well,' said Alasdair. 'If it's all right with everyone, Judith's agreed to help us for tonight's performance.' He glanced at Judith, who seemed illuminated from the inside. 'Sadly, she's refused to move up here and play with us permanently.'

Brent and Ella looked at each other. It was odd, thought Ella, that although they hadn't really had much to do with each other, they seemed somehow in tune.

'Well,' said Ella, 'if Judith is going to be playing in a band, I should be at the gig in case she needs a manager.'

'Good idea,' said Brent. 'No one will get anything dodgy past the Christmas Fairy, eh, guys?'

'I don't know if you're all really musical,' said Alasdair, 'but I've got a couple of guitars in the car. Fancy trying them out? One of them is a Fender Squier. Not the classic Fender but still a very nice guitar. Electric.'

Brent and Bill inhaled in unison, both extremely impressed. 'I used to play a bit of guitar,' said Brent. 'I'd love a go! What about you, Bill?'

'Oh. My. God,' said Bill.

Alasdair looked apologetically at Mia. 'I don't suppose you fancy some female company, do you? I've left Kate with Rebecca and, while she likes her cousins, Archie and Henry are only boys and Nell is too little. Would you like to save her from an evening of noisy computer games, Mia?'

If Ella really had been a fairy, she decided, she would have arranged for Alasdair to be rewarded with his weight in rubies. Her own instincts, backed up by the look of ecstasy on Mia's face, told her this would be very heaven for her.

'It won't be a late night,' said Alasdair. 'Should have everyone back by nine. Is that OK?' He addressed Brent for confirmation.

'I'm sure it's past Mia's bedtime,' said her uncle. 'But on Christmas Eve we can be a bit more relaxed, I'm sure.'

He obviously wasn't all that sure but Judith nodded. 'It's always later on Christmas Eve to make sure we all go to sleep easily.'

Mia, who'd been very happy at the prospect of spending an evening with Kate, suddenly looked worried. 'We will still hang up our stockings, won't we? Father Christmas – I mean . . .'

'Oh yes,' said Ella firmly. 'Father Christmas always knows where to go.'

It was arranged that Alasdair would pick up Judith and Ella in an hour, while Brent and Bill would take Mia to Rebecca and James's house to join Kate.

Ella extracted her make-up bag from the now very untidy suitcase in the utility room, and took Judith upstairs to the bathroom. When Judith's hair had been washed and mostly dried, Ella sat her down in front of the mirror. When she'd repositioned the bedside light so she could see better she set to.

'Do you wear make-up usually, Judith?' she asked.

Judith ran her hands through her hair, giving it a tousled look Ella rather liked. 'Well, a bit. But I'm not really into it. When I put it on it just looks silly.'

'I'll help you. It's just you'll be in the spotlight a bit, and when you put up a video on Facebook you want to be looking good.'

Judith didn't reply but seemed thoughtful. Ella went on, 'The thing is, it was pants that you couldn't go to that party, but it would be good if everyone knew you were doing something really cool instead.'

'Not all my friends know I play the violin. It makes me look nerdy.'

'Well, now it's time to show them how cool you are – you're an amazing violinist! I'm not going to do anything extreme, just bring out your lovely eyes, and put on a bit of lippy.' Ella concentrated as she applied eyeliner. 'But you're not worrying about doing this?'

'I should be, I know,' said Judith, trying not to

blink. 'Musically, I think I should be fine, going on what Alasdair said. But apart from exams and the odd little concert my music teacher arranged, I haven't performed, really.'

'That's about as much as I've done, to be honest,' said Ella, 'although we did put on quite a few plays and things at drama school. But you're with a band. You only have to connect with them and smile at the audience when you feel you can. Now, how does that look?'

'I look amazing! Me but better. Thank you so much, Ella. You're the make-up fairy!'

'YouTube taught me all I know,' she said modestly, feeling very pleased with her efforts. 'Now, what are you going to wear?'

A little while later, Judith, having decided on a V-necked pullover and jeans, said, 'Honestly, it would be easier to just put on a ballgown than it is to work out an outfit that looks like I've just thrown it on.'

'You are so right,' said Ella, searching through her own supply of scarves (her motto being there is no such thing as too many). 'But I think this pale blue number will just lift it.'

She looped a pale blue scarf round Judith's neck. 'You see? It brightens everything up without making it look like you've made an effort.' She paused. 'And if you get too hot, just take it off and throw it into the crowd! There'll be a stampede to get to it.'

Judith giggled. 'I don't think so, but I do think it's pretty.' She paused. 'I really want Mum and Dad to be proud of me, so I hope someone does film it. They've spent loads on lessons for me. It would be good for them to see me actually playing, for a band.'

Ella nodded. 'Have phone, will film. And you're right, apart from paying for the lessons thing, which I'm sure they were happy to do. We could email the link to them. It would be nice for them to see you having a good time even if it is without them.'

'Yes. I know Mum really hated having to have Christmas away from us.' She sighed but then looked up. 'But playing with a band is pretty cool! Even if it's up here, where no one will ever hear it.'

'You never know,' said Ella. 'They might have a good fan base. If I'd remembered to ask them the name of the band, we could look them up!' She heard a knock on the front door. 'That'll be Alasdair. We'd better go down.'

Ella sat in the front of Alasdair's estate car while Judith squashed in the back with two other members of the band. There was a van full of equipment and more band members following on.

'Hey!' said Ewan, who, Alasdair had told them, was lead guitar or squeeze box, depending, and about eighteen. 'I was stoked when Alasdair said we had a fiddle player. I'd have been even more thrilled if he'd told us how pretty she was.'

Ella smiled to herself in the front seat. Either Rebecca had done her work well and had told the band that Judith needed a confidence boost, or she personally had done a really good job on styling the fiddle player. She had had very good material to work with, she knew. Judith *was* really pretty and now looked even prettier.

'You'd better see how I play first,' said Judith.

Yes! thought Ella. She's going to be fine!

'Alasdair's a fussy guy. He wouldn't let you within a bar of us if he thought you couldn't play,' said Ewan.

'Someone needs to have standards round here,' said Alasdair, laughing.

'What an amazing house!' said Ella as they drove up the drive towards a huge Scottish Baronial pile.

'It's like a hotel!' said Judith, sounding anxious.

'It's "the big hoose",' said Fergus, who played percussion and harmonica – sometimes, he had boasted, at the same time. 'The owners put on a big party for the locals on Christmas Eve. We're the entertainment. It's a great tradition. But it is a bit spartan inside: these old houses cost a fortune to keep up and you're only warm if you're next to a fire.'

'Still, the room where we perform is great,' said Ewan. 'Big but not so big we won't fill it tonight.'

'Oh God,' muttered Judith.

'Good acoustics, too,' said Alasdair. 'I'll drop you lot off by the door and then park. The van will need help unloading. Judith, you don't have to do that, you're already doing us a favour.'

'I'll help!' said Judith. 'If I'm part of the band I must do the same as everyone else.'

'I'll be a roadie,' said Ella. 'It won't be the first time.'

Half an hour later, Ella was in the front row feeling extremely pleased with her Christmas Fairy achievements. Most of the success of the 'cheering up Judith' mission was down to Rebecca and Alasdair's band, but seeing Judith blossoming was delightful. The band treated her like one of their own. They teased her gently, but in a way that Judith could respond to, giving back as good as she got. She was glowing, maybe with excitement or even a bit of embarrassment at their remarks, but whatever the cause, it made her extremely attractive.

The fact that she was a very good violin player, who could sight-read brilliantly, helped a lot. Judith could relax into the music, knowing she was above the standard really required. She was part of a team and holding her own. Ella felt her work here was done.

So now Ella watched them finish setting up, see-ing Judith laughing at some joke Ella couldn't quite hear, thinking that being a Christmas Fairy was a very satisfying job. But at the same time she knew it wasn't really a career.

She was wondering if it would be wrong to go to the bar and buy a bottle of San Miguel, when some-one sat down next to her. It was Brent. Ella was thrilled to see him.

'Brent! What are you doing here? Aren't you look-ing after Bill? I know Mia was catered for but—'

'Relax! Bill, with those amazing guitars, is happily "putting down some tunes" with a neighbour's son, who's a bit older and was very happy to have the opportunity to escape from his parents' drinks party and go over to Rebecca's.'

Ella bit her lip. 'I bet Rebecca and James were supposed to be at that drinks party – or here at this one – and couldn't go because we left Mia with them.' Guilt flooded over her, punishing her for her smugness. 'I should go back! You can look after Judith.'

'Calm down, miss!' said Brent, laughing. 'You seem to have forgotten that Rebecca was already babysitting Kate and she's got a toddler of her own! I did offer to stay and look after everyone so she and James could come here but Rebecca said she had far too much to do and was grateful to Kate and Mia for keeping Nell amused.'

'Oh.' Ella's moment of panic subsided. 'That's all right then.'

'Now, let me get you a drink?'

'Thank you! I shouldn't really but I was just longing for a bottle of lager.'

'Look at Judith,' said Ella proudly after the first set. She and Brent were watching the video she'd made on her phone. 'She's really holding her own with the band.'

Brent nodded. 'She's very musical and really looks the part.'

'We can email this to Jenny,' said Ella. 'They will have been so sorry to miss Judith's moment of triumph.' She paused. 'She can also put it on Instagram or whatever she uses, so all her school friends can see it.' She smiled at Brent. 'They will be so jealous!'

Brent laughed. 'You really enjoy making everyone happy, don't you?'

'I do! But it's my job.' She became thoughtful. 'I may have got the kids sorted out but I haven't done anything to make your Christmas special. I was hired to help you too, if you needed it.'

Brent smiled down at her. 'There are ways you could make my Christmas special but I'm not going to mention them.'

Ella blushed, slightly regretting his last statement.

'I didn't mean anything like that!' she said indignantly.

'I know you didn't, but honestly? Having you with us has been amazing. Where did you learn to cook?'

Ella, relieved to be on safe ground, said, 'When you're an actor, you take a lot of different jobs. I've worked in some quite good restaurant kitchens and paid attention. I'm not brilliant though, as you'll find out tomorrow when I cook you Christmas dinner.'

'I'm sure it *will* be brilliant. But tell me, what is your favourite job, in between acting roles?'

'It's all in between acting roles because I haven't had any. Maybe I'm not much good, which is why I never get the parts. But having bothered to go to drama school I feel I can't give up on acting just yet. I love bar work. It's fun when it's busy, and when it's not busy, I love wondering about the people, making up stories for them.' She laughed. 'Sometimes, when I get to know them, it turns out I've been quite right!'

'Making up stories again – it's becoming a theme. And do you tell them you've been speculating about their private lives?'

She shook her head. 'No, but I do sometimes show them the sketches I've done of them. If they're not too beer-stained and blotchy.'

'I bet they love them!'

Ella nodded. 'I did suggest I sat up one end of the bar and did drawings of the punters but my boss couldn't see how he could make money out of it. They wouldn't drink much while they were sitting for me and I'd get the money for the sketch.' She smiled. 'So I stayed a barmaid.'

Brent looked down at her for a moment and seemed about to say something when a sound from the stage indicated the band was going to start playing again. The moment passed.

'That was so awesome!' said Judith as they drove back home with Brent. 'I never would have thought I could do something like that!'

'There you go!' said Ella. 'I said you were a brilliant fiddle player.'

'I know you set it up with Alasdair,' said Judith. 'They'd have managed without me, but I know I made it better. And they said if I could ever get up here and play with them again, they'd love to have me.' She stopped for breath. 'They even said they'd get in touch with bands down south and give them my contact details.'

'Maybe you should get your exams out of the way before you do too much,' said Ella, suddenly imagining how Jenny would feel if her clever daughter gave up everything to join a band because of what happened while she was in the care of the Christmas Fairy.

'But well done, Judith,' said her uncle. 'You were

really great. Your mum and dad will be so proud of you.'

'I expect you wish they could have been here to see you up there,' said Ella.

'Actually, not really,' said Judith. 'I would have felt a bit embarrassed. They've only ever seen me do classical stuff.'

'Now they'll know how versatile you are,' said Ella. 'Brent? Could you possibly drop me off at the house before you pick up the others? I've got things to do.'

'At this time of night?' Brent was surprised.

'It's Christmas Eve and I'm the Christmas Fairy, of course at this time of night!'

'Oh!' He frowned slightly, a bit guilty. He had obviously been going to ignore the stocking issue. 'I'm so glad you're here.'

Judith got dropped off too and agreed to stir the hot chocolate while Ella went upstairs. Judith was still in a happy bubble and, because of this, Ella was fairly happy too.

She quickly laid out the long knitted shooting socks that Jenny had provided, these being what they always used as Christmas stockings. She hoped that Mia wouldn't mind not being the one to do this but trusted that Judith and Bill would be able to jolly her out of any grumbles she might have.

Ella went downstairs to find the rest of the family in the kitchen, holding their hands out for mugs of hot chocolate.

'We had so much fun!' said Mia ecstatically. 'Christmas in Scotland is so much better than it is in England. They eat stuff called black bun.'

'The other day you were saying you liked it better at home,' said Bill.

'Don't remind her!' said Ella. 'Now, it's really late. It's time you lot were in bed.'

'We have to put a mince pie and a glass of sherry out for Father Christmas,' said Mia. 'And a carrot for the reindeer.'

Ella realised with horror that her reputation as the Christmas Fairy was going to be spoilt. She had no sherry.

'Actually,' said Brent, possibly interpreting her look of shock, 'in Scotland, Father Christmas prefers to drink whisky.'

'And we have some lovely home-made mince pies,' said Ella, who had even made her own mincemeat.

'At home we have Waitrose mince pies,' said Mia reprovingly, possibly not trusting that the home-made variety was good enough for such an important visitor.

'He must get thousands of Waitrose pies,' said Bill. 'He'll much prefer a home-made one. Can we have one now to test them?'

Ella beamed at Bill as she opened the tin. Mia, who was obviously very tired, was now happy that Father Christmas would enjoy his snack.

'And there are some jam tarts if any of you don't

like mincemeat,' said Ella. Everyone looked at her as if she were mad. 'Oh, just me then,' she said.

Eventually everyone had their teeth more or less brushed and was in bed. Ella sank on to the sofa and closed her eyes.

'You look exhausted,' said Brent. 'Let me walk you home.'

Ella shook her head, her eyes still shut. 'Nuh-uh. I can't go home until I've done a little favour for Father Christmas. He's so busy at this time of year I like to help out when I can. But everyone has to be asleep first.'

Brent laughed. 'Well then, let's share a dram and sit by the log burner.'

He got up to get the whisky but when he came back, Ella was on the verge of sleep. 'You just have a wee nap then,' he said. 'I'll check on the kids and tell you if it's safe to go up a bit later.'

'Thank you,' mumbled Ella.

'I think you could go up now,' said Brent softly.

Ella woke up. 'That was the most heavenly power nap I have ever had,' she said. 'I'm so sorry. You must have thought me dreadfully rude.'

'For not making polite conversation until midnight?'

'Is it that late? Golly, those kids have got stamina. Remind me never to go clubbing with them.'

'I definitely will remind you.' He was smiling. 'Now you go up and do your thing. We've got a big day tomorrow.'

'Oh, that reminds me. When do you usually open presents? First thing? After breakfast?' She didn't imagine they'd wait too long.

'After lunch,' said Brent.

'After lunch?' Ella was astounded. 'Amazing!'

'When Jenny and I were little we had to wait until after tea!' said Brent. 'But we ate the turkey at about six, so we didn't have that to go through first.'

'Poor little children!' said Ella. 'I'll make sure we're not a second late getting the meal on the table.'

When Ella had laid each carefully labelled and extremely fat stocking on the appropriate bed and come back down, she took the glass Brent offered her. 'This is nice,' she said, having taken a sip.

'It's a single malt from just across the way in Jura,' said Brent. 'Did you have to buy all the things for the stockings?'

'No, only a few little fillers and the chocolate oranges. Jenny did it all and had it Fedexed to me, with the actual stockings. She put each one's presents in a labelled bag.' She took another sip of the drink that felt like liquid gold, filling her with power, as if it were a magic potion. 'There were a few little mix-ups – not sure Bill would have really appreciated Frozen bubble bath!'

'Not at this time of year, anyway,' said Brent.

Ella laughed. 'Now I must be off. What time do you want me in the morning? And what time do you want your Christmas dinner? Please don't say one o'clock sharp!'

'Oh no. We never seem to get round to the turkey until about three. I'll do breakfast, but then we need you quite early.'

She laughed. 'You won't need me when you're all opening stockings and things.'

'I'll need you when I want to open the champagne, which will be about ten.'

'Not Buck's Fizz? I'm sure Jenny said you had Buck's Fizz.'

'I never add orange juice to champagne. I avoid extra calories when I can.'

Ella punched him gently on the arm and went to find her coat.

Ella arrived just before ten o'clock. There was a fair amount of hilarity and jolliness going on but Ella made a point of giving Mia a hug.

'Good stockings? Father Christmas come up trumps?' she asked.

'Oh yes. He knows what we all like,' said Mia.

'And the others? Did they have things they liked?'

'Uncle Brent's stocking was a bit random,' Mia said, frowning slightly. 'But he really liked getting one.'

Ella suppressed a chuckle. Doing a stocking for Brent had been a fairly last-minute decision. It included a caricature she had done of him from memory, on the back of a postcard. He'll know it's from me, she thought, but then realised he was unlikely to think it really was from Father Christmas – not at his age.

'I've got to get this turkey crown into the oven fairly soon, so, since you don't do presents until after lunch, I suggest you all go for a walk on the beach or somewhere, work up an appetite, while I do the sprouts and potatoes.'

The family, coincidentally standing in height order, with Brent at one end and Mia at the other, stared at her as if she had just announced she was the Queen of England and was about to give them all knighthoods.

'I don't think so!' said Judith.

Mia shook her head, sad that Ella could have said something so stupid.

'Not how we do things,' said Bill.

'We'll all go for a walk,' said Brent firmly, 'then come back here for drinks and veg prep.'

'When we were little,' said Mia, who at seven was obviously very grown up, 'we were allowed one big present *before* lunch.'

'But we're not going out and leaving you with all the work,' said Judith. 'You've been so kind to us all!'

'That's you told then,' said Brent, smiling down at her.

Inside, Ella was delighted, but as the Christmas Fairy she felt she should protest. 'But the turkey crown doesn't need to go in until eleven, not if you want to eat at three. It would mean hanging about a bit until then.'

'We can start the veg now,' said Judith.

'And the drinking,' said Bill. 'I'm allowed a beer on Christmas Day, and some wine if I'm sensible.'

'OK,' said Ella, seeing she was outnumbered, 'but I suggest you all open one big present to keep you amused while I cook.'

'That's a brilliant idea!' said Mia. 'I know just which one I'm going to choose.'

'We're all going to help!' said Judith. 'I thought we explained.'

'All right!' said Ella. 'If we're all chopping and peeling and putting little crosses in the bottom of the sprouts – if that's your tradition – shall we have some music on while we do it? We can have a sing-along. I brought my iPod. It's got a good Christmas compilation on there.'

'Christmas carols?' asked Bill.

Ella couldn't tell from his expression if he wanted to sing carols or not. 'Some carols, some nice folky things you might know and, of course, Wizzard and all those Christmas favourites.'

'Cool!' said Brent. 'Now, I'm in charge of drinks. Ella, what do you want? Champagne? Whisky punch? A cocktail?'

'So can we open a present now?' said Mia, the moment she'd been given sparkling apple juice in a champagne flute.

'Of course!' said Ella.

'Have *you* got presents, Ella?' asked Judith, concerned.

'I did bring one present with me,' she said.

'Are you going to open it?' said Mia, obviously feel-ing embarrassed that she was so much keener to rip off wrapping paper than anyone else seemed to be.

'Sure am! Can't wait!' said Ella.

She knew what was in the William Morris

376

wrapping paper her mother favoured. It was a vastly expensive, long cashmere cardi. While on the surface her mother had been very grown up about Ella spending Christmas away from home, she had become sentimental at the last minute. 'I want to give you a virtual hug!' she had emailed, with a link to a website so grand it had 'Lord' as a title option when you ordered. 'Tell me what colour you'd like.' Ella had gone for Dragonfly, a wonderful zingy blue that made her think of summer.

It was half past two, the turkey crown had been tested and declared cooked, and was now resting in a Christmas parcel of its own, consisting of foil and as many towels and tea towels as Ella thought they could spare. The roast potatoes and – randomly – the Yorkshire puddings (Ella had not been prepared for this but fortunately found a bun tin that would do) were getting their final browning. The gravy was perfect, so delicious that Brent had declared he'd be happy to have only that and the roast potatoes for his festive meal.

Ella had agreed, and just for a moment allowed herself to dream of a time when it could be only Brent and her, about to sit down and eat together. She banished the thought firmly. They would never see each other again after this Christmas, and on the day after Boxing Day they would say goodbye forever.

Now, Judith was playing the violin (either to herself or to her family, Ella couldn't tell from the kitchen), and everyone seemed content. She was just putting the finishing touches to the table. She was wearing her wonderful cardigan, having had a slightly teary telephone conversation with her mother, thanking her for it, and Christmas was going perfectly.

Ella tested the lighting, making sure there were enough fairy lights wound round things on the table so people could still see to eat if the main lights went off, and yes, they definitely could.

She was peeping into the oven to check things for brownness when she heard a commotion.

She went into the hall and saw the front door was open. There was a car and a very smart couple hugging Mia and Judith while Bill bounced up and down on the periphery. It didn't take a Christmas Fairy to realise it was Jenny and her husband. They must have somehow managed to sort out the emergency with his parents and got up to Scotland to join their children on Christmas Day.

Ella's feelings were desperately confused. It was a magical thing to have happened. Little Mia would be so thrilled to have her mummy and daddy there for Christmas Day and the other two would be pretty delighted as well. Brent would be relieved to have the responsibility of looking after his nieces and nephew taken away. Everyone could relax. Christmas would be 'proper'.

She should be pleased too. She'd done a good job. She should go out now and let herself be thanked for all her magic. But then what? She didn't really have a place here any more. She'd have to go back to her little room at Rebecca's, and only after she'd said goodbye to everyone and probably cried. (She'd had enough champagne to make this a serious anxiety.)

She made a decision. Even as she acted on it she knew it was impulsive, but it seemed like the only thing to do.

First she squashed another place setting on to the table. It wasn't easy as the holiday home didn't have quite enough knives and forks and spoons for everyone to have all three, but after a bit of fiddling she managed it.

Then she took the wonderfully brown roast potatoes and the beautifully risen (not a given) Yorkshire puddings out of the oven and put them on the side. She wrote a quick note saying 'Goodbye and love from the Christmas Fairy', added a funny doodle so they wouldn't go hunting for her, and then she retrieved her boots and outer layers and her rucksack from the utility room and went out through the back door. And all before the joyous reunion was over.

She had intended to go back to her room but she was worried someone in Rebecca and James's house would see her. She'd be drawn into their celebrations and she didn't want that. Unusually for her, she wanted to be alone with her thoughts. When she came to the turn in the road, instead of going home, she set off for the beach. A good stride out would help her clear her thoughts and get the champagne out of her veins.

It was unlikely she'd see Brent or the children again. And while she did really like the children it was the thought of Brent disappearing from her life that was tearing her heart in two.

The fact that she was quite pretty and had a friendly, outgoing personality meant that Ella was never short of boyfriends. But her heart was rarely engaged. And something about Brent had disturbed this happy state.

As she walked, Ella tried to work out why. While he was pleasant-looking, he wasn't 'drop dead gorgeous'. He was kind, to her and to his nieces and nephew, but lots of people were kind. He also made her laugh, but she had a lively sense of humour and laughed easily. There was something more, a connection, that she couldn't put her finger on, that made the thought of not seeing him again seem so sad.

She had nearly reached the beach, having walked along the road, looking at the distant hills, undisturbed by any passing traffic, listening to the seabirds, when she came up with a partial reason.

They'd only spent a couple of days together, but he seemed to understand her, to see beyond the superficial, entertaining façade she kept up most of the time. He'd gone straight to the crux of her Christmas Fairy invention – her non-existent acting career – and made her realise that after Christmas it would perhaps be time to reconsider her options. He respected her abilities; he made her feel she was worthwhile, more than just one of life's ornaments. She could be herself with him.

She stepped on to the beach just as she heard a car; she was glad to be out of the way. The car was probably off visiting a relative, or taking a relative home, or going to fetch some forgotten present. She felt very alone, very far from home and so sorry for herself, she almost shed an actual tear of self-pity.

She found a rock to sit on and pulled her rucksack off her back. She would do a sketch of the beach. It would remind her of a happy time although tears began to fall as she drew. She wiped her eyes and cursed the champagne.

'Hey,' said a male voice. 'I thought I'd find you here.' It was Brent.

'Why?' she demanded and then realised she'd sounded a bit rude. She managed a smile.

'Because I couldn't find you anywhere else,' said Brent. 'Why did you run away?'

She shrugged. 'You know why. My work was done; I was surplus to requirements.' She paused. 'And there wasn't room for me round the table.'

He laughed and pulled her in for a hug. 'There's always room for the Christmas Fairy.'

'Only on top of the Christmas tree,' she said into his coat, loving the feeling of his arms around her.

'Well, there's not room for me round the table either. You stay here, I'm going back to tell everyone you're fine, then we'll have our own Christmas dinner. I'll bring the makings and we can have a fire.'

When he had gone, Ella felt there was no reason why she should wait until he got back for the fire. There was plenty of driftwood and she had paper, matches and even firelighters in her backpack. She set to.

'I can't believe you've got a fire going already!' said Brent a little later.

Ella shrugged, hardly able to keep the smile off her face. 'I am the Christmas Fairy! What do you expect?'

'I'll have to rename you the Firelighting Fairy, but I'm not without skills myself.'

He sat down on the rock next to her, took off his own backpack and took out some foil-wrapped parcels. 'Here's some turkey, sausages, stuffing, all the lovely things you made.' He brought out another parcel. 'Here's a baguette from actual France. Hope you're impressed. Some amazing cheese, ditto, bottle of fizz, bottle of red in case you're fed up with fizz, and some truffles, also from France.'

'Did Jenny think I was terribly rude, just running off like that?' said Ella, guilt washing over her.

'I think she understood and was so pleased to be able to be with her family she didn't really care. And with us gone, they can at least fit round the table.'

'I do feel a bit bad, but really it was time for them to be together as a family.'

'And they are all so excited about it! Nothing like a bit of absence to make people appreciate family life.'

'I'm glad.'

'Now, fizz or red?'

Ella thought about it. Champagne did make her emotional and she was already emotional enough, but the thought of sitting on this beautiful beach, with the man she loved, on Christmas Day, made the decision for her. 'Champagne, I think.'

'I'll open the bottle,' said Brent, and then frowned. 'Um, you don't happen to have anything to drink out of in that magic bag, do you? I meant to bring glasses but forgot.'

'Plastic beakers aren't quite the same as crystal

champagne flutes,' she said, handing him a couple, 'but they'll do the job.'

'I think they're a vast improvement on crystal champagne flutes,' said Brent.

'Really?'

He nodded. 'It means I'm on a beach, with you, which is very special. Now,' he moved on quickly, 'food. I didn't bring a knife – are you surprised? – so we'll have to just tear things. Shall I make you a sandwich?'

Ella did have a knife but decided not to mention it. She wanted to watch him tear things.

He put his arm round her for warmth, and they huddled together, by the fire, eating chunks of bread and turkey, sausages, stuffing and even a few sprouts. ('Otherwise it's not really Christmas,' Brent had insisted.)

'I think that was the best Christmas dinner I've ever had,' said Ella, wiping her greasy fingers on her jeans.

'I'm certainly never going to drink champagne out of anything but plastic beakers from now on,' said Brent, also wiping his greasy fingers on her jeans.

'Hey!' she objected, catching his hand.

He caught her hand in return. 'Cold little fingers.'

Seeing her fingers in his big, protective hand made her stomach lurch. Along with desire and happiness came a surge of melancholy.

'Have we finished the fizz?' she said, taking her hand back.

''Fraid so. Shall we open the red?'

'Yes,' said Ella. 'It's Christmas.'

'Thank God it's a screw top,' he said, having found the bottle, 'or we'd have been screwed, so to speak.'

Ella rolled her eyes. 'You think the Christmas Fairy doesn't have a corkscrew with her at all times?'

'You!' He kissed her forehead. 'I brought Jenny's present for you.' He produced a package wrapped in silver tissue paper, with curly ribbons and a beautiful sticker shaped like a unicorn.

'She brought me a present?' said Ella, delighted and surprised. 'From Paris?'

He nodded. 'Open it. Jenny insisted I bring it. If I couldn't bring you back.'

Reluctantly, in case she spoilt the sticker, Ella teased open the package. Inside was a pashmina, in a pink so delicate it was like dawn in a Scottish winter. She opened it out and it seemed enormous. 'Goodness, it's beautiful!' she breathed, aware it would have cost a lot of money.

'Here,' he said, having wiped his hands again, on his own jeans this time. 'Let me put it on for you.'

Tenderly, he wrapped it round her neck. Although

it was big the cashmere was so soft it settled easily round her, feeling like warm marshmallow. Where his fingers touched her skin she shivered, but not from cold.

She cleared her throat, banishing the threatened tears. 'What a really lovely present.'

'Later we'll go back, and you can thank her in person. We'll have to walk though. I must be way over the limit.'

'I walked here. It's not far.'

As she gazed at the sea and the islands beyond, Ella couldn't help feeling intensely sad. She wouldn't want to be anywhere else, with anyone else, and they'd had a wonderful time, but it was nearly over. Soon they would walk back along the quiet road, go into the noisy house, full of Christmas. She would thank Jenny for her wonderful pashmina and Jenny would thank her for being the Christmas Fairy. Later, she would go back to her little room at Rebecca's, and the following day, she would start the long drive home, never to see Brent again.

He seemed to pick up on her feelings. His expression was tender as he looked down at her. 'Come on,' he said, 'let's finish the bottle. We might as well be drunk as the way we are.'

'I thought we were already drunk,' said Ella, holding out her beaker all the same. She was determined to appear jolly from now on, no matter what she was feeling inside.

'Not quite drunk enough.'

She wondered if she picked up a wistful under-tone to this statement.

They started to shiver in earnest and decided to put out the fire and go back along the road to the family. Brent put his arm round Ella, hugging her close. They walked in unison but didn't speak. They had been so happy for a little while on the beach but now they had to return to real life.

The family was delighted to see them both. Jenny and her husband, Graham, told Ella a million times how wonderful she had been. Mia hugged her, and Judith gave her a look showing gratitude she couldn't find the words to express. Ella had arranged for her to have a really good time and increased her self-confidence enormously.

More drinks were offered, but Ella opted for apple juice this time.

When she'd admired everyone's presents and eaten a mince pie, Ella decided she must go back to Rebecca's.

'I've got a long drive tomorrow. But it's so brilliant you were able to get back to be with the family,' she said to Jenny.

'I was thrilled too. We sang "Driving Home for Christmas" all the way!' said Jenny.

'You did, darling,' said her husband. 'I checked for traffic reports.'

'So you don't mind if I go?' asked Ella. 'I know I was booked for Boxing Day too but—'

'Of course you must go! You'll be able to have a bit of your own family Christmas if you do.'

'I'll walk back with you,' said Brent.

Ella was about to insist this wasn't necessary when she remembered her huge suitcases and the vast amount of stuff she had brought with her to ensure that Christmas was perfect for everyone.

'That would be handy, thank you.' She smiled broadly, and hoped no one could tell that it wasn't champagne that was making her eyes sparkle so brightly.

As they walked along the road, towing suitcases and carrying rucksacks, Ella wondered if Brent would ask for her telephone number. Would he make an effort to see her again? Did he want to? Or was his gentle flirting and kindness just that – kindness because she was helping keep everyone happy at Christmas?

He didn't ask for her contact details. He just brought all her luggage into the little holiday cottage attached to Rebecca and James's house. He put his hands on her shoulders and looked down at her.

'You'd better get back,' said Ella quickly, her heart and hope plummeting, a sixth sense telling her he wasn't going to be in touch with her again. 'They'll be missing you. It's Christmas.'

He didn't speak for a while and then he cupped her cheek with his hand.

'You're right. Happy Christmas to the best Christmas Fairy I've ever met.'

'Thank you,' she said, her smile taking every atom of acting ability she'd ever had. 'And a happy Christmas to you! Now I'd better get this lot sorted out.'

'Goodbye, Ella.'

'Goodbye, Brent.'

She turned away into the house before the tears that had formed escaped and fell. She knew when she was inside she might sob. The reason he hadn't asked for her number or anything was clear: he thought her far too young for him. He was ten years older than her and while she couldn't have cared less about this, he obviously did.

She'd said goodbye to Rebecca and her family as soon as she'd got her face back together, so she was able to set off smartly in the morning: so early, in fact, that she might be home by early afternoon. She'd sent her mother a text outlining her plans, and her mother had insisted it was too far for her to drive in one day. Ella had replied that it was fine and promised to stop if she got tired.

She staggered through her parents' front door at three o'clock and burst into tears. She passed it off as exhaustion and spent the rest of the day curled up in front of the fire and *It's a Wonderful Life*, with a box of champagne truffles, pressed into her hand at the last minute by Rebecca, who'd felt terrible about her leaving.

It had only been a few weeks since Christmas, but Ella had already given up all hope of becoming an actor. One dark afternoon, as she was teaching herself to touch-type while waiting to start her shift as a pizza-delivery girl, an email pinged into her computer. It appeared to be from Brent Christy, but Ella was wary. She hadn't given him her email address, and he certainly hadn't asked for it.

She clicked on it.

Hi Ella,

Or should I call you the Christmas Fairy so you know it's me and not a random Brent Christy?

My sister was a bit reluctant to give me your details. She thought if you wanted to hear from me you'd have made sure I had your email or phone number. But when she heard what I had to tell her, she relented.

The reason I didn't get your details was because I wanted to put some things in place before I got in touch. You spent all Christmas solving everyone's problems and making things work for other people; I wanted to do something for you.

Sadly, I can't get you a part in the latest Hollywood blockbuster, or even the next TV advert for stain remover, but could you come to the address below with all your sketches, drawings and stories? I have an idea that may interest you.

Ella reread the email several times, a smile of sheer joy on her face. She was going to see him again. He wasn't asking her out or anything, but she would see him!

And him wanting to see her doodles and stories was good too. She'd been doing a lot more since Christmas. She hadn't been able to get a pub job she fancied and so had gone for delivering pizza. She had a bit of time during the day.

Then she googled the address to see what she could find out. It was in Fitzrovia, and housed a small but very highly regarded children's publishing house.

A week later, she was walking along a London street full of extremely edgy (and expensive) food shops, self-consciously carrying the brand-new art portfolio her mother had insisted on buying for her. She was looking for the address on Brent's email. She felt sick and she couldn't decide why. Was it because she was insanely excited at the thought of seeing Brent again? Or was she utterly delighted and thrilled at the thought of changing to a career that suited her far better than that of a failed actor? She realised that either was enough to turn her stomach into a seething mass of conflicting emotions.

She found the discreet dark blue door with a brass name plate, cleared her throat, did some breathing exercises, and then pressed the buzzer.

She might as well not have bothered with the breathing exercises, she realised, as by the time she'd got to the top floor she would be out of breath anyway. However, she did them again before she knocked on the office door.

Brent was there, smiling widely, and for a moment they stood there beaming at each other until he said, 'Come in, Ella, it's so good to see you.'

'Me too! I mean, I'm really pleased to see you too.' Then she realised she'd probably shown an indecent amount of enthusiasm. He was so much better-looking than she'd remembered! 'I mean, this is a great opportunity.'

'Well, come in. The team is all very excited to meet you.'

As Ella followed Brent down the corridor she

wondered if he'd seemed a bit knocked back when she mentioned the opportunity.

She didn't have long to think about it because there were three people on their feet waiting for her to come in with Brent.

A quick round of introductions – Polly, Esther and Phillip – and everyone sat down again, including Ella, who took the chair Brent was holding for her.

'Well,' said Brent. 'You might have worked out by now that I work for a children's book publisher—'

'Actually, Ella, he owns it,' said Esther.

'It doesn't mean I don't work for it,' Brent objected. 'Anyway, I tried to speak to you about your sketches in Crinan, but Christmas kept getting in the way. When I got home I realised that that was probably for the best – it is a fairly democratic business here and I wanted everyone to look at your work to see if they felt the same about it.'

Ella, her fingers shaking and a bit slippery, put her portfolio on the desk and shoved it towards Esther. If she'd gone through this and Brent's team didn't feel the same about her work it would be dreadful. But on the other hand she'd seen Brent again and maybe she'd be brave enough to invite him for a coffee.

'Actually,' she said, having cleared her throat, 'would you mind if I went out and got a glass of water or something? While you look? There are a lot of stairs!'

'Sure, I'll show you,' said Polly. 'Those stairs are killers, aren't they? There's water out here.'

Once out of the room, Polly added, 'There's the water, there's the Ladies, and I must just say, Brent has been going on and on about how great you are ever since he got back after the holiday.'

Ella rubbed her lips together. 'I'm not sure that makes me feel better.'

'It should!' said Polly, laughing. 'Just come back in when you're ready.'

Ella took her time and only went back into the room when she was breathing more or less normally and had replaced her lipstick.

'Ella!' said Phillip. 'We all think your drawings and your stories are amazing!'

'Yes, we definitely want to publish them,' agreed Esther. 'We think you could be the new Lauren Child. You have just the right mix of edginess and warmth.'

Ella looked at Brent. He was smiling down at her as if all his Christmases had come at once. 'Of course there's a lot of work and effort and time before we'll have a book on the shelves, but I know that once we do, it'll be mega.'

'Oh my God,' said Ella. 'Does this mean I should cancel my shift at the pizza company for tonight, then?'

He nodded. 'I'm going to take you out to lunch to talk over the details—'

'It's only eleven o'clock,' said Polly mildly.

'Coffee first, and then lunch.' He smiled again.

'Who'd have thought being a Christmas Fairy could turn into this?' said Ella, who still couldn't take in what was happening to her.

'I thought it,' said Brent. 'The moment you made us all take part in that amazing story you wrote for Mia, and then showed me there were illustrations as well, I knew.'

'Really?' It was disorientating.

He nodded. 'Your stories are quirky and your drawings wonderfully economical – you get so much into just a few lines.'

Ella cleared her throat of the sudden lump that had formed there.

'I don't know if I believe in fairies,' said Brent, 'but I know I believe in you!'

But Ella still couldn't speak.

'Oh, take the poor girl out for a latte,' said Phillip. 'She looks like she needs one.'

'Go on, you two,' said Polly. 'We'll work out the details. Go and – have a date, why don't you?'

'How does that sound, Ella?'

'Wonderful,' she said. 'Just wonderful.'

# Read on for an exclusive sneak peek of Katie Fforde's brand new novel

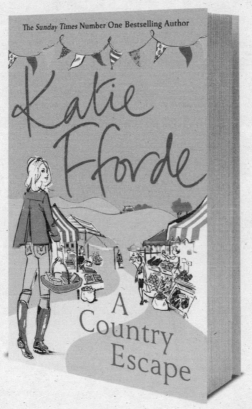

# Chapter One

The farm gate clanged shut behind her as Fran steered her little car up the steep track. Now she and Issi had found Hill Top Farm for certain – the name was written (not very clearly) on the post box – she felt a mixture of excitement and nervousness. This was going to be either a wonderful adventure or a humiliating mistake. She decided not to mention her feelings to her best friend. Issi probably guessed how she felt already.

'I always wanted to be a farmer when I was a little girl,' Fran said instead.

Issi, who'd just got back in the car having helped deal with the gate, seemed surprised. 'Really? I never knew that and we've been friends for years. I thought you'd always wanted to run your own restaurant.'

'That came later. I'd forgotten myself,' said Fran, 'but Mum reminded me at Christmas.'

'Do your parents think you're mad to do this?'

'Yup. But they're being supportive. My stepdad thinks I'll be back with them before the end of the month, but I'm in it for the long haul.' She paused. 'Which may only be a year, if I don't make it.'

'Come on,' said Issi, 'let's go and find this farm-house you might inherit.'

'It's not just the farmhouse, remember? It's the whole darn farm.'

Fran rounded a steep corner and tried to push her nerves to the back of her mind. Now she was finally here she realised no sane person would leave their comfortable life in London and move to a farm in Gloucestershire that they might not even inherit. No *sane* person, obviously, but maybe someone like her whose normal life had stalled rather, and who relished a challenge.

A couple of minutes later, they arrived, having bumped their way to the top avoiding as many potholes as they could. 'I'm not sure a Ka is the right vehicle for this track,' Issi said.

Ignoring her friend, Fran got out of the car. 'But look at the view!'

The farmhouse was on a plateau at the top of a

hill that overlooked hills and wooded valleys. Beyond them lay the Severn, a silver snake in the far distance, and beyond the river was Wales.

'I think I remember this landscape!' Fran went on. 'We came here once when I was a little girl. I'd forgotten all about it until we were discussing the farm over Christmas, and Mum reminded me. Mum said we'd all been here when Dad was alive, but I must have been tiny – after all I was only five when he died. But this feels faintly familiar.'

'It is stunning,' Issi agreed.

'Come on,' said Fran, 'let's look at the house while it's still light. It'll be dark by about four, so we'll need to turn the leccy on. I've got a torch.'

After failing to open the front door – 'I don't think people use front doors in the country,' offered Issi – they went round the back. The key Fran had been given turned smoothly in the lock and they were in.

'Wow! It is dark,' said Issi.

'Hang on. I think I've found the fuse box. I'll just get my torch out. There! We have light!'

They were in a fairly big farmhouse kitchen. The friends looked around in silence for a few seconds, taking it all in.

'An open fire!' said Issi excitedly. 'How lovely to have an open fire in a kitchen.'

'As long as it's not all I have to cook on,' agreed Fran, looking round. Although the central light was on, it wasn't very bright and created shadow-filled corners. 'Oh, look,' she went on, relieved. 'There's a Rayburn. Probably a prototype it's so ancient. I do hope it's not run on solid fuel.'

'But you're a chef. You can cook on anything!' said Issi, laughing at her friend.

'I'm fine with the cooking,' Fran agreed, 'but I have no experience of lighting fires. Oh phew, it seems to run on oil.'

'And look, there's an electric cooker as well. You're in culinary clover!' Issi seemed to find Fran's dismay over the cooking arrangements highly amusing.

'I'll be OK,' said Fran, more to herself than to Issi. 'I'm here to farm, not to cook, after all. And I really like all the freestanding cupboards and things. And the sink has a lovely view of . . .' She lifted the net curtain and peered through the window. 'Ah, the farmyard. But it's lovely beyond that. Come on!' Suddenly she was more excited than dubious. 'Let's go and explore some more.'

The sitting room, which was at the front of the house, was a good size, and the windowsill was covered in pot plants. Some had died, but the geraniums seemed to have survived. There was a three-piece suite draped in crocheted blankets, and a profusion of tables and whatnots covered in photographs. Fran picked a photo up. 'A woman and a cow, or maybe a bull. There's a rosette. How sweet!'

Issi joined her. 'They all seem to be of cows or

bulls. There's nothing to tell you anything about the old lady who owned them.'

'Except that she was really into cows,' said Fran, putting down the photo she was holding. 'Oh, look at the fireplace!'

'It's tiny. You'll need something else if you're going to warm this room up.'

'I know it's tiny, but look at the beam above it. I bet there's a wonderful original fireplace behind this little coal-burning thing. I long to take a sledgehammer to it!'

'I'd wait until you're sure you're staying put, but I understand what you mean,' said Issi, looking around her. 'It's not exactly shabby chic, but I do like it. This room could actually have been two or maybe even three rooms.' She looked up at the ceiling, which had large beams at intervals.

'It's "old-lady chic", that what it is,' Fran decided. 'And I like it too. Although I wish I could investigate the fireplace. I bet there's something amazing behind all this thirties stuff.'

'You said yourself, you're here to farm not to cook,' said Issi. 'If you thought you were going to miss cheffing, you should have stayed in London, cooking for the pub.'

'No,' said Fran determinedly. 'This time I'm going to work for myself and make my own decisions. But I suppose you're right, I can't knock the house around, not if I haven't actually inherited it yet.'

'So tomorrow you're seeing your aunt – cousin – what is she?'

'I can't remember exactly how we're related but it's by marriage and through my real dad. I'm Amy's – I suppose I'd call her Aunt Amy – I'm the only relation of her husband's she could trace. She's been running Hill Top on her own since her husband died. Now she's had to go into a care home she thought she should try and leave it to one of his relations.'

'Complicated,' said Issi, which Fran knew meant that she found it boring. 'Shall we investigate the bedrooms? They may be damp and we've got to sleep in a couple of them tonight.'

'Thank you so much for coming with me,' said Fran as they made their way up the stairs. 'This would all be a bit daunting on my own.'

'I'm just sorry I can't stay longer than four days. It's such an adventure!' Issi paused. 'Would you have preferred Alex to come with you?'

Fran shook her head. 'No way. One of the reasons we broke up was that he wasn't up for adventure. He seems very happy being an intern for his uncle in New York . . . Although going on the fact there are supposedly very few straight men in NYC I suspect he has another motive.' She sighed. 'No, I really don't miss him, apart from as a friend, sort of.'

Was she over Alex? Fran knew that Issi was still concerned about this, but she definitely was. He was a kind and lovely man but, when it came down to it, too safe and a bit dull. They'd broken up a few weeks ago after a couple of years together.

Fran realised they'd been going through the motions for a while but the catalyst had been this opportunity – challenge, even. If Alex could have hacked the countryside (unlikely) he couldn't cope with the uncertainty. A straightforward inheritance might have been different – but probably not. Fran, on the other hand, although terrified, was very excited at her new adventure.

A few minutes later, Fran and Issi were making up beds, helping themselves to soft, old flannel sheets they found in the airing cupboard. Then they found hot-water bottles and filled them, although they agreed they didn't think the house was damp. Then it was time for supper.

'So,' said Issi when they'd eaten most of the moussaka that Fran had made and brought with her, and heated up in the electric oven. 'You're seeing Amy tomorrow?'

'Yup. After my meeting with the lawyer. He said in his letter he's arranged for me to have a bit of money to run things with but I don't expect it's very much.' She sighed. 'It is quite daunting when I think about it. I know nothing about farming – and yet here I am. I could have said no when I first heard from Amy's solicitor but . . .' She paused. 'I wanted to challenge myself.'

'See if you can run the farm for a year and make it pay?'

Fran nodded. 'Of course I don't have to look after the cows myself. There's a herdsman. Amy would never let her precious cows be looked after by an ignoramus, which is what I am as far as farming is concerned.'

'And cows are quite big, aren't they?' said Issi.

'Are you afraid of cows?'

'More to the point, are you?'

Fran swallowed. 'I really hope not but actually – I think I am!'

Issi laughed. 'Let's finish the wine and then get an early night. You have to be up with the lark tomorrow. Better set your alarm for six. Get used to your new life.'

Although Fran knew Issi was joking, she also knew what she said was true. As for being afraid of cows, she'd just have to find out when she met them.

The next morning they were standing around in the kitchen, shrouded in layers of woollen jumpers and clutching steaming mugs of tea.

'It's the lawyer first? Then your Aunt Amy.'

Fran nodded. 'I'm not sure how long it will all take. Will you be OK here on your own?'

Issi nodded. 'I'm going to sort out the pot plants, and maybe do a bit of exploring. I might even move the furniture around a bit and clear out the odd cupboard. Would you mind?'

'Not at all. I'm so grateful you're here. I wouldn't grudge you a bit of entertainment. In fact I think you're going to have a better time than I am.'

'Shall we refer to your father's cousin's wife as Mrs Flowers for ease?' Mr Addison, the solicitor, a kind, tired man in his fifties, had attempted to explain Fran's relationship to Aunt Amy but it had become complicated.

'What do you think I should call her when we meet?' asked Fran, who was getting nervous at the thought of meeting a woman, who, although very elderly now, had apparently been formidable in her time.

'She'll let you know, don't you worry about that,' said Mr Addison. 'Now let's go through the finances a bit. Mrs Flowers has arranged six months of care in her home. She has set up an account with a thousand pounds in it for your use. There is a bit more money but I'd honestly prefer you didn't encroach on it. Although Mrs Flowers is very well looked after, she is frail and may need more than six months' care, which is going to be expensive.'

'But in an emergency?'

'You can apply to me.'

'And what about wages for the herdsman, and other people who work for her?'

'All arranged for six months.'

'But she wants me to stay for a year? What happens after the first six months? In July?'

He shrugged. 'I think she hopes the farm will be earning money by then.'

Fran noted his careful choice of words. 'You mean, it's not making money at the moment?'

Mr Addison sighed. 'Mrs Flowers has been slowing down for a while. Things have been let slip.'

'So I'm not taking on a going concern. Things are in a bad way?'

'I wouldn't say a bad way; just not a desperately profitable way.'

When she'd first heard about it Fran had thought it was a romantic, dramatic idea to have been brought in to look after the family farm, but she was no longer quite so sure.

'Is that you being tactful?' said Fran. 'You would tell me the truth, wouldn't you?'

Mr Addison's expression closed down. 'I have to act in my client's best interest. I'm sure you're going to do a good job.' He stood up. Fran realised he'd explained everything to the best of his ability but he obviously felt he could do no more.

'What happens if it turns out I'm afraid of cows?'

He shook his head and smiled. He obviously thought Fran was making a joke. 'I'm sure we don't need to worry about that.'

When Fran arrived at the care home, she'd anticipated it taking her a while to explain who she was. But no, everyone knew exactly who she was. And for the first time that day she wondered if she was dressed right. When she'd got up, after a night disturbed by an uncomfy mattress and strange noises, she'd just put on the clothes she'd worn the previous day, more concerned with getting down the drive, finding the solicitor and then the care home than how she looked. Now she wondered if leggings, boots and a tunic that revealed quite a lot of leg were acceptable.

Still, it was too late to worry about it now. She was following a care worker down a carpeted corridor, her boots scuffing against the pile.

The nurse stopped and opened a door. 'Mrs Flowers? It's your young relative.'

The room wasn't huge but it was bright and sunny. There were pictures on the walls and the furniture would have fitted into the décor of the farmhouse. Fran went into the room, not sure what to say.

'Hello – Aunt – Cousin – Mrs Flowers . . .' She paused. The old lady was sitting on a chair, looking very neat and upright.

'Better make it Amy, dear,' she said crisply. 'Otherwise I might die before you decide what my name is. And sit down, do.'

Fran sat and inspected her companion. Her eyes were bright and blue and shone out from a pink, slightly weathered complexion. Her thin grey hair was twisted into a knot on top of her head. She wore a long tweed skirt and a neatly ironed white blouse with a lace collar. She seemed bright, cheerful and well cared for. She had obviously chosen her care home well.

'Hello, Amy, it's lovely to meet you finally,' Fran said, sensing it was important that she appeared confident, even if she was anything but. The meeting with the solicitor had turned a year learning about farming and a bit of an adventure into a huge undertaking loaded with responsibility and concern.

Amy nodded, possibly with approval. 'Well, dear, I'm very glad you came. I didn't want my farm to go to rack and ruin while I'm in here.'

'But you realise I don't know very much about farming, don't you?' Amy obviously wasn't the sort of person who appreciated 'how are you' conversations, so Fran got on with what was on her mind.

'Yes, and – please don't take offence – believe me, if there'd been anyone else I would never have got in touch with you. But you're related to my late husband. It was his farm. I was eighteen when I married him.'

'Goodness.'

'The farm had been in his family for three generations. We never had children and it was a great sadness to us both to think it would all end with us. My husband died twenty years ago and I've been on my own since then. I've been worrying about who to pass it on to all that time.'

Fran was touched. 'I can understand that.'

'It's the herd, you see. They're Dairy Shorthorns and quite rare. I've known all those cows personally for years. Cows can live to be quite old, you know, if they're looked after. If I don't leave the farm to someone who'll carry on with it, it'll be sold. The herd will go, the land will be built on or ploughed up or something, and that would be a tragedy. It's for the cows, the farm, that I tracked you down and now here you are.' Amy smiled as if this was a satisfactory conclusion.

'I do hope I don't let you down.'

Amy shook her head. 'You won't. I remember you as a little girl. You liked the cows. You liked their red and white colouring.' This had obviously stuck in her memory. 'It's the herd that's important,' she repeated. 'The bloodlines. It must be kept going.'

411

Amy obviously felt extremely strongly about her cows, even given old people's tendency to repeat themselves.

'I see.' Fran offered a little prayer that she still liked cows herself.

'And you have Tig, my herdsman. I would never have left you my herd without someone to look after them. But you have to look after everything else, so he can look after the cows. I've paid him six months in advance so he won't leave.'

Fran wanted to ask why Amy hadn't just left all of her farm to Tig, but realised this too was to do with bloodlines. Tig was not related to Amy's late husband, and she was.

'And there's a bit of money to keep you going, but you have to run the farm for a year and then I'll decide whether you should inherit.' Amy's expression emphasised what a massive reward she thought this was. 'So you will try, won't you, Francesca?'

No one ever called Fran 'Francesca', not even her mother when she was cross. She realised she liked it. 'About the house—'

Amy interrupted her. 'I really don't care about the house. Do what you like with it. But don't let anything happen to the herd.'

Fran nodded, instantly thinking about the fire-place she could now investigate.

'Oh, and don't let that scoundrel who lives next

door have anything to do with you. He's always wanted my farm and it's your job to make sure he doesn't get it! Vineyards, indeed!'

'Tell me—' Fran began.

But Amy had closed her eyes and had apparently gone to sleep.

'She does that,' explained the nurse who appeared in the doorway at that moment. 'Bright as a button one minute, fast asleep the next.'

'When is she likely to wake up again?' asked Fran, who felt she really should find out about the scoundrel-neighbour as soon as possible.

The nurse shook her head. 'Not for a while. You'd do better to come back tomorrow, or as soon as it's convenient.'

'OK,' said Fran. She got up from her seat. 'I'll come back. I haven't learnt nearly enough about things.' She went to the door, stopped and addressed the nurse. 'But – are you allowed to tell me? She's generally well, isn't she?'

'Oh yes. She's very good for her age. I suppose she's always led a healthy outdoor life. Never smoked, never drank alcohol.'

'And nothing's likely to happen to her within the next six months?'

'I can't see into the future, but she seems well enough at the moment – although with the elderly you can never really be sure.'

'That's good enough for me.' Fran smiled. 'Thank

you so much for looking after her. I'm looking forward to getting to know her better.'

The nurse returned the smile. 'She's a great favourite with us all here.'

By the time Fran got back to Hill Top Farm it was early evening and nearly dark, she was freezing cold and wanting to open the wine even though it was really only teatime. After her visits, she'd spent a little time investigating the town, then she had got lost trying to get home and so most of the day had melted away. She pulled up in front of the house and saw lights peeping out from behind the curtains, which made the house seem welcoming. As she collected her handbag from the back seat of the car she realised how bright the stars were here, miles away from any light pollution.

Minutes later, Fran was in the sitting room, looking around it. The room, which had been cluttered and a bit claustrophobic, was now far more sparsely furnished. And every suitable surface supported a teacup with a flickering candle in it. It was welcoming and restful, just what Fran needed after her day.

'Wow! You've done some good stuff here – and lit the fire. And candles!'

'Tea lights,' corrected Issi. 'Knowing what a fussy-knickers you are about lighting, I put some in my bag. When I found all the teacups in a cupboard, I put them together. Good day?'

'It's gorgeous! So cosy and pretty. Daunting day – got lost coming home but I'll tell you later. But I can knock the fireplace out! Although not now, obviously.'

'You asked Aunt Amy?' Issi was surprised.

'Not specifically but she said I could do anything to the house as long as I looked after her cows.' Fran collapsed in one of the armchairs drawn up next to the fire and started tugging at the heel of a boot. 'I am so tired. I think it was meeting people and having so much information fired at me.' She looked around. 'It looks far better in here now. Thank you so much!'

'Well, I needed something to do and you gave me permission to play.' Issi paused. 'Although the changes haven't been approved by everyone.'

'What do you mean?' Fran pulled off the other boot. 'Who else has seen them?'

'You've had a caller. Mrs Brown. She's coming back tomorrow. She used to look after Aunt Amy a bit. She looked at everything I'd done and tutted. I reassured her that everything is still safe. I haven't burnt the nests of tables and whatnots and all the other clutter, but she was still a bit put out.'

'Where have you put it all?'

'There's a little room at the end of the house. It had quite a lot of things in it already so I just stacked more bits on top. I don't think you'll need that room. It's quite a big house, really.'

'Amazing. Is there wine?' The extent of her potential inheritance wasn't a top priority just at that moment.

Issi nodded, very pleased with herself. 'There's wine and there's dinner. I asked your visitor how to light the range and she showed me. Then I put in the lasagne you brought.'

'Sorry,' said Fran. 'Lasagne is a bit like moussaka but I wanted to bring food that was easy to heat up and didn't need saucepans and things.'

'I can't believe you haven't brought your pans and things.'

'I brought my knives but I didn't want to bring everything I owned. I've left a lot of stuff in my parents' garage.' Fran closed her eyes. 'I've got a lot to tell you but not until I've had something strong to drink.'

'It's still teatime really,' Issi objected.

Fran shook her head. 'No. It's dark. Winetime. At least, today it is.'

'I'll get it. Do you want your dinner early, too?'

'Yes please, Mummy . . .'

Fran felt revived when she had eaten and was ready to elaborate on how she had got on. 'I feel a bit in the dark still. Both the solicitor, and Amy – she told me to call her that – told me a lot but left out a lot. The solicitor said there's a thousand pounds for me to use and although there is more money, it has to be kept for Amy's care.'

'I know care homes can be expensive,' said Issi.

'But I don't need to worry about that for six months because Amy's paid for that much care. She's thought it all out. And there's the herdsman, who looks after the scary cows. She's paid him, too.'

'And if they're not scary?'

'It should all be fine!'

But Fran knew their cheerfulness was a little false. She might not be able to do this at all.

'I really want this to work,' she said. 'I've left my job and packed up my life to come here, and although I could go back to it I'd always wonder if I could have made a go of it. Very few people get chances like this. I can't waste this opportunity. It's my chance to make my mark on the world.'

# THE NEW NOVEL FROM KATIE FFORDE

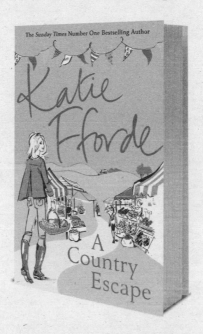

## A year in the country.
## A year to fall in love.

Fran has always wanted to be a farmer and now her childhood dream is about to come true.

Fran has been left a beautiful but dilapidated farm. She has one year to turn the place around.

It's either going to be a wonderful adventure or a humiliating mistake . . .

## ORDER YOUR COPY NOW